SNAKE OIL

ALSO BY KELSEY RAE DIMBERG

Girl in the Rearview Mirror

SNAKE OIL

A Novel

Kelsey Rae Dimberg

MARINER BOOKS

New York Boston

SNAKE OIL. Copyright © 2024 by Kelsey Mueller. All rights reserved. Printed in the United States of America. No part of this book may be used or reproduced in any manner whatsoever without written permission except in the case of brief quotations embodied in critical articles and reviews. For information, address HarperCollins Publishers, 195 Broadway, New York, NY 10007.

HarperCollins books may be purchased for educational, business, or sales promotional use. For information, please email the Special Markets Department at SPsales@harpercollins.com.

FIRST EDITION

Library of Congress Cataloging-in-Publication Data has been applied for.

ISBN 978-0-06-286795-7

24 25 26 27 28 LBC 5 4 3 2 1

To my parents

Illusion is the first of all pleasures.

—VOLTAIRE

If you want to build a better future, you must believe in secrets.

—PETER THIEL

SNAKE OIL

Dani

Saturday

"This is heaven," the woman says, shimmying her shoulders. "Heaven."

She takes a shot from Dani's tray and throws it back like tequila. Even in the dark hotel ballroom, her gold highlights look like they're reflecting a sunbeam.

Dani's serving samples of Radical Boost, a supercharged potion made with energizing adaptogens, powdered plum skins, and a jolt of ginseng. She's poured hundreds of shots today, stuffed garbage bags with empties.

It's the last day of the Radical Retreat. Liberated from homes and jobs, the two thousand women in attendance are ebullient. Over the weekend, they've enjoyed hot yoga classes, deep-tissue massages, inspirational talks on work and sex and divine purpose. First tentative, then bold, they've tried communal screaming, silent meditation, Reiki healing, vitamin B injections shot into bared butt cheeks. They've cinched on Radical bracelets—available in gold or sterling—and synced their Radical apps, marveling at the columns of step counts, pulse rates, and sleep scores.

Their first-day chignons and buttoned cardigans have given way to flowing tresses and flip-flops. They look years younger. Their bodies are loose and free, like they didn't realize how heavy their loads were until they set them down.

Dani's trajectory is the opposite. After working all week in Customer Worship and volunteering at the Retreat all weekend, she's so exhausted that her tiredness seems like a permanent feature, as fixed as the color of her eyes. She's subsisting on a diet of Radical Boost and cucumber-ginger smoothies. Her lilac T-shirt, emblazoned with Radical's call to arms, #bebetter, is stained with spills and sweat.

But the Retreat is a smashing success. SFGATE called it "the Coachella of wellness." Rhoda will be so pleased.

Lilac banners hang from the ceiling, decorated with an abstract symbol: an upside-down droplet of water, or a flickering flame, or maybe a snake. The fabric ripples gently over the bazaar, where women weave through booths, scooping up Radical products, scanning their bracelets to pay. Scanning to measure their blood pressure or read their aura. Scanning for a customized Radical Reset nutrition plan, or to take a cooking class with Radical's new CBD line (this the most raucous station, laughter spilling out).

When her tray empties, Dani holds it against her hip and leans against her booth. She watches the women, imagining what brought them here. A young mom tests lipstick on the pad of her thumb. Sinewy marathoners browse compression leggings. A woman with a knit beanie tugged over her bald scalp browses bottles of essential oils.

Dani looks away.

Heat rises on her neck. The smell of the smoothie stand is suddenly overwhelming: ripe banana, bitter tang of powdered vitamins. She abandons her tray, pushes out an exit into a fluorescent hotel corridor, runs for the bathroom.

Her cough is harsh and gagging. She wipes her forehead with the back of her wrist, feeling the cool ridge of her own Radical bracelet.

At the sink, she splashes her face with water. Her skin looks thin and creased, like a shirt worn too often. She digs in her pockets for lipstick.

Dani is twenty-seven years old. She's worked at Radical almost three years, and in that time, she's carefully, meticulously established herself. Her days are built with solid bricks of productive activity: work, meditation, exercise, cooking. She lives with her boyfriend, Trevor, who grew up here, who has a band and a business and Warriors season tickets. Yet for all of that, Dani's life in San Francisco feels tenuous, a wildflower clinging to a cliff off Highway 1.

So it's crazy, isn't it? It's illogical, really—impractical, definitely—that Dani is twelve weeks and five days pregnant.

When Dani slips into the dim, overwarm auditorium, Rhoda is already speaking. Her husky voice rasps into the microphone, so amplified it seems to pour from above.

"I was young and invincible. I had a very specific plan. Like a train timetable, every day, every year, tick-tick-tick."

Dani instantly knows where Rhoda is in her story, like a favorite book falling open to a page. Rhoda is at Stanford, with her track scholarship and her plan to study science and fulfill her childhood dream of changing the world.

Dani's supposed to be helping dismantle the bazaar, but she squeezes into the standing room section until she finds a gap between shoulders.

Rhoda strolls across the stage, dragging a spotlight in her wake. Her diaphanous green dress billows.

"Then I got sick." She stands solemnly still, hands pressed together.

Her face is projected on a screen next to the stage, so magnified Dani can see the quiver of a tendon at her jawline.

"It was ordinary, at first," she says. "A virus. A nasty flu that struck just before midterms and landed me in bed for two weeks.

"That first shower," she adds drily, "was better than sex."

But strange symptoms lingered. Exhaustion so extreme she sometimes went to bed for twelve or fourteen hours at a stretch. Her digestion was inflamed and unpredictable. Walking across campus exhausted her. Standing at the lab tables, her joints ached. She struggled to concentrate. She, Rhoda, who was always top of her class!

"All my life I was healthy. I ran track, I didn't need much sleep, I could eat anything. And suddenly I was a horizontal person. I was tired, I was dull. I didn't recognize this person. I didn't like her."

Dani can see it. The dorm room distorted by the prism of illness, like a cubist painting. Stale bedsheets, bleary hum of a neighbor's TV, ramen turntabling in the microwave. Rhoda leaning against the tile wall in the communal showers, flip-flops spongy and slick.

She visited doctors' offices like a penitent, one after another, blue paper gowns crinkling on exam tables, listing her symptoms until the concern fell from the doctors' faces. Impatience, or amusement, replaced it.

They dispensed their wisdom:

Too much partying, they said, though she was practically a monk. ("If a woman can be a monk," she adds, deadpan.)

Too little sleep, when she was sleeping twelve or more hours a day, and caffeinating whenever she was awake, just to remain that way.

Too much stress. Well . . . that was true. She had fallen behind in her classes. Was it only stress wearing her out, and worry over an imaginary illness compounding it?

The doctors hustled her out of their offices. "You're a healthy young woman." They all but patted her head.

Rhoda fumes. "They assumed that I was exaggerating, or imagining things. I was thin, strong from running. I wore makeup. They looked at my surface and didn't dig deeper."

Still, she listened to them. She told herself she wasn't sick. She pressed on.

"I existed on saltines and coffee, and when my stomach went nuts, I loaded up on Imodium and Advil. When I was tired, I bullied myself. I said horrible things to the mirror."

Finally, on her way to an exam, she fainted on the quad. She awoke on her back, staring up into a tree. A breeze wafted the leaves, swept over her bare legs. She couldn't remember the last time her body had felt simple pleasure. She couldn't recall feeling anything but bad. Something had to change.

Rhoda's voice is a musical instrument. Limber and expressive as a violin, but deeper. A cello. Resonant and throaty and sometimes so soft you have to lean in close to hear.

When she pauses, the audience holds their breath. The musicians' bows hover over the strings. Anticipation for the next note vibrates in the air.

"It's funny, isn't it? That a story of wellness begins in illness. Like pulling scarves from thin air, a rabbit from a top hat. Turning nothing—

bleakness, desolation—into something." She pantomimes, fingers drawing air from her empty palm.

"I was sick, and traditional medicine failed me, and to cure myself, I rejected it. I dove headfirst into wellness. I founded Radical and never looked back. That's the story you hear on talk shows, the success story. Sickness into health."

She holds up a finger. "But it's only sleight of hand. I've made you look one way, and you missed it. Look again.

"I was sick, yes, but the real sickness was one that's so pervasive, so insidious, so ordinary, we don't even recognize it.

"My body was suffering, and my response was to punish it. I treated it horribly, brutally. I would never treat another person that way. Not an animal. Not even my possessions. But my own body? I didn't hesitate.

"Our culture teaches us to ignore the simple ways the body communicates its needs. To power through hunger, tiredness, fear, pain. And, if you're a woman, you're also taught to criticize your body. To hate it for being too hairy, too loud, too wrinkled, or especially, God forbid, the wrong shape and size.

"We've got this beautiful, incredible body, capable of feats of agility and strength, but also of cooking dinner, singing songs, making love. But we treat it like a machine or fight it like an enemy."

Rhoda looks stricken. She puts a hand on her shoulder and strokes her arm.

The room goes filmy. Dani blinks hard. She's tracked down a dozen versions of this speech online, but she's never felt it like this.

Rhoda smiles. "This has been an amazing weekend, am I right?"

Applause.

Softly, she says, "I'm sorry to tell you: this is fake."

The silence is tense. She stretches it.

"There's a reason we call this a retreat. It's sheltered. It can't last.

"Wellness isn't a vacation, or a task you check off your list. It's a daily practice.

"When I look at you, I see a battalion of warrior women. Scarred, but hopeful. Hungry. Seeking as much from our bodies and spirits and hearts as this life can offer.

"If you commit to it, wellness can optimize every facet of your life. Unleash your superpowers. Imagine: if every woman felt radically healthy, we could save the world. That's my vision for Radical.

"When you go back to real life, take this with you: I'm giving you permission. You deserve to be better, every fucking day."

The crowd cheers. A full-throated roar.

Rhoda opens her arms, embracing them all. Their messy tears, their clumsy scramble to stand, heedless of purses sliding to the floor.

Dani feels warm, like her core has turned into a luminous gold flame.

On the huge screen, Rhoda's eyes glisten. She kisses her fingertips and flings them to the crowd.

Three years ago, Dani heard Rhoda's story for the first time. Within a month, she had packed a suitcase; sold her car, her house, and everything in it; and boarded a flight from O'Hare to SFO. She fell asleep over a patchwork of fields and woke to find the plane hovering impossibly low over the ocean. Seconds later, the wheels bounced on the runway.

San Francisco glowed with sun, as California as she dreamed. It was April and snow was shaking over Illinois, but here, cherry trees were blooming pink and white. Back then, she didn't know it wasn't always like that.

She had an interview with Radical that same afternoon.

The office was in a drafty warehouse in the Mission. Workers— "Radigals," they called themselves—leaned into their computers, intense as cavemen creating fire. An abstract silver statue of a woman danced in the middle of the floor.

The HR woman told Dani to touch the statue's foot. "It's good luck."

Dani glided her fingers along the intricate seams of the toes, the metal fogged with fingerprints. She didn't need luck. The universe had guided her here.

She found an apartment the next day, a one-bedroom on the top floor of a peeling Queen Anne Victorian in the Western Addition. The $2,300 rent supplemented with the proceeds of her former life.

Three years of watching cherry blossoms unfurl from tight buds.

Three years of being shocked by cold summers, though this one the coldest by far.

She kicks off her clogs at the door and changes into sweatpants in the bedroom, tripping over boxes overflowing with Trevor's startup paraphernalia: tangled cords, lanyards, T-shirts. Trevor himself is absent, off at a tech conference in Austin.

She worries, not for the first time, how they'll fit a baby here.

In the kitchen, she makes tea and checks the Radical app. Her activity score is high, but her nutrition score is low. Not enough calories, and most of them liquid.

She longs to fall into bed, but she remembers Rhoda's words. Nourishing the body is a sacred task. An investment that pays dividends.

She chops a pepper, whisks eggs, melts butter in a cast iron pan and pushes it around with a wooden spatula, because she never uses plastic, feels slightly sick every time she touches it, which is often, because plastic is everywhere: cart handles and packaging, her phone charger, chairs and coffee cups and yoga mats. One side effect of seeking wellness is hyperawareness of toxins you can never completely avoid.

While she eats, she scrolls the Retreat hashtag on her phone. Among the enthusiastic selfies and the grainy snaps of Rhoda spotted across the room, there's the inevitable snark from Radicalidiocy, the Twitter account devoted to mocking Radical.

@Radicalidiocy
Tickets to the @Radical Retreat cost $500, but once you're inside, it's all-u-can-drink Kool-Aid.

Surprisingly, they share a photo of the bazaar. In the camera flash, the dark ballroom is overexposed. The lilac draping looks mauve. Radical's bestsellers are bleached: rose quartz face rollers, energy-balancing crystals, and a jade egg.

@Radicalidiocy
Vaginas are as empty and vacuous as life itself. Buy this $200 jade egg and all will be well. #Radical #bebetter

The joke is stale, but the photo takes Dani aback. The tweeter was there. Dani might have seen her. Might have handed her a shot of Radical Boost and accepted her empty, lipsticked cup. She might have stood beside Dani during the keynote, silently mocked Dani's brimming tears.

Dani closes the window. She logs her meal on the Radical app, and her health score rises to 97, leaping to the uppermost level of a bar graph, color-coded from red to purple to blue to a slim segment of green, bright as spring sap. *Optimal.*

Rhoda

Saturday

Applause echoes in my ears as I stand in the shower, washing away makeup and sweat. Bits of my talk loop in my head, imperfections obvious in retrospect. I wrap myself in a towel and make a note on my phone.

After a speech, I feel spent and unsettled, exhausted and craving motion. I want to drive, to eat with my hands, to swim. I pull on a linen dress and cinch the belt tight.

Retreat staff crowd my hotel suite. The talk is jittery. Raw data streams across screens. The sales manager calls out numbers. We can drill down infinitely: sales by category, by time of day, by customer age and income. We can track movement through the Retreat, even map the audience's pulse rate to the transcript of my speech.

For now, total revenue is the only number that matters. The target is high. I believe goals should be almost impossible, requiring superhuman will to achieve.

This is our twelfth and final event. We started in the Northeast, leapt to Miami, hopscotched across the country, Chicago, Austin, Denver, and then snaked down the West Coast, Seattle, Portland, LA. Everywhere, women waited to meet me. They paid extra to have dinner with me, leaned over their plates to confide their secret desires. Strangers who knew everything about me. One even flagged the waiter, appalled, to tell him I dislike lemon in water, as if this trivia were common sense.

The numbers are in. We exceeded my goals. Shattered them.

The team's tension melts. Fingernails earn reprieve from teeth. Lungs deflate. Cheers fill the room, then laughter, louder talk.

For me, the pleasure of achievement is intense and brief as an orgasm. They're elated, and I feel cool, even restless. There was more we could have done; there always is.

I go around the room, thanking them, touching their shoulders. They've been with me the entire trip, waking at five, working past midnight. I call room service to bring champagne. I tell them to enjoy their Sunday. Sleep in, have brunch.

I don't tell them that next week we'll be working twice as hard.

Thirty minutes later, I'm driving under the arms of the Golden Gate Bridge in the cream-colored vintage convertible I bought when Radical was just taking off. Top-down is the best way to experience the Bay Area's patchwork quilt of climates. The cold damp over the water, the heat as I leave the highway for twisting country roads. A dry breeze skims the hills. Windmills lazily spin their arms. Approaching the sea, the air cools again. Pine forest. Green sap. Saline.

My drive is unmarked. An iron gate opens onto a stone house wrapped in vines. Perched on the edge of a continent, the backyard falls off a cliff. Steep stairs descend to a strip of gray beach.

I park and reflexively check my phone, though it doesn't work here. Before I left cell range, my assistant texted me a reminder: *interview*. Grimacing, I switch it off.

Untether. Disconnect. Recharge. The hardest thing to do, the most necessary. Work, like gravity, exerts a force. I should be stepping inside my office, not the quiet house; should be facing not the windows framing inky sky and sea, but a bright laptop screen, the top-secret file containing my pitch deck, which still isn't quite right.

The house is empty. I drop my bag and go out through the kitchen door to find Gavin working in the yard, his white T-shirt glowing in the dim. So far, the garden is mostly churned-up dirt, rough with roots and rocks.

Gavin's shovel digs with rhythmic crunches. Seeing me, he stands, propping his foot on the blade.

"You do realize you're working in the dark?" I hug him, breathing in his scent of sweat and dirt.

"I guess you're influencing me." He wipes his forehead, grinning. "Our laurel arrived today. I thought you could help me plant it tomorrow. You might have left the city entirely by then," he teases.

I planned to hire landscapers, but Gavin took over the project with surprising enthusiasm, buying native landscaping books and studying the layouts of historic gardens. He's planning a meadow, lush with flowers and trees.

In June, we'll marry out here, an intimate ceremony. Radical's photographers will capture every moment. (I remember a dozen undone tasks: writing a letter to accompany the bridal beauty collection, making a public playlist . . . Stop. Release.)

This house was Gavin's idea. When we met last spring, I actually slept at Radical HQ some nights. I showered and exercised and ate there. Sometimes, I didn't step outside for days at a stretch. Radical was growing, and I was going—that's all I could see.

Gavin reminded me that there's an intangible piece of Radical, our soul: my own inspiration. My well was almost dry, and I hadn't even noticed.

He showers, and I set out a dinner of octopus salad, delivered by my favorite restaurant in town. An unassuming spot in an old farmhouse, it recently won a Michelin star, and the ensuing crowds mean I can no longer eat there in peace.

The wine makes my head floaty. I draw my hair over my shoulder. "Will we get there, do you think?"

"Hmm." Gavin traces my palm. "You have a good money line."

"That's not real."

"I knew a fortune teller for a while, in San Diego. I learned things."

"I bet."

Gavin's fifteen years older than me. In the '90s, he launched a surfing website and sold it during the swell of the dot-com bubble. Ever since, he's been coasting. Traveling. Taking photos. Surfing. He studied deep meditation in Thailand and tea ceremony in Japan. He knows more about the spiritual side of wellness than I do.

After we go to bed, when I'm tucked in the crook of his arm, pulling a strand of hair through my lips, he snaps a selfie. I look disheveled, slightly smug but appealingly tired. Only Gavin captures me so unguarded. As soon as I get back into cell range, I'll share it on Instagram. *Tired but so grateful. Time for some rest . . . in theory.* I'll tag Gavin, who's grown quite a following himself, his grid a thirst trap of surfers and beach.

When I launched Radical, I didn't expect to reveal so much. The first video I shared was laughably unpolished: just me, washing my face in my apartment sink.

"The face begins at the nipples," I chirped, rubbing Skin Polish into my pristine, twenty-two-year-old skin. People didn't clean skin with oil back then; oil was the enemy.

Views ticked up, up, up. Comments flooded in. Gorgeous skin, gorgeous face, and then: Where did I get my robe? Did I take birth control? How long did I sleep at night?

In opening the door to my bathroom, I had pried a seal off my life. I started sharing my workout routine, my guilty pleasure snacks, my last-minute cleanse, my underwear drawer. I showed my childhood diary, promising to be a millionaire by age nineteen. There was nothing people didn't want to see. The more personal, and stranger, the better. I branched out: oil pulling and v-steams, cryotherapy, sensory deprivation, every detox known to man.

We're on this journey of discovery together, I tell my followers. I pour everything into Radical; Radical is all of me.

When the reporter from *Entrepreneur* rings the bell, I'm in the kitchen, chopping vegetables in a silk jumpsuit. Onions sweat in butter on the stove.

Jeremy Krill wears dark jeans, expensive Italian loafers, and a baby blue fleece with SAN FRANCISCO embroidered across the chest. The cold summer weather takes even prestigious journalists by surprise.

I settle him in at the kitchen island. Cooking for writers is one of my tricks. It's hospitable and familiar, while giving me an excuse to turn away, pause, as if concentrating on some critical issue of heat or seasoning.

"I hope you like mushrooms," I say. "This is a recipe from my first cookbook."

He sets up his recorder, his leather notepad.

We talk early days of Radical—starting the company in my college apartment, dropping out, growing fast, early employees working until dawn in the dusty shell of an old community center in the Mission, formulating products in the same kitchen where people microwaved lunch and made coffee. Making the leap into tech with our app, growing faster, faster, until we're nearly outgrowing the top two floors of a SoMa tower.

Jeremy looks properly boggled by our numbers. Even though his magazine is naming me Entrepreneur of the Year, he didn't take Radical seriously. His eyes dart around the kitchen, calculating how much I'm worth. Out the window, the sun condenses to a bright, shimmering yolk and splits across the water.

Gavin comes in, hair wet from surfing. He shakes Jeremy's hand, amiable, accepting his congratulations on the wedding, replying to the query of what he's working on with talk of the garden, effectively curtailing Jeremy's interest.

I pour the wine, and his attention returns to me.

"Pretty staggering rate of growth right from the start," he says, grasping for our groove. "What's your secret?"

I sprinkle bowls of mushroom bourguignon with fresh chives.

Thoughtfully, I muse, "In a world of skeptics, I'm open-minded. I don't dismiss anything. There's a vast world of wellness we're only beginning to understand, ancient traditions resurfacing and astonishing us with their wisdom. Energy, beauty, sex, spirit, mind, heart—they all have higher planes, infinite potential. I'm always asking: What would help me feel better, live better? Even as Radical grows, it's still incredibly personal. I can't work any other way."

Jeremy sits forward, his fork quivering in his hand. I brace for the inevitable.

"Your father was also in business." He watches me with all the concern of a hunter sighting a deer. "He was convicted of fraud. And here you are, Entrepreneur of the Year. How did your dad's fall from grace influence you?"

Gavin's foot moves to the lowest rung of my stool.

"I'm often asked that." I've mastered my tone: serious, unoffended. It implies that I've worked through this with a therapist, achieved closure.

"My dad made major mistakes, and paid a high price. He lost everything. He went to jail.

"I was thirteen. The most important thing to me wasn't business, obviously. It was the loss of my dad.

"As a CEO, the lesson I take is that authenticity is the central thing. At Radical, I've always taken that incredibly seriously. I promise radical honesty. Some people even say I go too far."

This bait is juicy: my sex diary, the full-body mud mask I wore in lieu of clothing on a magazine cover, the backless red-carpet dress that revealed purple cupping bruises.

"You don't have many boundaries."

"I'm an open book."

"You've drawn almost as many detractors as admirers."

"Inevitable, on the internet."

"Still. There are vocal skeptics of wellness. If it's real, or only snake oil."

Squeezing my napkin in my lap, I explain that some people are quashers. They take pleasure in tearing down ideas, mocking and dismissing.

"Even the premise, that wellness is 'fake': What does that even mean? Wellness is sleep and nutrition and mindfulness. Surely those are 'real'?"

It's a strain to keep impatience from my voice. "My followers are questers. They're curious, open-minded, optimistic. They want to explore."

The meal is almost over. It's been a straightforward interview, but I'm drained. Maybe it's the reminder that my dad won't walk me down the aisle, that he never saw Radical. He died soon after I started Stanford, but he'd faded to a ghost of his former self long before then.

Touch Greatness at Jake's, that was his tagline. His ads played on the radio. A memorabilia store sounds quaint now, but I was proud, living in our big house in a Seattle suburb, ignoring the classmates who bragged about whose dad was higher up at Boeing, because my dad flew me around the country. At arenas and stadiums and ballparks, we sat in floor seats and box seats and sometimes climbed the bleachers to rub elbows with real fans. *The hoi polloi,* he'd say. He wore swishing jackets and sneakers. His was the shrill whistle the TV microphones picked up.

Fraud sounds so serious. He forged signatures. The plastic-sheathed, UV-proofed treasures proudly displayed in the shop were fake.

I never knew why he did it, or how much he forged. Surely some of it was real. Hadn't we gone to all those games, met so many athletes? I shook their hands myself.

For dessert, there's pie from the bakery in town. Fetching cashew cream from the fridge, I linger, wait for my flushed skin to cool.

When I sit, I'm sure my face shows nothing, but Gavin presses his foot to mine.

Jeremy Krill cuts his pie with the side of his fork, chomps aggressively. "Do you expect Radical to reach a billion-dollar valuation?"

Tap-tap of my fork on the plate, like I'm considering this.

"A billion is an arbitrary number. A point along the journey to a larger goal."

Jeremy raises his eyebrows.

Nobody believes me when I tell them how big Radical is going to be. Then, when I surpass my own predictions, they forget that they ever doubted me, even suspect that I've come up short.

"Still," Jeremy presses. "It's a landmark. Do you expect your next financing round to make Radical a unicorn?"

My fork stalls. "I haven't announced a new round."

He lifts his phone, taps the screen, confusion creasing his forehead.

"We're off the grid," Gavin says, lacing his hands behind his head. "Disconnecting is crucial for health and creativity. In the future, being offline will be considered a luxury."

Disappointed, Jeremy drops the phone, but not the point. "I heard a rumor that you're about to open another financing round. Your, what, fourth?"

"I'm afraid my Legal Team wouldn't like me to comment." My teeth clash together. "Do you happen to know the source?"

"A Twitter account. One of your detractors, Radical lunacy, or something. I take it from your reaction that the post wasn't a joke."

"No comment," Gavin chimes in cheerfully.

"You promise radical transparency," Jeremy says, a challenge entering his voice. "You let your followers into every area of your life. Do you have any secrets? Besides the financing round, of course."

"I'm an open book." I smile. I hold up a finger. "But I don't like spoilers. I'm the one telling the story."

As soon as his headlights disappear, I get into my car and drive the opposite direction. I'm not even wearing shoes. The night air is freezing.

I'm announcing the fundraising round at the All-Hands tomorrow morning. The cherry on top of a successful Retreat. It should galvanize the staff, give us momentum through the summer, our slowest season, and into fall, our biggest. It's really fucking exciting, and it's my news to share. Very, very few people know.

So how did it get out?

The road climbs. Pines crowd in. The few houses beyond mine are rarely occupied. As soon as a bar of reception appears, I stop in the road.

@Radicalidiocy
A little bird told me @Radical is about to pass a hat around Silicon Valley's smartest VC firms. The company that sells powdered unicorn horn is finally becoming a unicorn.

@Radicalidiocy
The real question is, will Rhoda finally decide to share the wealth with her employees? Most don't own a single share of Radical.

Back at the house, I begin packing. Gavin is editing photos on his computer. He blinks at me through his blue light glasses.

"Bonfire or forest fire?"

"A small conflagration. Actually no, just the errant spark that might cause a fire. I'll stamp it out."

He gets up and puts his hands on my shoulders. "You're too tense to drive."

His touch travels down my back, and my body reflexively eases. I sidestep him, zip my bag. I need to get to the city, to call my adviser, to be Rhoda.

"I'll come with you, then. Warn you when you're doubling the speed limit."

"No, you stay. Work in the garden. It makes me happy."

In the car, I tie a scarf over my hair, and my head throbs like the silk is radioactive.

No one can understand the pressure I'm under. Usually, it gives me freakish energy, makes me capable of working without sleep or food. It sharpens my mind, keeps me five or six moves ahead of the rest of the room, clears my vision so the best ideas and cleanest solutions appear in laser focus against the fog of minutiae.

But sometimes, the pressure turns inward, holds its dagger to my throat. *You can't keep up,* it hisses. *You can trust no one, but you can't do it all yourself. You'll drop one ball, and your life will crumble. You'll be finished, a laughingstock. You'll fail.*

Cecelia

Monday

The customer is livid.

"I preordered this serum in spring, and it finally showed up today, smashed, oil spilled everywhere. You threw bubble wrap into the box but didn't bother securing it to the bottle!!"

"Not me, personally," Cecelia types. She can't help herself.

"I'm sorry?"

"I'm happy to issue a refund."

In the chat window, Cecelia's avatar is a brunette in a purple cardigan, eyebrows arched in a concerned expression. After she was assigned the cartoon self, Cecelia bleached her hair.

"Do you think that's an acceptable solution? I've been waiting MONTHS."

Cecelia resists correcting her. The customer placed her order in April, and it shipped five weeks later. Still, she has proof the bottle arrived broken. In her photo, she's holding the offending package over an antique blue Persian rug.

In the upper corner of Cecelia's screen, a clock ticks down the allotted time per complaint. She's down to thirty seconds, and it's obvious Blue Rug is just warming up.

"Unfortunately, the serum is out of stock. Our skincare products are made by hand in small batches, and they sell out quickly. I can put you on the list to ship as soon as we have inventory."

The official script attempts to simultaneously soothe disgruntled customers and fuel their desperation to acquire Radical's exclusive products.

Cecelia is amazed anyone believes Radical "handmakes" anything. Skin Polish alone sells tens of thousands of units every month.

But their customers do believe. The entire company floats on a bubble of collective delusion.

@Radicalidiocy
We could advertise skincare potions made by elves and they'd sell out, and then people would cry because elves are famous for their luminous skin.

The Core Team brags up Radical's average customer: a thirty- to forty-something woman with 1.4 kids. Highly successful. Extremely educated.

Not necessarily smart.

"This is unacceptable. Can I speak to a manager?"

Cecelia's countdown clock turns red and shakes furiously.

"I'll mail a complimentary sampler and get you on the waitlist for Skin Polish."

She marks the issue resolved.

It's seven thirty in the morning, and Blue Rug is Cecelia's third ticket. Customer Worship associates "process" 120 tickets per day, a supposedly reasonable target that barely allows time to use the bathroom. The thought of the mountain of tickets still to climb makes Cecelia's chest tight. In the CW portal, where team rankings are publicly displayed, her name is always at the bottom.

A ping announces a review. (Instant feedback provides "transparency" and "real-time lessons on improvement.")

Blue Rug gave her one star. "Dismal attitude. Didn't apologize, didn't care."

She's surprisingly perceptive. Cecelia never apologizes, on principle. Why should she, when it isn't her fault?

She guesses that Blue Rug is a Diane, the largest category of Radical shoppers.

A Diane is in late middle age and emulates Diane Keaton's style—casual luxury, neutral-colored clothing, no-makeup makeup. When life fails to live up to a Diane's expectations, her rigid perfectionism lashes into rage.

> **@Radicalidiocy**
> Scariest place on the internet is Radical's Instagram when a product sells out. Never tell a woman with a six-figure credit limit that she can't have something she wants!

Then there are the Chloes. Twentysomethings with twenty-step skincare routines, earnest questions about animal testing, and self-indulgent "unboxing" videos.

Thirtysomething Amandas have money to burn on forty-dollar-a-pop barre classes, hundred-dollar yoga pants in every color, and ten-dollar juices "powered" with vitamins.

A Josie is a young mom on a tight budget who still "invests" in Radical products.

But the absolute worst are the Michelles. Michelles follow Rhoda's advice ardently. They genuinely believe in the power of wellness. They send long letters describing problems healed by Radical's pricey snake oil, from hormonal acne to acrimonious divorce to literal cancer. Michelle testimonials are automatically sent up the chain. PR and Marketing pull quotes to feature in newsletters and splash across the website. Proof that Radical's mission is beneficial. That Rhoda's dream of "saving the world" by helping women is real.

> **@Radicalidiocy**
> A $100 chunk of rose quartz (mined for pennies in Madagascar!) cured my chronic pain and looks great on my bookshelf! xo, thanks, Rhoda!

It's strange, how strongly Cecelia dislikes the Michelles. More even than the insufferable Dianes. She hates them with a quivering fury that pulses between her lungs and heart like a toxic organ.

Cecelia marks her avatar as busy. She's the only one working in CW, a downside of taking the early shift, as the queue has 187 tickets and counting. The upside is that nobody's there to glare as she walks away.

The office is quiet. Rhoda designed the open floor plan to resemble some national park, so all the support beams are wrapped in faux rock. The desks are arranged not in rows but random loops, like aliens got high before making crop circles. It's a gift for Cecelia, who wanders through the pods of teams she has nothing to do with, stopping to read scribbled to-do lists and scan unattended inboxes, subject lines hinting at secret corners of Radical she longs to access.

Cecelia started the account with no agenda beyond releasing the pressure that builds up in her brain, day after day, listening to Radical bullshit, having to spout it herself. Nobody's allowed to joke. Everyone has to be "all in."

@Radicalidiocy
How does she do it? Subscribe to our podcast to hear CEO and Beautiful Privileged Person Rhoda West discuss how to get rich and still have time for weekly colonics!

@Radicalidiocy
Breaking: Four million people have downloaded the Radical app for tips on living whole, undistracted lives.

@Radicalidiocy
Seeking writer to promote wellness products. Must have experience in fiction. Magical realism preferred.

Even though she loathes social media—it's gamified to keep people hooked to their phones all day—Cecelia was gratified by the upward tick of followers. Early on, she had an unexpected success. The FDA dinged Radical for making false claims, and Cecelia's tweet was quoted in BuzzFeed.

@Radicalidiocy
The FDA doesn't appreciate that Femme Vitale absolutely delivers on its core benefit: making your medicine cabinet look like Rhoda's.

Cecelia's followers surged, and her ambition grew. More than mock Radical, she longs to tear it down.

She peers into Rhoda's private corridor. Sometimes her assistant leaves an intriguing sticky note on her desk. The light is already on in Rhoda's office. Cecelia imagines her pacing, snarling at the latest tweets, wondering how her big news got out.

At the Retreat, Cecelia was in the bathroom, shirking her mandatory volunteer shift, when two members of the Core Team walked in. She saw them through a crack in the stall door. Tall and willowy, as if being a manager requires beauty as well as brains.

As they languidly peed, one said, "I heard Rhoda's finally going to announce the new round."

"It would be insane if we didn't unicorn, right?"

"She's pitching, what, seven firms? And Jason, I heard, is getting in again."

"We're definitely gonna unicorn."

Flush.

Cecelia was thrilled.

She posted on Sunday morning, and comments rolled in all day, a rally building for Radical to share stock with the "Radigals" who toil for her.

Cecelia usually dreads the daily All-Hands meeting. Every Radical crowds into the lobby, an earth-toned rainbow of billowy caftans and high-waisted trousers. The air is thick with a headache-inducing smell of coffee, expensive shampoo, and cruciferous-forward green juice. A peppy pop song blares from speakers. *I'm happy*, the singer insists, snapping his fingers. *Happy!*

Is it Cecelia's imagination, or is the throng especially geared-up this morning? She imagines them booing Rhoda, outraged and energized.

"Can you imagine," a guy with a pubescent mustache says to his doppelgänger, "being so dumb you don't ask for options at the hiring table?"

The friend laughs like Beavis. Cecelia glances around at the Engineer dudes and Marketing girls who surround her. Nobody else looks offended.

Rhoda appears. In her white suit, she looks like a cross between a cult leader and an eager Realtor. She does a little dance, shimmies her shoulders until the music stops.

"Good morning!" Her voice is deep and throaty, as if she learned in business school that a masculine voice is more trustworthy. (Though Rhoda is proud that she didn't go to business school. Proud that she dropped out of Stanford, when most of the world would give a kidney for an elite education.)

"Thanks to everyone for showing up at our hometown Retreat. We shattered our goals. And, as you know, I set impossible goals, so surpassing them is a big fucking deal!" She pumps her fist. She's smiling, but her eyes scan the crowd like a hawk's.

For Radicalidiocy's profile, Cecelia sketched a caricature of Rhoda: a bubbleheaded blond with a cobra in her hands. But in real life, Rhoda is intense, even aggressive, always leaning forward like she's waiting for the sound of a starting gun.

"In more exciting news, I'm thrilled to announce that we're opening up another round of financing!" She puts a hand to her ear theatrically. "Nobody sounds surprised?" She rocks on her feet. "I guess you all have the internet."

Everyone laughs. They all sway, unconsciously imitating Rhoda.

Cecelia feels clammy. Her vintage polyester dress tightens around her body. The smell of old cigarettes rises from the fabric.

"In all seriousness, I'm excited to find partners who share our vision, so we can accelerate our zippy growth. But I also want to address a topic near to my heart."

Her voice is all concern, all warmth. "It's my dream to make stock options available to employees. As often happens, my dream got tangled in a net of logistics."

Pain winds up Cecelia's ribs. She tries to ignore it, breathing lightly, while Rhoda spouts bullshit and everyone gazes up like she's bearing a divine message.

"My hope is that everyone in this room already feels possessive of Radical. This company wouldn't be what it is without you." She stretches out her arms. "At Radical . . ."

Too late, Cecelia remembers why she always slips out early. Here it comes, the dreaded chant, the voices reciting louder and louder, ending on a shout:

At Radical, we share the Well, we quest harder, ignore the haters, always bebetter, can't be stopped, Radical, Radical, out on top!

Rhoda cheers. Her ponytail hangs down her shoulder like a snake.

Yes, there's someone Cecelia hates more than the Michelles.

Rhoda.

Dani

Monday

Dani is at the bottom of a pit, an anchor lashed to her ankle. Far away, something beeps. Hauling herself up, she fumbles to silence her alarm. Her eyes droop; the anchor drags. She's never been so exhausted. Never knew exhaustion like this existed.

As soon as she's vertical, nausea rushes in. She hurtles down the hall, bangs the bathroom door shut.

Not long ago, her mornings were carefully choreographed: meditation, shower, makeup, a daily affirmation scrawled on a Post-it stuck to the mirror. Now she vomits, collapses against the claw-foot tub, legs flopped on dusty penny tile.

The baby floating inside Dani is only the size of a lemon, not an anchor, not heavy at all. Her eyes close.

Up, up, get dressed, go. Lift is waiting.

This is the only affirmation she needs: Lift is ahead.

Only one elevator stops on the thirty-fourth floor. It opens onto a black-tiled antechamber, empty except for a brass sign that reads "Access to the Well Is Restricted. No Photography or Video. Visitors See Reception on 35."

Dani swipes her pass at the heavy door set into the wall. It opens with a suction sound, like a seal breaking.

Stepping into the Well, Dani always feels as if she's descended deep underground. The hall is cool and dim. Her reflection glides across the black tiled walls like a pale fish. It's silent apart from a low hum, as if the air behind the closed doors is pressurized. Dani's never glimpsed inside the rooms, with their mysterious, evocative names: Source Room, R&D, Panacea Conference Room.

Breathing the cold, pure air, Dani already feels better. In the Well, Radical develops all the remedies she relies on. Her Femme Vitale and Good Gut vitamins. The immunity concentrate she dissolves in water and the magnesium caramel she chews before bed. The oils she dabs on her wrists, for calm and focus and energy. The collagen-rich SuperYou juice she's sipping now, the only thing she can stomach for breakfast.

Thirty percent of the human body is collagen. It makes hair strong, skin elastic, muscles springy. Dani imagines thick, unctuous collagen coating her insides, plumping the baby.

The final door is the only one Dani's opened. Inside the Testing Center a worker in a white lab coat sits behind a counter. As Dani enters, she rises to shake a pill into a dish.

"Any new symptoms? Headaches, nausea, fever, rash?"

"Nope," Dani lies, accepting the dose of Lift in her palms.

The call for testers went out after the New Year: *Be the first to try Lift! Apply for the Radical Trials!*

Lift! For months, Rhoda had teased the mysterious supplement under development. Not for health or beauty, but to "center the mind, spirit, and heart."

Within days of starting the Trial, Dani felt the effects. Before Lift, her sadness was perpetual. It ebbed and surged, always worst at night. Lift broke the pattern. Nothing dramatic; she wasn't ecstatic. She simply felt *even*.

The improvement was so notable that, in March, when Dani confronted a stick with two pink lines, she never considered withdrawing from the Trial. If a mother is upset or stressed, the fetus essentially marinates in bad hormones, absorbing them into her foundational nervous system. Dani on Lift is good for the baby, too. Anyway, in spite of the attendant's symptom check, the risk feels small. Lift is natural, like everything Radical makes. Dani's only fear is being found out. The truth is written on her body: in the grease at the roots of her hair, the swell of her breasts and stomach, the woozy clench of her jaw. But the attendant doesn't notice. So far, nobody has.

Taking a seat at the long table, Dani opens the sleek, lilac-toned Radical app and navigates to Lift. The screen goes white, and unadorned text appears:

Good morning! Welcome to the world's first hybrid supplement.
Please follow the journal prompts and take your dose of Lift when
directed. Write freely: the deeper you go, the deeper the benefits. The
journal is yours alone.

Dani clicks.

Did you dream last night? What did you feel when you woke?

Dani tries to remember past the anchor and its heavy chain. She dreamed of her mom's garden. It was peaking: fragrant peppers and tomatoes heavy on vines, geraniums so red they stung the eye. But it was winter. The air was slate gray and wet. Wind shook the plants in their stakes. The flowers didn't have time to drop their petals; they simply shriveled.

Her mom was kneeling in the flower bed. Dani called for her to come inside. Her mom glanced over her shoulder. Her smile was radiant. "Don't worry!" She leaned back over the lilies, her gold cross pendant swinging.

Dani takes her time recounting the dream, trying to express how warm her mother had looked, even in the cold. Glowing with vitality.

The app swallows Dani's text. The screen goes black, reflecting Dani's face, and the thin gold chain under her collar, then it serves another question.

Take a moment to imagine a relaxing vacation, real or imaginary.
Where are you? Name one thing you can see, smell, touch, hear, and
taste.

In the spring, Trevor took Dani to Tent Rocks in New Mexico, the place that inspired Radical HQ. Whittled by ancient water, the canyon wound between mammoth rock formations. Compressed into red and bronze layers by the passing of eons, the rocks appeared strangely soft. They rippled and curved. Meandering along the twisting path felt almost mystical. (Like birth, Rhoda described it: feminine and holy.)

It was beautiful, although Dani was queasy from the altitude, or maybe early pregnancy. She leaves that out. She writes about the smell of dust, the heat of the stone and the startling chill of the shade.

Swallow Lift with 6 oz. liquid.

Lift is button-size, matcha-green. It's not chalky like a vitamin, or smooth like a gel capsule, or coated like medicine. When Dani puts it on her tongue, the shell is brittle as a seed. As she holds it in her mouth, it dissolves, airy and almost savory.

Her shoulders uncurl. Her tiredness eases, the anchor loosened.

Choose a word to define your day.

Thinking of her mom's garden, Dani writes: Bloom.

You've achieved Lift-off! Thank you for participating in the Radical Trials.

Dani's lifting her bag to her shoulder when a tall, dark-haired woman comes into the room, holding a manila envelope. The receptionist lowers her phone, but the woman's eyes land on Dani. Her heels clip briskly.

"Dani Lang? I'm Mari Kapoor. I'm glad I caught you. Do you have a moment?"

Dani's Radical bracelet hums three quick warnings: her pulse is high.

Mari is the Director of the Well. The genius, as Rhoda calls her, behind every release. Like Rhoda, Mari has a background in science, hence the uniform of crisp white coats and the pristine workspace. *We run the Well as rigorously as a medical lab,* Rhoda says. *Except our ingredients are entirely pure.*

"I want to thank you for helping with our project," Mari begins.

They know Dani's pregnant. They're going to kick her off the test. She'll be lucky if they don't fire her. Lying about her symptoms, jeopardizing the veracity of the Trial results, just because she selfishly enjoys taking Lift . . .

"It's an honor," Dani blurts. "Lift is incredible. The journal, the ritual—it really works for me." With an effort, she closes her lips.

Mari seems amused. "I'm glad. Your responses impressed us. We've sent a few up to Rhoda. She's interested in talking to you about a potential writing role."

Dani is stunned. Rhoda has read her writing. *Rhoda!*

"Customer Worship transfers need special approval," Mari says, sliding the envelope to Dani. "Here are the forms for transferring departments, for your perusal."

Her voice is impersonal, focused on the logistics, but Dani finds herself smiling apologetically. It's her habitual response to the condescension that inevitably accompanies the words *Customer Worship*, whether she's talking to someone at Radical, to Trevor's friends, strangers at parties, Uber drivers, baristas. Customer Worship doesn't fit into either of the city's two categories: Tech and Everyone Else.

"Rhoda's assistant will set up an interview." Mari stands, smoothing her crisp coat. "Good luck. Rhoda is very particular. You should be proud, however things go."

Dani takes the envelope in both hands.

Dani would have done anything to get in the door at Radical. Mopped floors, scrubbed toilets, worn a hairnet and served lunch. She feels lucky every time she rides the elevator to the top floor. Lucky as she passes between the sculptural pillars, designed to evoke the striated rocks of the canyon. Lucky as she follows the teal path set into the navy carpet, which winds through the pods, past the glass-doored conference rooms where future Radical projects unfold. (The full path is a quarter-mile loop; Rhoda walks ten or fifteen laps a day.)

Dani's lucky to be here. Lucky to be employee #55, with an enviable first-name-only email address, a coveted lilac track jacket with her name embroidered on the chest.

She sits at her desk, automatically checking the sidebar to confirm her avatar is still ranked at the top of the CW Team. She easily sinks into a flow, responding to tickets, words coming easily as apples picked from a low branch. She likes helping customers, even the ones her teammates find difficult. She's lucky to be in CW, truly, but the idea of writing for Radical fizzes inside her. Under her desk, Mari's envelope juts from her purse like a flag.

At noon, black-painted fingernails tap her desk. "Lunch? They're doing bao buns." Cecelia lifts her eyebrows in ironic enthusiasm.

She joins the thronged buffet line, while Dani goes for the bland safety of a hummus wrap. At a table, she takes a cautious bite. Crumbles of salty feta dot the creamy hummus. It's delicious, but her hunger is a coin that can flip, at any moment, to revulsion.

Cecelia drops her loaded tray and collapses in her chair like she's been toiling in a kitchen for hours. "What a circus." She squints at Dani's wrap. "That's it?"

"I'm not hungry," Dani says, averting her eyes from the squish of Cecelia's bao. She hasn't told anyone yet, apart from Trevor. Not even his parents. At some point, they'll drive down to Brisbane, sit in the dining room with the collection of antique stringed instruments, eat a flawless dinner with paired wines, and share the news.

Cecelia licks her fingers. "Aren't you pissed that Rhoda didn't give us shares?"

Dani hums. *Lucky*, she's still thinking, sipping her ginger juice. Lucky to be in the bright cafeteria. Lucky to have found Radical.

"What's up? You're all—" Cecelia describes a circle in the air over the table, searching for the word. "Something."

Cecelia is perpetually off in space, but she can be surprisingly perceptive when she tries. She might read the signs: Dani's puffy eyes, her ginger juice.

"I might get a promotion," Dani blurts.

"Really?" Cecelia's surprise is close to a recoil. "Will you be a Team Lead? Taking over for Holly, I hope." She brightens at the idea.

"To Marketing. But, I dunno. Maybe I should stay in CW." Dani smooths the wrinkles from her empty foil wrap.

Cecelia laughs. "Oh, sure. What'd they tell us, our first day? We're doing crucial work on the front lines with customers!" Her voice deepens to a parody of an old-timey news anchor.

They started in CW together. Cecelia found out Dani was new to the city and took charge of her orientation. They ate Bi-Rite ice cream in Dolores Park, ogling the skyline, Dani coughing in the cloud of pot smoke. They drank tiki cocktails in a fancy hotel in Nob Hill, and sipped espresso at sidewalk café tables in North Beach, and danced in the Castro wearing feather boas from a store that sold vintage clothing by the pound. They browsed paperbacks at City Lights, and Cecelia admitted that she wanted to be a writer. *If nothing else, I could write a memoir. How to Be Filthy Poor in Tech Paradise!*

"Good for you," Cecilia says now, drawing her legs from under the table. "Want dessert?"

Her flip-flops slap across the floor. She pulls the lever for soft serve, coiling the chocolate-vanilla swirl perilously high over the rim.

Rhoda

Monday

"Someone in this room is responsible for leaking the fundraising round. Whether you're aware of it or not."

The Core Team is silent. Heads of Marketing, Data and IT, Operations, People, and the Well. Smart women. Handpicked by me. Loyal, I thought. They sit straight, ignoring the punches of construction noise from the high-rise going up next door.

@Radicalidiocy
Radical's "Core Team" looks like a collection of Business Barbies from Mattel. #bebetter #orjustlookbetter

Women's effectiveness is ten times as likely to be linked to their appearance as men's. An all-female Core Team was crucial to me. The best candidates knew the research and presented themselves accordingly.

Everyone's all blown-out hair (except for Cam's spiky pixie), invisible makeup, manicured nails raking the tabletop. Our weekly meetings are bloodbaths. We review wins and fails, assign ownership to cross-departmental projects, and—most crucially—distribute budgets. The atmosphere gets as heady as a locker room before a match. Radical bracelets trap sweat, detect the rise of endorphins, assess the hammer of the pulse. Competition brings out the best in people.

"I'm going to assume the leak was unintentional, since everyone in this room stands to gain or lose in direct proportion to the success of this round. If you believe you know how it got out, speak up."

Silence. In the back of the room, Jason Percy, my first investor, my oldest adviser, stands, arms crossed. His nose is sharp, his head shaved in an attempt to one-up encroaching baldness. His glasses reflect the windows as he surveys the table.

I stride to the whiteboard, scrawl *Circuit*, the marker squealing.

"Going forward, remember this rule. Energy can only flow when a circuit is closed. This room is a circuit. Your teams are circuits. When a circuit is open, no information should move, period." I swivel on my heel. "Cara?"

Cara, Head of People, stands. "We're taking immediate steps. All social media sites will be blocked. We'll run a search in case the writer posted from Radical equipment. Log-ins, email activity, even keystrokes, if it comes to it. It's a sizeable search. If anyone has concerns about a member of their team, that could speed things up."

Cara is athletic and upbeat, a former volleyball captain. Does her aggressive cheerfulness mask secret cynicism?

"Are we sure they work at Radical?" asks Lisbeth, Head of Marketing. Milk-pale, with orb-like blue eyes, Lisbeth danced professionally before enrolling at Harvard Business School. Her Instagram has over twenty thousand followers. If she's tweeting, she's motivated by envy, or restlessness. At some point everyone wonders if they can do better than the boss.

"Have you read all of the tweets?" I ask.

Lisbeth scoffs. "Of course not."

I lean against the window. Construction shakes the glass. "Know your enemy. I've read them. They work here."

This morning, five minutes after the All-Hands:

@Radicalidiocy
Rhoda's message to Radigals who want stock: Visualize how hard you'd work if you had options, begin to work that hard, and the universe will manifest your desire. Probably. Maybe.

"Is searching computers a privacy concern?" asks Mari, Director of the Well. Mari has a medical background; her notions of confidentiality are outdated. I can't imagine Mari tweeting, she's too professional, but if it's her, I have real reason to worry. She's done brilliant work on Lift. Is she feeling underappreciated?

Cam, Head of Data, reclines in their chair. "As a condition of employment, employees agree that everything done on Radical hardware is visible."

Cam is sharp, efficient, unflappable. It they're behind it, it's to make some political statement.

I stroke my Radical bracelet with my thumb. Sometimes I check my profile in the system. It's reassuring to see the even lines: pulse and step count and 5.5 hours of sleep.

In the silence, everyone twitches, except Jason. He's still as a hawk on a branch. He's the only person in the room I trust completely.

An alarming crash comes from the construction site. Then a chorus of frantic shouts. Everyone turns eagerly to the distraction.

"A good place to end," I say. "A reminder of the importance of careful work."

I cross the room to open the door. The team, surprised at the release, rushes to collect laptops and coffee cups. They file out quickly, as if they're afraid I might grab them by the elbow. I stand in the doorway a moment, watching them disperse to their pods. The office hums. Radigals bend over computers, stride in pairs to meeting rooms, heads swiveling as they pass the flat-screens showing the latest numbers.

The troll, whoever she is, is an anomaly.

Back in the room, Jason's settled into a chair, awaiting our debrief. His legs are crossed, exposing his signature red socks—same brand as the Pope, he brags.

His dapper clothes were the first thing I noticed about him, a contrast to the khaki-and-branded-activewear venture capitalist uniform. We met at a mixer at the Rosewood Hotel, our elbows jutting over the glossy wood bar. I ordered a Coke in a glass, hoping no one would guess it was all I could afford.

"I prefer club soda with lime." Jason's voice was conspiratorial. "And ditch the straw." To my surprise, he pinched the skinny black stirrer from my drink with an efficient, fussy gesture, like flicking away a bug. "Voilà."

He wore a sweater the color of a robin's egg, cuffs rolled. A wry expression animated his sharp features, as if he and I were in on the joke. The mixer was stilted. The bar resembled a high-end furniture store: midcentury leather chairs and brass objects artfully scattered. I was twenty-three, and my ambitions for Radical felt insuppressibly big. It seemed that the furniture in the room should be levitating off the ground with the force of it.

Jason saw my vision as clearly as I did. By the end of the day, he gave me a check. By the end of the year, we did another round. He helped me recruit a team, scale our operations, charge through thousands of roadblocks. Radical grew and grew.

The tweeter is a pest, a flea—I want him to toss it aside like a straw.

"What do you think?" I ask.

His fingers drum the table. "If it's one of your team, it'll be a disaster."

I was returning to the table, but I stop. "'Disaster' seems excessive."

"Does it?" He directs his prosecutorial stare at me.

I walk up the room, making an effort to seem relaxed. "Most likely one of them said something to someone on their team, or worked on the deck in the open. You know how rumors spread."

He stiffens as I pace. He's warned me about it before. *Excessive energy is exciting, until it's irritating.*

"We need to take this seriously. Investors will be watching us closely. They'll factor the threat into their calculations."

"We were about to announce the round anyway. It's an annoyance, certainly, but a threat?" I lift the eraser and scrub the whiteboard clear, as if this was always my aim. "The worst she can do is distract us. I won't give her the gift of my attention."

"Your attention." He raps the table. "Ah. Finally, we get to the real concern."

I was about to sit beside him, but I stop, squeezing the mesh chairback. "What does that mean?"

"If your cabin had basic amenities, you would have known about the tweets immediately. The Rhoda I know wouldn't leave herself out of the loop." He pronounces *cabin* as if the word itself has mildew.

"I took one day off. Not even! The reporter from *Entrepreneur* came over yesterday. I'm their cover story, if you remember."

"At this stage, one hour is too long," he counters. "Investors won't tolerate anything less than one hundred and ten percent focus. All you talk about online is that wedding."

My temper propels me down the length of the table. "Do you realize how big the wedding industry is? The Social Team says those posts perform. The Merchandising Team wants to expand the collection. It's a growth area for us."

My ring twists, the diamond digging into my palm. I've gotten thinner since Gavin proposed. To plan a wedding and launch the Wedding Collection in a matter of months is an enormous feat. I wish I had a clone to help me.

Inhale. Exhale. "The wedding will give us a boost during our slow season. You've never expressed concern before. You said you like Gavin."

Actually, he said he could see why my followers like him. Hardly the same.

He holds up his hands in surrender, one of his favorite gestures, maddeningly superior.

"It's not personal, my dear. It's a business concern. You're taking your eye off the ball. You didn't open the pitch deck all weekend, and it's far from finished. We're presenting in one week. At this level, we can't be cavalier. This is a new playing field."

I stiffen. It's bad luck to mention it, even obliquely: the expectation that this round will value Radical at over a billion dollars—a unicorn. I've never promised it or predicted it, but the idea is airborne. Jeremy Krill said it outright.

I force myself to sit, fold my hands on the table. When Jason says investors are jumpy, he means himself. His eyes are bloodshot. Despite his accusation, we were both in the pitch deck late. It's been our constant companion, incubating like an egg.

"I'm confident, not cavalier. It's good that we're firing on all cylinders. Since when do VCs reward caution?"

He sighs, pinching the bridge of his nose. "Getting bigger means getting more careful, not less."

"Radical isn't going to be like Pique." I mean to be reassuring, but impatience clips my words.

Jason winces.

Pique was his last major investment. It was supposed to be that rare company, a landscape-changer. Every VC is looking for a legacy-maker, that early bet that pays off exponentially, the investment so canny that, in hindsight, success seems fated.

But Pique went the other way. The only thing more spectacular than its early rise was its swift and humiliating crash. The last I heard of the founder, he was wandering the Ferry Building barefoot, accosting tourists to ask if they'd ever had a great idea.

Jason raps his knuckles on the table, dispelling the jinx.

"Radical is a rare bird." His tone is conciliatory. "We soar upward on aerials nobody else seems to find. We don't want to be taken down with a slingshot.

"We close the leak. We buckle down the deck. We stay on the grid."

I nod, swallowing my urge to remind him that I know this. He forgets, sometimes, that I'm no longer the wide-eyed girl ordering a Coke.

"I'll find whoever's behind the Twitter account. The deck will shine."

An incomplete reassurance, but he nods. He checks his watch, idly running his thumb over the scratch in the dial. The watch was a gift from me, a vintage Rolex Submariner. The dealer came to my office with a briefcase lined in blue velvet. I almost laughed when he told me the price. It was old, and even scratched! I offered to replace the glass, but Jason refused. *It adds patina.*

"I'm late," he says. "Send me the revised slides tonight."

"This afternoon," I promise.

In my own office, I stand at the window watching construction on Rusher Tower. The bottom floors are sealed with gleaming windows. The top floors are still raw, hollow as honeycomb. Work carries on inside, sparks flaring in the dark, cords tangling like capillaries. I resent the intrusion into my expensive view, but I like watching the work.

Ten years ago, this block was derelict. Ugly asphalt, junkies shambling along with shopping carts or passed out in the doors of papered-over storefronts. Then a giant software company built a tower in the neighborhood. One by one, other startups followed. The city rebranded the neighborhood the "East Cut," and construction cranes proliferated like an invasive species, building skyscrapers, transit centers, public parks floating twenty stories in the air. The biggest tech companies in the world have addresses here, and when Radical outgrew our old office, I knew we'd join them.

We couldn't afford it, but I signed the lease anyway.

There are two acceptable sizes for a startup: the minuscule, working-in-the-garage startup that's all heart and innovation and brilliance, and the successful, glossy startup flush with money and buying up land in the future. When you're in between, you fake it. You style yourself as the company you hope to be. You go all in.

I rise up on my toes and sink slowly down, stretching my calves. I'm rationalizing. I'm honest enough to admit that to myself.

What Jason doesn't know—what nobody knows—is how urgent this round is.

Radical is almost out of money. Without a successful round, our cash flow will be seriously strained seriously soon.

Our spending has always been high, but the app cost far more than I anticipated. The bracelet burned money. Their release was such a wild success, I felt no compunction about downplaying the costs to the board. Especially since Jason had opposed the app, vehemently. It was our first major disagreement, a dispute that dragged on for weeks. If he'd learned of the expense, he would have stomped on the brakes.

Radical's mission is vast. My ambition is on a larger scale than a quarterly or annual or even decade-long forecast can convey. To quibble about the cost of changing the world is shortsighted.

So: another round.

On the surface, a fundraising round is simple. Private investors have a chance to buy a stake in a company. The owner gets cash, and investors get shares.

Imagine a company as a pie. The owner decides to sell a piece, and strikes a deal with a buyer. Say, 10 percent of the pie for ten dollars. Ownership is split, and the market extrapolates that the entire pie is worth one hundred dollars.

Then the founder offers up a second slice. After some haggling, it sells for twenty dollars. Suddenly, the value of the whole pie has jumped to two hundred dollars. The first investor's slice has doubled in value, and the new investor is betting that someday theirs will do the same.

A company is far more complex, obviously, but the lesson here isn't about fractions or math. It's that value is determined by the existing owners and those who want to buy in. That means value is subjective. To an astonishing degree, value is a matter of persuasion.

Investors need to feel tingles when I present next week. I need to spin a story, make them see Radical rising, accelerating, unstoppable. To draw them into a shared vision of the future, glittering and Technicolor as a fever dream.

I need the cash; Jason needs the confidence. Radical needs the fuel.

Dani

Wednesday

Dani's mom is calling, but Dani can't find her phone. Her purse gapes in her lap. Buzzing drones deep inside. She pulls out wallet, keys, ginger candies. Her CW headset. A stuffed bear from childhood. And finally, a jar of Radical Lift. When she opens it, the pills are melted into a gummy mass.

Too busy for your mother, Nadine teases on voicemail. *Just dreaming of you.*

No, that's not right. Thinking of you, not dreaming of you.

Dani opens her eyes.

Someone is standing in the door of the meditation room.

"Are you sleeping?" The voice isn't chiding but amused. "Dani Lang, sleeping at work. I never thought I'd see the day."

Dani presses her knuckles to her eyes. Her phone is vibrating beside her ear. She set a timer for fifteen minutes. Radical's podcast touts the benefits of a catnap, and Dani was aching for sleep.

It's ten to eleven. She almost slept through her interview. She sits up, groggy. "Insomnia," she says.

"Ugh, poor you." Cecelia pulls the door closed and flops on the floor beside Dani. "Don't we sell anything for that?"

The room is too small for two. Cecelia's perfume mixes with the smells of yoga mat and perpetual damp from the water feature built into the wall.

Dani draws her legs in. "I just nodded off." A yawn pops her jaw.

Cecelia's watching her, forehead crinkling with the understanding that something is off, some factor being left out of the equation.

"And what's your excuse?" Dani asks.

"Miserable cramps. It's like a skewer." Cecelia mimes a knife sticking into her stomach. "I'm waiting for the painkillers to kick in."

Dani rubs her temples. Her interrupted nap left her with a headache. Cecelia never simply has cramps: she burns with fire or acid. Her stomach doesn't just hurt; it's molten. She's always calling out of work, canceling plans with Dani. *My organs are melting.*

"I still think you should try Femme Vitale."

Cecelia rolls her head back against the wall, closing her eyes like she really is here to meditate. "Not for me."

"It's designed to help with your exact problem."

Cecelia only yawns, languid as a cat.

"Well." Dani stands, and dizziness overtakes her. Her vision floods black. She throws a hand out to catch the wall, and blinks her sight back. Her eyes are about six inches from the water feature. A tiny stream burbles past a tiny bonsai tree.

Cecelia has that look again. On the brink of guessing.

"I'm late for a meeting," Dani says. "Are you coming to my party this weekend?"

Cecelia fiddles with the hem of her dress. "Hopefully, yes."

"Ah," Dani says. She'll get another text, another excuse. "Well, I hope you do."

In the hallway, she pinches her cheeks. Her energy is draining from her head down to the baby, like sand in an hourglass, spilling and spilling. Soon, she'll be out of the first trimester, and her pregnancy app says she'll feel so much better.

Every week, Dani endures the app's cloying pink font and baby talk to read fetal development updates like chapters in a book. This week, the baby's head accounts for half of her mass. Her vocal cords are forming. Her eyes are shut tight. Dani hasn't decided, yet, if she should mention the baby to Rhoda. She touches her stomach, like touching wood for luck.

A ring of red rock frames the door to Rhoda's office. It's arid and porous and seems to hold the memory of desert heat.

Rhoda opens the door herself. "Nice to see you, Dani."

Her silk trousers billow as she ushers Dani in. She heads for her desk, where three computer screens fan like a hand of cards. A pair of worn leather mules are kicked on the rug, for when Rhoda slips off her heels for an intense work sprint. The opposite wall is hung with press clippings from carpet to ceiling.

Rhoda bends over her laptop to type. "One second," she says. "Have a seat."

Dani perches on the canary yellow velvet couch, where Rhoda hosts product launch videos on Instagram. She plucks at her shirt hem, smoothing it down. Out the window, Rusher Tower looms like a huge machine with the casing removed. Strips of insulation flutter from the unfinished top floors.

Rhoda follows Dani's gaze. "That'll be me, soon. I'm buying the penthouse. They took my view, so I'm taking it back."

Her smile is wolfish and sharp, the only thing about her that isn't perfect. She settles into an armchair, tucks a leg under her.

"How long has it been?"

Thirteen weeks, Dani thinks, a leap of surprise in her throat, but Rhoda keeps talking, "I interview everyone we hire, but I can't always remember the details."

Dani smooths her shirt again. "Three years. I remember when you came into the room. I almost had a heart attack."

Rhoda's dangling earrings pat her cheek when she smiles. They're jade beads, the same color as her eyes. Green, almost turquoise.

"It's not meant to be intimidating. It's crucial for me to meet every potential Radigal, no matter which team they're joining. I can tell a lot about people in a few seconds. It's all about energy. Negativity is contagious."

Rhoda studies her. Dani can't remember anyone looking at her so attentively. Everyone, including Dani, doles out attention in slivers.

"You're progressing nicely," Rhoda observes.

Again, Dani falters. Thinks of the baby curled in on herself like a slipper, skin transparent, heart beating like a propeller, *dut-dut-dut.*

"From CW to the Well to my office. Quite an accomplishment."

Focus, Dani.

"It's an honor to help with the Trial. Lift is my favorite Radical product. I mean, I love them all, but—"

"Lift is special. I agree. There's a reason it's taken years to develop. It's my grand symphony." Rhoda laughs. "I don't know anything about music, really, but that's the metaphor I keep returning to. Lift requires the perfect synchronization of many elements. Mind and body and spirit, all have to play in harmony."

Addressing a crowd, Rhoda speaks slowly, her low voice resonant. In person, she speaks rapidly. Her rhythm and pitch are as certain as if she rehearsed ahead of time.

"Yes." Dani feels painfully inarticulate, but Rhoda goes on.

"You prefer writing to speaking," she declares. "That reveals a careful personality. That's exactly what I need. After our last Well release, the FDA slapped us with a fine. They have rules about what we can claim. Never mind that the FDA is a bloated, big-pharma-loving bureaucracy that disregards thousands of years of global healing tradition."

She closes her eyes, exhaling.

"You can tell this is important to me. This role will handle all content for the Well. What I need is a writer careful enough to adhere to the rules, but clever enough to preserve the Radical Voice.

"The Voice is the soul of Radical. Image gets all the attention, and of course it's gorgeous, but Voice is the real conduit for connection to the customer. The Voice validates universal female experiences. Desire and pain and hunger and pleasure. Voice truly is *radical*."

"The Voice is like an incantation." Dani's so carried along with Rhoda's thoughts she's surprised to hear herself speak. Haltingly, she continues. "It sort of . . . carries you to a higher plane. Puts you in the Radical state of mind."

"An incantation, yes, exactly." Rhoda laces her fingers together enthusiastically. Her eyes cast over Dani's face again.

Dani hopes she's going to make another proclamation about Dani. She wants to hear Rhoda's vision of her, and then fulfill it.

"So," Rhoda says, "have you ever written professionally?"

The prosaic turn is a disappointment.

"In CW, obviously." Dani crosses her ankles. "I also took a poetry workshop."

"So that explains it. 'You don't have a body, you *are* a body.'"

Dani blinks. Rhoda's holding a palm up, reverent. Song lyrics? Then Dani remembers: she wrote the words herself, in her Lift journal a few weeks ago.

She was describing an epiphany she'd had after dreaming of falling from a carousel horse as a child. Her mom picked her up, pressed a napkin to her bloody knee. Her mom in striped capris and gold sunglasses, not much older than Dani is now.

When Dani woke, her fingers found the keyhole-shaped scar on her knee.

Everything about us, every thought, every dream, every movement, every memory, comes from the body. We treat the body like a vehicle that carts us around. But we *are* a body. Nothing more.

"I was working through a dream," she says slowly, trying to remember what else she's written. Mari mentioned Rhoda reading her journals, but somehow Dani didn't consider that Rhoda now knows about her dreams. Everything she's written.

She's never written about the baby. Should she mention it, right now? It would be radically honest, and Rhoda values that, but Dani dreads spoiling the easy energy between them. *Oh,* Rhoda might say, stopping Dani's heart.

"Those lines gave me goose bumps," Rhoda's saying. "Everything comes back to the body. Our amazing, mysterious conduit of energy and life."

"There are more cells in our bodies than galaxies in the universe," Dani recites.

Rhoda posted that last night, along with a photo of the night sky over the ocean. She must have gone to her beach house after the Retreat.

"You follow my Instagram."

In fact, Dani's scrolled through the entire Radical grid, thousands of posts, stretching back years to the very first: young Rhoda pushing a dolly stacked with boxes.

Dani found Radical at the darkest part of winter, during a spell of grief so deep she didn't think it would end. Her phone screen was a portal to a new life: Rhoda doing her nightly routine, droplets of Radical oils Pollocked across a white dish. Radigals doing yoga on surfboards. Rhoda in a lab coat holding a vial between her fingers. Radigals dancing under a glittering disco ball. Rhoda meditating on a beach.

When Dani looked up from her screen, she saw her situation clearly. Crushed sofa cushions and stacked dirty dishes, orange bottles of sleeping pills shaken like dice. The den of a hibernating animal, and she'd just scented spring. She found the job listing. She boarded the plane. She trusted the universe.

"This job will be much more demanding than CW," Rhoda says. "The hours will be long and unpredictable."

"It's my dream job," Dani hears herself say. She doesn't explain that she'll need maternity leave, that she might not be available around the clock. She'll figure it out. It's not a lie.

Cecelia

Fríday

She's lying on her stomach, elbows dug into the mattress, a hot-water bottle wobbling under her hip bones.

The egg-shaped face of her Team Lead, Holly, frowns out of her laptop.

"You see where I'm coming from. This is your seventh work from home day this month. Sometimes I have to track you down, only to learn you've stayed home without telling anyone."

Cecelia stifles a yawn. Her camera is off, her avatar grinning. "I didn't feel well."

Holly sighs. "If you're sick, you should take the day off."

Cecelia snorts. CW only gets five sick days, unlike the rest of the Radigals, who enjoy "unlimited" time off. Cecelia used hers up in February.

Holly swipes a piece of hair from her eyes. She looks tired. More green juice, Cecelia thinks. Less blue light.

@Radicalidiocy
Radical recommends syncing your body clock by getting several hours of sun every day, but Rhoda brags that she spends 14 hours a day at the office. What iz math?

A spasm of pain flares like a starburst through her abdomen, twisting the air from her lungs. Cecelia presses her knuckles to her teeth.

"The problem goes beyond working from home. To be honest, I wonder if you even want to work at Radical."

"Who wouldn't?"

Relax, she orders her abdomen, but hot wires are strung between her ribs, and someone is drawing them tighter. Tighter, tighter.

"Where do you see yourself in five years?" Holly asks.

Cecelia opens her eyes. The glare of overhead light on the cement block walls suggests an emergency shelter, or an underfunded municipal office. Her door rattles with the force of someone else's laundry spinning in the washing machine. Not here, she thinks, please.

Holly gazes upward. "You need to do better, Cecelia. You're on the front lines with customers, and I need you to care."

Her pause invites Cecelia to promise she'll try harder. To grovel.

Cecelia should. She needs the job. The paycheck, the health insurance.

"Oh-kay," Holly says. "I guess that's it from me."

Cecelia closes the meeting window. She peels the masking tape off her laptop camera and rolls it into a sticky ball. She opens a ticket. She's lucky, it's just an idiot who can't find her tracking number. Here you go, have a nice day.

Feedback comes in. Four stars.

Why can't she ever, just once, get five?

Footsteps clomp down the stairs, shaking dust into Cecelia's bed.

Through the particleboard partitions that separate her bedroom from Margo's garage, Cecelia listens to her landlady heave wet clothes into the dryer.

Margo is clever. She sectioned off an eight-by-ten corner of her garage and found a sucker desperate enough to rent it for $800 a month. Cecelia.

It wasn't supposed to be like this. She has a college degree! In journalism, it's true, but who could have guessed how quickly the internet would open its maw and swallow everything, newspapers and magazines and 98 percent of human attention? Cecelia won prizes for her writing. She had grand plans. More like grand fantasies. She imagined striding through airports, passing displays of her own books in newsstands.

Instead, what has she done? She was a barista for a while. She tutored rich kids, essentially writing their college application essays for them.

Her words won other people admission to Irvine and Berkeley. She quit. One dreary spring, she stood on the sidewalk asking people if they had a moment for the environment. Nobody did, so she read books against the clipboard.

There was always the complication of her pain. The suddenness of it, grabbing her, rough as a hand. Flattening her.

The job at Radical seemed ideal. Easy, mindless work, a regular paycheck. And there was Rhoda. A woman famous for enduring a mysterious illness, whose mission was to make women well. When Rhoda ducked into the room during Cecelia's interview—"just to say hello"—Cecelia actually felt a small thrill.

God, she was naïve. She actually bought a jar of Femme Vitale, Rhoda's "favorite all-around well-being enhancer that never fails to make me feel like a goddess. It's got everything essential to a female body. I credit FV for getting me through Radical's wild sophomore year. It boosts my energy and even calms my monster PMS."

Why did Cecelia believe this? Why did she start feeling better as soon as she placed her order? Even with her employee discount, it cost more than groceries. She was confident through the first week, clung to optimism the second, and finished off the thirty-day jar feeling no different, except her pee had turned sunshine yellow.

She found a chipper little disclaimer buried in the FAQs: *Not seeing results? Be patient. Our products work best alongside a holistic lifestyle: mindful eating, good sleep hygiene, and regular exercise.*

Cecelia was chastened. She hadn't worked out all month; her eating was junk.

Then she felt furious. As though, if only she'd tried harder, she might have cured herself. Illness doesn't work that way.

Chronic illness is entirely indifferent. It constantly confronts Cecelia with the bare, cold truth that she has no control. Illness doesn't care about work or romance, plans or ambitions. The pain will come, seething and toothed. If it ebbs, it does so randomly, with a threat to return in a week, or an hour. Illness doesn't negotiate. It definitely doesn't crack open to reveal a beautiful lesson.

That's the wormy lie at Radical's heart. Cecelia can't forgive Rhoda for talking about sickness as if it's a secret font of strength. When really it just takes and takes.

At noon, Cecelia cautiously opens her door. Margo's laundry is still tumbling. Cecelia treks upstairs with the cold hot-water bottle. Margo's bungalow is bright and messy, redolent of cat. Cecelia sticks a frozen burrito in the microwave.

When she turns the corner for the bathroom, she runs into Margo, who jumps, throwing her hand to her heart. "Cecelia! I didn't realize you were here."

"Lunch break," Cecelia says.

From the kitchen, the microwave makes an alarming pop.

Margo frowns. "I thought you were at the office during the week. I need the laundry all day."

"Fine." Cecelia closes the bathroom door and waits for her to withdraw.

One day, she thinks, this will all be a story I tell people at cocktail parties. *You'll never believe where I used to work,* she imagines saying, to uproarious laughter. *Customer service! Cecelia? Never!*

She can feel blood threading out of her. A clot drops into the toilet water, dark and oily as ink. There's blood on her thighs. She turns on the shower, undresses, heaps her clothes on the floor.

You'll never believe the hovel I lived in. I was broke. Loopy on carbon monoxide and fabric softener.

@Radicalidiocy
What does a founder do on Friday night? Orgy with the board?
Shut down brain for software updates? Lobby congress to abolish
weekends?

Dani's apartment door is flung open. Music and talk pour out like heat. The voices are all male and twice as loud as necessary, and Cecelia almost turns back. She hesitates by the bed heaped with coats, and notices a card stuck in Dani's dresser mirror. *Demure, Adorable, Natural,*

Intense. An acrostic Cecelia made in January, when Dani was depressed, missing her mom.

Cecelia stops tying her scarf. When was she last here? Dani's Christmas party? She forgot a white elephant gift and stole Dani's last tampon. She's sick; it's a valid excuse, she tells herself, every time she cancels plans, stays home from work, hides in bed. But nobody seems to believe her. Not even Dani.

The truth is, she hasn't really tried to explain her illness, to Dani or anyone else. The details are too humiliating. She doesn't want to be associated with that misery. She would rather be an enigma, or even a flake.

In the mirror, her face is dull. She swipes her pinky on Dani's lipstick, blots color across her cheeks. She's taken three Motrin, and her pain is a measly six out of ten.

Dani's strung fairy lights around the bookshelves. A record player spins feel-good indie music, lots of choral la-la-las. For every woman, there are five men. For every regular person, there are a dozen founders with business cards and earnest pitches. *O Startup! My Startup!*

Case in point: Trevor has hooked some innocent bearded man to his machine. White wires run up his arms and legs.

"You can't feel anything," Trevor enthuses. "It works on a circulatory level."

Cecelia goes through the French doors to the kitchen. The table is spread with bowls of dip, dripping wine bottles, the remains of a sheet cake crumbled across cardboard. Dani is leaning against the counter, holding a glass of water to her cheek. A short man in a tight fleece is talking her head off.

Seeing Cecelia, she smiles. "Fashionably late."

"Your apartment is like a clown car. I could barely get through the door."

"Trevor invited everyone." Dani looks exhausted. A bell chimes in Cecelia's head. Dani, flat on her back in the meditation room, sleeping.

"Are you feeling OK?"

"Of course."

"You're working too hard."

Dani waves her hand.

"She's up for a promotion." Trevor appears, bad penny.

"That's right. Any news?" Cecelia makes an effort, but her brightness is tinny.

"Rhoda interviewed Dani herself. She read all of Dani's journals. Says Dani gets the voice of Radical, which, for Dani, is like being told she's channeling a deity." Trevor pretends to bow down.

"Wow." Cecelia can't think of anything to say that won't sound sarcastic.

Half-zip fleece guy saves her.

"What do you think about stock options?" He says it like a challenge. She could kiss him. "I'm in favor."

His belligerence is gleeful. "It's an absurd custom. Entrepreneurs have to draw the line somewhere. If you want to get rich, start your own company."

Even though his buddy Trevor got a fat stock package from his first job.

"And what do you do?" Cecelia makes a bet with herself: trust fund kid slash angel investor.

"I'm a freelance industry observer-disrupter with a background in patent law. I look for technology adjacent to burgeoning product categories, and I patent them. When a company catches up to me, they have to pay me for a lease." His smile is red with wine. "What I'm really looking for is the wheel of the twenty-first century. Can you imagine the value of a patent on something like the wheel?"

"Dude," Trevor says, and Cecelia takes Dani by the elbow, escaping the conversation.

"So you think you got it?"

"Don't jinx it!"

"And you'll work with Rhoda? Did she really read your journal? That seems intrusive."

Dani's eyes slide to the floor, to her toes curled in blue striped socks. "Journaling is part of the Lift Trial."

Cecelia is about to argue. Dani doesn't always have to defend Rhoda.

A woman in a green dress sets a paper party hat on Dani's head, drunkenly croons, "Birthday girl!" She hands another hat to Cecelia, who twists the sharp cone in her hands.

"What is it, anyway? This magical Lift?" Cecelia really is curious. Teasing Lift's upcoming release, Rhoda only says it's bigger than anything Radical's ever done.

Dani tugs the elastic under her chin, too polite to yank the hat off. "It's hard to describe. It's centering. Introspective. You'd like it. It might help you find your direction."

Cecelia feels reprimanded. "Ha," she says, abashed.

Dani grimaces. "I only mean . . ."

A banjo twangs in the living room, and she turns eagerly toward the distraction.

"Oh, they're going to play." Dani's already stepping away.

"I'll meet you in a minute."

Incredibly, the nasal bung of the strings is drawing everyone to the living room. Cecelia is left alone with the empty bottles of Trader Joe's wine.

A man starts to sing. Plaintively.

Dani keeps cheap vodka under the sink, for the sole purpose of doctoring vases of flowers so the blooms last longer. Cecelia sloshes some into a mug, knowing she'll pay for it tomorrow.

A woman in chunky tortoiseshell glasses sidles into the kitchen.

"I can't bear bluegrass," she announces. She scoops up a pinky of frosting from the ruins of the cake. "How do you know Dani?"

"We work together."

The woman perks up. "At Radical? Amazing. I'm fascinated by Rhoda. Last week, I fell down an Instagram rabbit hole all about her morning routine. I ended up buying a jar of bee pollen. What even is that? I got it in the mail today, and I swear I didn't even remember ordering it. I was completely brainwashed." She laughs, unperturbed. "What do you do there?"

"Appease harpies."

Tortoiseshell tilts her head.

"Customer service."

The smile Cecelia gets is pitying, so she adds, "I'm getting fired soon, though. I'm not mission-oriented. It's a fatal flaw."

She rummages in her purse to see if she has her bus pass or if she'll have to burn money on an Uber.

The woman frowns. "I'm sorry. Or am I? I follow this Twitter account about working at Radical, and it doesn't sound great."

Cecelia stops. "Radicalidiocy?"

The woman nods.

"What do you think of this? 'Don't bees have enough problems without people eating all their pollen for I-forget-what-reason?'"

Tortoiseshell's face morphs from confusion to delight. She leans closer. "You?"

Cecelia shrugs. "I used to want to be a writer."

"Wait, I can't believe this. Have I introduced myself? I'm Leandra French. I'm the editor at Megaphone. Have you heard of it?"

"I'm not sure." Cecelia's disappointed at the pivot to Leandra pitching her own hustle, though it's typical.

"We're growing. We specialize in first-person stories about women's lived experiences. You might have read about Hank Keith?"

Hank hosted a home makeover show, popular for his warm personality and kitchen-demo-ing muscles. Then an intern came forward with her story.

"That was Megaphone? Wow."

Leandra beams. She puts the rim of her glass to her lips and speaks into the poison-red surface of her drink. "To think I almost didn't come tonight. Your account is one of my favorite things on the internet. Would you ever consider writing the inside story? What Rhoda's really like?"

"I'm just a peon." Cecelia is irritated. Even people who mock Rhoda love Rhoda.

"First-person stuff is my specialty. Megaphone is all about providing a platform for voices that have historically been designated as 'smaller,' as if that's synonymous with unimportant. Everyone's perspective is valid."

Leandra's passionate gesture splashes wine onto the photo collage taped to Dani's wall, mostly of Trevor and Dani, and of Dani with her mom, who looks just like her.

Dani invited Cecelia, when everyone else at work treats her like a leper. Dani loves Radical. On her tidy shelves, Radical products stand like soldiers, ready to battle the innumerable threats of modern life. Sleeplessness and tiredness and getting old and fat. And whatever Lift does. Happy pills. *It might help you find your direction.*

Leandra brays. "This joke about the vagina egg!"

"The account is anonymous," Cecelia says.

"Gotcha." Leandra closes her phone. "I suppose they'd sue you to the moon and back if they found you."

She's drunk, Cecelia realizes. Megaphone might be a blog with three articles, or if it is for real, Leandra might forget this conversation ever happened.

"I'm exhausted," she announces, that ubiquitous complaint that's really a brag. She fishes in her bag for a business card. "Email me. I want to hear your pitch."

Leandra slides out of the kitchen, careens into the lap of a guy with a waxed handlebar mustache and a striped shirt, a combination Cecelia can hardly stomach. He curls his arm around her shoulders, and off they go.

The business card is embossed in gold text. *Leandra French, Truth-teller.*

The living room's twinkle lights shine on Dani's face. She's lying against the couch cushions, idly tracing her belt buckle. She looks sick. Can't you overdose on vitamin A? Cecelia should warn her, but Dani will be armed with Rhoda's breezy blog posts, blowing away concerns like dandelion hairs.

Seeing Cecelia, Dani stirs, but Cecelia shakes her head. I'm leaving, she indicates, tapping her wrist, even though only people truly obsessed with tech wear anything as analog as a wristwatch.

Dani grimaces an apology, makes a futile motion toward the party. She seems to gesture to Cecelia's lateness, to her holing up in the kitchen where, for all Dani knows, Cecelia spoke to no one and sullenly drank cheap wine.

Cecelia shrugs. Next time, she indicates, rocking her chin.

Of course, Dani nods.

Even in gestures, they can lie to each other.

Rhoda

Saturday

Announcing the fundraising round is wonderful; cashing the check will be wonderful; the time in between is a gauntlet of double-edged egos, barbed tongues, loaded questions, and so many swinging dicks. All the VCs I'm pitching are men.

Jason's throwing a kickoff event at his house. "Let them see their competition and sweat." He was gleeful. "They'll be eating out of your hand."

His sedate suburban road is lined with Teslas, black and shiny as beetle carapaces. Gavin exhales a plume of oaky pot smoke. "We're late," he observes.

"We're making an entrance," I counter.

A uniformed caterer takes our coats, and we cross the foyer to a catwalk balcony. Jason designed the house so the foyer overlooks the "salon," a cavernous room decorated with his impressive art collection. Three dozen guests—*an intimate soiree*, his voice purrs in my head—mill around a pianist playing far too well for the occasion. Partners from seven firms, their wives and girlfriends in bright plumage, and a smattering of extras: actors in various stages of metamorphosis into investors, the keyboardist from a late-night show band, his producer wife in a cool maroon pantsuit.

Jason spots me. "Here she is!"

So the gauntlet begins.

Gavin and I descend the catwalk staircase. He reaches Jason first, and Jason answers his fist bump with a stiff wrist.

"Gavin! I just mentioned your name to Sam Carl. Do you know him?

He's launching a documentary project in Puerto Rico. Incredible work. I'll connect you."

Sam Carl was a pioneer in social media. Like Gavin, he took his fortune and retired young, a rarity in this world. He still appears at parties, hustling for support for various projects, all of which nod to charity while offering adventure for Sam. Apparently, Jason hopes he'll lure Gavin abroad. Keep me on the grid.

I take Gavin's arm. "Gavin's show opens next weekend at the Golden Hour Gallery."

Jason opens his mouth in a mime's exaggerated enthusiasm. "Congratulations."

"Where's Jennifer?" Jason's redheaded wife usually stands out in the crowd. She's an artist, as well—artistic, anyway. She mostly paints portraits with the subjects turned away. *I can't manage faces,* she admits with a laugh.

"Indisposed, I'm afraid."

I make the proper concerned murmuring. I'm surprised. Jennifer relishes a good party. She organized the app release celebration at a private Pacific Heights mansion (*old friends of mine, dead broke, would you ever guess?*). The party was Jason's mea culpa for doubting the app. He even gave a toast. *To Rhoda, our North Star!*

He offers his elbow. "Shall we?"

"I'll get drinks." Gavin strolls off, hands in his pockets. Women's eyes leap from their conversations to follow him.

"How do I look?" I ask Jason. My dress is slinky, slit to the knee, green for luck.

Jason presses my arm. "Ready to kill." The ritual response.

The guests are drifting in tides, awaiting our approach.

First up is Larry Ivers of Redwood. Toweringly tall and famously down-to-earth, Larry was an early investor in practically every tech company that's gone on to become a household name. To say he's revered by his peers understates it. His investment instantly legitimizes any startup. No surprise Jason steered his way first.

Larry shakes my hand. His eyes are brown and surprisingly guileless. "I noticed you source some of your magic ingredients from the rainforest. That happens to be one of my passions. I'm developing an eco-adventure resort in Brazil. Part recreation, part education, so folks come away inspired to take action."

"We use a sustainable harvester." I describe the Well, and he listens attentively.

It's easy to imagine trusting him, but I've done my research, and his track record with founders is patchy. He's thrown more than one founder over, forced them out as soon as the business had a growing pain. If I bring him on, he will consider me a separate entity from Radical, a lever to pull.

We're talking easily, Larry throwing a big laugh, when Jason edges in, apologetic. "I need to steal her, I'm afraid. More this week, of course, you're our first stop—"

I smile, but don't look back as Jason ushers me along.

Money isn't so valuable, really. In this room alone, the fortunes won and lost rival the GDPs of entire countries. Right now, money is cheap and plentiful. Outrageous concepts are getting outrageous valuations. Last week, a company that delivers pizza made by robots closed a round that valued them as high as a blue-chip auto company.

So I need cash: easy enough. The right investors are harder.

Other VCs step forward. They shake my hand, beckon their partners from across the room. They trot out anecdotes calculated to please.

The founder of Oort Unlimited tells me about his great-grandmother's potent herbal tea, passed down through generations. The buzz-cut senior partner at Afterburner confides that he thought yoga was "happy horseshit" until it healed an old football injury. Ken Lowell, the youngest partner at Riptide Capital, raves about the Radical CBD he tried at a music festival in the Sonoran Desert, "the next Burning Man."

Jason dances in and out of the conversations, making minute redirections, filling lulls, bolstering my laugh with his. Like a chef concocting a finicky sauce, he lets the conversation simmer, then whisks me along at the right moment.

"Quite a sunburn on Ken," he whispers. "He's a wild card."

"He's always tweeting about women not having the tech gene," I observe.

"Then what could be more satisfying than taking his money?" He steers me toward the bar. "Best for last," he whispers. "If all goes well, this firm will lead the round."

We approach two dark-haired men tilting their wineglasses like they're reading fortunes in the sediment. They look like twins, though I know from my research they're two years apart. Tall, with the narrow faces of racehorses, meticulous facial hair framing dazzling smiles.

"Rhoda, I want you to meet Chad and Brett Ephraim."

"No introduction is necessary in the other direction," Chad says. "Great handshake."

"Likewise," I say, and he laughs like I've said something absurd.

Chad is wearing an oyster-colored pullover under his navy blazer, while his brother is formal in waistcoat and tie. Otherwise they're effectively identical, with quick, jocular voices, expansive hand gestures, and roaring laughs, chins tossed back.

"We are huge Radical fans," Brett assures me.

"We bumped into Jason at the marina," Chad says. "When he mentioned that he's on your board, we practically tackled him."

They gab more, interrupting each other to tell their life story. A wealthy family, teen modeling careers ("humiliating," says Brett, "and lucrative"). After college (Yale), they worked on Wall Street ("the salt mines!").

"Then we realized we were approaching forty, and decided to hang out our shingle."

"Less than a year in, they've established themselves as visionaries," Jason says.

I give a slow nod. "Impressive."

My assistant assembled dossiers on every firm, and theirs was the thinnest. A couple fintech startups, a food-ordering app. Their money must be burning the proverbial hole in their bespoke trouser pockets. If they join the board, I can't imagine them parsing quarterly reports, challenging my forecasts. I can more easily see one turning to the other to say, "Remember when," and launching into a narrative of childhood summers, boats scuttled on the rocks. What a gift.

"Why don't you come up to Radical? I'll give you the grand tour."

"Take her up on that," Jason says. "You can't help feeling immersed in Rhoda's vision when you're up there."

Their teeth gleam. "Wonderful."

Jason slips around the bar and retrieves a dusty bottle. "Not a word to anyone else, but I pulled this from my personal stash. Less than a thousand made. You'll appreciate it." He fills our glasses generously.

We sip. The wine is cloudy, flecked with tiny motes.

"It's like a good memory," I say.

"Nostalgia!"

Grins all around. *Remember when* we met Jason at the marina.

I know he arranged the meeting, timed it to seem accidental. I bet he took them to the restaurant with the excellent views and mediocre food, and waited until they balled up their napkins to mention the opportunity. *You know* . . .

Jason chimes his glass, drawing the room's attention. "I have a surprise! In advance of their run at the SAP Center, world-renowned Aero Cirq will perform for us tonight. Please grab a drink and make your way outside for the show!"

There's a flurry of enthusiasm. Caterers push open the doors to the backyard, where chairs fan out from a makeshift stage. I find a seat beside Gavin. He curls a hand around my neck. "You're flushed."

The dusk is cool. The obsidian surface of Jason's swimming pool steams, releasing the day's heat. The light is fading fast, and I wonder how we're going to see.

Three figures dressed in black spring out from behind a curtain. They clap their hands, activating LED lights threaded into the fibers of their suits, even over their faces. The effect is creepy and mesmerizing. As they move, music comes on, flutes and drums. Indifferent to gravity, to the rigidity of skeletons, their bodies coil together and spring apart, like the mating ritual of snakes.

It's restful to let someone else perform. I sink back. Jason is in the front row, sitting sideways so he can watch his guests enjoy the show.

He's done well. Everyone seems all in. At our formal pitches this week, they'll air concerns. They'll have done their due diligence, found the Twitter feed, read up on the FDA complaint. But they won't push hard, I can tell.

My first time pitching Radical was quite different. I was twenty-three and clueless. I prepared as if I were facing an IRS audit, calculated every profit and loss to the penny.

On the big day, I woke with a sore throat. By the time I drove down to Sand Hill Road, I was experiencing a messy internal weather system. Sweaty and freezing.

"You are not sick," I told the mirror.

The conference room reeked of stale coffee. The partners (all men) slouched around the table, fleece vests unzipped. The angles of their laptops indicated their level of engagement. Angles under thirty degrees showed complete attention. Forty-five degrees suggested a stalemate between focus and a knee-jerk urge to check sports statistics. While I set up, a dude across from me spread to one hundred degrees.

Fuck you, too. I passed out hard copies of my pitch, and they flipped ahead to get the gist.

"This may be a strange claim in a room in which billions are managed, but good health is the most valuable asset anyone can possess."

The partner I'd emailed with, Andrew, smiled encouragingly. Did he assume I was nervous? I was not. I was frustrated at their inattention and at my head, which felt like it was stuck in a rice cooker.

"Over eighty percent of American women experience regular symptoms of fatigue, stress, and exhaustion. Ninety percent say they struggle to keep pace with modern life. Wellness is a timeless concept that's finally having its moment in the marketplace."

I sounded like a robot. I clicked a button, and the numbers slide popped up. The numbers slide was my friend.

"I started Radical as a limited product range, focusing primarily on skincare made without harmful chemicals."

I ran through the figures: Skin Polish, with sales tipping into the five digits when I dropped out of school, the addition of mood oils (calm, sleep, love) boosting demand to such a pace that I couldn't keep up. The investment from my mother ("a family friend") paid for office space and production help.

I left out everything that went wrong: the expensive, glitchy inventory software, suppliers ghosting me, delivery delays. We grew anyway. And now I was asking for real money, begging these men—each of whom could benefit from an application of Skin Polish—to cut me a check so I could build the company I actually envisioned.

The investors perked up with the numbers, but only slightly.

I opened a case and passed out my bestsellers.

They handled the glass bottles as if I'd given them something dirty, private, slightly damp. One spoke kindly, as though to a precocious kindergartner: "I'll pass this along to my wife. She loves this stuff."

The lights came on, clicked by a discreet secretary. I allowed myself to briefly press cool fingers to my forehead.

The men didn't confer. Their laptops were open and demanding attention.

Andrew slid my prospectus back and forth on the table.

"What you're describing is a solid foundation for a midsize business."

He drew his chin back, like he was politely swallowing a bite of a bad meal.

"Our resources are designed to launch large companies. Companies that can scale. Frankly, I don't see that potential here."

I hadn't expected a verdict on the spot.

"Maybe I didn't make clear the target audience—"

He shook his head, looking disappointed, as if it wasn't up to him.

Dots fizzed across my vision. I heard myself thanking them for their time.

Nobody was in the lobby, which was a relief as much as an insult. I didn't even fill my allotted half hour.

The secretary handed me a cone-shaped cup of water.

"Sit down for a minute," she said. "You don't look well."

"I've got the flu," I admitted. It was absurd not to have canceled. I'd blown it.

"You'll get other meetings. May I offer a piece of advice?"

I felt too weak to hold the water; its surface trembled and splashed my skirt. I couldn't set the cup down, though, thanks to its pointy bottom. VCs didn't want people to linger in their lobby.

"You're the first woman I've seen all week, and I want to help you.

"Women tend to prove themselves. Show their work. Men show their dreams. And that's just more exciting, because it's all hypothetical, it's all possible."

She had fantastic green metallic glasses that mesmerized me.

"They don't do anything, you see. They take meetings, and distribute money, and track the money. They want to feel like they're building something. Shooting the moon.

"Go bigger," she said. "Tweak your proposal until you think it's outrageous, that you'll get laughed out of the room because it's so over the top. They'll eat it up."

The words sunk into my brain like the rhythmic lines of a childhood story.

"I love Skin Polish, by the way." She took my empty cup. "It's a miracle worker."

After dispensing the most priceless wisdom of my life, she ushered me out. The next entrepreneurs had arrived, two men, one of whom was actually wearing a hoodie. I coughed wetly as I passed them.

Three days later, I woke with the clear-eyed blue-sky energy that comes after a fever breaks. I started over. I imagined Radical invading every corner of life. I inflated my numbers until they bulged like home run kings.

When I was done, my deck was brilliant, inspired, deranged.

The next VC I met was Jason. I didn't falter. My pitch flowed smoothly. Chin high, palms dry.

Here's the piece of advice I'd share with founders, if I were a sharer of advice:

You are a magician. You're showing the audience a bird. A ball. A coin. You make it dance. Make it fly. Make it appear and disappear.

In the back of everyone's mind is the knowledge that none of it is real, so you don't need to worry about distorting reality. You shouldn't think of reality at all. For this hour, for this trick, you are responsible only for making them believe in magic.

*

After the performance, the party loosens, the audience riding a secondhand rush of feeling pleasurably boneless and slinky. I mosey through the crowd, accepting and abandoning glasses of champagne. Women approach me to share their admiration for Skin Polish or Femme Vitale. Some wear Radical bracelets cinched among gold cuffs and chiming bangles.

I sneak off to the bedroom wing. The powder room will have the atmosphere of a urinal by now. Jason's bathroom is luxurious; it puts my beach house renovation to shame. The sauna door hangs open, exhaling a cedar smell.

I reach under the sink for the basket of tampons Jennifer keeps there. It's gone. Surprised, I check the drawers, even the medicine cabinet. They're bare. No face cream, no wax strips, no makeup. No second toothbrush.

I peek into her side of the his-and-hers closets. Empty except for a bottle of perfume abandoned on a shelf.

My surprise is already disintegrating. So this is why he's been red-eyed and irritable. *All you talk about is the wedding*. His own marriage is unraveling. He must be in a nightmare of lawyers, battles over real estate, his yacht, the wine cellar.

I make sure everything is as I found it, and shut the door behind me.

In the living room, I spot Jason beside a marble bust he found in Paris. Her twin lives in my office. I'm even more impressed with the party now that I know he put it together on his own. I imagine him arranging the acrobats, outdoing Jennifer even though she isn't here to see it.

I slip my arm around his shoulder.

"Shh," he says. "No gloating."

"I'm not. It's just such a nice party."

Quietly, he says, "Two of them have already asked to move their meetings up."

His face is a mirror to mine, glee glittering in his eyes, lips biting back a smile.

"You've done it," he whispers. "You've grown a unicorn."

Now I shush him.

We signed off on the final deck this morning. The numbers are beautiful. The future is bright.

Dani

Sunday

The party left a tide of debris. Empty cups, dirty plates, the lingering smell of alcohol.

The whole night, Dani wanted to cry. Especially when Trevor turned off the kitchen lights and the cake blazed with twenty-seven candles. Almost halfway to fifty-five. She blew them out, and smoke got in her eyes.

Fifty-five years old, can you believe it?

In the bedroom, Trevor pounds his keyboard. He hasn't taken a day off since she told him about the baby. His phone rings, and he answers instantly, his voice deeper and louder than normal, his upbeat tone halting as the other person interrupts.

Whatever he's being told is disappointing.

"No worries, I'll circle back later, I have a good feeling . . . OK, sure. Take it easy."

There's a long silence. Dani slides a pin into a red balloon and the air sighs out.

The doorknob rattles, and Trevor emerges, pressing his long fingers to his temples. His hair is pushed back from his forehead. It's thinner since he started SitFit.

Seeing Dani, he adjusts his expression to a smile. His face is dynamic, the skin creased around his eyes and his wide mouth, which twitches constantly, like he's so excited to talk he can never quite hold still. When she met him, he was playing with his band: a tall guy leaning over a bass, the pencil in his shirt pocket about to skewer his heart. They dated for weeks before she learned that he was high up in the tech hierarchy.

The small robotics company he worked for straight out of college sold to a massive search company. He stayed there for years, letting his stock options vest. On weekends, he trained for triathlons and tinkered with side projects. It was always his dream to launch a company. The idea for SitFit came to him after a long day of work, his muscles crabby with inactivity. Sitting all day is horrible for the human body. What if a device could trick it into thinking it was moving, even when it was still? His friend Mekin was a mechanical engineer; Eric, his college roommate, was in medical tech. Together they built a prototype and launched an LLC. Trevor is the CEO. The others kept their day jobs.

When she told him about the baby, he was slicing wagyu steak for their dinner. His hands stilled. He looked at her with amazement.

"Wow," he said, emotions flickering across his face, building into a grin. "Really?"

He kissed her, and the fire alarm went off as onions scorched on the grill pan. He wiped it down, oiled it, started again. He asked how she felt, and when she admitted to nausea, he vacuum-packed the steak and went out to buy bone broth.

Lying in bed later, he quietly said he wanted to keep trying SitFit, unless she wanted him to quit. "I have plenty in savings."

She shushed him, told him she knew he'd succeed. But truthfully, she worried, especially after SitFit's anniversary passed and still Trevor traveled to pitches and conferences, always returning disappointed.

Now he takes his hand from his forehead, flicking his fingers as though defeat can be shaken away like drops of water. "Want to give the baby some exercise?"

Every Sunday, Trevor runs on the Lyon Street Steps, a grand staircase along the green edge of the Presidio. The steps descend in tiers, from the pinnacle of Pacific Heights, past mansions and manicured gardens, block by block, all the way down to Cow Hollow. On Sundays, they're crowded with joggers and power walkers.

Trevor doesn't pause to enjoy the view, but plunges down. His SitFit T-shirt is quickly lost in the crowd.

Dani stretches, delaying entering the stream of sharp elbows. The day is sunny, but a cold breeze carries away any warmth. The Bay glitters like a live-action postcard. Picking her way around resistance bands and water bottles abandoned at the top, Dani starts down, dragging the anchor of her tiredness.

The flower beds are lush. Blue corydalis, like hundreds of tiny trumpets, dance in the breeze. Her mom's favorite. Dani bends to sniff, stands up dizzily.

Her mother's first diagnosis came in April. Dani was twenty, a sophomore in college. She went home immediately. The doctors were optimistic: they caught it early. Treatment went well. Textbook, they said. Nadine was thin, her joints stiff and her hair like a baby chick's, but she was energetic. In the fall, she drove Dani back to school.

The next year is like a wall calendar in Dani's memory: the last Christmas punch, the pink peppermint pie. The last spring daffodils. The last summer, Dani working in her mom's office, answering the phone. The final blazing gold of the ginkgo tree.

A warm November morning, a ringing phone. Her mom had collapsed in the garden. She was in the hospital. Dani better come home.

The cancer was back. Worse. The doctor told them the grim prognosis.

A painting of a dark woods hung behind his desk. An insensitive choice, really. Dani stared at it while her mom asked questions in a voice like a bird trapped indoors.

I'm only fifty-five years old, she said. *It's unfair. So unfair.*

Her voice was amazed, terrified, accusing.

November. December. January. A hospital bed in the living room, nurses always moving, machines always beeping.

Fifty-five years old. So unfair.

One morning, her mom sat up and reached for Dani's hand. Her eyes were bright.

She looked at the frosted windows and said, "It's the perfect time of year to decide what to plant. Short, dark days are for dreaming."

When Dani went to find the seed catalogs, the nurse warned her. This happens. A final surge of energy right before the end. Dani should prepare herself.

Dani shook her off. Who to believe, the nurse or Dani's own mother? Tapping her lip with her pencil, her favorite cardigan slipping off her shoulder. "You like dinner plate dahlias, don't you? We'd better do those."

She scribbled a list. Her handwriting was unchanged. Fat-bellied *b*'s, undotted *i*'s.

"We'll start the seeds before you know it. March is right around the corner." Worry twitched across her face. "I won't get to eat the tomatoes, but maybe I'll see them sprout. I'll think of you eating them."

"You'll eat them," Dani said.

In the morning, her mom was voiceless and gray. Dani held her bony, still hand. She wetted her lips with a sponge. Sat through hours as thick as granite.

Someone else owns the garden now, the porch swing, the ginkgo tree.

Dani's bracelet is buzzing, her heart buzzing, the air buzzing. No. Bees. Crawling in the flowers, round and furred as tiny bears.

"You OK, babe?" Trevor appears beside her, pink with exertion. "Don't overdo it."

Is she ready to go? They can get breakfast at Jane, go to the farmers' market, whatever she wants, it's her birthday!

She wants to forget the math. For her eyes to stop stinging with candle smoke.

Lift dissolves on her tongue like a soft firework. She feels her shoulders ease for the first time since her party.

Exiting the echoing Well, she's surprised to find someone else in the antechamber. Prowling with her phone held up for photos, cowboy boots scuffing the floor.

"Cecelia!" Dani's calm spills out of her, like water from a tipped glass.

"Oh, hey! I'm here to join the Lift Trial." Cecelia's grin is mischievous, mocking.

"How did you get up here?"

Cee sweeps her fingers against the tiled wall. "The elevator was open." She shrugs, unabashed. "I couldn't resist."

"It's restricted." Dani's astonished to find herself crying. She wipes away tears with her thumb, as if she can hide them.

"What's wrong?" Cecelia puts a wiry arm around her shoulder.

"Nothing. Allergies." Mascara inks her fingers.

Cecelia appraises her, skeptical. "You look tired. Let's get coffee."

Behind them, the Well door opens, and two workers emerge. Cecelia can't resist craning to see past them, her hand still on Dani's elbow.

Dani herds her onto the elevator. One of the Well workers is wearing too much perfume, sugar and musk, pungent as a clothing boutique. The elevator plunges down. Her stomach bobs like a balloon on a string. The women are talking loudly, but Dani can't hear them over the rushing in her ears. Heat climbs her neck. She breathes shallowly, counting floors, not even worrying what Cecelia thinks.

As soon as they hit the ground floor, she runs through the lobby and pushes out the revolving doors. She bends over the curb and throws up, her purse flopping from her shoulder, her hair plastering to her cheek.

Cecelia lifts her purse strap back into place.

"God, are you all right? You must be really sick, what are you doing at work?"

Dani leans forward, bracing for another wave, but it passes. She wipes her mouth.

At least the sidewalk is empty. Humiliation is worse than the scald in her throat.

Cecelia steers her toward a food truck. She buys a bagel and a Coke, over Dani's protests. "They're to calm your stomach, not poison you."

They sit on the steps. A seagull lands at Dani's feet, puffs its chest.

Cecelia kicks it away. "Are you hungover? You seemed sober at your party."

Dani chews. "I'm OK, really. It's just a thing." She's forgotten the satisfying blandness of bread, the way the crust creases and tears, yielding to soft crumb.

"Oh, Dani." Cecelia's staring at her, dismayed. "You're knocked up, aren't you?"

Dani hisses for her to be quiet.

"Shit," Cecelia says.

The bagel forms a hard mass in Dani's stomach. Too late, she realizes that she could have denied it. Blamed her birthday, laughed it off.

"What are you going to do?" Cecelia's sympathetic.

Dani pinches off a bit of bread and tosses it to the seagull. Its throat jerks as he chokes it down.

"But you're so young." Said like Dani's naïve, inept, unformed; like she can't possibly think her life is real life.

"I'm not at all young, actually." She rips off another piece of bagel, and the gull dives. *Halfway to fifty-five.*

"Well, don't waste it." Cecelia plucks the bagel from her lap. She doesn't eat, though, just holds it like a comfort object. "God. Does Trevor know?"

Dani nods.

"Did he cry?"

Dani picks up her bag. "I'm late for work."

"Sorry," Cecelia says, catching her sleeve. "I'm just surprised." She looks Dani over. "You're not glowing at all. How far along are you?"

"Only fourteen weeks."

"You should ask Holly to work from home."

"No!" Dani lowers her voice. "It's still too early to tell anyone."

"But look at you. Aren't you all about wellness?"

"I'm fine. I get motion sickness sometimes. Please don't say anything."

"What about the Well? You told them, right?"

Dani wipes her hands, rallies her energy to stand. "It's time for the All-Hands."

"Dani! You shouldn't be taking some random drug. What does your doctor say?"

Dani hopes Cecelia can't see how dizzy she is, balancing on her feet as if the sidewalk is moving. "Supplements are fine! It's natural." She blinks until the street stops bending and stretching like taffy.

Cecelia stays put. "I'm going to finish your breakfast." Her smile is strangely sad, slanting down. Maybe it's Dani's angle.

"Please don't tell anyone."

Cecelia scowls. "Obviously." She waves Dani off.

Dani feels an impatient kind of pity. Cecelia's negativity is worse every day, pervading not just Radical but everything. The way she interrogated Dani, probing every sore point, underlining every worry. *Negative energy is contagious*, Rhoda warned.

Dani was right to keep her secret. Everyone will react this way, as if her news is objectively bad, as if Dani's wonder at her transformation, the future uncurling inside of her, is nothing: a feather on the scale.

A foggy dreariness drags Dani all day. In the afternoon, she gets an email from Rhoda's assistant.

"Thank you for your interest in the Voice position! The next step is a writing test. Share your vision for a Lift launch. The ideal candidate will showcase creativity, clarity, and style. Please submit your test by Monday."

So there are other candidates. Disappointment opens a trapdoor in Dani's stomach. Somehow, speaking to Rhoda, she thought she alone was being considered.

Dani imagines her rivals. Smart women, with real experience. Not pregnant.

She walks the teal path, slowing as she reaches the Marketing pod. They're sparring over a disagreement, bold, capable, energetic. Now and then, one jumps up to rearrange pictures pinned on a rolling bulletin board. Their glamour seems drawn from a deep well of confidence. They get to construct Radical, to dream it into reality. While in CW, Dani is more like a handyman, fixing what's broken: if she does her job correctly, her efforts erase themselves behind her.

Rhoda

Tuesday

"I personally vouch for my people." Mari sits calmly on my couch. "None of them would dream of breaking their NDAs."

The controversy has leapt to Instagram. My latest post—a personal diary about hot yoga—is overrun with panicked questions. I drop my phone on the desk and pace.

"This isn't something we've discussed with any other team. The Well is practically hermetically sealed, by design."

Mari clears her throat. "If the writer was one of mine, she could say much worse."

I pause, silenced by this sobering fact. I've stopped in front of my first press clipping, from a tiny local magazine. "This Chem Major Wants to Clean Up Your Medicine Cabinet." I'm dressed in a lab coat, holding an amber vial of Skin Polish.

I was a one-woman show then. Oh, I was stressed. The sky crashed down on my shoulders on a weekly basis. What I wouldn't give for those problems.

There's a perfunctory knock at the door, and Jason barges in.

He nods at Mari and takes the armchair across from her. Crossing his legs, red sock flaring, he says, "From your stance, I assume I'm interrupting a postmortem."

I return to the couch. I will be calm. I will not be goaded into losing my head by this . . . writer, if I must call her that. Her blow landed in a tender spot, but I won't wince.

"We're discussing the potential source. Mari has assured me it's not internal. She's about to suggest an alternative."

Mari twists her fingers. "I hate to say it, since we owe a debt to the volunteers for helping us. And the program has been overwhelmingly positive."

I cut her off before she issues more disclaimers. "You mean the Trial."

She nods. "Someone could have overheard a conversation."

"I thought we vetted all the testers."

"We checked their applications for medical history. We didn't delve into, what? Loyalty? Their enthusiasm seemed genuine."

I should have screened them myself. I grind my heel into the carpet.

If it is someone in the Trial, she's had access to the Well for months. And this is all she's come up with? A vague insinuation, and not even about Lift itself, when I've said Q4 is riding on its release. Is she stupid? Biding her time?

"Do we have the data we need?"

"Given the recent adjustment to the formula, I'd prefer another month, at least."

My molars set. I don't look at Jason, but I see his red sock twitching from the corner of my eye. I led him to believe Lift was finished, under budget.

I wanted that to be true, but Mari insisted on tweaking it.

"Let's sunset the Trial," I say. "Only a handful of testers reported negative side effects. The adjustment was minute. There's no reason to expect problems."

Mari's about to argue, but I hold up a hand. Jason's heard enough.

"I appreciate your attention to detail, truly, it rivals my own. But we don't have infinite time. The app portion has been ready for weeks."

"The app," Mari echoes. Now it's her turn for disapproval. "And you've implemented the privacy protections we discussed?"

"Yes." I can't stand debating after a decision has been made. "The app is signed, sealed, delivered." I stand and head for the door. She follows.

"Dismantle the program ASAP. Make sure to revoke their Well access." I soften my voice. "I'm grateful for their participation, but it's imperative that the Well remain sacred. It's the source of Radical's magic."

Mari nods. "I understand. Though I don't believe in magic."

I'm amused at the way she says this, like it's a sign of intelligence. It's obvious to me: without magic, no medicine.

Jason's looking out the window, watching workers clamber over Rusher Tower, their tools contributing to the insidious percussion in my skull. He clasps his hands behind his back, stretching his shoulders. He swims laps every morning, part of his efforts to live to 150. I wonder whether he'll get to keep his black-tiled pool or if Jennifer will claim the house. I'm trying to gauge his mood. The Ephraims will be here soon, and I want to avoid an interrogation about Lift.

"I'm about to clear things up on social." My voice comes out too cheery. Since my first VC pitch, I've practiced using a low timbre. Calm, confident, unhurried. "Ironically, sales are up since the tweets. The writer didn't bank on that."

"So you still don't know who it is." He tips his head, cracking his neck.

"Twitter refuses to remove the account. They claim it isn't violating any rules."

"Legal shouldn't be wasting time on futile efforts. You need to stop privileged information from leaking." He draws back his shoulders, reining himself in. "I warned you to take the account seriously."

His tone is ominously even. A voice reserved for serious disappointments. A promise unfulfilled, generosity squandered. It's totally out of proportion here.

"I'm working on it. We employ two hundred people, it takes time." I check my phone, the clock obscured by notifications. "Can we discuss this later?"

The Ephraims are already our third pitch. We met Redwood yesterday. An enormous cross section of an ancient sequoia hung from the wall of the conference room like prize game. The pitch went like clockwork. Larry Ivers actually sat forward in his chair and rubbed his hands together. Then we visited Oort, and the partners cinched on Radical bracelets and compared resting pulse rates with rowdy good nature.

The energy is flowing, and I'm in the groove, surfing it. Pitching is a specific feeling: part dance, part battle, pure instinct. We need to stay in the zone.

"They'll ask, but nobody's really worried. Big companies attract quashers."

Jason turns away from the spectacle of Rusher. His tinted glasses slowly lighten. "And will you explain away your fib about Lift, too? Or did you think I missed it?"

My assistant knocks, saving me. "They're here."

Jason consults his watch. "Early."

I take the opportunity to slip behind my desk. "Can you go down to collect them? I want to post before it gets too late."

Jason sighs as he goes, displeasure trailing behind him like a cape.

I'll handle him later.

More urgently, I need to take social in hand. People love Skin Polish. They believe in it. Any disturbance to the ritual, even as trivial as a tiny tweak to the formula, risks puncturing that belief. That's part of what I mean by magic. A product isn't only its ingredients. A product is a bridge between a hope and a promise. The recalibrated formula—a simple cost-saving measure—is best kept backstage.

I search through old photos and find one of myself applying Skin Polish in a lighted vanity mirror.

radical We love it as much as you do! Never change, Skin Polish.
xo, Rhoda

The office is bright and busy, anticipation humming for the investors' arrival. The flat-screen TVs mounted on the wall cycle through performance stats. Everything looks good, until the CW numbers appear. The team is deep in the red.

I message Holly. My thumbs fly.

Looks like we have to go above and beyond today! Important to stay on top of this rumor. Please write a boilerplate script so the team can move quickly to catch up. Remember: queue ʒero!

When the brothers step off the elevator, I've just exhaled.

"Wow!" They take in the lobby, the sweeping view.

In the spotlight, my nerves vanish. My focus narrows. My attention springs into high alert, seeing the clues embedded in every gesture, parsing words for subtext, listening for the catch in consonants that indicates a bluff. Hoping for the elusive sight of a finger stroking a wrist, a sure sign they're sold.

"It's always a treat to show off Radical HQ." I lead them past the Radical Woman, and they gamely touch her foot for luck.

"Our gal Friday was smart to move into this building when she did," Jason says. "Real estate is in the stratosphere."

I laugh, like I didn't notice the diminishing nickname. I walk ahead, playing tour guide, describing my vision for an office that evokes nature and beauty.

"We're major ecotravelers ourselves," Chad says. He and Brett interrupt each other to list the exotic locales they've visited, the secret beaches and fading reefs.

As we pass, people freeze in self-conscious excitement. The Ephraims grin amiably. Even in their suits, they give the impression of having just stepped off a squash court. They seem oblivious to the impatience of Jason's stride, the tension in his neck.

When I suggest a peek into the Well, they're game. Jason overtly checks his watch. Even the sight of the outrageously expensive gift doesn't sweeten him.

"The Well is the heart of Radical," I insist, leading them to the elevator. "It's our source of innovation, past and future. We're at the vanguard of wellness, and we take R and D seriously. The next discovery is always around the corner."

I love going down to the Well, and don't get to visit often enough. As the heavy door swings open, the cool air envelopes me, as refreshing as if I've actually plunged into water. When Radical moved into the building, creating a separate space for product development was a priority, long overdue. The design came to me instinctively: a hushed, sealed space below the office, like a foundation, like deep roots, like . . . a well. The name stuck.

I let the Ephraims roam the Source Room, explore the walk-in coolers filled with rare herbs and leaves, flowers and fruits. They lift their noses to articulate the bouquet of smells. Rosemary, sap, dry needles, wet hay. Nectar, honey, sweetness of overripe fruit. They sample the bites I pluck for them: maca root and buckthorn berries.

"The ancient human diet used to contain hundreds of plants. Today, most people eat maybe a dozen. One of our missions is rediscovering potent raw ingredients, and finding new ways to deliver radical nourishment."

The Ephraims want to feel like adventurers. *Remember when we ground roots with the massive mortar and pestle!*

In the Testing Center, two doses of Lift wait on the table.

"With our upcoming release, we'll combine an all-new Well formulation with an immersive app experience to deliver what I'm calling the world's first hybrid supplement."

The brothers click through the journal prompts. They lift their cups, shake the pill like dice, a little nervous, I'm amused to see. Jason looms behind me, ticking like that watch of his. He refuses to try Lift, says he leaves the voodoo to me. *What Radical sells,* he once said, *is possibility. That ineffable, inexhaustible thing.*

My critics like to say Radical is fake. Snake oil. But what we manufacture is entirely real. The ingredients we source have been used as medicine for millennia. For many people, it works. I believe that. It worked for me.

For the rest, the worst we can be accused of is selling a placebo. Is that so bad? The placebo is miraculous, really. No matter what's wrong, a sugar pill helps. Believing that you're being treated makes you better. What a miracle! What an astonishing feat of human imagination! Belief can heal.

Believe in Radical, and you'll feel better.

Modern life is a chronic condition with a million miserable symptoms. In an age when the earth has been poisoned, and nature's been beaten back, and nothing is sacred—microplastics float in the sea, lead taints drinking water, even breast milk is laced with rocket fuel—to believe that you've found something pure . . . what is that worth?

It's priceless.

What I sell is a panacea for whatever you wish was better. Tired? Moody? Unbalanced? Unhappy? Take this. Breathe it in. It will help. At least, it will do no harm.

For years after my dad went to jail, questions nagged me. How had he justified tricking people? Did he ever feel guilty, wrapping up a false signature in tissue paper, taking a credit card and watching the face of the sucker bending to sign the receipt? (But he was never mean, would never have said "sucker," would have been chatting the entire time they were in the store.) Did he do it because he couldn't get his hands on the most exciting stock himself and wished he could? Or was it laziness, a shortcut? Plain greed?

Other people were quick to judge him. Cheat, liar, crook. Why did none of those judgments ring true?

Then, one day, I had my answer. It was simple. His lie never diminished anyone's joy. A customer's excitement at having tracked down, at long last, a prized artifact, a token of victory. My dad was doing them a service, still. What difference did it really make whether someone famous had thoughtlessly scribbled his name, bored and fulfilling a contractual duty, or whether my dad had painstakingly re-created it, keeping his hands steady and dry, determined to hit every curve, mimic every idiosyncrasy, to make an exact replica of the real thing?

Honestly, I don't believe it makes any difference. What he sold was an abstraction anyway. A feeling of connection to fame and talent and glory. He still gave people that.

I'll never be convinced that's wrong. If you believe it, it's all good.

"Bottoms up," Brett says, taking the pill like a shot.

"Red pill or blue," jokes Chad, following suit.

I know from experience: in a minute or two, they'll feel livelier. Brighter. Better.

We're waiting for the elevator when Brett speaks.

"We saw your Twitter troll laid into the Well this morning." His voice is casual.

I risk a wry smile. "Starting a rumor that a secret recipe has changed?

Very clever. I'm not surprised that our followers were on top of it. They feel ownership over the brand. I'm proud of that."

The brothers are listening carefully. They don't look skeptical.

By the time we get to the conference room, the pitch feels practically redundant, more encore than performance. Jason will let me take it from here. He insists on attending pitches, claiming his presence is reassuring—*you're the visionary, I'm the realist*—but his role is to vanish, like the Cheshire cat, nothing but a smile.

We're halfway through when he starts fidgeting with his pen.

"The Radical app launched a year ago, but it already generates half of revenue."

When I suggested the app, Jason said it was outside our wheelhouse; our customer base wasn't "obsessive" about data. *Men troll, women scroll.*

"I define wellness broadly, so you'll see the usual metrics like step count, sleep hours, et cetera. Obviously, data entry is boring, so the bracelet tracks the physical markers. We reserve manual entry for deep stuff. Energy, mood, dreams."

I'll give Jason some credit—his skepticism about "arduous" data entry haunted me while the app was in development. The idea for the Radical bracelet dropped into my head in the middle of the night. Sitting in bed, I sketched the entire concept in a half hour. Actually building it was a feat of engineering. And cost accordingly.

"People share all this information?" Chad's jaw hangs like it's been unscrewed.

"Not everyone fills out every field, but three of four app users input some data on a daily basis. And a staggering fourteen percent—our power users—complete it all."

"This is a gold mine," Brett says. "This could redefine the business."

Jason's fingers are laced together, and his thumb is circling. A signal we set up long ago, when I was new to pitching: give him an entrance, let him handle this.

"Data is a crucial component of Radical," I say. "But the Well is the essence of who we are and what we do. Our story, our community, everything flows from it."

"The Well was great, but it must cost a fortune." Chad thumbs through his documents, as though I've put a price tag on the Well slides.

"Data is the future," Brett declares.

Jason's nearly wringing his fingers, but I don't want to let the point go by.

"The only reason we can collect such high-quality data is thanks to the Well."

Jason interjects. "It's a delicate balance. We don't want to pivot overnight, but Radical will follow the areas of greatest growth."

The effort of concealing my outrage makes my voice come out close to a hiss. "Radical's brand is incalculably valuable. We're a community first."

"This is a matter of lively debate on the board," Jason says, in a tone of finality. "Radical is in very reasonable hands."

The brothers visibly calm.

"Gotcha," says Brett, nodding at Jason.

What is the boiling point of blood?

"What the fuck was that?"

We're back in my office, the brothers happily waved off, carrying child-size Future Radigal track jackets for their daughters. I considered every detail—I could have achieved perfection.

I toss my laptop onto the couch, wanting to throw myself beside it, pound the cushions with my fists.

Jason displays infinite patience. "I knew the Well tour was inviting trouble. The expense is ostentatious. Even the Ephraims were going to notice."

"They loved it. They were getting the big picture. Until you cut in."

"You forced my hand. You were tunneling us deeper and deeper. I signaled you." He wags his thumb, exaggerating. "I could have reset the course sooner."

"Your energy was dragging us down from the minute they arrived."

He lifts his eyes to the ceiling. "I'll take your word on my energy reading. Let's talk about facts. Even if you don't consider expense, the Well isn't as ideal as you suggest. First the FDA fine, now Twitter making waves. And Mari mentioned issues with Lift? You're pouring time and money into a faulty product, when the app is generating one hundred times the growth. That's foolish."

"Your fixation with the app is ironic, considering that you opposed it from the beginning."

He throws up a hand. "This again! You can't keep using that as a trump card. One disagreement doesn't erase my years of work building Radical, making it what it is."

"The story we're telling—"

"We've outgrown stories! This is reality. For them to buy in, they need to know we'll deliver huge numbers. That means scaling data. You can't always flirt and wink and keep the kimono closed. We're spending like there's no tomorrow, and there will, indeed, be none, without their money."

"I can't believe you said that." My mouth feels flooded with lemon juice. "Kimono!"

"It's an expression. Outdated, I'll grant you. But the kernel of truth remains."

"You sabotaged our meeting. You embarrassed me. Where is this coming from? Is it because Jennifer's left you?"

Jason rears back—surprised, about to yell?

But he chuckles, shaking his head. "So you know."

He pinches his nose. Suddenly, he looks old. When we met, he had darker eyebrows, didn't he? And his lips weren't bracketed by those stern lines.

I'm wrong-footed. I should offer sympathy, but I can't bring myself to apologize. Knowing him, he'll slyly apply it to the entire day.

"She left two months ago. You can't blame my questioning you on high emotion."

He takes his coat from the rack and shrugs his arms into the sleeves.

"You need them more than they need you. Repeat that like one of your mantras."

He adjusts his cuffs, speaking as if dictating to a secretary. "We have three more meetings. Prepare yourself to smile and pretend you're listening to the advice of people with decades of experience."

He leaves, wiping his hands together, prim and superior, like I've wounded him, like I'm so unreasonable.

Like it isn't my fucking company, my fucking customers, my app, my data.

Like any one of them could ever build anything like this.

I feel shaky. Have I eaten today? I can't remember. I pace the office circuit.

Radical transparency has always been a core tenet of the company. The things I know about my customers! A priest wouldn't hear more. I won't blindly chase the most profitable short-term: gutting the Well, trading our soul for an algorithm that extracts personal information and turns it into something as tedious as a pop-up ad. That would destroy the relationship I've worked so hard to build. We can be so much bigger—the Well, data, all of it—if only Jason and the others don't get impatient and spoil everything.

I'm careful not to project anything but calm on my walks, but suddenly I'm halfway across the office and can't remember getting here. I was blacked out, rage-blind.

I'm passing the CW pod. It's almost empty. The flat-screen is a livid red.

The Team Lead, Holly, is slouched at her screen, a crocheted shawl over her shoulders. When I come up behind her, she jumps.

"I know," she says. "I'm answering tickets myself."

"Where is everyone?"

"Several people are working from home today. We're in constant communication on Slack." She gestures to her screen, as if it shows her team diligently working away, and not a hole growing deeper by the second.

"Half the team is out? Why would you allow that?"

She twists the ends of her shawl.

Ah. She didn't authorize it.

"I expect everyone in tomorrow."

Returning to my office, I pass the cafeteria. The raucous noise of communal drinking spills out the door. There's even a sign: COME ON, GET HAPPY HOUR!

Irritation surges through my veins. Has everyone lost their minds? We're in the middle of fundraising. Customers are jumpy. And my employees? Complacent.

In my office, I open Slack. The Customer Worship channel should be all business. Instead, it's nothing but silly GIFs. Jokes about how they'll never catch up.

If I could do everything myself, I would. Imagine if I could multiply myself, what Radical could be.

I begin to type.

Dani

Tuesday

Guiltily, Dani ducks out of the office midafternoon, leaving the queue deep in the red. Customers are in an uproar, in spite of Rhoda's reassurance. Who would believe a vague accusation (*shortage of snakes for your snake oil?*) over Rhoda, who famously uses every product herself?

Her doctor's office is close enough to walk, but she didn't realize it's inside a medical complex. She hasn't stepped into a hospital since her mom died. Passing through the sliding glass doors feels unlucky. She dresses in the paper gown and perches on the end of the papered table. Holds her breath as the doctor slicks cold goop across her stomach and probes with a plastic wand, searching the oceanic hum of Dani's insides.

Dut-dut-dut. The baby's heartbeat leaps into the room.

"Good," the doctor says. She passes Dani a towel. Her stool glides away, and she taps at her tablet, efficiently skimming Dani's questionnaire.

"Hmm, a lot of supplements. You really only need a prenatal with folic acid."

"They're natural." Dani's at a disadvantage, wiping her stomach with the rough towel. She's about to explain Radical, but the doctor interrupts.

"For obvious reasons, we can't test supplements on pregnant women, so we can't prove they're bad." The doctor taps her pen, speaks slowly like Dani might be not so smart. "But conventional wisdom is that you don't need anything excessive."

Dani imagines Rhoda onstage, deriding doctors' devotion to conventional wisdom. This doctor isn't interested in the feeling of protection

Dani's routine lends her. The touchstones of morning and evening self-care. Dispensing drops of Skin Polish into her palm, tapping her forehead, cheekbones, throat, fingertips moving as swiftly as her mom's made the sign of the cross at church.

"Any other questions?" the doctor asks, without curiosity.

Dani shakes her head. She won't come back here. The energy is wrong—she knew it right away. Her instincts have been stronger since she found out she was pregnant.

She hadn't planned it. She stopped taking the pill, because she didn't like interfering with her hormones. She intended to use the rhythm method, with the help of Radical's cycle tracker, but going off the pill made her periods irregular. When the app alerted her that she was late, she hardly registered it. Then, two weeks late, she glimpsed herself in the mirror. Blue veins striped her swollen breasts. Fast and certain as a coin dropped into a fountain, she knew. First, that she was pregnant and second, more surprising, that she was glad.

All week, she'd dreamed of her mom. Nadine digging in the garden, laughing with the phone gripped under her chin, scooping ice cream, turning up the car radio, as vivid as if she'd just stepped out of the room. Nadine, as she had been before. Healthy.

For a long time, these old memories were crowded out by Nadine's illness. They were a gift. A sign from the universe. *You'll be a mother yourself.*

At fourteen weeks, the baby is the size of an orange, with translucent skin, so Dani imagines the membrane of segmented citrus, wrinkled and filmy. The baby's lungs pull in fluid. A fish, an orange, a ghost waiting to be born. Why should there be ghosts after life but not before?

She doesn't know the gender yet, but she's calling the baby Naomi. Naomi, Nadine. Not identical, but echoing.

Back at the office, the CW pod is vacant. It's almost five, and Tuesday-on-Tap is underway, the cafeteria raucous with Beyoncé singles and hammering basketballs.

The queue has grown. Dani rubs her eyes, opening a new ticket.

A Slack alert pops up: *Rhoda has posted in the Customer Worship group.*

Rhoda

Hi @CWsquad. When I saw the queue this morning, I made a note
to thank you for your hustle at the end of the day. Nothing CW can't
handle, I thought. We even encouraged you to use a script, which we
NEVER do, because individual responses are crucial to the Radical
relationship. We prioritized making life easier for you.

Rhoda

But, somehow, we've only fallen farther behind. Every time I passed
the pod today, it seemed oddly empty for a team dealing with a fire
alarm. It's unfathomable to me that anyone thinks it's OK to prioritize
personal business or leisure over their PRIMARY job. I don't want to
hear excuses. We don't do excuses at Radical.

Rhoda

I'm willing to chalk today up to a learning opportunity, a crash course
in the Radical values of teamwork and ownership. I know you can all
#bebetter.

Dani closes the window, guilt thick in her throat.

*Dani, you, especially, disappoint me. You want to rise at Radical? You
snuck out in the middle of the day, and when you returned, you were disheveled and distracted. Of all the days not to hit your quota, this was the wrong
one. You're disappointing me, Dani. Have you even started your writing test?
They say women can have it all, but frankly, I don't know if I see that for
you. We accept no excuses at Radical. We need energy, and not just the metaphysical kind.*

Cecelia

Wednesday

The CW Team is heads down, toiling in the queue. Holly passes out chocolate espresso beans like a general distributing cigarettes in the trenches. Her pep talks are more panicked than peppy. "It's never fun to get called out, but it happens to every team eventually. Let's pull together! Queue zero!"

Opposite Cecelia and one desk over, a knight's jump, Dani's clamped into headphones, probably listening to Radical's podcast. Suddenly, her pregnancy is obvious. Her sweater swallows her, exposing only her fingers darting over the keyboard.

It was a risk, tweeting after Dani caught Cecelia trespassing in the sacrosanct Well. But in the elevator, as the Well workers gossiped, Dani was oblivious, staring at the floor numbers going down. (In retrospect, how obvious: her pallor, her gritted teeth, her purple-shadowed eyes.) Even Cecelia knew the product under discussion, the lauded Skin Polish, a dribbly gold-green oil sold by the half ounce, like drugs.

The Well girls weren't impressed with the reformulation: "At this point, it's basically tea-tree oil, thoughts, and prayers."

Dani should have been appalled, but she wasn't listening. The second the doors opened, she raced off the elevator to be sick.

Rhoda stalks by the CW pod, and they cower like mice in a hawk's shadow.

In response to Cecelia's tweet, she posted a black-and-white portrait of herself preening into a mirror, satin robe tumbling off her shoulder. *Never change, Skin Polish.*

The blatant lie hasn't entirely reassured customers.

"Can you check if there's any OG Skin Polish in the back? Pretty please?"

As if Radical is a corner apothecary with a dusty backroom rather than a vast warehouse with a digital inventory system.

"No," Cecelia replies.

Instant feedback arrives: "I'd give zero stars if I could."

Cecelia needs a break. She's unleashed chaos, but it's mostly fallen on her own shoulders. She heads for the bathroom. Her period is on day nine. She's literally drained. Pain is diffuse across her stomach, crackling like static electricity.

Dani is standing over the bathroom sink, swishing water in her mouth. When she looks up, their eyes meet in the mirror etched with loopy cursive: *You Look Fabulous!*

Dani's eyes are bloodshot, her lips colorless.

"Please take a sick day," Cecelia says.

Dani tugs paper towels from the dispenser. "We're way too busy."

It's so ludicrous, Cecelia laughs. In the echoey bathroom, it sounds manic.

"What, are you afraid Rhoda will throw another tantrum?"

Dani sighs, pressing the towel to her face. As if Cecelia is what's tiring her out.

"We fell behind," she says. "It's our job."

"Right. It's our job to lie to customers."

"What are you talking about?" A worry line bisects her eyebrows like a smudge of ash, the symbol of a true worshipper in the church of Rhoda.

"Skin Polish," Cecelia prompts. "The changed formula?"

"You mean the Twitter troll?" Dani rolls her eyes. "They obviously made that up to get attention."

She opens the door with the paper towel. "You coming?"

I wrote it, Cecelia wants to say. You were there when I heard it! It's one-hundred-fucking-percent true!

She shakes her head. The door swings shut.

You Look Fabulous! Cecelia looks slapped. Her own frown line sunk deep.

*

Her anger needs an outlet. She posts, reckless:

@Radicalidiocy
Under no circumstances may any Radical employee go to the doctor during work hours. Any employee feeling under the weather should listen to Rhoda's TED talk and drink green juice.

Perversely, she *wants* Dani to guess. Dani's always dismissing Cecelia, diminishing her.

Like yesterday, when Cecelia was processing Dani's news—pregnant! so young!—Dani snapped. *I'm not young, actually.* Impatient, condescending. *Grow up, Cecelia!*

But Dani's younger than Cecelia. And ahead of her, in every way. Cecelia has no relationship, no apartment, no pending promotion, no plan. All she has is her writing. And what is that, really? The brittle asides of a ghost, which Dani barely hears.

If Dani reads the new tweet, she gives no sign. She doesn't take her eyes from her screen. Doesn't join in as the team swaps GIFs: a runner falling off a treadmill, an actress chugging wine from a bottle. Cecelia contributes a frazzled cat in outer space, the animation zooming in on its mouth, which contains an identical wide-eyed space cat, and another, ad infinitum.

Rhoda pops in: "Still under an enormous backlog. Is it the time to google cats? If a customer gets disenchanted, we lose them forever. In other words, that meme is literally costing us thousands in potential revenue. This isn't rocket science."

Such a perfect blend of condescending sarcasm and exaggerated offense! But don't worry—every team gets reamed at some point!

Cecelia fishes out Leandra French's card. The metallic lettering flashes. Gold, Cecelia thinks, or fool's gold? Leandra might not even remember her.

She scrolls to Rhoda's screed and snaps a screenshot.

Story Idea: Bullying CEO. Two-faced founder. Rhoda yells at people on Slack all the time. I can dig into it.

The reply comes quick: *The toxic reality inside a wellness startup—yes, please!*

*

The next day, while her teammates battle the queue until it calms from red to orange and Holly leaves ribbon-wrapped eyedrops on desks and Dani nurses a bottle of SuperYou, Cecelia digs into the archives of Slack.

The entire company uses the messaging app. Each team has its own thread, where they discuss ongoing projects, deadlines, mistakes. Cecelia has unfettered access. What an oversight! She can enter any team's chat, and scroll the conversation threads back and back. She can read everything Rhoda has ever said.

She starts with the Marketing Team, betting that Rhoda has screeched at them more than once. As she scrolls back, one day, then two, it's quickly clear why Radical didn't bother restricting access. The chatter is unbelievably tedious. The conversation unfolds in reverse chronological order. Dialogues constantly reference earlier discussions, sending Cecelia digging for meaning. Worse, everyone chats at once, small talk and inside jokes braided into business jargon like some nightmarish AI-generated free verse poem.

By lunchtime, Cecelia is only a month in, with no sign of Rhoda's rage.

Surfacing from Slack, she finds her teammates eating sad desk lunches. She heads to the cafeteria, where everyone lucky enough not to be in CW is happily speculating about Radical's prospects. Rhoda's headed south to pitch another VC firm.

Cecelia slurps her ramen, reenergized. If she writes fast enough, she might spoil Rhoda's round.

Back at her desk, she leaps from group to group, giving up on understanding—all she needs is a rant.

Quality Assurance. Merchandising. Fulfillment. Rhoda is everywhere. She drops into conversations like a parachuter, abrupt and startling, demanding statistics as urgently at midnight on Friday as midday Monday. She knows every detail of every project. Does she ever sleep?

Unfortunately, she's also relentlessly positive. She sends praise hands, thumbs-ups, "NAILED IT!" with a hammer emoji.

*

Friday afternoon, Cecelia finally finds something. One weekend back in January, the Data Team didn't reply to Rhoda for an hour, and she threw a tantrum.

Delighted, Cecelia snaps a screenshot. She stands to stretch, and sees shadows dragging past the pillars. It took two whole days to find one example.

Dani stands, too, rubbing her eyes. Cecelia knows how they feel: dry and scratchy, like her eyelids are full of crumbs.

Dani looks at Cecelia, surprised. "I'm not sure I've ever left before you."

Luckily, Holly calls her over to pat her on the back. On the rankings, Dani's avatar has climbed to impossible heights. She's answered twice as many tickets as anyone else.

It's six thirty, and the bright young things at Radical are toiling into their eleventh hour for the reward of a free burrito. The savory aroma of green chile drifts across the office. At 6:40 on the dot, everyone swarms the cafeteria.

Tech bros grab burritos and beers, annex the foosball table, manspread out on the couches. Marketing and Social pump the rosé tap like 1950s carhops. Take a shot every time you hear the word *unicorn*.

Cecelia accepts a burrito from a woman with tired eyes and a hairnet, wonders what she must think of them all.

She eats at her desk.

As she scrolls, people file back to their pods. They shrug into coats, load laptops into bags, apply lipstick in their camera's selfie mode. In pairs and groups, they prance onto the elevators. Outside, the city's restaurants are warming up like ovens. Bodies crowd around tables and candles are lit and waiters tuck wine keys into their aprons.

Cecelia hasn't been on a date in months. The festival of aches and pains in her torso is too lively. She can't imagine sitting across a table from someone, chatting, flirting, worrying. Does she mention it? Make a joke? Or hide it? Until when? At some point, she's going to cancel on them, or rush to the bathroom, or double up in pain in the movie theater seat.

They'll lean away from her. Try to put space between themselves and her illness, like she's contagious, if only with bad luck.

Sorry, I'm not really looking for anything serious . . .

Or they'll be skeptical. Accuse her of being overdramatic. *Hysterical*, a word that originates from the Greek for uterus.

The final elevator leaves. The overhead lights switch off, until only the panel above Cecelia's desk shines. Spotlights illuminate the craggy pillars, leaving the rest of the floor in shadows. White noise whistles from the ducts like wind through a canyon.

She walks to the cafeteria. Her wrists feel hollow, probably the onset of carpal tunnel. Filling a mug with rosé, she checks Rhoda's Instagram on her phone.

While her lackeys hustled for burritos, Rhoda shared a selfie taken in the mirror of her gas-guzzling vintage convertible.

radical What an amazing week. Talking to really smart people about the big dreams I have for Radical. I did my best. Now I have to trust the universe to bring the right team together. xo, Rhoda. #CEObehindthescenes #girlboss

@Radicalidiocy
The universe is forging itself in the fire of stars, shuffling dimensions like decks of cards. Not, emphatically not, stage-managing your life.

After Cecelia posts, the room drops to silence, as though the office sensed it. She stands still, holding her breath, until she realizes the HVAC system turned off, that's all. Laughing, a little tipsy, she refills her mug.

The overhead lights track her across the floor. Her thrifted cowboy boots scuff the carpet. Even her mouse wheel is loud, a rolling *r* as she scrolls.

It turns out some groups are locked: Core Team, People Team, the ever-elusive Well.

Cecelia realizes she's still wearing her Radical bracelet. Everyone wears one, everyone has the app on their phones. *We need to use the tools ourselves in order to best assist customers . . .*

She spins it on her desk as she reads the App Team thread. Numbers, launch dates, features. Now and then Rhoda spits an accusation—"How did we miss this bug before release?"—but it never escalates. Everyone apologizes. They act like she's reasonable.

Cecelia yawns. She drags her cursor wildly, like spinning the wheel on that old game show, the slow click-click-click of fate—the universe!—deciding her hand.

Someone asks Rhoda about budget, and she replies: "Let's move to @RadOrg."

Cecelia follows. The most recent conversation is from this afternoon:

Jason
What can we do to prevent another backup in CW? Do we need added headcount? Important that customer experience remains seamless.

Holly
Part of the problem was a top performer missing a half day. On top of a perfect storm of other people being out plus an already busy queue plus the twitter rumor.

Rhoda
A single contributor shouldn't impact the numbers so dramatically. That's a problem.

Jason
Agree.

Rhoda
Didn't we project that the top performer will need replacing in Q3?

Cecelia fumbles her bracelet. It rolls off her desk.
She reads again, blinking. Rhoda is talking about Dani.

Holly
Haven't gotten confirmation, but that's what the program indicates. Could be early q4.

Jason

?

Rhoda

Part of the early results of Lift Trial. Lets us assess diff factors that may affect productivity and pivot accordingly. For example: a worker having a baby. We can go more granular, too. Still a pilot test, but fascinating results so far.

Jason

I'll say! Wow!

Rhoda

Back to CW. @Holly, so we will need 1 HC just to break even?

Holly

I'd predict 2 HC to break even. Forecasting a busier workload in Q4.

Rhoda

Hire them now & we can train while top performer still with us.

Jason

Jason

This product sounds 🔥 🔥 🔥

Rhoda

More to share soon!

Rhoda

@Holly We want to set everyone up for success and CW only works if it's actually good service so don't hesitate to send up a warning flare at the first sign of trouble instead of waiting for the ship to be underwater.

Cecelia's bent close to her screen. She doesn't quite believe that the words say what they say. That they're firing Dani. That when Holly called Dani to her desk to thank her, she had just conspired with Rhoda to fire her—after she trained the two people needed to replace her, of course.

Dani's desk is neat, her chair tidily pushed in. Her lilac Radical mug is rinsed and ready for the morning's coffee, or Matcha Goddess juice, or whatever. Dani thinks she's being promoted. She believes Radical is exactly what Rhoda says.

Cecelia snatches up her phone to text Dani, to warn her, to be outraged on her behalf. *They're assholes, they don't deserve you, fuck 'em.*

She hesitates.

Dani won't believe it. Even if she does, even if Cecelia sends the proof, she'll deny it. She'll be furious—with Cecelia. She'll want Cecelia to keep quiet. *Don't tell anyone.*

If Cecelia writes the story without telling Dani, that's also a betrayal. Flip a coin: either way she'll lose.

Her screen has gone dark, and her reflection hovers in it, intense, almost quivering. This is bigger than she even hoped. Rhoda is breaking the law. Firing a top employee for being pregnant! It goes against everything she stands for, all her fake rah-rah bonhomie—saving the world one woman at a time. This single conversation rips the mask off her persona. Exposes her. Isn't it better for Dani to know the truth?

The screenshot is as loud as an old-fashioned camera shutter.

Leandra's reply clinches it. *Jaw on the floor. Is this for real?*

No going back now. Cecelia skips up the stairs, pushes out the heavy door to the roof. The night is bracingly cold, tingling on her skin. The pitch-dark outline of Rusher Tower interrupts the glittering skyline like a thumb fumbled over a camera lens.

Cecelia dances in place. Her cowboy boots slide, but it's exhilarating, not frightening. She hoots. Imagine Rhoda's face when the story comes out! How arrogant she must be to say those things and expect to carry on forever, loved and admired!

Cecelia caws. She's young enough, if she stops wasting time. Here's her chance, a fork in the road, a rope tossed into her palms. She wants—she needs—to escape.

Dani

Saturday

"Will you be all right?" Trevor slings his duffel bag into the trunk. "You're not going to work all weekend, are you?"

Dani's worked until midnight every night this week, Trevor sitting across the couch on his laptop, their feet tangled in the middle. Dani floats on top of the CW rankings like a grinning cheerleader atop a pyramid.

"No," she lies. "I'm going to take a break."

Trevor is driving to Tahoe for a weekend at Slim Riley's house. The former grunge rocker has reinvented himself as an angel investor. Dani can't shake the image of his thrashing hair and tank tops. Trevor met him this week, and their connection was solid enough to merit not just a follow-up meeting but a getaway. Trevor's packed his swimsuit and banjo, a $300 bottle of bourbon and a twelve-pack of Radical Reboot.

"Good luck," she says.

He kisses her. His hair is shower-wet, his cheeks razor-pink. On his T-shirt, lines of electricity zing off the outline of a man. SITTING IS THE NEW SMOKING.

"Do you think this could be it?" he whispers.

"Of course," Dani says. She has a new understanding of his breathless hope, the nerves jittering in his muscles. How badly he wants this.

She waves until his car turns the corner. In the quiet, the early morning is perfect as a glass bowl.

Dani is going to walk.

On the bus last night, she listened to a Radical podcast about creativity.

Rhoda interviewed luminous women: designers, musicians, a screen-writer. They all recommended walking.

Get out. Go. Look. Listen. Wander. Get lost. Don't think.

Don't think!

Dani's already far from thinking. Panic pinballs around her brain, scattering all thoughts except a chorus of self-doubt. *You're running out of time, you'll never make it, you've got nothing, that's a bad idea, that's worse. Failure, failure, failure.*

So, walk.

She stops at Jane, her favorite coffee shop. Ahead of her in line, a man holds a baby in a sling. Dani watches, entranced, as the baby yawns, then burrows her chin down into sleep, cheek squished against the fabric.

She pries her eyes away. No babies. No ticking clock. No pressure.

She wanders Japantown with her decaf cappuccino. Here's the sea-food restaurant where she and Trevor used to get sushi before seeing a film at the indie theater. They should do those things again, before the baby comes. The idea is flimsy as the litter scattering in the wind. They're too busy.

As she heads downtown, the buildings get taller. The shadowed side-walk is as cold as the bottom of a canyon. The once-elegant neighbor-hood has gone seedy. Filthy awnings shield ornate stone entrances. Metal gates shutter outdated storefronts: a luggage shop, camera store. Outside the corner grocer, crates of conventional fruit shine like plastic. *Conventional wisdom.* Dani needs to find a new doctor, needs—*Stop!*

She's almost to Market Street. Heading for the office on autopilot.

This isn't wandering. She's not getting lost in any sense of the word.

On a whim, she boards a cable car going north on Powell. She hangs on to a pole, the breeze skimming her skin as they glide past Union Square's grand hotels, apartment buildings like wedding cakes. The hill steepens, and Dani holds tight as they surge upward. The city spreads in every direction, cream and white and faded pastel. Sun pours over the hills, blue shadows pool in the valleys. When the car flattens to cross intersections, she can see all the way to the water. Crossing California Street, she spots the Bay Bridge, a trick of perspective making it seem suspended between buildings.

At the pinnacle of the hill, she disembarks. The bells of Grace Cathedral are chiming the hour. The rising, pealing song seems too intricate for the heavy bells. The cathedral looks ancient, Gothic, like a shipwreck hauled to a hilltop.

She follows the song through the heavy doors and blinks her way into the dark, cool church. It smells of incense and damp stone. Pillars vast as redwoods stretch to the vaulted ceiling, where the light seems thick as honey in the dusty, ancient air. On the ground, the air is blue and cool and compressed, like water at the bottom of a well. The stained glass windows are saturated shades of purple, blue, and red.

Nadine would have loved this. She went to church every week. Knew the rituals like dance steps: fingers dipping into water, rising and sitting and rising in the pew.

Dani walks slowly, taking it in. The high ceiling draws her mind upward, out of itself. The architecture facilitates the act of marveling.

The rasp of a match makes Dani turn. A woman lights a candle beneath a statue of Virgin Mary. Her hands move in gestures Dani remembers well: shaking the match to extinguish it, drawing the sign of the cross through the curl of smoke.

The idea drops into Dani's head. A trinity. App, Lift, bracelet. A ritual. She has a vision of the product page, not done in the warm neutrals of the rest of Radical's line, but in bold jewel tones, like stained glass.

She spreads her work across the kitchen table. Laptop, notes, sketches. She gets up only to make a fresh pot of tea, to open a Radical Boost, to eat a bowl of cereal at the sink. By midnight, she's written twenty pages. She spends Sunday whittling it to ten. Before she can second-guess, she sends it to Rhoda.

The sun is setting. Fooled by the soft sky, she leans to open the window, craving a summer breeze so strongly that the cold air feels like a mistake.

When her phone pings, she snatches it, as if it might be Rhoda, finished reading her test, delighted with it—

Of course it isn't. The CW group text is blowing up. Someone shared a link to an article: "The Toxic Reality Inside a Wellness Startup." The thumbnail: a black-and-white photo of Rhoda, eyes blotted out by red asterisks.

Just a quasher—why is she compelled to read it? She's only giving the site clicks.

The author is anonymous, but she recognizes the voice immediately. The smug disdain of Radicalidiocy, nothing new.

Then she takes the phone in both hands.

To understand who Rhoda really is, you need to hear Lauren's story. (Lauren isn't her real name, of course; I'm using a pseudonym to shield her identity.)

Lauren is a believer. In spite of her lowly role in Customer Worship, Lauren is "all in," as Rhoda likes to shout. Lauren religiously uses Radical products. She adheres to Rhoda's advice, whether that means avoiding nightshades during tomato season or spending a fortune on smelly natural deodorants.

Lauren wears her Radical bracelet proudly. She checks in with the app like a responsible teenager with an overbearing parent. She even volunteers to test unreleased Well products, which seems rather dubious given that she's pregnant.

Every sentence is worse than the last. *All in, CW, Trial.* Each line a bright arrow aimed directly at Dani, making the fake name futile. And then: *pregnant.*

Dani's shaking. Cecelia! She promised not to say anything—looked insulted when Dani asked. When she was already tweeting, already angling for this . . .

She's hiding it. I found out by accident, when I caught her getting sick at work. I was worried, but she refused to take a break. She's hoping for a promotion and needs to prove herself.

I thought she was being silly. They should support her! She's a top performer, and wellness is the cornerstone of Radical . . . isn't it?

As it turns out, that's bullshit. Rhoda knows Lauren is a top performer. She's going to fire her anyway.

A chilly breeze gusts over Dani's hands, the tops of her legs, settles into her socks. She forgot to shut the window. She stays in the cold while she reads the rest.

Cecelia writes about Rhoda chastising the CW Team, self-pityingly describes their busy week, while Cecelia lags and Lauren hustles. Lauren sounds witless, insipid, a paper doll with a Radical account—is that how Cecelia sees Dani?

The story could end there, with the CEO acting as though people who make $40,000 a year without stock options owe her 24–7 hustle, blood, sweat, and tears.

But it gets worse.

After the uproar, Rhoda entered a Slack group along with the Customer Worship Team Lead and a member of the board. Here's their conversation.

There's another Slack screenshot. Dani clicks to expand.

Rhoda
Didn't we project that the top performer will need replacing in Q3?

Rhoda is talking about Dani. These are her words, not the tweeter's. Dani's phone drops to the table. Her notes for the writing test drift in the wind. Her eager scribbles, festooned with exclamation points.

Rhoda

Sunday

All weekend, I have a feeling of suspension in my stomach, like a half-court shot arching through the air: hurtling trajectory and tight-throated anticipation. The pitches wrapped Friday. It's out of my hands. I can only hold my breath and wait for the drop.

On Sunday, Gavin and I drive south along the Embarcadero. The Bay is like a sheet of hammered metal under the sun.

"'When did you fall in love?'" he reads aloud. "I met Rhoda at a party. The hosts had a penchant for psychedelics, and everyone was letting loose. Rhoda was standing over the offerings, interrogating our host about their origins and effects. I've never seen such intense curiosity."

He turns the camera on me. We're hosting an ask-us-anything on Instagram. Hearts and flames float up the screen as people comment.

"You lured me into the master bedroom," I say. "I thought it was presumptuous, but it turned out, they had one of your pieces hanging there. A photograph of a girl floating in the ocean. It was beautiful."

Gavin pivots back to himself. "That's Rhoda's shameless pitch."

I laugh. "Gavin's show opened last night at the Golden Hour Gallery, and it's incredibly beautiful, and you should all go. His pictures resonate positive energy. This . . . pleasurable serenity. That's how you made me feel, when we met."

Gavin leans over to kiss me. I laugh, tightening my hands on the wheel.

"'What's Rhoda like in person?' I'll be honest. She's been fasting all weekend, and she's a terror." He cuts a grin at me.

I wave my elbow in protest. "Only a mini-cleanse."

"Right. She got to have a cup of tea and four olives for breakfast this morning."

More questions roll in, and Gavin fires off answers as I park. The gallery is in the Dogpatch neighborhood, surrounded by cookie-cutter luxury lofts. Gilt letters on the front window declare *Since 2008*, reminding everyone that they were here before Zuckerberg put his name on the hospital, before gentrification spiked like a fever.

Lisbeth's wife, Ashleigh, is the owner. She's cajoled us into an encore appearance, so Gavin can meet a major admirer. She sweeps across the room to greet us, the silk sleeves of her haori billowing. She herds Gavin toward a trio of women in Gucci loafers.

I check my phone, even though I can't expect a term sheet until Monday, at the earliest. No reason to worry. The pitches were smooth, apart from the Ephraims, though they hardly seemed to notice the fault line trembling under the conference table. I eased off the Well talk in our final meetings, and Jason was wise enough to keep quiet. Our audience was rapt. So eager to see the rabbit, it practically leapt from my hat.

I stroll the gallery. In Gavin's photos, the ocean is muscular and dangerous. His people look heroic. Surfers face towering waves, walk out of the sea with dripping hair.

My fingers tick against my hip, calculating. Not how much we'll bring in, but how much I'll give up.

In my head, I own all of Radical, from the first iteration of Skin Polish to the unimaginable thing we'll launch in twenty years, from the distant servers that store our data to the screws holding together the office furniture.

On paper, I own 58 percent. This round will leave me holding less than half, which is terrifying to the point of queasy, like a dream in which you wake up in a bathtub of ice and someone's harvested your kidneys.

Thankfully, my supervoting shares give me about 70 percent control. That will drop after this round, but not enough that I won't have final say.

That may rankle some investors, Jason warned me, though plenty of my male counterparts do exactly the same and nobody is scared off. He's only priming me for the negotiation. He wants the highest valuation we can get, the biggest splash, the most ostentatious feather in his cap.

I do, too, of course—but not to the point of giving up control.

I gaze at a towering wave, like a gaping mouth, closing down on a tiny figure inside. He's bent nearly level with the board, surfing fast, staying ahead from inside.

My phone buzzes. As I reach for it, Gavin and Ashleigh round the corner.

Ashleigh is beaming. "Fifteen gone!"

Gavin rakes his fingers through his hair, abashed. He doesn't see himself as part of the art world, like he wasn't part of the business world, but I persuaded him.

The nearly sold-out show feels like a good omen. I set my purse on the bar as Ashleigh pours glasses of boozy seltzer, chattering about the wedding.

"Lis and I are going to make a long weekend out of it. We're staying in that fantastic B and B over Berg. They let you gather your own eggs in the morning."

"The chef is doing our food," Gavin says. "My sole contribution to the planning."

Behind us, the sliding door that leads to the living area upstairs squeals open. Lisbeth dashes into the gallery, bare feet slapping the floor.

"I can't believe you're here. Haven't you seen this?" She brandishes her phone, which shows a photograph of me, my eyes slashed with neon red asterisks.

"THE TOXIC REALITY INSIDE A WELLNESS STARTUP."

Gavin drives. I can't unfasten my eyes from my screen.

Editor's note: At Megaphone.com, we believe all voices are valid, no matter how small. To protect the author, we are keeping her identity anonymous.

Bold, to accuse me of retaliation before I'm even aware a shot has been fired! Though obviously she'll lose her job, whoever she is.

In San Francisco, the question is inevitable. "Where do you work?"

When I answer, eyes widen, jaws drop.

"Do you know her?" Their voices are hushed and reverent. Women think they know her. They think they love her.

Her being me, of course. My name being the currency that the author trades for attention. It's obviously the same writer as Radicalidiocy. The mosquito in my ear given a megaphone to shout her complaints.

The big bombshell is my Slack speech to the CW Team. She quoted the choicest lines. I sound like a harpy. (Never mind that I was justifiably angry, reprimanding a team for a very real failure. A man would have been blunter, while I was supposed to scold them in song, perhaps, woodland creatures frolicking at my feet.)

I've missed ten calls from Jason, and another is incoming. I silence it. He must be livid. He'll see this as more evidence that I didn't take the Twitter threat seriously, that I've taken my eye off the ball. Knowing him, he'll have tracked me online, watched the ask-us-anything with Gavin, worked himself into a frenzy of outrage.

I'm scrolling faster now. I've got the gist, and I'm already mentally drafting my response. Then I get to the screenshot.

The scariest things in the world are those that can't be destroyed. Plastics. Nuclear waste. Private conversations preserved in the amber of zeroes and ones.

A Slack conversation fills my screen. Holly, Jason, and I discussing Radical's Lift data program.

This is bad. The program is still in beta; there are members of my Core Team who don't know it exists. It's not ready to roll out, certainly not ready to defend to the public.

We pull into the dim parking garage.

"You go up," I tell Gavin.

He thinks I'm joking. "Oh, come on. Nobody died."

"Don't nag." I'm taut as a drawn bow. I don't want anyone near me.

I sit in the reek of oil and exhaust. This is my fault. I failed to lock the Slack group. Failed to move us to email. I was caught up in the satisfaction of showing off Lift's value to Jason. That petty impulse will cost an outsized penalty, the way gangsters got locked up for tax fraud instead of murder. To use an exaggerated metaphor.

I read the article again. Slowly, this time.

When I'm through, I almost laugh. She's missed it. She sped past the scandal—Radical collecting data, *health* data, analyzing it in a self-serving way—and grasped at a straw instead. She's accusing me of planning to fire Dani for being pregnant. (Why change her name and disguise nothing else? Stupid.)

The accusation will be easy to rebut. Promote Dani. Apologize for the misunderstanding.

Finding the author will be even easier. She's given away too much about herself.

Gavin left a note on the table: RUNNING. I fold it in half, sharpening the crease with my fingernail, as I dial Jason.

"Rhoda," he says, "thank you for getting back to me."

"I know, I know," I say. "I was delayed. It's a ridiculous article. Their claim is totally false. If they'd bothered seeking a comment, I'd have told them so. But I suppose that would have interfered with their *first-person truth-telling*."

Ranting is like scratching an itch; I want to dig my claws in. I resist.

"I'm about to set the record straight." I head down the hall to my office.

"Slow down," Jason warns. "This is extremely delicate." He's primed to lecture.

"It's simple. I'm not firing 'Lauren,' I'm promoting her. I can easily explain."

The cleaners have come through, tidied my crystals into a bowl, slicked the desk with oily spray. I lift my laptop lid.

"I know your instinct is to address your followers directly. But we are on the brink of bringing on new investors. We cannot be hasty. We need to think through every possible scenario, every option."

"I don't need you to remind me of the timing. All the more reason to respond."

"Rhoda." Jason raises his voice for the first time. But he only sounds exasperated, not angry. "I know we tussled last week. Let's set that aside. This is more important. We need to work together."

Tussled? An urge to offer up another word is in my throat like a cough. I swallow.

"Are you going to suggest that I hire a PR person again?"

"I'm going to suggest that we hire an attorney who specializes in reputation management."

I distrust his calm. He only wants to control me.

"That sounds expensive. Especially since I can clear it up right now."

At last, he cracks. His voice resumes its usual acidic sting. "What will you say? Will you admit that you shout at employees on a public forum? That you don't like pregnant women?"

"That's hardly fair."

"That's not the worst thing people are saying. The article is gaining traction."

"It's a tiny website. Nobody's heard of it."

But on Twitter, my notification tab is overrun. The article is spreading. Viral. A gross word, but a fitting one.

"Inevitable, a story like this," Jason says. He can tell he's scored a point. "People love nothing more than raising their torches and joining a witch hunt."

I push my fingers into my temples. My skull feels oddly shaped, like the bones are poorly soldered together.

"We'll come up with a playbook. We will survive this."

It's generous of him to say "we." Or arrogant. Nobody knows who the Jason in the Slack conversation is. Nobody cares. I'm the one exposed. Still, he might have blamed me for Megaphone—relished it. But he didn't.

"It will be easy to find the writer," I offer. "She's in CW. Stupid to admit it."

"Do you think it is Lauren herself? The 'friend' she keeps referring to?"

"No."

I think of Dani, perched nervously in her seat, smoothing her shirt. A nervous tic, I thought. Endearing.

It was a coincidence that Holly emailed me about Dani's data the next day. She was one of a few Team Leads testing the data pilot. *Am I reading these results right? She hasn't mentioned anything yet, but we'll need to plan . . .*

I admit to initial disappointment. Pregnant! Maternity leave is a hassle, especially early into an important role, and there's always a risk the mother won't come back.

Still, Dani appealed to me. Thoughtful, serious. Peaceful as a crane. A true believer. She understands Radical's magic. *Incantation*, she called it.

If only I'd given her the job! I hesitated, and Lisbeth wanted someone else, insisted on the writing tests, and it fell from my priorities.

Really, it will be an asset to have a mother in the Voice role. Most Radical customers are mothers.

Jason deploys his most persuasive voice. "Let's follow my instincts on this one. I know just the person to help us. First thing tomorrow, I'll pick you up."

I'm still skeptical when he suddenly says, "Once more unto the breach!"

Our battle cry! We haven't used it in months. In the old days, we passed it between us whenever things went wrong. Jason was a perfect partner in that turbulent growth phase, as Radical alternately accelerated and threatened to implode, when we were hanging on as much as driving. He was that rare person energized by bad news. We were always working or talking about work, day and night. We stayed late in the empty office, the remains of takeout congealing in boxes, whiteboards crowded with ink, laptop chargers tangled. When I had a 3 a.m. epiphany, I called Jason without hesitating. Sometimes, we sat in silent thought, phones sighing like seashells in our ears, until the solution came to me, and the talk got fast again, overlapping. I had the ideas; Jason knew how to execute.

Oh, we argued. *Tussled.* We traded absolutes, until one of us (usually Jason) would bend. He'll bend again. We'll close the round, and he'll relax. Forget the Well. Leave me to it.

And if he doesn't, I have the supervotes. I have control.

"Once more unto the breach," I echo.

Gavin's doing sit-ups in the living room. He breaks, breathing heavily. "Is Jason melting down?"

He doesn't expect an apology for my petulance. *Your emotions are your emotions*, he says. *You never have to be fake with me.*

"Amazingly, no." I perch on the couch. My last Instagram post is filled with acrid comments. My inbox is a traffic jam of nasty messages. Nobody asks whether it's true.

I'm spurred to respond, regardless of the truce with Jason. But as my thumbs hover over the keys, no words come to me.

Jason's right: if I don't get it exactly right, I'll make it worse.

Out the windows, fog drifts over the water like smoke. I think of Gavin asking *bonfire or forest fire*, when the Twitter troll leaked my fundraising round. *A spark*, I sneered. But it caught. The fire is growing.

He's trying to cheer me up, telling me he can think of a thousand worse things his friends have done. VPs and CFOs and COOs.

It's easy to imagine the men laughing on their surfboards, unscathed.

I almost confess to my fear, but naming it would give it power. If doubt infiltrates my mind, it will ruin me. My work relies on confidence, on pure, unflinching action.

I stare at the oil portrait over the mantel. I commissioned it for my last birthday. I wanted the artist to paint me like a warrior queen, commanding and regal.

She painted me seated, dressed in emerald velvet. My smile is coy. I'm holding a stalk of straw in one hand and a ball of gold thread in the other.

I hated it at first. The fairy tale reference seemed infantilizing, vaguely insulting, as though what Radical sells is without value.

Over time, it's grown on me. My skin is radiant, the main source of light in the otherwise dark portrait. My eyes are watchful. When I pace the living room, they seem to follow. The angle of my hands suggests cunning and skill.

The writer's voice hisses in my brain. *The only wellness Rhoda West believes in is the health of her bank account. The only wellness she's devoted to is that of her sales curve. The only thing radical about Radical's workplace is her hypocrisy.*

I know people—smart, capable, excellent people—brought down by a single anecdote.

It's not going to be me.

*

The lawyer ushers us into his opulent office, our steps hushed by thick Turkish carpets. Don't miss the photos on the wall, a still-frame history of triumph: long-haired Bill Orson with diploma, tousled Bill Orson giving a news conference after an acquittal, balding Bill Orson on the steps of the Supreme Court.

No sign of his most famous client, the country music star charged with assault for punching his girlfriend in full view of a hotel security camera. His label dropped him, his agent left. He hired Orson. A dig into the woman's past turned up nude photos, some with whips and handcuffs. The subtext: she liked it rough. Incredibly, the tide turned. The jury was persuaded. The singer recently won a Grammy.

"You want to associate with this guy? With his reputation?" I whisper to Jason.

"He's the best. Nothing scares him."

"What could, at the rate he charges?"

Orson, tactfully deaf, beckons us into a conference room perfumed with coffee and pastry sugar. The table is spread with a full china tea service.

"Most important meal of the day." Orson twinkles. His white hair rises in tufts, giving him an elvish look in spite of his tailored suit of fine walnut-colored silk.

"I've read the article," he announces, pouring cream. "Nasty piece."

"Jason thinks we need a professional to handle the fallout."

I drop a sugar cube into my coffee. Clever, the tiny spoons and rattling porcelain. Props for clients to fiddle with, while Orson observes whose hands tremble. My spoon lands smoothly, of course.

"But you're not sure," Orson says. "You've established a connection with your followers. Maybe you can handle it yourself. Save money and stay in the driver's seat. I appreciate that."

He nods, flattering me, the word *but* hanging in the air.

"The trouble is, you're being attacked on two fronts. First, the actionable claim of discrimination. It hasn't emerged as a concrete legal threat, but it could. The other is softer. Reputational. That's my wheelhouse."

He sets his coffee down and cups his hands, tracing a sphere in the air.

"Your audience is your world. Now there's outside interference." He wags his fingers, miming chaos. "I manage that outside element. The noise you don't want."

Jason chimes in. "We'd be entering a partnership. A two-way street." He's sitting forward, forearms on the table, too intent to even pour himself a juice.

"What exactly do you suggest?" I ask Orson.

"First, disavow the illegal firing. If you were planning to let the pregnant employee go, don't. Dispute the article's claims, loudly and often."

"That seems logical." I throw a pointed glance at Jason, but he dodges it, leaning forward to take a wedge of pineapple from a platter.

Orson goes on. "Bigger outlets will be less inclined to pick up a story with one anonymous source. Any new information—online gossip, employees talking—will escalate the situation."

I select a croissant from a platter, tap it against my plate, shaking off crisp shards.

"Our People Team is reminding the staff of their NDAs as we speak."

Orson is unfazed. "She's smart," he says to Jason.

Jason concentrates on slicing his pineapple like steak.

Orson presses his fingertips into the table. "By the end of the day, I'll know everything there is to know about Megaphone. Who edited the piece? Do they employ fact-checkers? Who owns the site? What's their financial situation? We'll go after them, aggressively."

"Get them to retract the story," Jason adds. "Take it down, issue an apology."

He knows I'm tempted to attack Megaphone, but I can't react emotionally.

"The writer has a platform of her own. She'll keep vilifying me."

"A lawsuit would be entirely justified," Orson says. "That would silence her."

"She'll tell her followers I'm suing her. She'll be a martyr."

He purses his lips. "I have to challenge you on that. Not many people can afford to be reckless in the face of a lawsuit. She strikes me as vulnerable. Not much money, no connections. Will she continue to tweet after her article has been disavowed and a court has stepped in? I highly doubt it." He settles his hands over his stomach, satisfied.

Jason breaks the silence. "It's a strong game plan we can share with investors. Keep it about business, take the focus off the personal slight. Distance yourself."

I dissect the last of my pastry. Doubt nags me. Fear, spreading like frost, making my instincts brittle and stiff.

"I can take this problem off your plate," Orson says. "I know the countermove to every action she might take. I can escalate, as much as we need, until we win."

"You told me yourself," Jason adds. "Giving her your attention is handing her a victory."

The writer is a black hole of negativity, curdling my creativity, dragging my momentum. To fight her myself will plunge my energy lower, even if (inevitably) I win.

"I'll have a name by lunchtime."

Dani

Monday

Dani brushes on another coat of powder. Her skin has a sickly, bilious look. *You're not glowing at all*, Cecelia said when she caught Dani being sick. She pretended to sympathize, but they'd just gotten off the Well elevator, and now Dani understands: Cecelia was eavesdropping, picking up dirt for Radicalidiocy.

Dani dispenses a drop of Radical Calm and rubs her wrists together.

Her shelves rattle with Radical's signature glass bottles—on her tiny salary.

Lauren is stupid. Pathetic. Oblivious of impending betrayal.

In the mirror, Dani spots the acrostic Cecelia made her stuck in the frame. *Demure, Adorable*—She snatches it down, rips it in half.

A meeting appears on her calendar: 11:00, with Holly and Cara, the Head of People. It can only mean one thing.

Rhoda's always emphasizing radical honesty. In the interview, she told Dani how much energy matters. And Dani withheld crucial information from the Trial.

And still, here she is, slinking into the Well, desperate for one last dose of Lift.

"No symptoms," Dani tells the attendant, avoiding her eyes. To swallow Lift, to feel the whirling in her chest settle, to take a full breath, to plan her apology, her plea . . .

"Dani Lang?"

Dani nods. Her mouth feels stiff, her makeup cracking around her lips.

"Your Trial is complete." The attendant smiles, like this is good news.

Dani's disappointment is crushing, and irrational. Somehow, in spite of everything, she still hoped that the conversation meant something else.

"We've collected all the feedback we need. I'll take your Well pass."

The attendant's hand is out, insistent.

A spotlight tracks Dani through the office. Whispers travel between pods, hissing like a slow gas leak. *Is that her?* Her stomach is suddenly enormous, poorly smuggled under her skirt.

The CW Team is silent, surreptitiously texting from their laps. As Dani sits, everyone stares without turning their heads. Sweat films her upper lip, clamps like a hot cloth at her neck.

Cecelia's desk is empty. Maybe she's quit, or been fired, though she didn't tweet about it. *Crickets from Radical,* she wrote this morning, *and not the kind crushed up in low-cal protein bars.*

Holly's gone. Her iced coffee, straw still topped with paper, drips on her desk.

The CW queue is endless. Public anger is like a whirlpool, sweeping people up in its current, circling, spiraling, deeper and deeper until they're drowning in outrage.

I was shocked to read the revelations about Rhoda's horrible treatment of employees. I've been a loyal customer since day one. Never again.

So disappointed. I'm a proud feminist and believed this brand was in line with my values. So much for being better.

I hope all those essential oils give you some kind of uncurable cancer!

Dani sets her fingertips on the keyboard like she's about to play a difficult piece on the piano.

Thank you for your note. We're grateful to have passionate followers. Our customers demand the highest standards, and it's a privilege and a key factor of Radical's success that we strive to meet them. We're still reviewing the recent account of Radical's workplace. We'll have more information and a plan of action shortly.

The weight of eyes landing on her is palpable, like small tickling flies.

She leaves for the All-Hands behind the others, leans against a pillar in the back. The ridges dig into her shoulder.

The Core Team arrives, and the music cuts off.

The whispers intensify. *Where is Rhoda?*

"Probably begging the board to let her keep her job."

"She's just trying to run her company."

"She's toast."

"We all are. Investors are going to peace out."

Cara steps forward, her smile bright as a pageant winner's. "With our fundraising round and other exciting growth, Radical is experiencing more press interest than ever, so it's a good time to do a quick refresher on a document you all signed when you started: the NDA."

She holds up a packet of paper and shakes it like a pom-pom.

"I don't know about you, but when I see a legal agreement, my eyes jump to where I sign. But this one's important, so bear with me.

"An NDA is an agreement that an employee won't share private information about a company. Radical's NDA also includes a non-defamation clause."

Dani spots Cecelia, front and center. Her red lipstick is flagrant.

"You probably have an unspoken agreement with your friends—you're not going to spill their secrets or talk trash about them. This is the same, except it's a formal legal agreement with Radical."

Cecelia rises on her toes, so delighted she can't hold still. She wasn't up all night, lines of the article echoing in her head.

Cara skips the cheer. The Core Team rushes off, and everyone else lingers, murmuring, unsatisfied. It's not like Rhoda to stay silent. Not unless . . .

Misery lodges like a bone in Dani's throat. She looks for Cecelia in the drifts of Radigals, but she's slipped away.

Back at Dani's desk, an origami shape perches on her keyboard. A cootie catcher, its four points like the beaks of hungry birds. Cecelia's restless fingers are always folding papers: menus, napkins, Holly's team meeting handouts.

I'm sorry, it says inside, very small. *It's shitty.*

Dani unfolds all the flaps, but there's nothing more.

She asks the girl who sits next to Cecelia if she's seen her. Olga is going to law school in the fall, as she frequently reminds everyone, so she's detached from the scandal.

Olga pulls out an earbud. "She goes up on the roof a lot. Did you know there's, like, half a deck up there?"

There's something nihilistic in abandoning the fire-red CW queue. In an hour, she's being fired. Tomorrow, she'll be gone. She ignores the warning on the emergency exit door, and pushes out into the concrete stairwell. No alarm sounds. She climbs up, her steps echoing, and shoulders through the heavy steel door to the roof.

The day is cold, briny, and gray. The white roof shines like a migraine. It has an abandoned, dystopian look. Huge air ducts burst upward. Hulking metal boxes hum mechanically. Somewhere beyond the obstructions, the gunshot report of tools carries from the construction site. Dani calls Cecelia's name, but her voice is tiny.

Cautious, she takes a step. The roof moves. Her knees clench, and she feels it again, through the bones of her feet. The building is swaying in the wind, lightly but definitely.

Go back, her body screams, but the nihilistic streak that's brought her this far is determined. She walks toward the noise. Her knees feel hollow but they hold. A strip of gauzy fog drifts by, trailing beads of moisture along her skin. A cigarette butt rolls away from her toes, stubby as a piece of chalk. She's reached a clearing, where a U-shaped concrete bench faces an empty concrete urn. Olga's deck.

When she lifts her chin, Rusher is ahead. Fog slides over it, revealing the gleaming black tower, like a magician's trick.

On the edge of the roof, a woman sits with her feet dangling over the side.

"Cecelia!"

She startles, tilting back. Her leg kicks up, like she's in a tippy boat. The wind snatches her cry and blows it over the edge. Dani's hands are on her mouth. The ground is so deep, she thinks, nonsensically.

Cee catches her balance and turns to Dani, crimson mouth opened accusatorily.

But it's not Cecelia. It's Rhoda, in dark sunglasses and a dark sweater, her protest faltering as she recognizes Dani, too.

"Dani!" She brings a cigarette to her lips. "You scared me."

Dani approaches Rhoda slowly, as if reluctant to come close to the edge. The poisonous smoke hangs between them, like an accusation.

"It's a great place to think," Rhoda says abruptly. "A lesson in perspective." She swipes a hand across the view.

Dani shields her eyes. Workers crawl over Rusher like ants. A crane reels up a bundle of steel beams. She doesn't need to come up here to know that she's small.

"What matters? Building things. Altering the landscape. Moving a pebble in a stream, and diverting the flow of water. *Intention*."

Impatient, as if Dani's arguing with her, she flicks ash into the abyss.

"Nothing makes me angrier than quashers trying to tear down what I've built. They're destructive. They think they're being insightful, as if criticism is inherently truer than praise. If they were in charge, none of this would exist. There would be no towers, no cities, no innovation. Nothing grand, nothing that lasts."

Behind her glasses, she might be irritated, impatient for Dani to excuse herself, leave her alone. She takes a final inhale, then taps the cigarette out on the ledge.

"I allow myself two a week. It's a way of balancing my control over my health with a recognition that it's impossible to eliminate the toxic from life."

Turning a millimeter in Dani's direction, she squints. "I bet you disapprove. You're a purist."

Dani shakes her head. "No." The word evaporates in the wind.

"Whoever wrote the article is a purist. They were so intent on their own idea of me they missed the point entirely. I'm sorry you had to read it."

She's watching Dani, waiting for a response. Is she apologizing for the article, or her words? Dani rubs her arms, shivering. She remembers her interview, the easy understanding that passed between them, like an electric current.

"The writer assumed the worst of everyone." *I'm not Lauren*, she wants to say.

Rhoda nods. "Negative energy."

"I should have told you at the interview," Dani says. "I never meant to hide it."

Rhoda shakes her head. "You're not being fired, Dani. You never were. You're leaving CW to be the Voice, of course. What else could that conversation have meant?"

She cocks her head, challengingly, and flashes her wolfish smile at Dani's stutter.

"I don't blame you for doubting. You must have felt as bad as I did, reading that."

Relief sweeps over Dani like a wave. *Of course.* Wasn't her first instinct, reading the story, that it had to mean something else?

"Thank you! I didn't know what to think—"

Rhoda nods. "It's easy to take words out of context, twist their meaning. What disturbs me is how easily people believed it. After everything I do. How open I am."

A frown briefly creases her forehead. She smooths a hand over her hair.

"I'd better go in. The negativity is spreading. Legal is trying to find the author of the story. I'm in for a day of difficult conversations. Not your concern, of course."

She stands and grasps Dani's hand with her cool fingers. "Congratulations. It's reassuring to have you at Radical. A believer, like the writer said. But she didn't know what it meant, really."

Her eyes meet Dani's, that easy understanding flowing between them.

Dani's decision is swift, reflexive, like tearing down Cecelia's card.

"I know who wrote it. If it helps."

Cecelia

Monday

The bartender fills Cecelia's glass until sake trembles at the brim.

"Shockwaves!" Leandra shouts. She's reading the choicest reactions aloud. "'The revelations are sure to send shockwaves through Radical.'"

She raises her glass to Cecelia. "Incredible. I knew Rhoda was a lightning rod."

The waiter brings dish after dish, all ordered by Leandra from the menu that doesn't list prices. At the end of the night, she lays down an AmEx Black.

"How old are you?" Cecelia blurts. She's drunk. The paper lantern lights smear.

"Twenty-four," Leandra replies, scrawling her name illegibly across the receipt. "I don't count chickens, but this story has momentum. We're blowing up!"

She kisses Cecelia on both cheeks and gets into her ride. Cecelia stumbles home. *Shockwaves!* She sleeps with her phone, alerts humming in her dreams.

In the morning, she's punished by rare sunshine. She chases an espresso shot with a Reboot, squinting at the hulk of Rusher. After the Radical story settles, she'll need another idea: something bigger, something new. Construction, earthquakes, the way growth and destruction surge through California like waves . . .

Everyone is in their seats, working or putting on a good show of it. Polish your résumés, people, Cecelia thinks, although perhaps all of Radical won't crash, just Rhoda.

Rhoda no-showed at the All-Hands; Rhoda is on the ropes. It was Cara who sent the email, at lunchtime yesterday, announcing Dani's promotion to Voice. No mention of the Slack conversation plotting the opposite. Radical's ploy is transparent: pretend the truth is whatever they say it is.

Leandra howled when Cecelia told her the blatant maneuver, and Cecelia pretended to laugh. Really, it bothers her, a murky, silty dread at the pit of her stomach, persisting in spite of the retweets, the anti-Radical flood, the shockwaves. Dani took the job. Dani sided with Rhoda.

It was Leandra's idea to draw Dani into the story—*she has to come alive on the page, win the reader's sympathy*. So Cecelia invented a pseudonym, made Lauren a shiny, simpler Dani. She knew Dani would be upset, but told herself she'd realize Cecelia was defending her. But instead of waking up to Radical's bullshit, Dani burrowed deeper into it. *Join me in congratulating our new Voice, Dani Lang!* She must know they're using her.

She's already at her desk, one leg tucked under her, as if she's been at it for hours.

"Cecelia Cole?" The peppy HR woman snuck up behind her, the one who delivered the NDA spiel yesterday, her Teflon grin deflecting any idea of impropriety. No sign of a smile now. "Will you come with me?"

She strides ahead. Cecelia was expecting this, sooner or later: the conference room door held open, the paperwork spread across the table. A cardboard box on the floor is piled with Cecelia's desk junk. Two women in navy sweaters sit rigid and serious behind laptops.

"Members of our Legal Team," Cara says, shutting the door with a decisive click.

So Rhoda's not coming. Cecelia is strangely disappointed. She'd imagined a satisfying confrontation. Walking home last night, she'd practiced her lines.

"Your employment at Radical is terminated, effective immediately."

Cecelia plays dumb. "Why?"

HR doesn't crack. "Consistent underperformance. Your Team Lead has documented numerous conversations in which she alerted you to this problem."

With a snap of a binder clip, she unleashes paperwork.

"Is this my severance package?"

"Being fired with cause negates any right to severance."

In the small room, Cecelia can smell last night's sake rising from her pores. The number of her final paycheck is printed on top of the page. A pittance. Not enough for her phone bill, let alone rent.

The lawyers avert their eyes. Their skin is smooth as if polished, not a hair out of place. She refuses to be embarrassed in front of them. *You're drones*, she wants to shout. *Didn't you read the article? Rhoda's breaking the law. Rhoda is a criminal, and also an asshole!*

"This is a copy of the legally binding agreement you signed at the start of your employment. Termination does not release you from your NDA."

Cecelia riffles the pages. "Rhoda's own words seem to cause the most trouble."

This is enough to make the lawyers' brows lift, but HR is smooth. No wonder she's on the Core Team. "I suggest you review the document closely. If you violate the terms, Radical will aggressively pursue legal action."

She opens the door, and two men in suits lumber into the room. "Security will escort you out." She pushes the box at Cecelia.

It's too large to carry easily. Cecelia hikes it onto her hip, and it digs into her ribs.

The bulky men don't offer to assist. They march her past the empty pods. It's All-Hands time. Cecelia cranes to see into the lobby. Rhoda's back! Standing in front of the windows, speaking in her drugged monotone, so Cecelia can't tell if she's apologizing, denying, resigning . . .

Radigals shift from hip to hip, skeptical. Megaphone got to them.

"Here we go." The security guards are impatient, bored. The elevator's waiting.

She'll never step into this office again. Instead of participating in a mandatory cheer, she walks into the sunshine. She carries her box to the park across from the Ferry Building and dumps it out. The sleeve of her lilac track jacket stretches after her. Goodbye to all that.

She strolls north along the Embarcadero, away from the startup crowd with their pale indoor skin and hunched phone necks, though she's also on her phone, checking on the story. The numbers are trending up, gaining traction. People are coming up with new hashtags. She smirks: #fireRhoda is catching fire.

She posts, refusing to worry about the NDA crumpled in her purse.

@Radicalidiocy
I was fired from Radical this morning. Speaking up leads to termination. Rhoda can't handle #radicalhonesty after all. #fireRhoda

Her tone is serious, but her mood is sailing. She leans against the sidewalk railing. The Bay glimmers. Ships pass under the bridge, easing toward Oakland from a world away. A yellow kite dips and soars.

She's done it. She's untethered from Radical HQ, the Michelles, the one-star zingers, the bottom rung of the ladder. She's escaped. She's free!

Rhoda

Tuesday

"Disappointing," Pilar says.

"Reckless," adds Barry.

"It's not like you," says Faye, "to open yourself up to such an easy attack."

My board sits spaced around the table like the numbers on a clock: Pilar, Barry, Faye, Jason, somber-faced. Their reprimands are obvious, but I listen patiently. We all know they have no power over me. What they really want is reassurance.

When I tell them we've retained Orson, they relax, and I'm grateful to Jason. He sits quietly, hands laced, looking contrite himself. *We should have moved offline*, he told them, apologizing. *Heat of the moment.*

He's handling the fallout among prospective investors. *A delicate balance between soothing their worries and weakening our leverage.*

Dani is promoted, the writer fired. All that's left to do is tell my side of the story.

Standing in front of a room full of people, a lot of energy streams at you. Anticipation, skepticism, hostility, hope. Even boredom generates a dull frequency.

"Good morning." My voice is amplified with a clip mic. Ahead of me, a tunnel of empty floor leads to a camera on a tripod. Radigals crowd around it.

Sunshine streams through the windows, falls across my shoulders. Sweat prickles the back of my neck, but hopefully the effect is glowing, wholesome.

"This isn't a typical All-Hands, as you can see. We're streaming live to our global audience. Thank you for joining us."

Tension hangs in the air like smoke. It will do everyone so much good to dispel it.

"I want to address a recent article about my leadership at Radical. I'll be clear: the accusation in the article is false. I am not and never was planning to fire a top Radigal who happens to be pregnant. I was preparing to promote her."

I glance at the camera, but don't stare into it. I'm not Nixon.

"I'm devastated that my words were misunderstood. You had a right to be upset, even outraged. I assure you, Radical fully supports working mothers."

An apology should be told andante, at a walking pace. Too fast, and it feels spit out, ungenuine. Too slow, and it feels dragged out, resented.

"Still, I owe you all an apology, especially the Customer Worship Team. Last week, I took my stress out on hardworking Radigals. That's not who I want to be as a leader, especially as a female CEO in the male-dominated business world. In response, I've hired a leadership coach to help myself and the Core Team balance heart and hustle."

The leadership coach is real. The Core Team and I will sacrifice an afternoon to pretending we're interested in being therapists as well as bosses.

"I was reminded of our incredible heart these past few days, as Radigals put their heads down to address customer questions, even if you shared their concerns. I'm also grateful to our customers. You hold the highest standards, and it's a key factor of Radical's success that we strive to meet them."

I spot Dani tucked beside a pillar. Her face is flushed. Does she recognize her words? I smile, my first of the meeting.

"Today, as always, this cheer is for you."

Radical, Radical, out on top!

As soon as we're done, I make my exit. No questions, no doubts.

In my office, I strip off my wilted shirt and change into an identical one. I feel good. Last spring, I tried kambo, an ancient detox ritual using venom from Amazonian frogs. A healer scorches a patch of skin on your arm and daubs it with the toxin. The effect is instantaneous. The body basically turns inside out, a complete purge.

It was the worst hour of my life, but afterward, I felt clean and light, as if air threaded my veins instead of blood. That's how I feel now. Flayed, lightheaded, relieved.

I dive with renewed energy into my busy morning.

I meet with Lisbeth to rearrange the social posting schedule. She suggests that we move up our influencer features.

"In other words, I shouldn't show my face for a while," I joke.

She lifts a shoulder. "Up to you."

She's still sulking about my unilateral decision to promote Dani.

I relent. "Let's cool off for a few days. But Wedding needs to come back by the weekend to stay on schedule."

Content is already planned through the month, culminating in the dress reveal.

"What will Voice do?" Lisbeth asks. "Given that Lift isn't launched."

"Dani can review all of the Well copy. Remove errors and add energy."

Lisbeth raises an eyebrow, registering the rebuke. The FDA fine took her by surprise; she immediately tried to deny responsibility. Dani will report to both of us.

I tilt my phone up from the table. No news from Jason.

"I've never had a manager complain about gaining an asset. If you're overstaffed, we'll discuss it at the next Core."

She slinks out.

My assistant ducks in. "That ran short. Mari wants to see you. OK to call her up?"

I've just sat at my desk. Work—real work—calls to me, but I stand, smiling. "I'll go to her."

Actually, stepping into the cool hush of the Well is clarifying. As the door hisses shut, it seems to seal out the negativity, the furor of the week.

In the Well, only the essential exists. Behind the doors, earnest work courses along, the alchemy of transforming raw ingredients—leaves and roots and oils—into the magic of a Radical potion.

Of course, Mari doesn't believe in magic. Her office is as sterile as a science lab, as though she's a sensitive chemical compound. I know what she's going to say before she says it:

"It's too smart. There should be a line between the information we collect and the data we compile."

I nod, respectful. "It's only a pilot. We're working to balance privacy and value."

"Dani had no privacy," she counters.

"The tools are incredibly powerful. They enhance the customer experience."

"Do you even realize you're spinning it?" Her dismay is genuine.

"Data will fuel Radical. Let us expand the Well, invest in research, bring our mission to the biggest audience." My hand is stretching toward her. I want her to see it: the future stretching before us, unfolding in every dimension.

She shakes her head. "This is how great visions are corrupted, voluntarily and with enthusiasm, in the name of money."

My patience snaps at the way she pronounces *money*, like it's a deadly sin. I hold my temper. "You're missing the bigger picture."

"I can't work for a mission I don't believe in." Her chin is raised.

I sit back. "I'm sorry you feel that way."

Sometimes, if I stop persuading them, people suddenly come around. It makes them nervous, being held to their word.

But Mari removes her bracelet with melodramatic dignity, setting it on the table between us. "It's not worth the trade-off."

I expected a stiff-backed statement of dissent for the record. Not this. She's lost all proportion.

"I wish you'd reconsider. You'll never command resources like this again."

I gesture toward the door, the humming intensity of the Well. I spared no expense.

She lifts a shoulder, like the point is too shallow to consider.

I leave, stiff with fury. At least her energy won't be tainting the Well. Let her go work for a pharmaceutical company: see how she likes that moral compromise. Or she'll find a job at a research lab, eke progress along, begging for funding every inch of the way. What a waste!

When I studied science in college, they told us it was a privilege to devote your life to an incremental increase in collective knowledge. I balked at the idea of creeping along with a slow pack, yoked to tradition, hampered by arcane rules. Purists, believing in process over promise. Even then, it was obvious to me that a few smart people shaped the future, and I was going to be one of them.

I walk the teal circuit. My shoes rub my ankles. While I was downstairs, fog drifted in, blindfolding the windows. The pillars are dark red. People duck behind them as I pass. Faces squint from the pods. They're all unfamiliar.

I interview every person. I'm so careful. How did this happen, an office of strangers, people who might love Radical or leave it? People like the writer. As I predicted, she's made a public performance of her firing. Posted a photo of her Radical gear spilled on the ground.

@Radicalidiocy
I've been cut off from all my Radical employee perks: starvation wages, high-copay healthcare, and swag.

In this instant, I would trade this luxe office for our damp warehouse in the Mission, its pitted concrete floor and cracked windows, the shared bathroom in the hall; we kept a roll of toilet paper on the reception desk, and if you had to go, you took it with you. Every one of us would have given a kidney for Radical.

We celebrated every milestone because we sweated for every milestone. The first day we hit $100K in sales. The week we hit a million pageviews. Every holiday, we celebrated our biggest season yet, popping champagne and roller-skating around the office, a disco ball scattering coins of light. Nobody questioned whether it was worth the hustle. Everyone worked around the clock, Sales helping CW, Social pitching in with QA. Even Jason spent evenings boxing orders, dressed in red velvet blazer and Santa hat.

It's easy, now, to take our success for granted, as though it was inevitable. Back then, we felt the weight of every brick we laid. The customers recruited and retained. The cult-status products. The rallying Voice. We built that. Manifested Radical from almost nothing. From sheer belief.

Glossy Italian leather chafes my anklebone until the skin breaks.

In my office, I check Megaphone. The story stands. Not so much as an editor's note alerting readers that the facts are under dispute. And firing the writer has only given her more time to tweet.

@Radicalidiocy
Rhoda's apology is like the snake oil she sells: emptiness presented in a pretty package. Nothing has changed at Radical. #fireRhoda

The hashtag is proliferating. #fireRhoda.

If I were reassuring investors or staff, I'd tell them to be patient. But I'm seething.

I call Jason, but he doesn't answer. He texts a bee emoji—our shorthand for busy. I picture him talking to investors, my name in their mouths. As long as the story is up, the round is in jeopardy.

I dial another number.

"If you've made any progress since our meeting, I can't see it."

"Rhoda," Orson says. "Hello. I was just about to call you."

The red-eyed Rhoda on my screen is like a mirror. "Didn't you promise to get the story down? Every minute it's up costs me more than your exorbitant billing rate."

A sympathetic hum. "The editor is more stubborn than anticipated. Principled."

"Principled? Keeping a disproven story online?"

"We're wearing her down. The gears of the law grind slowly. Rather the opposite of the startup world, I'm afraid."

"I don't have time. My board is anxious. My employees are discouraged."

He clears his throat. "If expedience is our aim, I wonder if you know the identity of Lauren?"

I pause in my pacing. "Yes."

"I wonder if she might corroborate our side of the story. Confirm that she divulged her pregnancy, for instance."

I hear Orson's pen click. "I can make it easy. Prepare a statement for her to sign. We'll need it, anyway, if we're proceeding with the lawsuit."

When I told Dani she was being promoted, she was like a phoenix: burst into stunned flames. She volunteered Cecelia's name. She understands loyalty.

"Fine. Send it over, if it will move things along."

Dani

Wednesday

She hasn't officially started her new job, but Dani's already learning a secret language. Stock options. Vesting schedules. Shares.

"This package is generous," Cara observed, "especially given the timing. You're priced on the old value on the cusp of an investment round."

It boggles Dani that she owns any part of Radical. The pillared office and the hushed Well, the progress tallying on flat-screens.

"One last form." Cara clears her throat, holding a fist to her lips as she skims the final paper in a tall stack. She lets out a little "huh," and quickly smiles, covering it.

"The Legal Team slipped this one in on us." She slides the sheet across the table.

"Given the publicity associated with your promotion—specifically, the false claims published on Megaphone—Legal has prepared a simple statement. Setting the story straight, so to speak."

Her smile is like a question mark, compelling Dani to nod along.

"Wonderful. Look it over and sign." She taps her pen on the line.

Dani's own throat is dry, her eyes weary of densely worded legalese.

This form is different than the others. The name of a law firm is printed on top.

I, Dani Lang, affirm that I granted Radical access to my app and bracelet data as a condition of the Lift Trial. I openly shared my health information, and to my knowledge it did not influence my advancement at Radical in any way.

Dani bites the end of her pen, too distracted to notice the plastic against her teeth. The detached language is opaque, but it doesn't feel quite right. Cecelia's latest tweet comes, unwelcome, to mind. *Close your eyes. Imagine that down is up, up is down, and when Rhoda said she was going to fire Lauren, she meant promote!*

"I'm not sure," she says, and Cara nods, empathetic.

"It's only a formality. Our outside counsel needs this to clear up the issue with Megaphone." She grimaces. "I'm sorry to end on a down note. Rhoda is eager to resolve that, you can understand. And I'm sure you are, too. Ready to move forward, start your job off on the right foot." Another smile, encouraging Dani to mirror her.

Dani signs, her tired handwriting producing an inarticulate zigzag. It reminds her of the hastily scribbled names on the congratulatory card the CW Team gave her after the promotion. *Nice move, Machiavelli*, someone had scrawled in anonymous green ink. Cecelia, Dani thought, instantly. But Cecelia was already gone. Dani didn't even see her go. Suddenly, her desk was occupied by a temp with blue mermaid hair.

Dani tidies the papers into a sharp-edged stack that strikes the table like a gavel. Cecelia is still tweeting, remorseless, committed to her cause. Dani has her own life.

At eight, a car draws up to a huge brick building guarded by stone lions.

Dani lifts the hem of her dress. Trevor smooths his suit jacket, which tops a SitFit shirt. NEVER NOT MOVING. He reaches for her hand, grinning.

The Bastion Club is exclusive. Members-only, tech-only. The admissions process is secretive, the fees astronomical. Its brief history is storied: an eight-figure deal riding on a hand of blackjack, a baby leopard serving as ring bearer in an online retail baron's wedding, reclusive CEOs debating ideas in the steam room. Order the Big Deal, a $700 tequila shot, and the bartender comes to your table with the bottle handcuffed to his wrist like the nuclear codes.

Slim Riley added them to his guest list. The weekend in Tahoe went well. Trevor expects a term sheet any day, his startup getting started at last.

Dani's new dress sweeps the black marble floor. The floaty layers of persimmon-colored gauze transform her into someone confident, who doesn't gawk at the crystal chandelier, or point to the neon letters on the wall: *Impossible is nothing.*

The concierge wears a white gardenia in her updo. With a swipe of her finger, she checks their names on a tablet. "Your table is in Safari."

It's like walking onto a movie set. No: like stepping into an actual movie. Warm light, low chatter, the clink of heavy silverware, the chime of ice cubes, an underlying hum like an old record. Everything glints: gold and brass, wood and glass. A taxidermized lion crouches on a platform above the dining tables, his muscles frozen in a tense ripple, teeth bared.

Trevor's eyes leap from table to table. "That's Learson Urzi!"

He points to a man with dark, curly hair hanging past the shoulders of his crisp white shirt. He's gesturing with his fork as he speaks, transfixing the rest of the table.

"The VR king. He's going to be like Steve Jobs and Jeff Bezos rolled into one."

Trevor whispers more names—VCs who rejected him, overrated founders, brilliant engineers, a pro baseball player. Their own table is already occupied by the SitFit staff: perpetually single Eric, whose basement-dwelling look unsettles Dani; gregarious Mekin and his wife, Natasha, who wears chunky glasses over her beautiful, bony face. She's a VP at a grocery delivering app, and a huge fan of Rhoda's.

"Drama!" she whispers, wanting to hear about Megaphone.

Dani rolls her eyes, camouflaging her distaste for the topic by exaggerating it. Luckily, Natasha has no idea that Dani herself is Lauren.

"Did you see? Hashtag-fire-Rhoda. I mean, there's no way, right?"

Platters of food arrive, distracting her. Mekin claps his hands, directing the dishes around. They're gourmands, famous for their dinner parties.

"We ordered everything worth eating!" Natasha announces.

Sizzling merguez sausage and tomato sauce, a fava bean curry, stone bowls of Marcona almonds, tagines under volcano-shaped lids.

The talk turns to Slim Riley's quirks—he stays up late, and freewrites ideas for inventions and societal improvements in black leather Moleskines, which fill an entire wall of his cavernous barn conversion. Every few minutes, someone whispers another name: an early investor in Google, the godfather of AI, the fashion designer who invented *that* ubiquitous wool sneaker. Trevor is almost levitating from his seat. Meeting Dani's eyes, he lifts his brows twice, playful. *Believe it*, he seems to say. *It's real.*

"Dani has news, too!" He lifts his glass, and she holds her breath, wondering if he'll share Naomi, but he announces her promotion. (Of course: for all of them, news means work, their beating heart.) They pound the table, generously heaping their satisfaction onto hers.

Dani is flushed. Her cheeks are sore from smiling. It's tempting fate, celebrating when she hasn't even started the job, before Slim's signed the check. The worry is fleeting. The night is charmed. The movie rolling around them, nobody calling cut.

"This one's on me," Trevor cries, intercepting the bill, waving away protests with a flap of his hand.

In the bathroom, a vast marble trough sink sits in a ring of individual doors, each labeled with a deadly sin. Bizarre. Greed and Envy might make sense for a tech club. But Lust? Rage? Dani takes Sloth, fitting for her exhaustion.

When she emerges, Rhoda is washing her hands at the sink.

"Hi," Dani says. Her excited voice echoes in the marbled room.

"Well, hello." Rhoda blinks. "What brings you here?"

She shakes water from her fingers and tugs a towel from a ledge of rolled white cloths. Dani hangs back. It would be too intimate to scrub her hands while Rhoda twists her rings in the towel, checking her reflection with perfunctory satisfaction.

"My boyfriend's startup," Dani explains, unable to resist mentioning Slim's name, presenting it to Rhoda proudly. Building a picture of her life that isn't Lauren, that fits the woman who finds herself in the Bastion Club with Learson Urzi, with Rhoda West.

"Congratulations," Rhoda says. "It's hard to beat that early excitement. When everything is still possible. I almost envy him."

She yawns, hugely, her face contorting. "When this is over, I'm going to sleep for a week."

She tosses her towel in a hamper and waves over her shoulder as she goes. Her perfume lingers, orchids and a hint of scorch.

After the cheek kisses and the hugs, the giddy *how-much-do-you-think*s and *don't-even-say-it*s, the table breaks up.

Trevor nurses the last drops of his drink, then ropes his arm around Dani's shoulders, singing one of his band's songs. "My hot-air balloon heart, up, it goes, up . . ."

Dani's embarrassed to meet Rhoda waiting for the elevator. Gavin is with her, a handsome stranger Dani knows well. He sees them first, grins at the spectacle.

"Rhoda West!" Trevor shouts.

Rhoda turns, wearing her public expression of reserved friendliness.

"You must be Trevor." She offers her hand. "Dani's told me about your company."

Amazingly, Trevor's drunkenness only slightly smudges his manners. He shakes Gavin's hand—"I'm a big fan"—though Dani knows he thinks people who made money in the dot-com boom just got lucky. *Like people who got rich selling Beanie Babies.*

Gavin holds the elevator doors, and Trevor stands close to Rhoda.

"What advice would you give someone aspiring to be in your position?"

A presumptuous question, but Trevor is earnest and Rhoda seems amused.

"You know, it's incredibly simple, but almost no one is capable of it."

"Try me." Trevor leans in, smitten.

"You have to be willing to put the company first, no matter what. To sacrifice anything that gets in the way. Sleep, time, money." She waves a hand, like these are frivolities. "Anything. You do what it takes to survive another day."

Trevor nods, intent. "I get that."

Rhoda smiles. Wry? Doubtful? "Then you'll go far."

The doors open, and she strides out. The valet has already pulled up her convertible. She settles in, adjusts the mirror a millimeter. Gavin draws a vape pen with an impossibly elegant gesture. Her scarf trails over the backseat as they roar off.

"What a night!" Trevor shouts, uninhibited. This late, the downtown block is deserted except for the Bastion. The buildings echo his words in agreement.

It's happening. They're joining this world. Dani *owns* some of Radical.

Cecelia

Thursday

Unemployment agrees with Cecelia. She wakes at her leisure, strolls to the cheapest coffee shop for a two-dollar drip. She claims a bench at Crissy Field and watches the water, the bridge she secretly thinks is beautiful, corny as it is in photographs. She's convalescing, in recovery from employment at Radical. Her relentless pain has ceased. It's stunning, like silence after prolonged noise. Maybe Rhoda was onto something with wellness, though not the kind you can sell.

After Rhoda's public apology on Tuesday morning, Megaphone got more pageviews in an hour than in the site's entire history. Leandra called Cecelia late that night, breathless.

"She only drew attention to the story! I love it! This is how truth starts to catch fire, little sparks at first, then huge flames."

Not an ideal metaphor, maybe, since literal wildfire smoke films the horizon this morning. But fire is a fitting image for the energy—it's unstoppable. Cecelia's tweets surge every time. She ends every one with #fireRhoda. The hashtag is blunt, thrillingly assertive. *A call to action*, as Radical managers would say.

Radicalidiocy is flooded with messages. Supporters, women with anecdotes of their own terrible workplaces, reformed Radical fans who felt disenchanted but couldn't put their finger on why until now. Cecelia can't keep up with the responses.

On Wednesday, Leandra texted Cecelia. *Radical's trying to bully me into taking down the story. We're striking a nerve!!*

@Radicalidiocy
Fire sale! Radical is offering a free, unlimited silent retreat
for all critics, quashers, and concerned citizens. #belouder
#fireRhoda

The only cloud to the silver lining is that Cecelia is broke. Leandra
didn't pay her—*our pieces are testimonials; payment would muddy the
waters*—but she has no doubt of Cecelia's potential. She knows people at
the *Chronicle*. She has a blogger friend and a friend with a newspaper and
an ex-boyfriend who's taken photos for the Cut. *You were meant to write.
Nothing will stop you.*

Cecelia tips back her cup, slurping the last drops of coffee. She'll
make connections, pitch a few stories. She has enough saved for another
month's rent, if she scrimps. She imagines her future self laughing at her
worries: *I ate beans! Not even with rice! I didn't want to stay in my landlady's
kitchen long enough to boil water.*

A lime green Smart car is parked outside Cecelia's house. As she starts
up the driveway, the door opens. A tall man telescopes out of the driver's
seat and calls out.

"Cecelia Cole?"

He's wearing mirrored sunglasses and carries a manila envelope under his arm. He looks like a reporter, like he chases things for a living.
Finally—someone come to ask her about Radical.

She steps toward him, and he thrusts the envelope at her. Startled, she
takes it. It's lightweight, slim, bent in a curve from his grip.

"You've been served," he says, walking backward. "Have a nice
day."

Before she can speak, he's folding himself back into the car like a spi-
der tucking itself back into a hole. He must have left the engine running.
The tiny car makes a hairpin U-turn and speeds away.

Confused, Cecelia opens the envelope. Inside are a dozen typewritten
pages. Her name is on the first page.

STATE OF CALIFORNIA

DEFENDANT, Cecelia Cole

SUMMONS TO COURT

The text is dense, convoluted, every sentence a traffic jam of clauses tucked inside other clauses, sentences that interrupt themselves to clarify, to specify, to disclaim. She hacks her way toward meaning, like wielding a machete through a jungle.

Radical is suing her. Accusing her of breach of contract, conversion, whatever that is, and unjust enrichment. Rhoda, suing Cecelia over riches! The tweet writes itself!

There's an alarming line, buried toward the end. "Plaintiff is entitled to damages to be determined by the court."

Wind riffles the pages. It's ordinary printer paper. It doesn't look official at all. She considers opening her hands, letting it blow away.

Leandra's phone rings to voicemail.

"I got some papers from Radical and am wondering if you have a lawyer, or someone to look at them."

Cecelia's voice is astringent, too loud. Margo's dryer drums the wall at her back.

"She's probably just trying to scare me. Anything to shut us up!"

The steaming scent of artificial lilac seeps into her brain through her nose, threading a headache through her synapses. She lies down for a moment and wakes to late-afternoon light slanting into her eyes.

She has a new text from Leandra. *Swamped today, talk tomorrow? Maybe take the foot off the gas, if you're concerned?*

Rhoda

Friday

Finally, Orson calls. "Excellent news. Megaphone issued a full retraction. I'm quite pleased with how quickly that came about."

I would call it glacial, but at least it's happened.

"Gears are turning now," he says, ringing off.

I check Radical's social. We risked a return to Wedding content this morning. I asked Gavin to write about his prep, and he surprised me with a beautiful essay about the spiritual preparation for committing to sharing a life.

In the post, he's carrying his surfboard up the beach, arms over his head.

radical Surfing, you ride every wave alone. For a long time, I
believed life was that way, too. I overlooked the best part: the group
gathered at the birthplace of the waves. Floating on your own
boards, together.

The metrics are solid, but they should be better. Ordinarily, a photo of Gavin, especially shirtless, overperforms.

Just then a Molotov cocktail streaks into my inbox: Redwood has bowed out of the round.

Within seconds, Jason bricks off my calendar for the rest of the day.

Palo Alto holds no nostalgia for me.

I spent two years at Stanford, kicking with impatience as everyone spoke of founders like they were trading cards: age, net worth, company valuation. Everyone wanted to join their ranks, but most didn't have what it takes. I already knew I did.

As soon as Radical took off, I left. My professors cautioned against it. They said I was gambling my education on a dream, as if education began and ended on campus.

Jason arranged meetings with every VC firm. *Strategy sessions*, he called them, as if we're already partners who will pull together to solve this. Clever, if transparent.

When I arrive at Oort, his Tesla is already in the parking lot. He's seated in the conference room, which goes quiet as I enter.

Ignore it.

"I promise radical transparency to my customers, and I'll treat you the same."

My voice pours out of me like oil. I acknowledge the outcry. But the vast majority aren't our customers—they're villagers with pitchforks. It's pointless to appease them.

"We don't want to blow this out of proportion," the Managing Partner says. "In fact, we're intrigued. Jason was telling us more about your program. Using data to drive business operations. Lots of opportunity there."

No kidding. He's practically rubbing his palms together.

"But," he continues. "Given your strong personal connection to the brand, we're worried it will be a struggle to rebuild your image. We have to consider whether the valuation we discussed is still accurate."

"The story is already down. The worst of the storm is past."

"But the story will never go away." A paternal smile. "People have screenshots."

The next meeting is the same, and the next. Fiddle-leaf figs in windows, black leather chairs my skirt slips on. Men in branded Patagonia vests, lacing their fingers together, feigning disappointment.

By four o'clock, I feel brittle. The skin of my face is stiff, like it's covered in drying paint.

Last stop is the Ephraim brothers. In the parking lot, I swallow two Forward March capsules. They contain caffeine and rhodiola, a Taoist herb that hones concentration. When I take my seat, my pulse is humming, but I no longer want to rest my forehead on the high polish of the table.

"What concerns us is the optics," says one of the brothers. Brett? "The story punctures a hole in the entire Radical narrative."

"Does it?" A headache snaps like a rubber band at my temples. "My emphasis has always been on individual control over wellness. You could say that self-determination is actually a core feature of our narrative."

The other brother leans forward. "What Chad means is, I think, the centrality of the female customer to Radical's audience base."

"There are all kinds of women out there." I smile. "Thankfully."

"But those Slack conversations . . ." Chad shakes his head. "They're so aggressive."

On the wall behind him is a blown-up photograph of himself kite-surfing, hair drenched in spray. ("Taken by drone," he bragged when I came in.)

Jason is as calm as a suicide hotline volunteer. "The story has come down."

"I hear your concerns." I make an effort to sweeten my voice. "And, if it seemed like my customers were responding to the story, I would share them. But our sales are steady. Let's not react as if the worst-case scenario occurred when it didn't."

Brett strokes his goatee. "To be blunt, we worry about the risk of recurrence. Someone else coming forward. Some other dust under the bed."

My smile stings.

Smile, they tell women. Smile! You'd look so pretty if you smiled. It makes me wonder whether men have any idea how much a woman can express with a smile. Happiness, occasionally. Irritation, impatience, disappointment, misery. Anger, fury, rage. Smiles absorb insults, combat come-ons, acknowledge moronic jokes, deflect questions that shouldn't have been asked and won't be answered. The queen chess piece would wear a smile as she sideswipes the king.

Jason puts his hand on my back. "Rhoda started Radical when she wasn't old enough to legally drink. She's grown up with the brand. Women connect with her personal journey. It's powerful stuff."

Somehow I'm in the position of three men looking at me as though I'm an object to be debated rather than the subject of the action.

I put my bag on the table.

"I have complete confidence in what Radical and I have to offer." I stand. "If you're interested in a zero-risk company with a cardboard CEO, I'm sure you can find one. But it won't be a rocket ship and it won't put your firm on the map, because a million middle-aged Midwesterners already have it in their mutual funds. I'll be disappointed if you drop out of the financing round, but it's ultimately your call."

Jason catches up to me in the parking lot. His Tesla is parked at an angle so he can get into those silly lifting doors, proof that men stop maturing around age eleven.

"I've never known anyone to get scolded for playing with matches and then bring gasoline to their apology."

"They don't care about the transgression, only the fallout. A minor scandal, and their faith is already shaken. I'm not sure I even want them in the company, if this is their idea of backing."

He glances back at the office windows, as if they're spying on us from behind their beige UV-filtering shades. "They still know Radical is the best. If anything, they're more convinced. I've had more than one firm reach out to inquire about the data. This is just smart business. Trying to get more for less."

"If they were smart, they wouldn't antagonize me." I toss my purse into my car. "And if anyone else asks you about a Radical program, refer them to me."

"My role is to play the diplomat. You knew that when you asked me to handle investors this week."

"And look how well that went," I snap, feeling as hot as if I did toss a match.

Tech buses as big as yachts hem me in. I imagine coddled workers staring at me from behind the tinted windows. I put my roof up.

My phone is suspiciously quiet. My fury is still hungry, so I feed it.

@Radicalidiocy
Down to my last few dollars. About to get a crash course in fasting.
Luckily, Rhoda promises starvation has positive side effects.

"She's still tweeting."

"More persistent than we expected. Strictly speaking, she's allowed to tweet. It's difficult to forbid someone from using your name." Orson sneezes. "Excuse me. Our summer weather has given me a cold."

"At this rate, she might entice a headline-hungry lawyer to her corner. Our lawsuit will become a circus."

"I have every confidence—"

"I don't."

"I see." Poor man, realizing he has a difficult female client. "There are other levers we can pull."

"Such as?"

"Observation," he says, slowly, savoring the word, "can be extremely helpful. I have an associate who specializes in information-gathering. Where does she live? What is her daily routine? Where does she go and when? Whom does she meet?"

"I'm not interested in her personal life."

He chuckles. "You'd be surprised at the things we turn up. Plenty of behavior people wouldn't want public."

"She doesn't strike me as easily embarrassed."

"Observation can be motivating for other reasons," Orson says, carefully. "Especially for the subject who has been slow to comprehend the seriousness of her situation. People notice when they're being watched."

The freeway narrows, approaching the city. The lanes clot. Billboards advertise phone networks and B2B software. We're doing our first billboard campaign for Lift. If we close this round, that is. I drum my steering wheel. *Don't make it personal*, Jason warned. But I think of the conversations being held around the raw-edged conference tables along Sand Hill Road. Everyone clawing for leverage. Trying to overtake me.

"Do whatever you need to do."

Cecelia

Friday

The story is down. Her story, gone: no warning, no debate, just an email from Leandra in the early hours of the morning. (*Unfortunately, I have no choice.*)

Editor's Note: Earlier this week, we published a story about the wellness company Radical and its controversial CEO, Rhoda West. While our anonymous source offered what we believed to be substantial documentation of their story, it has since come to our attention that central facts are disputed by others at Radical. As such, we are removing the piece from our site. We apologize to our readers. Rest assured, Megaphone will continue to represent the spirit of reform and questioning.

Onward,
Leandra French

No hint, in this self-serious speech, of Leandra clinking her shot glass against Cecelia's, shrieking "shockwaves," of her glee as Megaphone's readership soared, her fist-pumping declarations of struggle and truth to power. She surrendered. Dropped the story. Dropped Cecelia. She's not answering her phone, her texts, her email.

Cecelia spends Friday alternately despondent and determined. She doesn't need Megaphone—her Twitter still has an audience. They understand the subtext below Leandra's disclaimer. *Folding like a cheap tent! What did Radical pay you?*

Cecelia retweets them all, but she's exhausted. Her pain is back. A throbbing cramp, like a hand grabbing her insides and giving them a good twist. She shakes a jar of Advil and a single pill rolls out. Should she take it now or save it? She gulps it down.

Rhoda posts a photo of the ocean. Fog like thunderheads on the horizon, blue sky above.

radical Wow. This week took me by surprise. What started as a storm turned into an opportunity to soul search. You let me know the kind of leader you expect me to be, pushing me to grow. Thank you for being here. May you find the silver lining in your own clouds. xo, Rhoda #bebetter

@Radicalidiocy
Wow, what a journey! From employed to unemployed. Applying for COBRA today; I wonder if they'll cover Radical's #snakeoil?

Cecelia checks her bank account. The number has dwindled, in just one day! Her cell phone bill autopaying, last month's credit card statement mocking her with stupid expenses. Food trucks and coffee shops incrementally accumulating to bankrupt her. That Uber to Dani's party! (Where she met Leandra. Hadn't her antennae gone up at Leandra's drunken laughter? Her buying bee pollen under Rhoda's spell—her carelessness.)

In the morning, Leandra posts a photo of her breakfast on Instagram.

leandraphone Eddie's, most authentic brunch in the city. Getting my greasy spoon fix.

Cecelia orders an Uber she can't afford. Restless, she waits for it in the driveway. A white Jeep is parked across the street. Not her ride: different car, different license. The driver is staring behind douchebag aviators. She avoids his eye, tense after the Smart car, that nasty trick with the envelope. When her Uber arrives, she flips him off.

The car heads uphill, climbing out of the sunny Marina and plunging into a fog as dense as cappuccino foam. It swallows treetops and rooflines, droops like a wet shawl over the underdressed shoulders of the long line outside Eddie's. There's a cry of protest as Cecelia goes right in.

Leandra's cozied up in a booth with her mustachioed man. Today he's wearing a porkpie hat.

At the sight of Cecelia, she chokes on her coffee. Wiping her mouth, she makes a show of being pleased. "I'm so clumsy! Cecelia! Where did you come from?"

Cecelia slides in across from her. "We need to talk."

"We're just finishing brunch," Leandra says, as if the meal is sacrosanct.

The table is crowded with greasy plates, where more food than Cecelia has eaten all week congeals in puddles of maple syrup. She slaps down the court summons.

Leandra looks wary. She flips through the pages gingerly, like she doesn't want to leave prints.

"I know a lawyer who specializes in NDAs. I can give you her number."

Already she's pushing the papers back at Cecelia.

"Isn't this somehow Megaphone's issue? You ran the story."

Leandra rubs the bridge of her nose. "You had the legal agreement with Radical. We did what we could to shield you."

Cecelia never appreciated how irritating it is that Leandra uses the collective "we" when Megaphone is all Leandra, a one-woman show.

"Look," Leandra says, as defensive as if Cecelia spoke aloud. "I'm hardly getting off unscathed. Radical's come after me, too. I expected some heat, but this is beyond."

Porkpie squeezes her hand.

She flags the waiter as he passes with a pot of coffee, and they all stare at her mug as he refills it.

"Thank you," she says loudly. Cecelia bets that she prefers six-dollar cold brew but this place, with its drip coffee in mismatched mugs, lets her pretend she's down-to-earth.

"I'm not happy about taking the story down. I resisted the pressure, even after it was clear I was risking a lawsuit myself. But your friend

Lauren signed an affidavit that her pregnancy wasn't secret. That backed up Rhoda's story, and my lawyer felt . . ."

She keeps talking, but the air disappears from Cecelia's lungs. She saw Dani hiding behind a pillar after Megaphone came out. Her pale misery. She interpreted Rhoda's conversation exactly as Cecelia did.

"Did you give her a heads-up about the article, confirm your facts?"

Cecelia shakes her head. "But we have screenshots of what Rhoda said."

Leandra sighs. "I don't like to fold, but what can I do? Megaphone isn't helpful to anyone if it no longer exists. Look what happened to Gawker."

She digs in her purse for a fat wallet and bypasses a full house of credit cards in favor of cash. Crisp twenties. Cecelia almost expects Leandra to hand her a few, but she tucks them under a plate.

"What about our momentum? All our readers?"

Leandra hitches a leather jacket up her shoulders. "I'm sorry it turned out this way. Think of it as a trial by fire. Journalism is a tough business."

"I can't afford to be sued. I can't afford rent."

Porkpie finally speaks. "Look at the papers again."

Cecelia nearly spills them out of the envelope in her haste.

He taps the front page. "California State Court. If you can't fight it, just leave."

"Are you kidding?"

"What are they gonna do? You didn't murder someone."

"But I love California."

Leandra tucks her soft, floppy purse under her arm, like a stuffed animal for a rich woman. "You need to take ownership of the situation, Cecelia. You're casting yourself as the victim, but have you considered how you endangered my livelihood?"

The waiter swoops in for his cash, stacking the plates on his forearm, swiping the table with a rag. Cecelia's in the way. Get out, Cecelia.

Rhoda

Sunday

The waiter pours Gavin a ceremonial swig of wine. He sniffs, swirls, savors.

Gavin and I are having dinner at Atelier Crenn before he leaves for a week of surfing in the Maldives, his unofficial bachelor party.

The chef brings the bread tray. The butter is carved in the shape of a unicorn. Gavin gushes. The feeling of a jinx falls over me like a shadow. As soon as she leaves, I slice off the horn.

"No one else will drop out," Gavin says, chewing his crust. "The story's down, right? Lining the proverbial birdcages."

"No one has committed."

"It's Sunday. Even VCs go home sometimes. Introduce themselves to their kids."

The first course is beet ceviche served under a ceramic cloche shaped like a beet, complete with dirt-speckled leaves. Gavin fills my plate. I have no appetite, especially for the red, earthy-smelling mince.

Since we left the Ephraims', Jason has gone silent. Technically, he's not ignoring me—he returns one-word replies to my long, wondering texts, considering scenarios, sending new slides about the data pilot. *Gotcha*, he'll reply. *Good thought*. Sulking.

The meal marches on. Who came up with the idea to divide dinner into a dozen plates? It reminds me of a pitch deck, every course building onto the last, showing off. The foamed vegetables and charred citrus seem less like food and more like the wildest ideas from a late-night brainstorm.

" . . . look at land," Gavin's saying.

I blink. Our plates are cleared. The waiter sweeps crumbs with a tiny broom.

"A winery." Gavin sounds like he's repeating himself. "Something small, with a house, a garden. Can't you see it?"

I tease him about wanting to crush grapes with his feet. He laughs but persists.

"Really. It's something I've been thinking about since I started working on the garden. A buddy of mine knows a place coming up for sale."

"It sounds idyllic. Maybe when I retire."

"I'll manage it. You'll come on weekends." He thumbs the stem of his wineglass. "I'm tired of this city. It's a hamster wheel, everyone scurrying after the next idea. I want my life to have a different pace. Sync with a more ancient rhythm."

Dessert is a scoop of green sorbet surrounded by dots of sauce, like the numbers on a clockface. I think of Jason's watch, worn less for information than as a reminder. *Tick, tock. Go, go, go.*

"You're forgetting Radical. I'm still on the hamster wheel."

"But Radical fits, don't you see?" He reaches for my hand. His engagement ring catches the glow of candles in its thick metal curve. "It's about growing things, nourishing the body. We can cultivate herbs for the Well."

I consider a farm. Hills, a stone house. Not wild like the ocean, not exciting like the city. Rhythmic, seasonal, repeating. A bowl of birdsong and insect wings.

Gavin isn't as surprised as I am when I agree.

In the morning, the Ephraim brothers send over a term sheet. Jason's call is almost simultaneous, as if he was forewarned.

"Let's consider this carefully," he says, and instantly I know what to expect.

The valuation is short. Not by much, but that's irrelevant. Almost doesn't count.

"My gut says they're anticipating negotiation," Jason says. "That they'll boost the valuation if we accept their terms. They know the number we're hoping for."

I think of the snap as I sliced the butter horn off the unicorn. But it gets worse.

They want to eliminate my supervoting shares. Reduce my voting power to less than half.

"Absolutely not." I hope to sound amused—the idea is absurd—but I snarl.

"I warned you that weighted shares would be contentious. As Radical levels up, investors expect more stability. A conservative balance of power."

"I can't accept less than fifty-five percent."

"I have a strong feeling we can push for that higher value."

"It's only their opening offer. Let's try for both."

There's a second of total silence. He doesn't even sigh.

"You told me never to show fear," I remind him. "Remember?"

Quietly, drily, he says, "Once more unto the breach."

On my way to a Merchandising meeting, my phone rings. I pounce.

It's only Orson. He has "interesting intel." The writer lives in an illegal sublet.

"I've taken the liberty of alerting the landlord." He's pleased as a cat dropping a dead mouse at my door. "As I said, it's simply a matter of pressure. Make our path the easiest for her to take."

"How true."

When we hang up, I feel cheered. The Ephraims are running a transparent play. Only a small tick upward gets us to a unicorn designation. Jason's right: they're deliberately withholding, trying to corner us. We can outmaneuver them easily.

The Merchandising Team unveils the final Wedding Collection, but only a fraction of my mind engages. Mentally, I redraft the deal.

Fifteen minutes into the meeting, Jason texts *911*.

Afterburner has bowed out.

I feel the round begin to fishtail, to veer toward the guardrail. For all their talk of boldness, investors have a herd mentality. They're easily spooked.

The gilt packaging fanned across the conference table suddenly looks cheap, like party favors on a clearance rack. The team watches me anxiously. I make a gesture that I hope reads as apologetic and leave, phone to my ear.

"I'm on my way," Jason says. "We need to close soon, or it'll fall apart."

Four firms left. The Ephraims will calculate that I'm desperate, that I'll be grateful for any deal to go through. They'll tighten their terms, take every advantage.

I feel like my blood has been replaced with Boost. I can hear the metallic growl of a revved engine, ready to accelerate straight at an opposing pair of headlights. I won't swerve first.

Every hour, Jason sheds a layer of clothing. Scarf, sweater, then his sleeves are cuffed, and finally, as the sun sets and Rusher Tower goes quiet, his shoes. His red socks prowl the length of the window. We've alternated pacing and perching in front of our computers. My assistant has come and gone with sustenance; the liquids are drained, solids congealing on plates.

The illusion of friendliness from Jason's soiree is gone. Oh, no one is anything but polite. *Our firm is thrilled to fuel Radical's flight—on condition of x and y and z.*

With each exchange, we inch closer. One board seat, we're agreed, one observer. The valuation is down to 800. Afterburner dropping out was like topping a tree, shearing off the maximum ceiling. We can't lose anyone else.

Numbers are scribbled on the whiteboard. What we need. What we can give up. We compromise on everything, but the sticking point is my voting control. I want fifty-five percent. They're not budging from forty-five.

The headlights are closing in. Tires scream on asphalt.

Radical needs this. I have no choice but to accept. If I accept, I could lose it all.

A call comes in. Jason's voice is jocular. "Ken! Hi!"

He swivels on his heel. "No! I don't— That's a mis— Listen, let me take you to dinner. Are you hungry?" He twists his wrist to check his watch.

Hanging up, he unrolls his sleeves, buttons his cuffs, hurries into his jacket. "Ken is getting nervous. I'm going down to talk to him."

"I'll come."

"No." He grabs my hands. "He needs someone neutral now. He wants to lower his guard and worry out loud, and he can't do that in front of you. All you can offer is a sales pitch, and he's already heard it: truly, he has. Now it's time for me to play my part."

He gives me a bracing squeeze. "The deal is close. It's just a matter of settling nerves. Go home. Have a drink with Gavin. I'll call you the second I know anything."

I don't tell him Gavin's halfway across the planet.

I loiter in the office. On the whiteboard, our initial, optimistic numbers, erased throughout the day, are still faintly visible. I douse the board in cleaner, scrub until it's blank.

I text Jason, but all he says is *on the front lines.*

I go home and stare at my portrait, wonder how to turn straw into gold.

He calls after midnight. "I talked him down. We did it."

He sounds ecstatic, relieved, triumphant.

"Will he agree to fifty-five?"

"He did come up." His tone is too positive; he's about to disappoint me.

"He's agreed to forty-nine percent. A generous lift."

"Give up control?" When his call came in, my pulse surged, but now it seems to fall away. "I should have come with you. I can go to them tomorrow, all of them."

"No, my dear." His voice changes. Shredded with tiredness, one string away from snapping. "I've spent the past four hours on Ken's couch with his golden retriever's head on my knee. My pants are ruined. The round was nearly ruined. You're lucky we have any terms at all."

It's the closest he's come to blaming me since the Ephraim pitch. I bring my hand to my cheek. My skin tingles. My fingers smell of chemical cleanser.

"I know how you feel," Jason says, gentler. "Every founder goes through this at some point. Almost every founder," he amends, before I quibble. "But Radical carries on. Bigger than we ever dreamed, in the old days."

I stare at my portrait. Her hands tip, revealing the sight of straw becoming gold but not the secret to the magic. It looks effortless. That's the hardest part. Out the windows, the lights on the Bay Bridge flash and dazzle over empty lanes. Across the water, above the foothills, a line of cerulean blue signals the approaching day.

Straw into gold, I think, straw into gold.

Cecelia

Tuesday

Chestnut Street has so many restaurants, you'd think nobody in the city had an oven, or a plastic knife and a jar of peanut butter, in Cecelia's case. She pushes open her twentieth door of the day: an Italian bistro, cramped quarters cozified with yellow paint.

The bartender scans her résumé with the resigned dread of someone being panhandled. "No restaurant experience? Well, go ahead and leave an application."

She should invent a fake bistro—say it closed, the manager moved overseas . . .

Stepping outside, she smells cigarette smoke. A white Jeep is idling at the curb, windows half-down, releasing the swell of classical music along with the nicotine.

Not a Jeep, *the* Jeep. Since the weekend, it's been a constant presence on Cecelia's block, usually parked straight across from her house. The driver is a nondescript middle-aged man in aviator sunglasses. He doesn't go into any of the houses. He just sits. She knows he's taken her picture—saw him lift his phone when she stepped outside.

Cecelia hurries up the sidewalk. Her reflection drags across the gleaming glass storefront displays: $300 strappy sandals, Technicolor shampoo bottles, trays of canelés so caramelized they're scorched. From the corner of her eye, she sees that her high bun is saggy, her linen dress striped with wrinkles.

At the crosswalk, she glances back. The white Jeep is still parked down the block. From here, she can't see the driver.

She detours to the Safeway for a pack of bagels (onion, not her favorite but on sale). When she comes out, he's not in the parking lot. Maybe he isn't following her. Maybe it's nothing, only her imagination turning her general dread into a tangible threat. It's stress, as her doctors loved to say. Stress! If stress can thread pain through her abdomen as meticulously as an electrician wiring a lamp, then certainly stress might morph her logic, make her believe an ordinary car is stalking her.

He's probably an Uber driver taking a break (though he parks for hours on end). Or a rich guy's driver (in a Jeep?). He's nobody. For all she knows, he goes to Chestnut Street every day, grabs a bottom-heavy takeout bag or a frosty iced coffee. Lots of people, Cecelia is learning in her unemployment, spend their whole day killing time.

There's an empty table outside Starbucks, and she claims it. She unwraps a bagel and chews slowly. Starbucks is probably hiring, but the burnt coffee smell gives her a headache. Ditto the beep-beep of grocery store checkout lanes, the sizzling oil of fast-food kitchens. She pinches the nubs of seasoning off the bagel. She'll apply for unemployment and just exist for a while. She should spin it like Rhoda would—a sabbatical! Though Rhoda obviously isn't going to lose her job. #fireRhoda is dwindling, from thousands of tags to just twenty-three today. Not that Cecelia's counting.

She trudges home and the Jeep is outside.

She lets herself in through Margo's front door and peers out the living room window. The driver's staring at his phone. He's a method actor, pretending to stake out a house. He's unemployed. He's a Unabomber. He's a writer with a block.

In the kitchen, she heats the kettle and fills her hot-water bottle. A cramp throbs at her side. She should write about this: her pain, the exhaustion, the doctors, the futility. She could tell the real story, not Rhoda's Disney version of it.

She recoils from the idea. Pinning her helplessness onto the page.

She's just crawled into bed when Margo raises the garage door. Daylight pours around the cracks in her doorframe, and she tugs her quilt up, protectively, as if the Jeep driver can see her. Margo eases in at her

usual ponderous speed. The stern drone of NPR news reverberates off
the concrete walls until she cuts the engine. Her heels clomp up the stairs,
and dust showers onto Cecelia's scalp. The garage door closes with reassuring heaviness, leaving Cecelia in the dark.

Hardly a minute passes before the steps shake again.

Margo knocks on Cecelia's door with a force that swings it open.

"Uh, excuse me?" Cecelia sits up, her dress twisting around her legs.

Margo, still dressed in her scrubs, brandishes an envelope. Her face is
hot and harassed. "You've gotta go."

Not another envelope, Cecelia thinks, but Margo puts it in her
hands. The letter inside is addressed to Margo from Arlow Property
Holdings, Ltd.

> It has come to our attention that Margo Jackson is in violation of
> Rental Agreement for unauthorized subletting of Unit . . .

"Are you serious?"

As soon as Cecelia speaks the words, she recognizes their idiocy.
Radical idiocy, ha-ha-ha! Of course Margo doesn't own this house. A
single woman with no family fortune—obviously she's renting. And
a renter certainly wouldn't alert her landlord to the drywall shanty in
her garage.

"You're out," Margo says. "I can't lose this place."

"You can't just evict me," says Cecelia, though that's irrelevant.
Margo could change the locks. In five minutes, Margo could pack everything Cecelia owns and drive it to the dump.

"I need some time," Cecelia says, hating her panic. "I can come and
go through the back door."

But the back door passes through Margo's kitchen, and the yard is
fenced.

"One week." Margo relents, like she's granting a huge favor. Before
she leaves, her eyes scour the corners of Cecelia's room, as if she's already mentally collapsing the walls.

The room is dreary, miserable—but it's Cecelia's.

She strides outside. The white Jeep appeared on Saturday, snapped her photograph Sunday. The garage door was open, she thinks, probably her door, too; he must have seen her entire setup. What a coincidence!

The street is empty.

Rhoda is lying face-down on a massage table, black stones marching up her spine.

radical My biggest beauty secret? RELAX. The busier life gets, the more important it is. Stress makes our bodies behave like we're being chased by lions: we take shallow breaths and our hearts race and the tiny, frightened amygdala bosses the entire brain. Slow down. Breathe. All is well.

@Radicalidiocy
It is so stressful to suppress dissent and silence criticism! I like to unwind by getting a hot stone massage and suing my critics.

Cecelia stakes out Rhoda's post, but the comments are positive. *Go girl. Ignore the haters. Gorgeous!* While Cecelia's tweet drops into an abyss.

Dani

Tuesday

Lisbeth is last to arrive in the mornings. She sashays to the pod, wrapped in a camel coat, and luxuriantly peels off layers of outerwear from gloves to earbuds, surveying her team. Brigette, silver hoops threading her lip, nose, ears, and eyebrows; Kim, granny glasses and botanical tattoo sleeve; Jia, dark eyeliner and expensive headphones; Laurel, cap of brown hair and a short story published in *The New Yorker*. They handle social, email collections, newsletters, video scripts, photo shoots, blog features. Their currency is pageviews, click-throughs, conversion. In their world, Dani is broke.

Lisbeth's wide eyes fix on Dani as she unwinds her scarf. She's so pale her skin is almost blue, and she exaggerates the effect by wearing only white, fawn, or severe black.

"I thought we'd run through the data aggregator this morning, if you're free."

Her smile seems sarcastic, and Dani thinks of the message scrawled in green ink: *Nice move, Machiavelli*. Some of the team must think Dani doesn't deserve to be here.

Lisbeth clicks through the data aggregator quickly.

"We track everything. Pageviews, time on site, revenue, obviously. You can see what people add to the cart, what they abandon, time of day they shop. Demographic info: age, location, income. The websites they visit after leaving Radical."

She sounds bored, while Dani's awestruck at how much they know.

"We study those numbers so we can try to move this one."

Lisbeth opens the net sales graph. It's eye-popping.

"Our objective is simple, really: sell more this month than last. The Well is tracking behind." She points to a dip in the line. "You'll look for ways to bring it up. Tweak a newsletter. Adjust the home page. Run some A/B tests."

Dani hardly registers this challenge. It's all she can do to take in the size of the numbers. Living in San Francisco, the word *billion* is bandied about so casually she's never stopped to consider what it means. One thousand millions. A digit with nine zeroes trailing after it. Rumor has it, that's what Radical is worth.

But somehow, Radical always felt small to Dani. Intimate. Radical is Rhoda, sitting on her yellow sofa with her legs drawn up, demonstrating a new product, splashing it onto her hands. It's Rhoda gushing about the rare microherb grown exclusively for Radical at a tiny farm upstate, bending over a sprig of green, twisting it toward the camera to show its heart-shaped leaves.

The massive size of Radical gives Dani vertigo.

"You've hit on our greatest challenge," Mari says. The Well Director meets Dani at the elevators for a tour. "The scale of Radical versus the scarcity of key ingredients."

She's as formal as Dani remembers from their brief meeting, when she told Dani about the Voice role. She doesn't congratulate Dani on getting the job. Her lab coat is crisp, her hair held back with a sharp pin. She lowers her eye to the retina scanner outside the Source Room.

"Radical is large enough that we have clout with suppliers. We can generally get what we need. If costs become prohibitive, we retool the formulas. Like with Skin Polish. I still don't know how that leaked."

Before Dani can register surprise—didn't Rhoda deny that Skin Polish had changed?—Mari ushers her into a cavernous room.

"This is the Source Room, where we store raw ingredients."

The walls are lined with stainless steel doors. Mari opens the first, and Dani steps into a vibrant, chilly Oz. Leaves of every shade of green, pale sage and mossy and emerald, and grasses with wormy white roots, and berries bright as beads. The air smells sweet and fresh, like a meadow. Dani gently touches a leaf as soft as velvet. There's no sense of scarcity here, only abundance.

Mari holds up a stoppered bottle of pale green liquid. "Rhoda's planning an entire line around this. It's distilled from a tea leaf. Very rare. It only grows on the shaded side of a mountain range in Japan. Its vitamin concentration is higher than almost anything on earth. We're calling it the fountain of youth."

Gently, she sets the vial back. "I will miss this. Radical always gets the most interesting ingredients. The privilege of a blank check."

"Miss it?"

"My last day is Friday." Her clipped voice closes off the subject. "So, Lift."

She shows Dani key ingredients, explains their purpose. Hesitating, she brings a paper bag down from a shelf. Inside is a fungus, brown speckled with black, like scorched toast. Its smell hooks in the back of Dani's throat.

"This is chaga. Very powerful, but it can cause nausea. It was a problem for some testers." Her eyes drop briefly to Dani's stomach. "If I remember correctly, you didn't report any issues."

Dani shakes her head. The smell is under her tongue, like a taste.

Mari shrugs. "It doesn't affect everyone. Rhoda's decided to go ahead with the formulation. I've given you access to all of the Trial data. Reviews, journals, et cetera."

More data. Dani's suddenly tired. Her bracelet buzzes.

"Dehydrated?" Mari's eyes flick down. "It's a feat of engineering." Her tone is dry, Lisbethian. Her own wrists are bare. "Rhoda will have to fill you in on the bracelet and app. Last time Lift released, we didn't have either."

"I thought Lift was new. The way Rhoda talks about it—"

"Her white whale. It was one of our earliest releases, but the original formula had unforeseen interactions with some medications. We pulled it almost immediately."

"Oh." Dani thinks uneasily of the pill she swallowed this morning. She's cleared to take Lift again, her pass granted full access to the Well.

"I don't always agree with Rhoda, but I see why she pursued Lift. A natural antidepressant—not that we're coming out and calling it that. It could be a game-changer."

She puts the emphasis on "could," as if it's up in the air.

"Good luck." Mari returns the chaga to its shelf and escorts Dani to the exit, rather abruptly. "It will be fascinating to see the launch. I know Rhoda won't settle for anything short of spectacular."

Dani hears it again: the hint of skepticism.

Upstairs, she grabs a Boost in the cafeteria. Eyes follow her, little flies. Her cardigan drapes her stomach. Naomi is the size of a pear. Her skeleton is ossifying. Her ears are on the front of her face, slowly shifting to the sides of the head. A surreal image, fetus by Picasso.

Twenty-five weeks to go. Dani has months to settle in. To prove them wrong.

Cecelia

Wednesday

The apartment listing says Nob Hill, but it's the Tenderloin. A lonely tree shades the windows. Needles glitter in the roots. The building emanates a chill, like a Victorian orphanage. The agent unbolts the locks and swings the door. She and Cecelia peer into the grim room. The battered plastic blinds let in just enough light to show that the carpet is stained, but not with what. The bathroom door is ominously cracked.

At $1,950 a month, this is the cheapest place on Craigslist. A "garden" level studio, water included. Nightmares, too.

@Radicalidiocy
If I hadn't been fired, I'd move into Radical HQ. I could live like a queen. Sleep in the meditation room, eat free food, become immortal with free access to the Well.

A tumbleweed blows through her Twitter feed. She posts anyway.

She takes the bus home. She blew her dinner budget on the round-trip ticket.

At least the white Jeep is gone. She didn't realize how much she dreaded seeing him again until her relief.

The side door to the garage isn't quite closed. She definitely locked it when she left. She twisted the flimsy knob to check. Probably Margo carelessly opened it.

She's gone, too, thankfully. Cecelia skirts the oil patch on the concrete and shuts herself into her room. She never appreciated what a bargain it is. Margo even shares her Wi-Fi. (Inadvertently: Cecelia found the password on a scrap of paper in the silverware drawer.)

She'll eat a stale bagel and watch a movie.

She shifts clothes off her bedspread, searching for her laptop. Her bed is like an animal's nest, redolent and wrinkled, roughened with crumbs. Under a damp hair towel, she finds her charging cord (slightly frayed; is it a fire risk to sleep with her hot-water bottle?). Her laptop isn't plugged in.

She checks her backpack: nothing.

She unplugs the charger and wraps the wire around her wrist, trying to remember if she brought the laptop with her to trudge between coffee shops and restaurants and bars. She left the backpack on a café table while she ordered ice water at the counter. Opened it carelessly on a crowded bus, digging for Advil. Fuck.

The balls of her feet ache from her shitty dress shoes. Her back aches. An organ behind her ribs aches, sharper when she breathes, like she swallowed a thumbtack. Her throat aches at the thought of losing her laptop. Everything's on it—her writing, her emails, her credit cards.

She searches every inch of her room. Nowhere. She ventures upstairs, but Margo's rooms are scrubbed and tidy. She's probably worried her landlord will pop in for an inspection, like maybe he'll overlook the squatter in the garage if the red silk pillow is perfectly centered on the sofa.

The picture window frames an empty street. Clouds are lowering over the houses.

The Jeep watched Cecelia leave. Then Margo. The side door was unlocked.

Every day he follows her, she loses something else.

Back in her bedroom, the mess seems unfamiliar. It feels infiltrated. Her hairs prickle with an animal sense of something wrong. A smell, barely detectable, of strange soap, stale car, newspaper.

Her phone pings a notification. Radical is trending on Twitter.

"EMBATTLED WELLNESS STARTUP CLOSES FUNDRAISING ROUND."

Radical is worth $800 million.

No mention of Megaphone, in any of the articles Cecelia skims. Only oblique references to accusations and rumors.

"CONTROVERSIAL SHE-EO FALLS SHORT OF UNICORN HOPES."

At least Rhoda didn't reach a billion. Maybe Cecelia had some impact, but she feels no satisfaction. So Rhoda can't brag. Cecelia is unemployed, broke, evicted. Her fingernail hold on the city is slipping.

On Instagram, Rhoda shared a photo of herself onstage at the Retreat. Her hands are open, welcoming applause.

radical Brimming with gratitude. Can't wait to build Radical's future together! xo, Rhoda

@Radicalidiocy
If I'm radiating at the same frequency as the universe, then the universe is fucking raging. #notblessed

Cecelia walks. The neighbors' pastel houses have their blinds shut against the evening, their doors tight as closed mouths. Nobody would bother to notice the Jeep driver break into the garage.

Her anger propels her. She climbs the bluff up from the Marina.

Of course it starts to drizzle.

Lights come on in apartment windows. Normal people are unwinding from work, cooking dinners that smell of garlic and tomato and ginger. They're watching TV and talking to lovers, friends, children. Cecelia's an outcast, slouching under the shell of her backpack. Life turned out to be a game of musical chairs, and everyone knew it except Cecelia. They rushed for the seats, and she's left standing.

Rain falls determinedly now, spiteful. Cecelia's hair is soaked. The sidewalk is so steep she could put her hands on the ground and clamber up. Signs warn parked cars to turn their wheels in. *Prevent runaways.*

A tall, gangly man strides up from behind her. She thinks of the man unfolding from the tiny green car, and her pulse hammers, but he lets himself into one of the metal-gated doorways, a citizen of the indoor world.

The houses grow grander with altitude. Mansions with every window lit and no sign of life inside. Cecelia could move in. They'd never know she was there.

At the pinnacle of the hill, she looks back. Rooftops descend in tiers to the foggy water. Windows and streetlamps and headlights shine in the wet.

Beauty is San Francisco's greatest trick. It can make you forget how shitty it is to live here, how cold and gray, how expensive, how arrogant, how performatively liberal, how fucking hilly. Cecelia should leave, like Leandra's boyfriend said. Where do writers live now? Detroit?

Cecelia doesn't want to live in Detroit.

She walks down Divisadero. The houses give way to skinny Victorians with downstairs storefronts. Their windows advertise boutique yarn, cocktails, tapas, Thai. A double-decker tech bus roars up the street, an indiscreet Trojan horse bearing tech workers from the Valley.

By the time Cecelia crosses the belt of traffic on Geary, she's drenched. At Dani's street, she checks her reflection in a liquor store window. Bunches of plastic grapes cluster around an alarmingly orange cheese wheel. She wrings her hair out.

She buzzes, and Trevor answers. For once, she's glad to hear his voice. The latch clicks open.

The stairwell smells of rosemary and garlic. Dani's door is ajar. Her apartment is humid, the heater blasting. Trevor's dubstep leaks from the closed bedroom door. Dani's fairy lights glow in the living room. A crocheted blanket stretches over the couch. Cecelia longs to curl up under it.

Dani's in the kitchen, stirring a pot on the stove. She's wearing her mom's old gingham apron even though there's an alarming stain down the front (not blood, not gravy, but chocolate sauce from her mom's famous cake).

"Hey," Cecelia says.

Dani startles, her wooden spoon shaking golden broth across the floor.

Cecelia goes for the paper towels, but Dani steps efficiently ahead of her. She has to bow her knees to bend. Her stomach has swelled to a neat round dome.

"Trevor let me in," Cecelia explains. "Why don't you sit down? I'll stir."

Dani's smile is polite. The kind a hostess would offer a guest she hardly knows.

"You sit. Is it raining?" She turns her back on Cecelia, stirring the pot.

Cecelia takes off her sodden backpack. A purple Congratulations banner hangs above the window. Maybe Dani had her baby shower. Tiny cakes, stupid games. Cecelia can't think of anything worse, and she's stung by her exclusion. She reaches up and flicks the letter C with a fingernail. "Congratulations."

"Oh," Dani says, embarrassment cracking her shell. "I started my new job. And Trevor's startup had a big milestone, too." Her chin bobs. She turns back to the pot.

Cecelia sits at the table. Daffodils trumpet from a green vase. Cecelia imagines buying flowers. Owning a vase. Scissors to snip the stems.

There's no way Dani needs to stir so much. "Smells good. Chicken noodle?"

"Lentil. With fresh turmeric," she says, talking fast, like she's trying to keep Cecelia from saying what she's come to say. "It helps with my tiredness."

Cecelia doesn't mean to sigh. Doesn't mean to bring her hands down on the tabletop so that Dani's tall green vase tips alarmingly, the perfect daffodils swooning.

"I'm sorry. I cannot stand any Radical bullshit right now. I just can't."

Dani's shoulders hike as the vase wobbles, showing more concern for her flowers than for Cecelia, who feels like the rain has absorbed into her bones instead of evaporating.

"Don't you mean Radical idiocy?" Dani asks. Her voice is surprisingly hard.

Cecelia strokes a drop of spilled water running down the side of the vase. The flowers are aging, the edges of the petals browning, the smell of rot stirring in the water.

"I was going crazy, working there. Writing about it made it bearable."

"Oh," Dani says. "So glad I could help."

"That's not—" She's taken aback. Dani's blows are mild but direct, landing clean. "Rhoda was so nasty about you. Didn't that bother you?"

"Saying I'm a top performer? That I do the work of two people?"

Cecelia groans. "It's sick that you think like that, in terms of your value to the company. As if your pregnancy would diminish it. Like it's not something to celebrate."

"Celebrate!" Dani laughs. "When you found out, you looked like you were going to be sick. You just used it in your story."

On the stove, the pot gurgles, spitting a splatter that hisses on the gas burner. Dani turns on it vengefully. She snaps the heat off, setting the lid over the pot like she's trapping a rat.

"I always knew you didn't like Radical. I didn't realize you held me in contempt for liking it."

"No," Cecelia argues, but Dani holds up a hand.

"How much more pathetic could you have made me sound?"

"That's not at all what I meant. I was writing about Rhoda. The hypocrisy of everything she does—"

Dani rolls her eyes. "You could have just quit. Nobody forced you to work there. You didn't have to drag me into it. Radical actually matters to me. You have no idea what I went through before I found Rhoda."

"You mean Rhoda's bullshit story? The fever that grew into a billion-dollar company?" Cecelia hates the sound of her own voice. "Being sick is nothing like that. The only thing Radical does is make people feel worse, like they've failed, because they couldn't magically cure themselves."

Dani's stroking the apron tie, winding it around her thumb. "How would you know, Cee? All you do is mock it."

Here it is, the chance to confess: the grinding pain, her exhaustion, her anger at how unfair it is, how absolutely unfair, like a fairy tale curse. To admit she did try, with no effect. To explain that she can't be optimistic, only to be disappointed, over and over.

"Rhoda helps people," Dani says.

"Rhoda," Cecelia snaps, "is suing me. She's having me followed.

Ever since I got fired, a white Jeep has been everywhere. I got evicted. My computer is suddenly gone."

Her elbows bang the table, and the flowers shake their heads. She sounds insane. Maybe she is. The laptop might only be lost. The white Jeep comes and goes. The idea that Rhoda's behind it is so unlikely that Cecelia has trouble believing it herself.

Dani closes her eyes. Her face, bare of makeup, looks faded with exhaustion. She's wearing her sheepskin slippers. When Cecelia used to come over after work, Dani would put them on the second she crossed the threshold. *Mr. Rogers*, Cecelia teased.

She wishes, suddenly, that she could unbraid the conversation. Start again.

"I know you're having a hard time," Dani says. "You should talk to someone. It's not productive, blaming all your problems on Rhoda. It's not healthy." She says the last word emphatically, confident in her authority on that subject.

At once, Cecelia's energy plummets. She might lie down on the floor if Dani weren't leading her out of the apartment, holding the door, brittle with politeness again.

Cecelia's jeans stick to her legs as she descends the stairs. Outside, the rain has stopped. The sidewalks gleam, reflecting the streetlights and neon signs. Divisadero has come alive. Noisy groups spill from bars. Cecelia crosses at the intersection. Puddles wrinkle under her feet. Behind her, there's a screech of brakes. A car with a hot pink mustache on its fender stops in the crosswalk. A man jogs across its headlights. His hands are thrust in the pockets of his khaki jacket. His elbow grazes Cecelia. His face is featureless as a pencil sketch. It's the man from the white Jeep.

Cecelia stumbles off the curb, plunging her boot into a puddle. A laughing girl in a minidress drags her back onto the sidewalk.

The man idles outside the liquor store, studying the garish grapes on display.

Cecelia ducks into a pizzeria. The high tables are crowded with jovial drunks. She orders a slice and drops her wallet. Coins spill to the floor.

A dopey-eyed guy scoops them up and drops them into the tip jar.

Cecelia's mouth opens in protest, but Khaki Jacket appears beside her.

He bends to level his face with the display of pizzas. The slices glitter with oil.

"Here you go." The cashier holds out a plate, but Cecelia's backing away, bumping into tables. Outside, a bus comes to a hissing stop.

She runs for it. The doors jerk closed behind her. She grabs the handrail as it surges away. The man is standing at a table, shaking cheese over his plate with a delicate flick of his wrist.

Rhoda

Thursday

The harbor is full, hundreds of white boats stabled like horses. Actually, with their tall masts, what they really resemble are unicorns. A sore subject.

Jason's boat towers over its neighbors. ("Her" neighbors, he'd chide.) He's standing on the dock, gripping a bottle of champagne by the neck.

"Ahoy!" He waves. "Don't mind the fog—we're not lifting the anchor. Settle in. I'll just pop into the galley to make our drinks."

The boat bumps against the slip. I recline on a deck chair and hug my knees. Over the slate ocean, the encroaching fog is substantial and icy as a glacier.

"I thought we were going to your house," I call.

Jason emerges from the galley carrying two coupe glasses. "It was sunny half an hour ago." He passes me a drink. "We did it, my dear. As you say, 'Radical, Radical, out on top!'" He salutes me.

I sip. A French 75, my favorite. A curl of lemon floats at the rim.

I don't feel like cheering. The headlines were nasty. "Scandal-Shaken She-EO Falls Short." They browsed Radicalidiocy for vinegary quotes.

According to Orson, the writer is packing her bags, getting ready to leave town.

"We can move for a default judgment and settle things up quickly and quietly. And that," he said, satisfied, proud, "will be that."

That is hardly that. I've lost control of Radical, and we've fallen short. A few weeks ago, either of those disasters would have seemed impossible.

If I'm radiating at the same frequency as the universe, then the universe is fucking raging.

I take a deep breath of the cold, bracing air.

I haven't lost control. I'm still equal to the rest of the board. I would have to lose the confidence of every single member to be overruled—impossible. Jason remains the second largest shareholder, after going in again this round.

He seems sanguine in spite of the shortfall. In spite of the trousers ruined with dog drool, the nearly ruined round. He crosses an ankle over a knee. No red socks today. Just Top-Siders, soft with wear.

He cocks his head. "You're thinking: we fell short. What's to celebrate?" He lifts his glass, speaks before he sips. "Hence the private party. Not even Gavin invited."

"He's out of the country."

"Ha. So that's the only fact you can dispute." He twists his empty glass by the stem. "The round was bloody, but it's done. In five years—hell, in one really good year—no one will remember the numbers."

"You're going to say we live to fight on." I try to sound light, but I'm tired.

"Life is one battle after another, my dear. The time in the arena is your reward."

"So I'm the gladiator. And you're . . . the emperor?"

He rears his head in amusement. He holds out his fist, pauses for drama, and slowly twists it up.

I'm glad to make him laugh. It almost feels like the old days, just the two of us in slightly uncomfortable surroundings.

He takes our empty glasses into the kitchen—*galley*—for refills. His dad had a boat. A small one, nothing like this. A shabby sailboat, taken out in all weather to toughen Jason up. An accountant, he considered life a balance sheet and fatherhood as a debt paid with obedience, so Jason followed him into finance rather than becoming an entrepreneur. He's a crucial character in Jason's foundational myth. Someone to blame.

My dad came off well by comparison. I told Jason how he really was. Not the stuff that makes headlines, but the small, daily things. His enthusiasm, his suit jackets, and grubby sneakers. The way he introduced me to his friends, customers, athletes as "the future president."

Jason comes back out carrying our glasses and a bottle of champagne under his arm. I stand to grab it. Heavy. He must have opened a second bottle.

"Thank you." He sits, tugging the hem of his trousers. "Sip slowly. I didn't stint."

The champagne is bone-dry, the bubbles almost hard. I think of the brothers eagerly guessing tasting notes at the soiree. *You've done it*, Jason whispered. Our glee.

"I've made the mistake of overemphasizing value in the past." He sits over his knees, leaning into the advice. "Direction is more important than speed. I have no regrets about coming lower when it means we got the right partners on board."

It's rare for him to reference Pique. Is that what went wrong? They rushed ahead, believing their own hype? Startups are like Rube Goldberg machines; things can fall apart all at once.

"You're right," I say. "If nothing else, it's better that we weeded out the quashers. The universe made sure the right people came through."

"Actually," Jason says, dry as the wine. "I consider it a master class in persuasion. The universe took a backseat role." He flicks his lemon peel over the deck rail.

I sip my drink, swallowing my irritation. Let him take the credit; it doesn't matter. The boat creaks against the dock. The fog creeps closer, stretching tentacles of cold mist.

Jason dances his feet in place.

"To think we could be poolside right now!"

"What do you mean?"

"Jennifer." He packs each syllable with disdain. "She got the house. Probably hanging her faceless little watercolors as we speak. I heard she's auctioning off her half of the art. Note that I use the term 'her' extremely loosely, since she neither picked it out nor paid for it."

I've never heard him talk like this. He tugs the bottle up from the floor. His face is twisted nastily, but somehow relishing the wound. I'm trying to guess what went wrong—an affair, or something equally humiliating and abrupt. The neck of the bottle clanks down on the rim of my glass.

"I rescued this bottle from my cellar. God knows Jennifer wouldn't appreciate it. When I met her, she was drinking skinny margaritas."

This is so petty I have to laugh. "I'm sorry. I really am. I'm surprised your lawyer couldn't keep the house. Didn't you build it before you even met Jennifer?"

"My lawyer couldn't hold on to my sock drawer. But that's irrelevant. I gave it to her."

I spill a big splash of champagne in my surprise. It hisses on the polished deck.

Jason smiles. "Believe me, I'm tempted to go over in the dead of night and burn it down. But! Had to be done. I needed the money to go in again."

I gasp. It's common for existing investors to put more money in during a new round. Show they still have skin in the game. But Jason contributed a sizeable amount of cash.

"I had no idea." I balance my glass in one hand and wipe my wet palm on my skirt. I'm touched. He's putting all his chips on Radical. Next time, we'll get there. *Once more unto the breach!*

He lies back and crosses his ankles, pressing the wrinkles into his trousers.

Suddenly, I realize. "Are you living out here?"

"It's all mine. What a luxury. Some nights there are even stars."

I can just see him padding around the cabin, with its upscale fixtures and scaled-down proportions, nothing quite big enough.

The fog is in the harbor now, swallowing the red-and-white buoys. I was on the ship's maiden voyage. Jason could hardly steer us out of the harbor. Jennifer and I were weeping with laughter. Gavin was there, too; it was his first time meeting Jason. He stood beside Jason as he veered and overcorrected, encouraging him. Jason probably resented that more than our laughter. Or maybe not. His tempers are strong, but he swallows them. After tonight, after the champagne wears off, he won't talk about Jennifer again, or the house. They'll be like Pique.

"Still planning to go through with it?" he asks. "Gavin, marriage?"

"Of course."

He tuts. "The young insist on making mistakes for themselves, and thus, human progress is stalled, chasing its own tail."

"You're in the aftermath. Your perspective is skewed."

"He'll slow you down. His laziness will be a rebuke to your work."

"He's going to open a winery. He's looking at vineyards."

Jason cackles. "Ah! My dear, you've just proven my point. He'll lure you away. You'll make accommodations. Slowly but surely, your edge will erode."

I start to protest, but remember Gavin calling the city a hamster wheel.

"Then again," Jason says, thoughtfully. "Maybe you wouldn't mind taking a step back. Maybe you're even tempted?"

Now it's my turn to laugh. "Not even a little."

"Why not? Enjoy the rewards of your hard work. The exhaustion will only get deeper. The hits will come harder. It never stops feeling personal."

Personal, he always warns. *Don't make it personal*. But that's what's so exhilarating. To go all in. To sprint into the arena, to fling yourself into the fight.

"I can't imagine anything else." It's simple but true.

The dock light beside Jason's boat turns on, the glow smeary and diffuse in the fog.

"I should go before I can't find my way."

"Always a wise policy." He rises with me, taking my elbow. He's tippy, swaying with the boat. I steady him. He points out the lights of the marina's restaurant.

"Thank you." I kiss his cheek. "I'm sorry again, about the house."

He pats my hand. "Radical will be worth it."

Cecelia

Thursday

Cecelia's last night in the city, and she's spending it in the garage, packing a suitcase. She's bringing only what's practical, leaving the rest behind. Yes gray sweater, no too-big cowboy boots. She leaves for Portland tomorrow. Her college roommate has a pull-out sofa. Cecelia can work at the big bookstore, maybe. Get a bicycle and take up knitting.

She walks back and forth across the concrete floor, sharp dust caking her feet. No more cinder-block cell, no more CW, no more Twitter metrics. It's almost a relief. She'll bring her favorite coffee mug, but only after she finishes the lukewarm beer she filched from Margo's fridge.

Margo's old-fashioned mantel clock sings out its full song, twelve chimes. When it stops, Cecelia notices the silence, thick as dust.

Is the white Jeep outside? She dragged the recycling bin in front of the side door, so she'll hear any disturbance. (She imagines Dani closing her eyes in exasperation. She wouldn't believe someone followed Cecelia down Divisadero, even less that Rhoda arranged it. Cecelia can't prove it, but she saw the Slack archives. Rhoda controls everything, down to the smallest detail.)

What is Dani doing now? Sleeping, Cecelia imagines. Her Radical bracelet tallying the correct number of hours.

And Rhoda? Cecelia doesn't have to guess. She posted a picture of herself on a yacht, champagne flute held high.

radical Slowing down to savor this milestone, to marvel at what we've built. This toast is for you.

Her dress is so long it sweeps the deck, but she won't trip and fall overboard. She's untouchable. She's won.

Cecelia kneels on her suitcase and drags the zipper closed. Done.

Lying down, she opens Twitter. Her engagement is meager, but she has a new message, from a user named @JoannePVoose. The subject: *Story of a Devoted Fan.*

Probably a Michelle, writing to scold Cecelia. She yawns, settling deeper into bed.

My mom, Carlene Voose, was a devoted Radical fan.

Carlene Voose. What kind of name is that?

My mom died several years ago. I've always blamed Rhoda.

Cecelia brings the phone closer to her face.

I'll never forgive Rhoda for what she did to my mom. She refused to take any responsibility. She dismissed me. She never even apologized. I'm haunted by the idea that she's hurt other people, too.

Technically, I'm not supposed to discuss what happened with my family, but I signed the agreement when I was in the middle of a hurricane of grief.

I read your story on Megaphone with sympathy. But it was your description of the way Rhoda hounded you that changed my mind. She can't treat people this way.

Holding her breath, Cecelia reads Joanne's story.

When she's finished, she blinks, lifting her eyes. Her room is the same as it was five minutes ago: heaps of rejected clothing and stuff lying in shadows against the wall. Except it suddenly seems faded, like it's already in her past.

This is it. The proof she's waited for. Rhoda's snake oil isn't harmless. Cecelia isn't crazy, she's not just negative. *She was right.*

Cecelia could tweet right now. She imagines a butler bringing Rhoda her phone on a tray, the tweet waiting on the screen like a scorpion.

Except that Joanne added a postscript. *I'm sharing my story with you for personal resolution. I would appreciate if you exercised discretion in how you use it.*

This knotted request reminds Cecelia of Dani: tentative, too considerate to make her wishes clear. (Though Dani wasn't tentative when she asked Cecelia not to tell anyone.)

She checks Joanne Voose's profile, but she only shares animal videos. She doesn't follow Radical. Rhoda doesn't follow her. Has probably forgotten that she exists.

A scraping noise cuts through Cecelia's thoughts, drawing the hairs on her arm straight. It sounds like someone's running a key along the garage door. She draws her knees up. When it stops, the silence buzzes. Her eyes are fixed on her door.

It's 2 a.m. Every noise is amplified and distorted. She forces her jaw to relax.

Rhoda's probably sleeping now. Probably drove home sloshed from the yacht (in fact, she has a chauffeur, but Cecelia imagines her convertible careening, running people to the curb). She's probably half forgotten Cecelia by now. The bug has been crushed.

Cecelia's chest is tight. She exhales. There's no rush. She can exercise discretion.

Cecelia leaves the house at noon, carrying her tote bag and a single suitcase. She leaves her key in the lock. Across the street, the white Jeep sees it all. She ignores him, walking with her chin up.

She feels light and clear. She's been swaddled, insulating herself, holding herself at a distance. Because of her pain, she thought.

The bus rears uphill, tracking her walk to Dani's, passing the apartments she envied, the towering mansions, the clutter of colorful Victorians. The bus hurtles across Geary, and Cecelia pulls the cord.

Trevor opens the door holding a can of beer. Not his first, by the look of him. He rubs his eyes with the back of his hand as she asks if he can keep her suitcase.

"Just for a day. I'll be back tomorrow."

Playing the gentleman, he takes her bag and slings it into the hall closet. He almost falls in after it.

"Are you all right?" Her concern is reluctant.

Trevor collapses on the couch, Dani's crocheted blanket under his dirty jeans. "I just lost a potential investor. I opened the email expecting a term sheet, and instead—"

He spreads his arms, bewildered.

"Didn't you have a good job before?" Cecelia asks. "Maybe you should go back."

"Ah." He taps his finger to his chin, like she's said something wise. "But how to give up the struggle? That's what it means, to be an entrepreneur. Or a writer." He nods at her. "We struggle, and then success is sweet."

Cecelia is surprised he remembers she's a writer. Then embarrassed—of course he knows about Megaphone. Not that he seems to remember now.

"Tell Dani I'll see her tomorrow."

He gives her a double thumbs-up.

Cecelia is light now, only her tote on her shoulder. She walks fast, forgetting to check the cars parked on the street. She's thought of her next tweet: *One woman's snake oil is another woman's poison.*

Dani

Friday

Rhoda hoists a saber and slashes the cork from a bottle. Champagne gushes, and one of the new investors, a handsome bearded man, laughingly thrusts his glass under the flow.

The lobby windows are fogged with the excited exhalations of two hundred drunk people. Waiters whisk trays of champagne around the room.

All day, there's been a carnival atmosphere. Everyone rushing from pod to pod. Dani spent the afternoon blowing up balloons with the Party Planning Committee, a helium shortage leaving them grounded. The balloons drift around the lobby like a tide. Now and then, one pops, and shrieks puncture the hilarity.

On the wall, someone from the art department drew a unicorn in pencil, omitting a single leg. When Rhoda entered the room with her phalanx of investors and Core Team, she pretended to stroke its back.

She raises the saber and chops another bottle.

"Disarm her!" the bearded investor shouts. The hawklike adviser with the shiny head applauds with his fingertips.

Lisbeth and the rest of the Core Team are dancing, throwing their hands in the air and shimmying their hips. What are they worth now? What is Dani worth? Not real money, but something better: a piece of this.

Another chant rises: "Speech, speech!"

"Thank you, thank you, I love you all, you beautiful humans." Rhoda's voice is husky, raspy with overuse. "Let's raise our glasses."

There's a sparkle of breaking glass.

"Hold on to them now!" Rhoda is jovial. "To all of you! To Radical! To our favorite siblings, the Ephraim brothers!"

Everyone cheers.

A photographer climbs onto a table, and Radigals press together.

"Say billion," she says, and some joker shouts, "Eight hundred million!"

At nine, a surprise arrives. A band Dani loved in high school is performing. The guitarist plays his famous riff, and everyone screams. The dance floor thrashes. Dani takes a break from the fray to order an ice water at the bar.

A drunk guy somehow gets hold of the saber and takes a wild swing at a bottle. The cork fires upward, cracking one of the copper pendants with a crash that sounds catastrophic.

There's a stunned beat, then the lead singer catcalls into the mic, and the drunk guy is reabsorbed into his pushing, shoulder-clapping group.

"Dani!" Holly appears beside her and seizes her wrist. "I just got a text from the ice sculptor people. They need someone to help. Someone sober." She giggles.

In the elevator bank, a group of Engineers and Dev guys is herding balloons into a pile. They double over in laughter as balloons bounce out of their arms.

The ice sculpture is pushed against the wall. It's the Radical symbol, the flickering flame, as tall as a mailbox, balanced on a rolling cart that seems too small for the task. Dani pushes it away from the drunken antics, into the quiet hallway outside Rhoda's office.

Surprisingly, the light is on. Dani hesitates on the threshold. Presumptuous as it is, she wants to congratulate Rhoda herself.

She knocks, but Rhoda must not hear. She's standing at the window. The glass is flecked with rain. Rusher Tower is pitch-dark against the skyline.

"Rhoda?"

She jumps, brings her hands to her chest. She's holding something white in her fingers, maybe a tissue.

"Oh, Dani, it's you." She drops her fists to her sides and inclines her chin to the window. "My penthouse is getting wet."

Her skin is blotchy, like she's eaten nightshades. Only an hour ago, she was dancing, her skirt flaring out, but now she's standing as stiff as the pillars in the lobby.

"It's a joke, Dani. Tonight, everything is funny."

Dani's lips twitch obediently. She asks about the ice sculpture, awkward, trying to justify her interruption.

"Roll it anywhere and watch the thing melt."

Rhoda gives one of her impatient smiles, waving her empty hand to shoo Dani. Her other is still clenched at her hip.

Back in the hall, the drunken group is busily stuffing their gathered balloons into an empty elevator. Plastic squeaks as they cram them in. A curled ribbon sticks out of the doors like a tongue. Dani pushes the cart past. The mammoth ice carving is coated in a sheen of moisture, like sweat.

Holly rushes her. "My hero! Let's get you a drink! Fizzy water!"

She drags Dani away, abandoning the sculpture in the middle of the lobby. The crowd flows around it, hardly seeming to see it.

The band has gone. Someone's setting up the karaoke machine, plugging in a whining microphone. High heels are scattered across the carpet. Dani sips her Reboot, swaying to Whitney Houston, Usher, and then, when the entire room starts to sing along to "Sweet Caroline," she joins, swept away in the chorus, singing like she loves the song she hardly knows, because in the moment, they all do. *Ba-ba-bah!*

"The grown-ups are gone!" someone shouts. Rhoda's left. The board and investors, too.

It's late, and Dani's tired, but she wants to stay to the very end. The night is a beginning, bright and shining. She'll remember it.

Rhoda

Friday

"Closer, closer." The Art Director adjusts Jason's elbow, nudges Pilar's shoulder.

The investors, board, and I stretch out our arms, showing off Radical bracelets. I'm flanked by the Ephraim brothers, who smell of Santal 33 and flash teen model smiles to the camera.

The photo will go out with a press release vaunting the bracelet's technology. Time to bring Radical PR back to business.

In the lobby, the energy is giddy, on the edge of wild. The tension of the last weeks finally bursting, exploding in a drunken swirl across the ersatz dance floor. Drinks are flowing. Tonight, we crush the past under our feet—our faltered hopes and tarnished reputation—and leave it behind. The party is an arrow into the future.

Jason holds my arm. He's beaming, munificent, like a prince among peasants.

The brothers present a champagne saber, betting me that I can't use it. I surprise them with the strength of my swing.

After that, corks pop incessantly. Music surges. Cara booked the band, and I don't recognize it. People are singing along, close to tears. I missed the teenage music scene. I went to high school in Nevada. As opposite from Seattle as possible. From wet to parched, granola to glitz. I knew no one and liked it that way. I worked, ran, worked. There was a motor inside of me, and I couldn't stop moving.

The lead singer screams, and Radigals scream louder. I feel younger, even though I don't know the words. We dance. Minutes scatter and spill like sequins.

Deep into the evening, the Ephraim brothers flank me.

The ditzy brother, Chad, bumps his cheek against mine. "This is the most beautiful company party we've ever attended!"

"We looked for your fiancé," Brett says. "We wanted to congratulate him."

"I hope you're taking a long honeymoon," Chad says. "You deserve it."

Across the floor, a camera flashes. My smile widens. I can't be caught looking any less than delighted.

"We'll be lucky if we get away at all. Radical's so busy."

Chad grips my shoulder paternally. "Another reason to be glad of the lighter load. We have a list of potential partners. Smart people, really excellent."

Brett takes his elbow. "No shoptalk. This is Rhoda's night. Has it sunk in?"

His friendly condescension makes me wish to hoist the saber again. Luckily, in that moment, there's a loud crash. A light fixture breaking. Everyone gasps, then covers their shock with cheers and catcalls.

When the Ephraims turn back from the distraction, I'm in control.

"Jason mentioned something about creative leadership structures, but we haven't had time to discuss it."

Brett's shoulders ease. "Of course! Nobody's in a hurry."

My teeth bite together hard. I advise them to grab some Reboot before they leave.

The lobby pillars glow red. The faces of the drinkers seem distorted, their eyes dark. What are we celebrating? We didn't even hit a billion.

My board skulks on the perimeter, like vultures. They own more of my company than me, forced the door open and wedged themselves in. Jason isn't with them.

I find him in the men's room, preening in the mirror. His surprise is almost comical, his mouth a perfect O.

"You're replacing me?"

His pupils dodge. He pretends to adjust the buttons on his jacket. "We're celebrating you. Didn't you notice?" He tuts, smiling mildly.

"Is that why you wanted the Ephraims to lead the round? So you could turn them against me?"

His eyes rise with infinite weariness. "If you're referring to the leadership suggestion, that was tactical. We needed to close the round. No need to get emotional."

"I am emotional." I step closer, inches from the razor-straight line of hair across the back of his neck. He stiffens. "I built Radical. I've given it every scrap of myself. I held nothing back. You could never build anything like this."

In the mirror his eyes are locked on mine, as if he's hypnotized. A muscle throbs in his cheek.

"In fact, what can you do, Jason? Write checks? Since checks went digital, you're not even as tangible as a flimsy slip of paper. You're an email signature. You're dispensable." My voice is a long hiss.

He snaps around. "Is that so? When we met, you were an arrogant girl drinking Coca-Cola in a cheap dress. Without me, you'd still be mixing essential oils in your bathroom."

"I needed you then, it's true. The way a runner needs a starting gun. Let's not pretend it hasn't been me running, every step of the way."

"Always the sports metaphors," he says. "I wonder why you don't distance yourself from your dad's petty crime."

"Enough." I hold up both hands. His gesture, and so useful. Completely silencing. My voice sounds pressurized. My ears have popped. "We'll find a dignified way to transition. It doesn't have to be like Pique."

Even in the gentle pink lighting, he looks scarlet. I don't wait for his retort.

The lobby is hot and pulsing with light. The music buzzes inside my bones. My chest is in overdrive. I can't possibly go back in there. I retreat to my office.

Every object invites smashing. The marble bust on my desk, a gift from Jason. The vases of victory flowers, sent from VC offices.

Jason beat me to every meeting. I'd find him chatting cozily. *I'm the realist.*

He gave up his house to grab up more shares. *Radical will be worth it.*

He let me think he was siding with me, when he was laughing at me, mocking my sentiment. *Once more unto the breach!*

My anger is electric. The lights seem to surge with it.

Then my eye catches a scrap of white. Someone left a flower on my laptop. I pick it up, and realize it's a piece of paper, folded into an origami shape. Between the folds and creases, words scrawl in messy pen.

Tick-tick. There's a tapping on the window. It's raining harder. Drops glide down the glass, blurring the view, the skyline dark and huddled under the storm.

Dani

Monday

The sun appears, and the rain-soaked city shines. Dani sheds her jacket and the fresh air feels novel on her skin.

A security guard stands outside Radical HQ, calling out good morning, bantering: "Some party Friday night! I've got celebrities in my building!"

Dani lingers, tilting her face up to the sky. Behind her, a siren whoops twice. A police car surges along the curb and parks across the alley. Its red lights flash silently.

The sidewalk clots as people slow to stare. Dani glances back, but there's nothing to see. A radio crackles through the driver's open window.

By the time Dani takes Lift and heads to the All-Hands, she's forgotten about the police car. She's the first in the lobby. The music hasn't even started yet. The smell of stale booze lingers from the party. The cracked light still hangs askew, almost jaunty, like a tipped hat. Sun pours in through the windows. Dani stands by the glass, letting it fall over her stomach.

"This is sun, Naomi," she whispers.

The baby is seventeen weeks, the size of Dani's palm. Her fingers are exploring the uterine walls, imprinting the whorls of fingerprints. Over the weekend, Dani found a new OB, Dr. Melinda. Her website describes her as a "natural birth evangelist." On Instagram, she talks about the power of breath and feminine energy, posting birth videos that inspire and terrify Dani equally.

"Can you see it from here?" Holly stands beside Dani.

"See what?" Dani follows Holly's gaze down.

In the shadows between Radical HQ and Rusher, a white ambulance, small as a sugar cube, creeps up the alley. The narrow, shadowy gap between the buildings is already crowded with a fleet of police cars. Tiny figures mill around the dumpsters.

"You haven't heard? They found a body outside Rusher." Holly rises on tiptoe.

Dani draws back, as if from something catching. "That's awful. Did a worker fall?"

"I heard it's a woman. People are saying she jumped." Holly leans forward, shuddering. "God, even this gives me vertigo."

The lobby is filling up. Everyone pushes to the windows. Dani gladly gives up her place, taking refuge by a pillar. Her coworkers press their palms to the glass, their clogs wobbling under their ankles.

The lobby is strangely quiet. It takes Dani a moment to realize why. Rusher Tower is silent. The constant hammering and grinding of construction have stopped. The long arm of the crane is still.

Somehow, this is more ominous even than the unhurried ambulance.

Cara enters the lobby at a jog. A single line between her eyebrows undermines her smile. She claps her hands for their attention.

"Forgive the late notice, but today's All-Hands is canceled. Everyone gets an extra ten minutes in their morning!" She leaves immediately, ponytail swinging.

The gossip is like the buzzing of bees, furious and redundant.

"When I came in, a white van was pulling into the alley. I swear it was CSI."

"They made it hard to jump off the Golden Gate. It'd be easy to break into Rusher."

Dani's muscles squeeze in a kind of sympathetic panic.

Returning to her desk, she cuffs headphones over her ears. Here is her blue mug, her roller of lavender oil, the framed Mary Oliver quote about her one life. The accident is horrible, but she, Dani, is fine.

She has her first Voice 1-on-1 with Rhoda this afternoon. She intends to arrive prepared. She opens Radical's Well product pages and begins making notes.

Next to her, Jia keeps her phone open to the local news site, refreshing the story every few minutes, though the headline doesn't change. Slack notifications ping like a carnival arcade. Dani mutes them.

She doesn't usually have time for Meditation Monday, but this morning, she joins the group heading for the lobby. Everyone veers toward the windows. Dani stands apart with her back against a pillar. By now, the ambulance must be gone, and maybe the police, too. Soon, Rusher construction will resume.

"A large group today," the instructor observes. She unfurls her mat. "Breathe out your tension. Release your worries. Anxiety has no benefits."

Dani sinks slowly to the ground. Her back aches from the morning at her desk. A radiating pain that makes her twist, stretch forward, lean back, trying to escape it.

Your center of gravity is changing, the pregnancy app warned; *expect some aches and pains!* Making it sound mild, manageable. Not this electric current.

"Set your worries against the vastness of the Grand Canyon."

Dani closes her eyes. She's never been to the Grand Canyon and has a feeling that the pictures she's seen, the cubist blocks of orange stone, don't convey the scope. She thinks of Tent Rocks instead. Wandering through the curving stone paths. But the image is claustrophobic. Like she'll soon be lost.

When she opens her eyes, Cara is hovering in the back of the room, making checkmark motions with her finger, her lips moving silently. She makes a note on her phone and strides out, too absorbed to notice the startled looks behind her.

"Square breaths," the leader intones, but she's lost them. They've broken form. They scoop up phones.

There's news. Or only a new rumor. The woman had a key card in her pocket.

Whispers: *Is it one of us?*

Everyone in the neighborhood carries a key card. Half the city must. It's morbid, drawing themselves into the drama.

Still, back at her desk, Dani opens the spreadsheet someone's made to take a roll call. Dani's own name has already been verified. Missing names are highlighted in red, and then in blue as they're tracked down. Eliza's at the dentist. Lisa Ling on vacation.

Nobody is missing.

"Something's up," Laurel says. "The Core Team is sealed up in Diana. They look tense."

"They always look tense," Kim says.

The laughter is too loud.

Rumors spread faster now. Dani's filter can't keep them all out.

It was a homeless person. A suicide. A drunken accident. A murder? Someone might have lured a woman into the empty site, disposed of the body. She was dressed up—is this gossip or fact? Sequins, high heels.

It's impossible to tell what's real information and what's conjecture, speculation, or pure invention.

What a relief to collect her laptop and head to Rhoda's office for their meeting. Rhoda won't be gaping at the window. She'll be at her desk, refusing to disrupt her work.

When Dani knocks on her door, it isn't quite latched and pushes open.

"Oops," she says, apologetic. The lights turn on overhead. The room is empty. It smells stale, like a vacuum cleaner, as if Rhoda's been out all day. She's left her laptop on her desk, so probably she's just stepped out.

Dani's back pain will not let up. She sits on the couch, bending forward, worrying that she's crushing Naomi as she reaches, lower, hunting for the stretch that will ease the pain. Her fingers trail on the carpet.

The doorknob rattles, and she straightens so fast she's dizzy.

A bald man walks sideways into the room, talking over his shoulder. "Handling the release of information will be crucial. You can appreciate our perspective—"

He holds the door for a man in a dark suit, who's so tall he instinctively ducks as he crosses the threshold. He scans Rhoda's office with a proprietary attitude, like he's viewing real estate. Seeing Dani, he blinks, obviously startled.

Dani doesn't have time to wonder about that, because two police officers follow him.

In Rhoda's pale, airy office, they're entirely incongruous. They seem to carry their work with them, the discord and violence, in the thick fabric of their uniforms, on their heavy belts.

The bald man finally turns, his mouth still open. At the sight of Dani, he closes it with a click of his teeth.

"How did you get in here?"

She recognizes him now. Rhoda's adviser, she can't think of his name. She's never heard him speak. She's surprised at the acidic authority in his voice.

The man in the dark suit glances between them. His eyes are small and shadowed, his voice laconic. "Not Rhoda West, I take it?"

In contrast to his lazy voice, his body is restless, twitching with excess kinetic energy. His fingers move in soundless snapping motions. He's as tall as the twin investors at the party, but he doesn't seem like their type. He doesn't have that executive gloss that's easy to recognize and hard to describe. That look, as if they rip open every morning from a shrink-wrapped package: just what they ordered.

Rhoda's adviser scoffs. "Of course not."

"I'm meeting her," Dani says. Why does it sound like she's lying?

Eight eyes stare at her. Then one of the police officers turns, as if bored, and strolls to the window, peering down like all the others. An egg-shaped humidifier on Rhoda's desk suddenly activates, releasing a hiss of moisture.

"Meetings are canceled," Rhoda's adviser says, but the tall man holds up a hand.

"Have you heard from Rhoda today?"

Dani shakes her head. Her mouth is dry as linen. The room feels as overheated as the party. She's afraid she might faint as she crosses the floor. She concentrates on walking in a straight line.

The investor shuts the door behind her. The latch clicks, and his voice resumes. She leans against the wall, regaining her balance, listening to the muffled voices.

More police are in the lobby. They're clustered around the emergency door. Cara's bright ponytail is their nucleus. Her voice carries. "We're deactivating the alarm so you can go up."

What if Dani told them there is no alarm? That they can simply push through and climb the echoing staircase, that they'll need to use a shoulder on the roof door. That Rhoda liked to go up there.

Her team is in a frenzied huddle beside the pod.

Laurel gives Dani a breathless update: "Nobody's seen Rhoda all day."

But Rhoda's adviser was just talking about her. *How we release information will be crucial. You understand our perspective.*

Our perspective, which must mean his and Rhoda's. The two are yoked.

Everyone's phone pings with a new email. The office is closing for the day.

Dani

Monday

Everyone goes across the street to Ground Floor, a windowless bar in a luxury tower. The walls are papered in shiny fuchsia paisley, like the inside of a designer handbag. It has a fun-house effect on Dani, dizzying and unreal. She crowds into a booth with the Marketing Team. By the time she has one arm out of her coat, she regrets coming. She pulls the sleeve back on, wraps herself in the comforting down.

"It must have been after the party."

"You mean—all weekend?"

"What was she doing outside? It was raining."

She went up there to think, Dani doesn't say. She toys with her zipper.

Jia inhales. "Well—I mean, everyone knew how badly she wanted to unicorn."

They groan in protest, but she holds her ground. "You never know what's going on in someone's head."

"Hi, team." Lisbeth slides into the booth across from Dani. Her face is even paler than usual. "I see our efforts to contain the rumor haven't worked."

She rakes her hair back. Cowlicks swoop off her forehead; she must have been pushing at it all day.

They lean toward her, wanting more.

She sighs. "Officially, I know nothing. Unofficially, things aren't looking good."

Gasps. Murmurs of protest, even though they've been discussing it.

"It might not be her," Dani says. Her voice isn't soft and reverent, like theirs, but flat and harsh. She sounds like she's the heartless one.

Lisbeth has been slouched back, fatigued, but now she puts her elbows on the table. "Here's the thing. On Saturday, the chairman of the board had a party on his yacht. He invited the new investors, the Core. Just a casual get-to-know-you outing."

She lowers her voice. "Rhoda didn't show. At first we assumed she was making an entrance. Fashionably late. We waited. We tried to reach her. But she never showed up."

"What did you do?"

Lisbeth lifts a shoulder in a helpless gesture. "We sailed anyway. Everyone assumed she was hungover. It was actually embarrassing. But now—" Her face is tragic.

They all look into their drinks. They're having mimosas, which seems inappropriate to Dani, almost festive. Though next round, Lisbeth buys her a freshly squeezed orange juice, sweet and pulpy and reviving.

Jia chews her thumbnail. "What happens now? If it's her," she adds, glancing at Dani. "What happens to Radical? Not to make it about us, but . . ."

Lisbeth says, "Radical will keep going."

Dani tightens her coat around herself. Impossible, she wants to say. Someone would know for sure if Rhoda were gone. She's a force, like the sun, or the fog.

"It's going to be a huge story. Whenever her name comes out," Laurel says. "What are they waiting on? Telling Gavin?"

"He's surfing in the Maldives," Lisbeth informs them. "Bachelor party."

Everyone is quiet a moment.

"How high is that, anyway?"

"Thirty-five stories."

"I heard when people jump off the Bridge, their body basically explodes. And that's landing on water."

Dani can't swallow. The pulp is like hair in her mouth. She holds her glass to her lips and spits.

That's why the news has been so slow, she realizes. Because they can't be sure, from whatever they found.

"God, she was so beautiful," someone says, but Dani's already leaving.

Dani and Trevor sit on opposite ends of the couch, feet tangled in the middle, scrolling their phones.

Radical is still containing the rumor, as Lisbeth put it. Their statement reveals nothing: *Radical leadership is cooperating with the SFPD. We are unable to comment on the active investigation and ask our customers, followers, and friends for patience. Be assured that the spirit of Radical is strong.*

But on Reddit, there's a new rumor. Rhoda's key card was in the dead woman's coat pocket.

On Instagram, Rhoda's last post—celebrating the investment round—is filling with new comments. *I can't believe it. Way too young.*

Grief is horribly familiar. The physical ache of it. Dani's body like a sponge, soaked in misery. After her mom died, she felt like she'd been run over by a truck. Her body collapsed. She had no energy, no interest.

She got a job at an airport coffee shop. Her brain was dulled by the fluorescent lights and droning PA system, the roar of hand dryers, the hiss of foamed milk. Refreshing the tureens of coffee every hour, diving for the lid of the creamer pitcher in the trash, why did someone always throw it away? Every task drained her strength.

At night, she lurked in chat rooms with strangers who shared her vague symptoms: fatigue, headaches, pain that migrated around her body. People offered up their diagnoses, often self-pronounced, their cobbled-together diets and meds. Dani's doctor prescribed antidepressants, anti-anxiety meds, birth control. Nothing helped.

As time passed, Dani became invisible. Not a single person whose hands brushed hers as she gave them coffee, coins, pastry looked at her. In the bathroom mirror, her face was a ghost's, hovering as other faces came and went busily. Her body was a weight she hauled around. Her hair hung like ivy in her eyes.

Then she found Radical. Rhoda was a lighthouse, throwing a beam into the fog, guiding Dani out of it, back to shore. What will Dani do without her?

"Listen to this," Trevor says. "Here's Rhoda talking about a deprivation tank: 'Floating in the water, my body feels weightless. After a while, it seems to stop existing. My mind quiets. I feel powered down. I rest, radically.'"

He shakes his phone for emphasis. "Doesn't that sound morbid to you?"

Something in Trevor is unhinged by Rhoda's death. A young, purposeful founder cannot die. They have too much determination. Their lives are perfectly controlled. A pointless accident on the heels of an achievement, at the height of strength—he can't handle it. Can't stand that random chance has such power, that mistakes and bad luck could overpower will.

Dani hates his theory, but she knows how he feels. Rhoda's death seems wrong to her, too. Impossible. Like a mistake.

"The suicide rate among perfectionists is wildly high," he says.

"She liked to go up there to think. It was raining. It would be easy to slip."

She doesn't say that she knows from experience. The smooth, shiny white roof, the skinny railing.

She doesn't tell him about finding Rhoda alone in her office during the party, subdued and strange. She can't remember if she thought so at the time, or if hindsight colors her memory, darkens the shadows and pelts the window with harder rain.

"Maybe they were bringing in new leadership," Trevor says. "That's common."

Dani closes her phone. "I'm going to bed."

She lies rigid on her back, aware that she should roll to her side but too tired to move. The pregnancy app warns against lying flat. The weight of the uterus presses on a crucial artery, cutting off the blood supply, which sounds dire, though the app waters down its own warning. *If you do wake up on your back, no worries!*

Maybe there should be worries. Safety requires constant vigilance.

Trevor comes to bed, whispers into the dark that he's so sorry.

He sleeps. Dani eases his arm from under her neck. Pigeons shuffle on the windowsill. She thinks of her interview with Rhoda. Her obvious pleasure at Dani's language; words traded between them with their precise connotation understood. Her intensity, the spark of her interest. Rhoda was more alive than anyone else.

Her thoughts are running a counterargument to Trevor. He should know; he met Rhoda. Didn't he feel her energy, leaping and flashing like a flame? She listened to his pitch with generous attention. *I envy him*, she told Dani, even though a moment later, she lowered her voice and confided, *When this is over, I'm going to sleep for a week.*

Dani

Monday

San Francisco is a city that sleeps, and deeply. Dani drives on deserted streets past darkened apartment buildings and shuttered stores.

At every stop sign, she considers turning back. It's a wild guess. A stab in the dark. Crazy, is what it is. Hope cut with delusion into something unstable.

The gas pedal of Trevor's ancient Range Rover shakes under her feet, sensing her lack of commitment. She presses harder, speeding across the Golden Gate, icy wind whistling in the cracked windows.

When this is over, I'm going to sleep for a week.

When Dani recalled Rhoda's words, she sat up in bed. She felt a rush of clarity, as though she'd just remembered where she left something important.

Rhoda goes to her beach house to disconnect. When she's there, she drops offline. Then, suddenly, she'll return, post a photo of the sunset over the ocean, or the foggy shore. She'll write about feeling radically rested.

It's possible, isn't it? The investment round closed, and instead of going out on a yacht to schmooze, Rhoda did the opposite: took time to recharge.

Gavin is across the globe, Rhoda's advisers and managers all at Radical. It's possible nobody thought to check the beach house.

Dani dressed silently and took Trevor's keys without waking him. The impulse was too fragile to confront with reason. She's wide awake, no chance of sleep anyway. If she's wrong, she'll come back. No one will know.

*

After midnight, she leaves the freeway for a narrow country road that dips and twists around unseen obstacles. Her headlights glint on wire fences, catch the glittering eyes of a raccoon as it scurries across the lanes. She drives so long she's afraid she's lost. Then she passes an old-fashioned gas station, defunct pumps under a winged horse, an incongruous painting of a goat over the door. It's the cheese shop Rhoda's shared on Instagram. Next comes the VW-bus-turned-coffee-cart, then the general store with a hand-painted sign, Eggs Fresher Than Your OS. This is it.

Rhoda's address isn't public, of course, but Dani spent an idle Sunday on Google Maps, exploring small towns up the coast until she found these places Rhoda's photographed. From there, it was easy to search real estate listings, discover the oceanfront property sold last year, a blurrily photographed stone house perched on a cliff.

If Rhoda isn't here, then Dani's visit will be a pilgrimage. A chance to see the place Rhoda loved so much.

At the peeling farmhouse (now a Michelin-starred restaurant), she turns onto a narrow road into the woods. Tree branches graze her windows. The dark is molasses thick. A panicked moth rushes into her lights, as though fleeing danger rather than rushing to meet it.

Rhoda's driveway is a narrow gap in the trees. An iron gate, formidable as something from a fairy tale, stands open. Dani drives through. Her turn indicator ticks like a clock as she eases along the gravel. The drive curves sharp as an elbow, and then the house is ahead: a stone mansion, with every window lit. Rhoda's cream convertible is parked at a careless angle, gleaming in the moonlight.

Dani grips the steering wheel. Her breath is loud in her ears, rushing.

She was right. Rhoda is here.

She stumbles out of the car. Pine and salt perfume the air. Laughing, she realizes that the rushing noise was the ocean. The house is perched on the rim of a continent, half a world of water surging up the beach. The sky is crowded with stars, arching across the curvature of the sky, like a vast overturned bowl. Dani hasn't seen so many stars in years.

Rhoda is alive.

*

Rhoda's doorbell chimes. It's one thirty in the morning, but she must be awake, with all the lights on. In interviews, she says she stays up past midnight, her creativity flowing late.

Dani's thoughts are jittery as birds, now flowing in a swooping mass of urgency, now scattering into a hundred anxieties. Who cares if she wakes Rhoda? She has to tell her.

The door opens, and Rhoda peers through the screen. She wears a long white nightgown, her hair falling down her shoulders.

"Dani?" Her confusion is evident. Her eyes sweep the driveway, take in the Range Rover parked behind the convertible. "What are you doing here?"

She steps out onto the porch. Her toes curl against the cold. The porch light glows over her. Its artificial flame casts jumping shadows over her face, so she looks impatient, then angry, then afraid.

"Dani? Are you sleepwalking?"

Dani blinks. She's staring. The reality of Rhoda is overwhelming. She has no idea.

"You're here," Dani says, faltering. She doesn't know where to begin.

"Me?" Rhoda's eyebrows lift.

Dani laughs. Giggles, until her stomach crimps and her cheeks sting.

"Breathe," Rhoda commands. "Tell me what's going on."

Dani wipes her eyes. "You're alive."

Rhoda pours a kettle over a Chemex, and a cloud of steam rises with the potent, oily smell of dark coffee. Her hands don't tremble as she passes Dani a mug.

Dani, on the other hand, is shaking so hard she has to press her forearms into the counter. The shock of the day has broken over her like a wave.

When Rhoda first heard what happened, she stood entirely still, staring without seeing, tendons taut in her neck. Dani thought she might scream, but then she blinked, seemed to wake.

"For a second, I had this intense feeling that I had to be somewhere.

Like I could run and fix it." She exhaled, a controlled sound, and Dani was embarrassed at her own collapsed giggles.

"I'd better make coffee," she said. "I want to hear everything. Leave nothing out."

But she seems to suspect Dani is omitting something. She insists Dani explain, again and again. Behind her, the wall of windows is stamped navy. A single pendant lamp casts a spotlight as Rhoda paces the length of floor between sink and island.

"They thought I was dead?" She stretches the *I*, as if it's ludicrous, absurd.

Though Dani felt the same way. As though Rhoda's death wasn't merely tragic but impossible. And she was right.

Rhoda's nightgown drags like a cape. "How could anyone make that mistake?"

Dani tries to explain the escalating rumors, to convey the confusion, but with Rhoda in front of her, it all feels flimsy. Recalling her own misery—sitting on Rhoda's couch in the stale office, seeing police fan out between the lobby pillars—is like describing a bad dream: artificial, unless you experienced it.

Then she remembers the rumor that sunk her into real despair.

"They found your key card. With the body."

Suddenly it occurs to her, as it should have from the instant Rhoda opened the door: the body didn't disappear when Rhoda reappeared. A woman in a dress, someone who looked like Rhoda.

Rhoda stops walking. Her skirt settles around her ankles. Her eyes fix on the windows, which have lightened to a grayer shade of blue. Vases of fluffy white ranunculus stand on the sill. Remnants of Rhoda's relaxed weekend, like the wine bottles lined up on the floor, the dishes in the sink, the scorched matches piled on a brass dish beside an arrangement of beeswax pillars.

"My key card? That doesn't make sense." Rhoda's fingers tighten into fists, then she shakes them out.

"I must have lost it," she says, resuming her pacing, impatient. "That's not enough, to make that kind of assumption. They should have been more careful."

"The body wasn't identifiable. After that fall, it probably exploded."

It's perverse, repeating the words that made Dani feel ill. It's the pent-up tension from Rhoda's questions, her exhaustion, the two cups of coffee seething in her veins.

Rhoda looks aghast. She sinks onto a stool. "God. How horrible."

She scrubs her face with her hands. "I just don't understand why nobody tried to find me. People know I come here."

Dani mentions the yacht, and Rhoda squints. "Jason's boat? I forgot all about it."

She traces a vein in the marble counter. "I came here straight from the party." She glances up. "It sounds strange. Driving into the night like that. It was impulsive."

Dani nods. She understands. To leave the pulsing party hungry for silence. She imagines Rhoda's key in the lock, lights going on in the empty house, the seashell sound of waves, Rhoda falling into bed in her travel clothes.

"You wanted to wake up here," she says.

Rhoda touches Dani's hand. The lace cuff of her nightgown is soft as silk. "Yes, exactly. You understand."

They're quiet for a moment. Dani remembers her own impulse, driving through doubt along the winding roads to Rhoda's.

"I was alone all weekend. I wanted to think. I worked in the garden and walked on the beach and swam." Rhoda's voice is soft and quick, almost defensive. "I didn't talk to anyone. I didn't hear anything. If I'd known, I would have come straight back."

She presses her forehead. Reality must be sinking in, more painful than the shock. She's experiencing the slow, tumbling feeling of disaster everyone else felt yesterday. She blinks at Dani. "You must be exhausted."

She takes her upstairs to a tiny blue bedroom off the landing. There are pajamas in the dresser, the shirt folded crisply around the pants like they're straight from the store. Dani sinks into the feather bed. She'll never be able to sleep. She'll just lie down a minute. She hears Rhoda moving around in the next room. Packing, she assumes.

Unconsciousness grabs her like strong arms, pulling her underwater. Or, that's what happens in her dream. Dani's struggling against a dark, slippery tide of water, not at the beach but splashing across the roof of Radical HQ. The water floods the top floors of Rusher Tower, lapping at Rhoda's penthouse. Through the unfinished walls, she sees the beach house sofa, vases of flowers bobbing on the waves. Rhoda stands in an empty window, wearing her swimsuit.

Dani wakes to the sound of feet slapping down the stairs.

Was Rhoda just standing in her doorway?

Groggily, she climbs out of bed. Her sleep was so intense, it felt long, but when she checks her phone, only an hour has passed. It's almost five. She dresses and hurries downstairs, wondering if Rhoda's gone back to the city.

The back door stands open, cold air gusting through the screen. Over the ocean, fog drifts like smoke. Dani crosses the grass, dew splashing her ankles. The lawn drops off abruptly into a sheer cliff. A narrow wooden stairway plunges to the shore. Rhoda's left her sandals and towel above the tide line.

It seems impossible that someone should own this. The cliffs curve like hands, cupping Rhoda's beach. The rock is striped with black and green moss and patches of scrub, where lacy white flowers bob in the wind, and a long blade of blue grass bends under the weight of a black caterpillar. Overhead, gulls gust like kites.

The stairs deposit Dani on gritty sand.

The waves are dark wrinkles to the horizon. As they approach the beach, each peels away from the mass and rushes the sand in a vain attempt at breaking free, before dissolving into froth and spilling back into the whole. A hundred yards from shore, black rocks jut from the water, collared with frilled white waves. Rhoda is far beyond them, her head small and dark. She plunges under, vanishing again.

A wave surges up the beach to Dani, and she dips her fingers in the suds. Glacial.

There are dead things along the tide line, weeds and rotting fish and clots of plastic. Rhoda's dropped her towel uncomfortably close to the muck. Dani picks it up, brushes off the sand. It's not a towel, but a thick, wooly coat. As Dani shakes it, a piece of paper falls at her feet. It's folded in the shape of a cootie catcher.

It tips in the breeze, threatening to skip like a stone. Dani snatches it up. The folds are loose, and she hardly has to pull one back to see the familiar handwriting inside.

Rhoda,

My article really got to you, didn't it? I expected to be fired, but the rest of it? Wow.

You should be careful how you treat people.

Does the name Carlene Voose ring a bell? It's terrible, what happened to her. You should be ashamed of yourself, though I'm sure you're not.

You're a fraud. You can't keep it up forever.

xo, as you say,

Cecelia

Carlene Voose. The name sounds familiar, like a brand of candy, or an old movie star.

"Rhoda!" A ragged scream, and Gavin runs past Dani into the water. While Dani was reading the letter, Rhoda was swimming in. She's only a few yards from shore. She stands, the water waist deep, and Gavin wraps his arms around her, making them both fall back.

"That must be Rhoda West," a flat voice says. The tall man from Rhoda's office walks up the beach, still wearing his suit. Only one policeman follows him this morning.

Dani shoves the note deep into the coat pocket.

The detective—that must be who he is—stops beside her. He has a five-o'clock shadow. Five in the morning, Dani thinks. The edges of the paper dig into her palm.

"I thought you said you hadn't heard from her." He doesn't stick around for her to defend herself. He steps toward Rhoda, his shoes pressing hard shapes in the wet sand.

Rhoda and Gavin emerge from the water, Gavin helping Rhoda like she was the frenzied one. Her long limbs are stark against her black bikini. The detective introduces himself as Lowell, and while he shakes her hand he blatantly looks her over.

Dani brings the coat to Rhoda.

"Thanks, Dani." She grabs it, icy droplets flying from her skin to Dani's. She swings it over her shoulders. The note doesn't fall from the pocket, and she doesn't tuck her frigid hands into them. She's already turning back to the detective, speaking in a quick, apologetic tone.

"Dani found me last night and told me what happened. It was a complete shock. I only came up here for a break. I never imagined what I missed. I certainly didn't intend to contribute to the confusion."

Rhoda's face is all concern. Her anger is gone. Extinguished in the frigid water.

"Do you have any idea who it is?" she asks.

Lowell looks uninterested in the question. "You weren't on your phone at all? I can't stay off mine more than five minutes."

Rhoda nods. "It's important to consciously disconnect now and then. I find it's crucial to declutter my mind and make space for creativity."

"Uh-huh. What did you do with yourself?"

"I gardened. Swam. Relaxed. Work has been hectic." She's concentrating all her attention on him, not flirting, but accommodating. Gavin looms behind her, kicking at the sand.

"I imagine running a billion-dollar company is hectic." Lowell looks up and down the beach. "Nobody saw you? Neighbors?"

She shakes her head. "Isolation is the attraction."

"When did you come up?"

Rhoda glances at Dani. "Saturday morning. I didn't notice the exact time."

Gavin takes her shoulders. "Rhoda is being polite, answering your questions, but you can see she's alive. We're both freezing. We need to get dressed and get back to our lives. You have questions to answer yourselves."

"It is urgent that I get back," Rhoda adds. Unlike her to placate.

"Of course. After a long swim, of course," says Lowell. But he heads for the stairs, the police officer following, Rhoda not letting them get too far ahead, and Gavin sticking to Rhoda.

Dani trails behind. The stairs are endless. A band of pain stretches under her stomach, delves into her upper thigh. She holds the railing, breathing hard.

Near the top, Rhoda appears above her, snakes of wet hair waving from her head.

Dani's dizzy. She clings to the rail.

Rhoda grabs her elbow and hauls her up. Her fingers are cold and strong. "You OK? It's a long climb. Rest a minute. They're gone."

She gazes out at the horizon as Dani breathes hard. A line digs between her eyebrows. Dani can sense currents moving fast behind her eyes. She pulls the lapels of the coat closed against the wind. Does she even remember Cecelia's note in her pocket? She obviously read it, but then she folded it back closed, sunk it deep.

"I don't know why I told him I came up Saturday. Thanks for going along. I didn't expect them to be so intense." She draws the coat tighter, protectively, like she's remembering the detective's scrutiny.

"He wouldn't have understood," Dani says. That's why she hid the note, too. Instinctively shielded it from the unblinking stare.

Rhoda smiles, distractedly. "But he was right. I shouldn't have delayed. I've got to get back. You can follow me, if you want. There's good coffee in town."

But Rhoda doesn't stop. She accelerates past the VW bus, startling the people waiting in line, reading newspapers. Rhoda's own face might appear in those pages. Do any of them recognize her?

Outside the general store, a woman sets out bouquets of flowers. Daffodils, dahlias, fluffy white ranunculus.

Rhoda tears along the country roads, the din of her engine rising with the incline of hills, her taillights winking at Dani as they zip downhill. In her wake, Rhoda leaves spit gravel, a vulture startled from a fence post, sheep scattered from their communal cluster like broken pool balls.

Dani hasn't turned on her GPS, and when Rhoda twists out of sight, one turn, and then two curves ahead, Dani has no idea where she is. She's surrounded by post fences and grassy hills and still windmills. She hits the gas, and a biker appears out of the mist ahead of her, a wasp-yellow figure speeding straight for her windshield. Dani swerves to the shoulder, her car chewing gravel. His delayed shout sounds far behind.

Dani stops. The engine ticks. The gray country road stretches ahead, empty. Dozens of blackbirds sit on the power line, crowded as words in a sentence. Suddenly, they rise into the air, a swarming cloud, erasing it.

Rhoda

Tuesday

Flowers are heaped on the sidewalk outside of Radical HQ. *xo, Rhoda,* a card reads. The metal shells of burnt-down tea lights circle my photograph.

My ears hum. *You were dead,* Dani said, and the police trampled my beach, but I didn't feel the weight of it until now. The air surges like the ocean. I almost stumble.

A hand grasps my elbow. "Good morning, Rhoda," Orson says. "Rather a strange circumstance, isn't it? We'd better head inside. You never know what an errant camera might capture." He steers me away from the flowers.

I stand straight, berating myself for being caught off guard. The hard click of my shoes on the cement is reassuring. I step ahead of Orson and drive through the doors.

"Thank you for coming on short notice. I don't know exactly what I'm walking into here, but I know it's messier than I'd like."

His forehead tightens, fractionally. *Messy.* Poor choice of word.

Pointless to wish I'd slept. Tiredness is a weakness, not an excuse. Things are about to become nonstop, as Jason once warned me.

The board is gathered in Athena. Jason's voice carries to the hall. "And yet—"

When I open the door, their faces crater. Jason stumbles back, his bad knee crumpling. He catches himself on the table.

Their silence has gravity. Like the drop of a roller coaster, snatching breath from throat.

"It's really me." My lips feel novocained. "I heard the news this morning. I expected to find confusion, but I see that you all believed the worst." I set a hand on top of my head, a runner's trick, a way to keep posture erect for optimal breathing. As I turn to draw Orson into the room, I glance at the projection.

- Internal messaging for staff & stakeholders
- Messaging for customers: reassure, reaffirm, remember
- Leadership transition

The screen goes dark. Jason's closed his laptop. His face is gray and wet, eyes wide, like a market fish on ice.

"Rhoda, reincarnated," he rasps. He licks his lips. "You chose an inopportune time to disappear."

"I took a long weekend at my beach house. It's no secret that I go there to disconnect. I've never come back to anything like this."

"How could this happen?" asks Pilar, with real dismay.

"I see I did the right thing, bringing our attorney along." I introduce Orson.

Jason sinks into his chair. His arms are limp at his sides. How quickly did he draft that PowerPoint? *Leadership transition*, tucked in like an afterthought.

"The immediate aftermath of tragedy is often confusing," Orson says. "In the absence of information, rumors proliferate. Let's be glad the police never formally identified the body as Rhoda and the media was fairly restrained. The police are aware of the circumstances, and will obviously take their investigation in a new direction."

Chad Ephraim honks. "That's a lot of words that leave out the real issue. Rhoda going MIA has landed us in an untenable situation."

I balk. "I had nothing to do with the creation of this situation."

His cheeks quiver like water about to boil. "When your investors throw a party in your honor, you attend. You don't drop off the face of the earth. I've never heard of a CEO going off the grid without a word. It's wildly irresponsible."

I wonder how long they idled in the harbor, waiting for me. I could apologize—and of course I'm very sorry, now, that I didn't attend—but I won't allow the implication that I'm not free to do what I want.

"I needed to recharge. Frankly, I'm baffled that nobody thought to look for me."

Jason lifts his hands, a conductor hushing the crescendo. "In hindsight, of course, everything looks different. We had no reason to doubt the evidence presented to us. We were reeling, cooperating with police, keeping the situation from devolving into a circus. You can't possibly understand what we've been through, the past twenty-four hours."

His voice cracks. His sharp eyes are bleary, shadowed with purple-green bruises. Even Jason, after his day of scrambling to claim control, must have lain awake in bed, blinking in the dark, trying to square the impossible equation of my existence ending.

"Emotions are high," Orson says. "The fact is, the death will continue to impact Radical until it's resolved. And Rhoda had every right to decompress. The situation is extraordinary, not her actions."

Jason pushes himself to standing, a weak attempt to hold the head of the room.

"Orson's right, of course. Let's meet in a few days to reassess." He rambles, resorting to cliché: one step at a time, take the temperature, circle back . . .

On their way out, Pilar and Barry and Faye touch my shoulder. "Thank God, it goes without saying, we're so relieved."

I can't speak, and hope it passes as quavering emotion. Part of me is fuming at being blamed. The other part is terrified. I felt the energy in the room. They weren't entirely happy to see me. It's taboo, they'd never admit it, but the fact is, this complication is less appealing than a straightforward tragedy.

I'm colder now than when I was in the water, diving under the waves.

Jason follows Orson and me to my office.

I can tell instantly that people came in while I was gone. The air is disturbed. More pressingly, my laptop is gone. When I sit in my chair, the recline tips me back.

I adjust it, pointedly. "I hope you didn't hand my computer over to the police."

Jason opens his bag. "I took it as a precaution. I didn't want anyone touching it."

Except himself. Did he open it? I'll check with Cam.

I square it in its place, visualize my own thoughts tidying, too. The situation calls for clarity, a swift, righting action.

"While I appreciate the board's concern, I see no reason we can't set the record straight and move ahead. Whatever happened, it has nothing to do with Radical."

"Are you sure about that?" Jason asks. He's standing at the window, arms crossed, the back of his charcoal blazer drawn tight. "A woman, wearing your coat, holding your key card. How does that happen?"

Orson clicks his pen. He's settled on the couch, legs crossed. "Can the police be so sure it was Rhoda's coat? It may have been a similar style."

My eyes travel to the coatrack in the corner of my office. I keep a trench there, in case of sudden swerves in weather, but it's empty.

Jason turns, and I meet his gaze, hoping he reads my expression as general concern.

"The key card is genuine," he says. "Security checked it."

Orson holds his pen in two fingers, dropping it on his knee, catching it on the bounce. "Rhoda may have lost her key." Bounce-catch. "These puzzle pieces may have suggested a certain picture yesterday, but today it's clear that they don't fit.

"More crucially," he continues, "going forward, nobody talks to the police outside my presence." He levels a look at me. "You mentioned speaking to them."

I explain their finding me at the beach, and he listens carefully, giving the impression of absorbing not just my words but also their subtext, the understatements, the evasions, and, on a still-deeper level, his own reinterpretations, the defenses he could employ, the deft and seemingly careless explanations he'd toss off.

"Fine," he says. "And have we checked that no one from Radical is missing?"

Jason's attention seems glazed. The shock of losing control has hit hard. He looks old—his age, I suppose. He wants to live forever, has funds set aside in his will to freeze his brain in a cryogenic chamber filled with the brains of other wealthy, egocentric men, in the event that some future society might be inclined to reanimate them.

He blinks. "Not that I'm aware of."

"There's our first order of business."

"Cara should have done it, but I'll make sure of it," I say.

"And if someone is missing?" Jason asks. His glance has sharpened.

"If it's a Radigal, it's a tragedy," I say. "And if it's not, then . . ." I catch myself before I shrug. "Then it's purely a matter for the police."

"Our lobby is wallpapered in caution tape. Radical went home last night believing the worst. This isn't going to disappear."

"Every office in the building has stairwell access," Orson says.

From down the hall, I hear Radigals arriving in the lobby. Word of my return is out. Their voices are indistinct, a simmering white noise.

You have no idea what we've been through . . .

Even Dani wasn't purely glad to see me. Her eyes were searching, worried. She wanted an explanation, a story to make sense of the confusion. Under pressure, I made mistakes. Silly lies, contradictions. She was sympathetic. Supplying explanations for me.

When I look up, Jason is staring at me, fingering the cuff of his jacket. As my phone returned to range, my inbox filled with his messages. Peevish, then angry, then anxious. Midmorning on Monday, he left a final, bleak message: a few seconds of silence, then a sharp inhale. "We can't find you. Call me."

I think of the flowers piled on the sidewalk.

So much emotion. So many questions. I'll have no privacy. I wish I'd gone home to shower and dress, armor myself in makeup. I feel raw, salt in my hair.

Orson is still talking. "Piece by piece, we'll distance Radical from the situation." He draws his hands apart, like it will be so simple.

He turns to me. "To begin, let's make your return official."

On cue, my assistant comes in with my green juice and a watery look. Behind her is Gavin, hair damp from the shower. He wraps his arms around me again, like he's afraid I might disappear.

I close my eyes, wish that my office was empty, that I had a moment to myself.

Jason clears his throat. "They're waiting."

"Bring him along," Orson says, clearly wanting Gavin as an example for how the rest of the world should react.

I'm practically marched out through the pillars to the feet of the Radical Woman.

A sea of lilac. Everyone is wearing their Radical apparel, their first-day T-shirts and anniversary track jackets, holiday fleeces and volunteer jumpsuits. Their faces tip up at me. The Core Team huddles in. Everyone wants reassurance that I'm real.

Suddenly, I know exactly what to say.

"How lucky am I, that this is my life. How incredible, to have you all in it.

"I spent the weekend at my cabin. After our celebration, I felt exhilarated and proud and completely spent. I needed to unplug completely, to recharge and rest.

"Early this morning, I heard the news you lived with for an entire day. I can only imagine the misery, confusion, and worry you all felt.

"I wish I had answers, but unfortunately, I don't. It may be days, or longer, before the police know more. I can assure you that Radical will continue doing everything in our power to assist the investigation. Our first priority at Radical is ensuring that you all feel safe. The People Team is arranging for a grief and trauma counselor to be available in person and online. Don't hesitate to use them. Everything you're feeling is valid.

"What I do know, without any doubt, is that we will get through this, together. Looking at all of you, I see that Radical's spirit is strong. Let's sing it loud, shall we?"

I stretch my hand out toward them. "At Radical . . ."

They take over the chant, their voices straining with emotion.

As we shout our final promise—*out on top!*—my eye snags on a flash of yellow amid the lilac. Police tape, sealing off the emergency stairwell.

I look away quickly, but it hangs over my vision like a bright camera flash.

All day, I'm present. The catharsis is heady and draining. I walk the teal path. I post to social. I wear my track jacket.

Orson manages the police, the media. Inevitably, my name sticks to the story. "Rhoda West Calls Fallen Woman 'Tragic,' Police Ask Anyone with Information to Come Forward."

Another day, a week at the most, and it will drop out of the top stories, tumble to the middle pages, below the fold.

I make it to happy hour. Every drop of wine is like a gulp of sleeping potion. I've already sent Gavin home, sagging with jet lag. Finally, I can follow. As I wind my scarf around my neck, I hear a call of dismay: the rosé tap has gone dry.

In the garage, I plunge my hands into my coat pockets, looking for my keys, and Cecelia's letter falls out, like a receipt for my stupidity. I forgot it was there.

I found it on my desk, during the party, folded like a flower. She must have snuck in, unnoticed in the hubbub. I imagine her lingering in my empty office, savoring her trespass, trailing her fingers over the surfaces, listening to the rain ticking on the windows. Did she steal my trench— for spite, or to keep dry when she went out?

I crush the note in my hand. I don't know for sure that it's her. Nobody does.

At home, I hold the letter over the gas burner on my Wolf range. The hood vacuums away the smoke, but fine ash drifts across the white countertop.

Dani

Tuesday

The Marketing Team gathers around a high-top table in the cafeteria.

"If any of you feels overwhelmed or troubled after the turmoil of the past days," Lisbeth is saying, her voice flat as a server offering up a daily special, "don't hesitate to reach out to me or the People Team."

She's wearing a cream blazer—an homage to Rhoda? The rest of them wear their lilac track jackets. They seem collectively shy, after the candor around the bar, their slumped, finger-bitten emotion exposed today as unnecessary. Lisbeth is especially distant, encased in shiny, invisible makeup, her hair impeccably straight.

"Our task today is to control the community fallout. The powers that be hope the customer response will be minimal, but we all know that the social channels absorb the bulk of the impact. Rhoda wants personal replies to every good-faith comment and message. I'm more worried about conspiracy theories. Don't hesitate to block trolls."

"Do they know anything?" Jia asks. "Who is it?"

Lisbeth lifts an eyebrow. "That's the question. Nobody knows, and we're not speculating." She claps her hands. "OK. Here's hoping the weather is mild out there."

Dani aches like she's doing manual labor, carrying heavy buckets, hauling stones. She replies to the outpouring of comments with heart emojis, words of support. *We feel the same. Thank you for being here.*

Was this some kind of publicity stunt? someone asks.

Dani shows Lisbeth, who smirks.

"That would be bold. Still, deleting it might seem overdefensive. Stick to the script. Went to recharge, et cetera." There's an edge to her voice—disapproval? Disbelief?

Imagine her surprise if Dani told her she found Rhoda. Described the lit-up house, the moonlight on Rhoda's car. Rhoda answering the door in her nightgown.

But Dani won't tell. Through the All-Hands, she braced for Rhoda to single her out, thank her. Rhoda didn't. She spared Dani the attention, the throngs of questioners.

Dani didn't even tell Trevor. She drove straight to work; as far as he knows, that's the only place she's been.

He texts: *Such a relief! I knew it wasn't possible.*

Most customers echo his sentiment, although for every joyful comment, there's a question: *Who is it? What really happened?*

We're all waiting for answers, Dani types.

It's not a Radigal. Cara confirmed this morning that everyone is accounted for. But they know nothing more.

Cecelia must be relishing the drama. Even Rhoda's death is a fraud!

For the first time in a week or more, Dani opens Twitter, but Cecelia's gone quiet. Her last post was before the weekend: *One woman's snake oil is another woman's poison.*

Strange that she didn't say anything about the body. Dani scrolls, but there's no mention of fraud, or anything from her letter. At a furious post about the universe's energy, Dani closes her phone, rubbing her forehead. She's so tired, she can conjure the exact pressure of her mattress, the sink of her pillow.

She walks the teal path, stretching her achy muscles, and glimpses Rhoda in a conference room, surrounded by managers, her adviser, Gavin. Her sleeves are pushed up, and she's making an emphatic gesture. She seems untouched by the sleepless night, recovered from the shock of the news. Dani brought her back; Dani fixed it.

As she makes a smoothie with extra SuperYou powder in the kitchen, a shadow passes by the door. Police, crossing the lobby toward the roof. Her hand trembles, and pink powder spills across the counter.

*

In the afternoon, Lisbeth pulls Dani aside. "Crisis. People are posting photos of the party. We don't want to seem insensitive. I need you to comb Radigals' socials. Ask them to take everything down, even private posts."

The party has its own hashtag (#radicalround4). Video clips of the band playing, drinks clinking, people dancing, cheeks squeezed together.

Dani remembers the party in a chaotic way, as if someone spun her by the shoulders and released her. Why does she remember so many bangs and pops? A light cracked with a cork, a glass shattered. Balloons snapping underfoot. The chop of Rhoda's arm swinging the saber. In her memory, their joy is frenzied, as if they sensed disaster dangling over their heads by a thread.

Someone on the People Team shared the group photo. Dani forgot: they all pressed together to grin up at the photographer. *Say billion!*

Dani zooms in on Rhoda. She stands in the center, her smile perfectly poised. Her adviser is beside her, hand on her shoulder. Behind his gleaming head, a girl makes a duck face with her lips.

Dani brings the phone to her nose.

The girl's lips are bright red, her eyeliner heavy as a rebellious teen-ager's.

It's Cecelia.

It can't be, but it is. Cecelia, standing brazenly behind Rhoda.

Dani texts Cecelia the photo with a string of question marks. *You were there?? How did I miss you?*

As soon as she hits send, she realizes the obvious: Cecelia must have avoided her. Ducked behind pillars, blended into the crowd.

When she actually worked at Radical, she skipped every event. Why did she crash the party? Dani can only imagine what she thought about the nostalgic pop band, the three-legged unicorn, the twin investors and their champagne saber!

But she didn't say anything. She didn't mock the party. Her Twitter feed is abandoned. Her last post garnered just two likes.

*

At Cecelia's house, the garage door is shut. Dani knocks on the side door, splinters scratching her knuckles, but there's no response. Dani climbs the front steps and rings the doorbell.

The landlady answers. Margo. Cecelia always said her name sarcastically, as if it were an alias.

"Is Cecelia home?" Dani asks.

Margo tightens her grip on the door. "I live alone."

But this is the house, Dani's sure. She even recognizes the orange cat who appears between Margo's ankles, arching its back luxuriantly.

"I'm a friend of hers," Dani says. "I haven't heard from her lately."

Margo scoops up the cat, cuddling it to her chest, roughly petting its head, dragging the fur so its green eyes stretch at the corners. "She moved out."

The cat springs free of her grip and runs back into the house. Margo starts closing the door, but Dani steps into the swing.

"When did she leave?"

Say yesterday. Over the weekend.

Another shrug. "Thursday or Friday. She didn't say anything. She left a mess. If you get a hold of her, tell her I've thrown her stuff out."

The door slams.

Dani drifts to the end of the driveway. The street is serene, the green lawns and pastel houses like drawings in a children's book. Dani's worries buzz like flies. She climbs into Trevor's car, draws her hair up in a higher ponytail. So Cecelia moved. She said she had to. Dani can't be surprised that she didn't say goodbye, after their last conversation. She might be deleting Dani's texts as they come in.

Did she go to the party just to spite Rhoda? In a way, she's as fixated on Radical as any superfan.

Maybe she crashed just to deliver her strange note. Couldn't resist one last jibe before she left.

Trevor and Dani sit on the couch, feet tangled, laptops open. Jazz plays on a record, a rattling snare drum. Trevor's foot twitches along. For him, the drama is over. Founders are immortal again.

Rhoda posts a photo of Radigals in their lilac.

radical Tired, reeling, and grateful. xo.

Dani knows what happened—Cecelia lost her phone. In the chaos of the party, or the mess of her move. She loses things all the time: credit cards, keys. Once she left her phone on top of a paper towel dispenser in the bathroom of a dive bar, and it was sheer luck that Dani found it later that night.

That's it. She lost her phone, and she's too broke to buy a new one. She can't tweet or respond to texts or even read them. Dani leans her head back on the pillow.

"Long day?" Trevor asks, nudging her foot with his.

Dani sighs. She didn't plan to mention anything (it's nothing!) but she hears herself saying, "I'm just worried about Cecelia. I haven't heard from her."

Trevor snaps his fingers. "I totally forgot. She came over the other day." He springs from the couch and heads down the hall. She hears him rummaging in the closet.

"Cecelia came here?"

He returns rolling a suitcase. "She left this. She's going to come back for it."

Dani snatches at the handle. "When did she bring this?"

He scratches his chin. "Friday." He nods. "Definitely, Friday. I had a weird day, and it totally slipped my mind."

Dani doesn't ask what was weird about Friday. She kneels on the carpet and unzips the suitcase. It's crammed full. Cecelia's favorite red sweater, her jean jacket jangling with vintage pins, a dog-eared copy of *Franny and Zooey*, a dirty velvet pouch stained with inky mascara.

Cecelia's retainer case rattles in Dani's hand. Cecelia wouldn't leave all this behind. Any minute now, she'll press the buzzer, appear at the door, bedraggled and hungover, with the excuse that she met a bartender at the party.

"She said she needed to talk to you. She had something to tell you."

Dani turns on him. "What did she say, exactly? Talk, like in general, or something to tell me—something specific?"

Trevor shakes his head, bewildered. "I didn't think it was a big deal."

Dani smooths Cecelia's red sweater over her lap. "She was at the party."

The couch sinks as Trevor sits. His hand is warm on her back. The music clashes in the background, as Dani thumbs a hole in the sweater cuff. A tailor can mend that, weave matching string across the tear.

"We have to call the police," Trevor says. "They'll be able to track her down."

His voice is gentle. He knows they won't. She knows, too. Has known, on some level, since she saw Cecelia in the party photo, scrunching her lips.

"Not yet," she says, standing. "If I don't hear from her, I'll call in the morning."

She closes herself in the bathroom. Moving automatically, she runs the tub, testing the temperature with her knuckles.

Her mom loved taking baths. She soaked for hours, candles precariously lining the rim. The water almost jellied with oils and bath beads, all of it from the mall, artificially fragranced, colored with toxic dyes, loaded with chemical preservatives. Pretty poisons. If only she'd had Radical, Dani sometimes thinks, it might have been different.

She pours a measure of Radical Bath Brine and steps carefully into the tub. Her stomach is soft like rising dough, not the taut, inflated balloon she associates with pregnancy. She spreads her fingers over her veined skin. She imagines stress dissolving into her body like bath beads, passing through the placenta and into Naomi. She takes even, deep breaths. Nadine would gather the hair off Dani's neck, smooth it from the nape, divide it into strands and braid them loosely. *Not your fault*, she would say, but Dani sent Cecelia away when she had nowhere to go. Cee was soaking wet, her chin lowered, shoulders slumped. Dani can practically smell the turmeric from her soup, feel the wet night chill seeping through the skylight, and the warmth of her own house as she shut her door. In the kitchen, she ate her soup at the table with candles lit, purging Cecelia's bad energy from the room.

What if she had called out to Cecelia to wait? Asked her to come back inside, take off her shoes. Lent her pajamas, ladled soup into two bowls. Cecelia could have stayed over. She used to crash on Dani's couch. They'd take the bus to work together, Cecelia producing an uncapped eyeliner from the bottom of her bag and drawing a smooth line through the bus's jolts. If you'd told them, then, that Dani would push Cecelia out into the cold rain, that Cecelia would go to a party and purposely hide from Dani—they would have stared with as much confusion as Rhoda answering her door to Dani in the middle of the night.

Rhoda

Thursday

Orson calls at dawn. It's urgent.

The clouds are still pink when we meet in my office. The skyline shines as if rinsed. A beautiful start to a day that's going to get ugly.

"The deceased is Cecelia Cole," Orson says, without alarm or surprise. He doesn't react when I draw breath through my teeth.

"In light of her"—Orson hesitates—"complicated relationship with Radical, they want to speak to you again. I'll make sure their questions remain factual. Did you see her at the party, speak to her, et cetera. They may want to revisit your weekend. There's no need to elaborate on your explanation."

Energy brims under my skin. I have to pace.

"We've been over that. Is it illegal for a woman to go to her own house?"

"Your absence may be interpreted as flight. We want to shed any whiff of strangeness. It's perfectly natural that a busy, successful CEO takes a break. Maybe you thought you told someone. Jason? Your fiancé? But it slipped your mind. Hmm?"

I walk to the window. "I might have mentioned it to Gavin."

The night's fog is evaporating, rising like steam from the Bay.

"Do you have any idea how she got into the party? Did she have building access?"

"HR would have taken her security pass when she was let go."

Orson clears his throat, tactful before he probes. "It seems that she was indeed wearing a coat with your pass in the pocket. A pale green trench," he says, like he's reading from a catalog.

"Sage," I correct. I turn, pretend to check the coatrack. "It must have been hanging there."

Click-click. "And you keep your office locked? Of course, that would be easy to forget, the night of a party. She might have taken it," Orson muses, as if talking to himself. More sharply, he adds, "But don't speculate negatively about her. You're concerned, regretful. As a young, appealing woman, you'll be very sympathetic . . . if you act sympathetic."

I bounce my fist against my thigh. I will not look sympathetic. A dead whistleblower. She never stopped tweeting. Her numbers were down, her sympathizers losing interest, but they'll come swarming back now.

"The lawsuit will come out. They'll make her into a hero. And me a villain."

He doesn't argue. He pushed the lawsuit on me. He arranged for his minions to watch her. My jaw is clenched.

"Will anyone find out? About the . . . surveillance?"

"No reason anybody should."

"Did they attend the party, by any chance?" I don't even know who "they" are.

"Not to my knowledge."

Good line, I'll have to use it.

He checks his watch. "Let's focus on the matter at hand. The police will be here any minute. Keep your answers simple. If in doubt, say you can't remember."

I crave a cigarette. I imagine sneaking up to the roof. The absurdity of it almost makes me laugh, but I have to look somber. *Regretful*, as Orson put it.

At the knock on the door, he stands, smoothing his vest. "You are innocent. Remind yourself of that morning, noon, and night."

My hands jerk, involuntarily. I cover it by reaching to check my hair. The way he said *innocent* conjured its opposite.

"Well done," Orson says, patting my hand as he leaves. "We'll get through this."

I feel spent, a husk. Unbidden, a memory of my dad surfaces, from an evening midway through his trial. I passed his open door and saw him sitting on the edge of the bed, staring at the turned-off TV with amazed dread, as though it was a crystal ball showing his future. His suit jacket hung from his fingers and puddled to the floor. It was the moment I understood he was going to jail. He'd given up, and so he'd already lost.

I'm slouching, staring at a marble bust on a shelf. I stand, straighten my jacket, buzz my assistant. Clear my schedule. Bring coffee. Prepare for a long day.

The news sites update. "Body Identified as Former Radical Employee Cecelia Cole." Somehow, they have her staff photo. Her fate gives her smirk a tragic aspect.

Within hours, Megaphone publishes a letter.

Dear Megaphone Community,

I was shocked to read the news that Cecelia Cole was found dead outside of Radical HQ.

Cecelia was the author of a recent exposé that shone a light on the toxic environment at Radical. After the story was published, Radical fired Cecelia, and aggressively pursued a lawsuit against her.

The circumstances demand a thorough investigation. Radical's resources shouldn't preclude public accountability.

Cecelia was a fierce advocate for truth. I hoped to continue working with her, sharing her searing, brave voice. Her death is a real loss. Join me in demanding #justiceforCecelia.

Leandra French
Editor, Megaphone

Share your stories. Raise your voice.

Jason swoops in, dressed for a game of golf canceled for my benefit. "From bad to worse. A dead whistleblower. What a disaster."

I snap. "Don't call her that. That's a gross exaggeration."

He raises an eyebrow. "Do you seriously think anyone is going to call her anything else? Tell me you have some grasp of the situation."

"I only just found out myself." I won't tell him about the detective on my couch, his dark, unblinking eyes like a camera with a long exposure.

"My dear, your beach house excuse may have worked for the weekend, but you are back in the real world now."

My dear, he says, a parody of our old rapport.

"We both know why I didn't stick around to sail with you and the Ephraims after the party."

As if he seriously expected me to board the yacht, recline on a deck chair, and endure his maritime vocabulary and the Ephraims' childhood anecdotes. After they schemed against me—*creative leadership structures!*—and Jason met my eyes in the mirror and hardly bothered to deny it.

I imagine him lifting the anchor after I didn't show, a broad shrug of his shoulders forgiving me for my hangover—thus planting it in everyone's minds. Playing host in his Top-Siders. Unimaginable that a week ago, I reclined on that deck. Laughed at his impression of an emperor turning his thumb to decide my fate.

"I hope you have a plan," he says, ignoring my bait. "You're in a real trap. If you call the death a tragedy, you'll sound like a hypocrite. You'll have no control over the messaging. You'll be under a microscope: everything you say, every gesture, every expression. For instance, when you clench your jaw, I know you well enough to know you're frustrated at being told something you resent. People less familiar will come up with their own interpretations. And they won't be flattering."

"Aren't you my adviser? Shouldn't you have solutions?"

"You never want my advice." Hands in his pockets, he ambles over to the wall of press clippings, looking proprietary, like he's imagining which of his Japanese watercolors he'll mount in their place.

"A good run," he says. "Look how far you've come. You've sprinted and rallied and built something beautiful."

He strolls to the windows, lacing his hands behind his back. "People don't appreciate the miracle of entrepreneurship. They don't understand the effort it takes to build something, when destruction is the overriding force of nature. Erosion, entropy. We triumph over them—for a while."

He's backlit, staring down into the alley with a grave frown, like a camera might be rolling.

"That's quite a speech."

He doesn't break character. He faces me, solemn. "My advice is to resign."

I'm stunned, like he's struck my solar plexus. I try to cover it with a laugh, but I sound as breathy as a panic attack. "How convenient for you if I stepped down."

"This has nothing to do with our disagreement. I'm thinking of Radical. You worked so hard to build it. Leave, and you give us a fighting chance. Stay, and you'll drag us down.

"You survived some hard knocks to your reputation. Many founders don't. None, I think, could survive an incident of this magnitude."

I want to cover my ears. He's so good at pouring poison. He maneuvered me so cleverly during the investment round. *Radical will be worth it.*

"That will never happen," I say.

I'm glad when the others descend on my office. People, Marketing, Legal. Their energy is frenetic. What-to-do-what-to-do.

Someone suggests a scholarship in Cecelia's name.

Pay all funeral expenses, another proposes.

A donation to victims of suicide. Or a foundation for aspiring journalists?

Jason watches me, impassive, his arms crossed.

My phone alerts me to my assistant canceling my dinner reservations for the month. Suddenly, my social calendar is blank apart from my wedding, two weeks away.

It won't happen. The thought drops into my mind, certain as an epiphany.

No. It's only anxiety. Bad energy breeds paranoia, doubt.

I close my eyes. Quiet my thoughts.

The death is a tragedy. We can't corporate away a tragedy. We have to honor it.

When I open my eyes, everyone is still arguing. Cara's ponytail sags at the nape of her neck; Lisbeth's decorative eyeglasses slide down her nose.

"There's a news van outside," she announces, reading her phone screen. A fresh wave of dismay rises.

"Enough!" I tap my desk with a pen. "I want to hold a vigil tonight. Someone find out whether we need permission, please? I don't want to get in trouble with the city."

City, I say, not police. A microscopic verbal gymnastic, requiring only quickness of thought and hyperawareness of my image. Nothing I'm not used to. Jason's wrong. I'm not trapped.

Dani

Thursday

Hundreds of candles illuminate the vigil, doubled in the glass walls of Radical HQ. Radigals are outnumbered by strangers. Women dressed in black, wearing pins that say *Remember Cecelia*. Flowers are piled on the sidewalk, teddy bears, heart-shaped balloons. Cecelia would have hated this.

Speaking into a microphone, Rhoda thanks them for coming. "We're here to mark the tragic loss of a young writer, a free spirit. Anyone who wishes to speak should do so."

Holly goes first, stammers awkwardly about Cecelia's offbeat humor.

Then an angry woman seizes the mic. She rants about speaking truth to power.

Rhoda stands beside her, candles lighting her face, which shows no impatience, no defensiveness. The gentle glow is interrupted now and then with the bright flash of a camera, startling as a lightning bolt.

Of all Dani's emotions, the most recognizable is guilt. Guilt for Cecelia, gone. Guilt at the impersonal eulogies. Guilt at the voice in her head, whispering that Cecelia wasn't really like they're describing her. Cecelia wasn't a principled crusader. She slung accusations regardless of who she hurt, or whether they were even true.

Rhoda thanks the speaker calmly. She gives no sign of the whiplash she must feel, pivoting from the shock of her return to the news of a Radigal's death—an ex-Radigal.

Dani's candle flame is doused in a puddle of molten wax. Her throat aches from the smoke. She pushes through the crowd. Strangers glower, scandalized at the disruption.

At the fringe of the memorial, Dani kneels to straighten a teddy bear that's tipped over. She left her own flowers here, wrapped in velvet ribbons. Daffodils for Cecelia, and lilies for Carlene Voose.

In the dark, sleepless middle of the night, Dani searched for Carlene online and found an obituary in an Oregon newspaper, three years old.

Beloved Mother, Daughter, and Sister, Carlene Voose (59) passed away peacefully, surrounded by family. A longtime resident of Eugene, Carlene was treasured by generations of art students. She was an avid traveler, dog lover, and generous spirit.

Dani swallowed. Her throat felt clogged, as if by an egg, hot and hard. *Fifty-nine years old, so unfair . . .*

The obituary included a photograph of a laughing woman on a beach, shaded by a floppy hat, her hands open to the breeze.

It's awful, what you did to her, Cecelia wrote.

What could Carlene Voose have to do with Rhoda?

Dani shut her phone, lay back on the pillow. The fan ticked above her. She was furious with Cecelia. Shaking with it.

Cecelia would use anything as ammunition.

Dani misses the signal that ends the vigil. The candles are extinguished all at once. Smoke films the air, and the solemn gathering dissolves into a crowd of bodies eager to get away. Dani is jostled into a reporter, who quickly brings her microphone to her lips, which curl in artificial sympathy.

"Would you care to share how you're feeling? How has the loss affected you?"

Before Dani can react, the reporter's attention shifts. Eagerness leaps into her face: "Rhoda!" Her soft lisp replaced by a bullhorn.

Rhoda must have walked right past Dani. She's hurrying up the building steps, her coat flying open behind her. She doesn't stop, and the reporter and cameraman huddle together in frustration.

If they knew Dani had found Rhoda, they'd chase her down the sidewalk.

The neon red sign of the bus stop seems miles away. Dani's back aches.

You can afford an Uber, Cecelia sneers, in Dani's head. *Now that you're the Voice.* To spite her, Dani waits eighteen minutes for the bus.

In the morning, fog hangs outside HQ like lingering smoke. Rhoda doesn't emerge from her office. People are drawn into it. The Core Team, Rhoda's adviser, dark-suited lawyers. Rhoda's assistant rushes in and out with trays of coffee and sandwiches.

The flat-screens tell the story. The CW backlog shades darker every hour: orange, rust, red, maroon. Instagram is under siege. Newspaper headlines end in forty-point font question marks. The Megaphone editor, Leandra French, is on the attack.

A whistleblower dies and a CEO hides, she writes. *Save your candles. We want accountability.*

She retweets Cecelia's posts about getting evicted, losing her health insurance. Radical was suing her, and Leandra posts the court documents on Megaphone.

Cecelia couldn't afford a lawyer, she writes. *She was terrified.*

Dani thinks of Cecelia banging the kitchen table, making the flowers sway. *I cannot take any more Radical bullshit.* Anger radiated off her like smoke, acrid and unhealthy. Dani recoiled from it.

It's obvious, now, that Cecelia was miserable. But she made it so difficult to sympathize. She picked fights about everything. Radical, Rhoda, the use of turmeric in soup. Dani is arguing in her own head, defending herself against a phantom Cecelia.

Did Rhoda drive her to the rooftop that night? Was this Cecelia's final message? A last, desperate protest of Radical's hypocrisy?

The accusation surges through Radical HQ, the teal path like a telephone circuit, lighting up with the gossip. People claim to have seen Cecelia at the party. Drinking too much. Dancing alone. Word is out that she liked to go on the roof. What tipped her over the edge? The three-legged unicorn? The endless bottles of champagne? Rumor has it Radical spent the equivalent of a year's CW salary to book the band.

The social channels are overrun. Lisbeth takes the "extraordinary step" of restricting comments. The uproar leaps to Twitter.

"Will she apologize?" Laurel asks.

Lisbeth purses her lips. "I can't say." She joins the migration to Rhoda's office.

"She can't apologize," Jia says. "That would be like admitting it is her fault."

"Poor Cecelia," Laurel says. "It's so spiteful, though. Think of going to a party, and planning that . . ." She shudders.

Dani wants to correct them. Cecelia didn't plan it. She left her suitcase at Dani's house. She was coming back. Leandra's wrong.

But they'll ask why Cecelia was at the party, and Dani can't explain the note, folded in Rhoda's coat pocket like a beetle. *You're a fraud.*

Sitting at Dani's kitchen table, Cecelia made wild accusations. Rhoda was following her, ruining her life. Why didn't she mention Carlene Voose?

Dani's eyes sting. The words on her screen are blurry. She's scanning the Well product pages, removing anything that references the "events," as Lisbeth put it: partying, slaying, leaping, falling. Around the Marketing pod, everyone is wading through such tasks. Jia pulling Wedding newsletters, Laurel scrambling to update the blog landing page. They consult each other in whispers. *Is this bad? Is that?*

"Femme Vitale saved my life," a pull quote declares. Dani wonders if she should delete it: the mention of saving a life might remind people of the opposite. Come to think of it, Femme Vitale nods to Fatale. If she stares long enough, every earnest word on the page sounds suspicious.

The day marches on, dreadfully. The white noise hissing through the office seems to rise in pitch, higher, higher.

In the afternoon, Lisbeth taps Dani on the shoulder. "You're being summoned."

Rhoda's office is hot and stagnant. Behind her desk, Rhoda types into her computer with staccato jabs. Her hair is pinned up, but otherwise she shows no concession to the atmosphere. Her dark blazer is buttoned over a gray turtleneck, and she hasn't even cuffed the sleeves.

A man from Legal, tie unknotted, jacket hanging loose, fills a mug from a tureen of coffee, releasing a bitter, scorched smell. The yellow sofa, occupied by Cara, is well-creased. Lisbeth sits on the arm, fanning herself with a hand.

"I only need Dani," Rhoda says. "I'm sure everyone has plenty to do."

The others skulk out, one by one, Lisbeth last, asking whether she should close the door, then doing so with ostentatious courtesy.

Rhoda's typing slows to pecks. She closes her laptop and rubs her eyes.

"A week of bad news." Her face is blotchy. As she stands, she glances out the window at Rusher. Her fingers flex. For a moment, she's just as she was the night of the party, when Dani found her in the dark. A bit of white crumpled in her palm.

"I've been meaning to thank you, Dani." Rhoda sits on the couch, gesturing for Dani to take the chair. "I appreciate your discretion."

The word hangs in the air like a smell.

She rushes on. "You're so intuitive, Dani. It's an amazing quality. Driving all that way to find me. I'm grateful. I probably didn't take the shock very well. You must have thought I'd lost it, going out for that swim." Her tone is mild, self-deprecating, but she watches Dani closely.

Did Rhoda see her read the note? Rhoda's coat over her arm, paper trembling in her hand.

But she goes on. "When my mind is overwhelmed, I always center my body. Stress can be paralyzing. It's important to release it."

Her voice is confiding, vulnerable. She does this: holds her perspective up like a glass to the light, inspecting it. Dani understands. The swim was strange but also logical. A cold jolt of water, clearing her mind, straining her muscles until she exhausted doubt and fear. Emerging from the water calmer, even though police waited on the shore.

"I'm sorry about Cecelia," Rhoda says. "You were close, weren't you?" She seems to remember Megaphone, and her mouth twists with rare awkwardness. "Even if it was complicated. It must have been a shock to hear the news.

"I thought the vigil would give us a chance to heal. The energy wasn't what I expected." Her hands squeeze, a pulse of frustration.

Dani feels conspicuously mute. She wants to agree: the vigil was spoiled. The news was a shock, even if she was the source of it. She called the police on Wednesday, endured a day of silence before the news was official.

Rhoda crosses her legs. "I have to ask a question. It may be a little sensitive."

Dani thinks of Cecelia's spidery handwriting, the creased note.

"Do you know what Cecelia was doing at the party?"

Dani's ears ring.

"It's just, we're not sure how she got in," Rhoda says.

"I had no idea she was there," Dani says, too defensively.

Rhoda holds up a hand. "I only ask in case she spoke to you. We're trying to understand what she was doing there."

She adjusts her bracelet into place on her wrist. When she speaks again, her voice is hesitant. "Did she ever mention being unhappy? Wanting to hurt herself?"

She looks up, her forehead tense. Leandra's accusation has invaded her office, too.

Dani shakes her head. "It was an accident. I'm sure. She liked to go up to the roof. It must have been slippery. Cecelia wasn't always careful."

Her guilt is immediate. Like she's betrayed Cecelia. Blamed her.

"A horrible accident." Rhoda's voice is reassuring, gentle. "We'll probably never know what happened, exactly."

She's holding her wrist again. Is her bracelet humming? She might be dehydrated, overtired. Dani's own health score is dismal. Her sleep nearly nonexistent, and when she finally succumbs, guilt follows her into her dreams.

"I appreciate your candor. If you don't mind, let's keep this conversation between us. It seems best for me to stay out of the fray."

Dani flinches. *Fray* sounds minor, petty. But Dani's the one being petty. Picking at syntax when Rhoda is preoccupied with larger issues.

She walks Dani to the door. "Grief is exhausting. Be gentle with yourself. Don't torment yourself with questions."

But in the middle of the night, Dani drags Cecelia's suitcase into the living room. She searches every compartment, every pocket, slips her fingers into the torn lining, hoping to find a note, folded like a flower, containing answers.

Rhoda

Saturday

I'm standing on a stranger's balcony, gazing over the crumpled topography of the city. Coit Tower juts from a dark, leafy hill, its cylindrical form as ominous as a watchtower.

The sliding door opens, and a woman in a yellow dress teeters out in precarious heels. Ice tinkles in her glass. She clutches the rail with her free hand.

"Doesn't this height make you nervous?"

"Excuse me?" I need to be nice, in case she's on Twitter, or Instagram, or runs a vindictive publishing platform. At this point, I probably need to be nice to everyone I ever meet. A wearying thought.

"Because it could have been you." She shivers.

I glance back into the living room, at the circles of bland conversation, strained by my presence. They'd rather be talking about me than to me.

Marty, our host, usually throws rather different parties, the sort where you have to put your phone in a locked, signal-proof pouch before entering, and guests prance about in masks, terrified and titillated at the risk of being recognized.

I abandoned Gavin in there, when he didn't want to come in the first place.

"If I skip it, everyone will think I'm hiding," I told him.

I changed my outfit four times, my hair crackling with static, until I was suddenly furious at having to soften myself. I put on a sleek dress with a dramatic slitted skirt. An overcorrection, but it suits my mood.

The woman shakes her mojito, wafting mint. "Did she really jump because she was going to be homeless? Poor thing."

The door slides open again.

"Lonny! So nice to see you." Jason strolls leisurely across the balcony. He accepts her glossy cheek kiss. "Annie's looking for you. Something about ice."

"Oh, I told them . . ." She hurries inside.

Jason joins me, pretending to admire the vista. "I'm surprised to see you out on the town, at a time like this." His wrists dangle over the railing. He's not wearing the watch I gave him, the snake. "And lingering near a high drop, too."

"Don't be ridiculous."

He laughs his soft, breathy laugh. I imagine his toes curling in their red socks. He puts his back to the view, fixes his gaze on me.

"You're the optics expert. I admit, your vigil was a nice effort. A shame it didn't change the story." He clicks his tongue.

Photos of the vigil did make the news, but they showed only the angry women in their Remember Cecelia badges, as if they organized it. I only appear in lurid headlines.

"QUESTIONS DOG SCANDAL-SHAKEN RADICAL FOUNDER-CEO."

"CONTROVERSIAL RADICAL SHE-EO ENTANGLED IN WHISTLE-BLOWER DEATH."

The board is meeting Tuesday. They're reading the papers like tea leaves.

It doesn't matter that they're only selling the most sensational story. There's no proof Cecelia intended to jump, still less that it was a symbolic gesture. If that was the case, why didn't she tweet about it? She was hardly subtle.

But I can't say a thing. Can't speculate, especially negatively, about Cecelia.

Jason rocks on his heels, scoring an unanswered point.

"I came out as a courtesy, to tell you I'm here with a date."

"Has the ink dried on your divorce papers?"

"It's a friend. Maggie Walker. You may know her."

"You're joking."

Maggie is the Valley's favorite female CEO. One of the old guard. She has no personal brand, no charisma, just a wardrobe of neutrals and a hard-nosed approach to costs.

Jason pats my hand. "My dear, being at the top of the food chain doesn't mean nobody below you has teeth."

"Why is Maggie interested? She only works with dinosaurs."

He smiles smugly and turns to go inside.

I catch him by the sleeve, and he recoils, as if he's afraid of me.

"This is as much your fault as mine." I twist his shirt tighter. "Every time I've been aggressive, pushed boundaries, it was with your encouragement. Even the lawsuit was your idea. Why am I the villain?"

Jason shakes himself free. "That's the unwritten rule, my dear. You were in the spotlight. You got all the glory. Now you take all the blame."

He straightens his cuff. He knows I've noticed his absent watch. "Did you think over my advice?"

"Of course not."

He shakes his head. "Don't wait too long. At some point, you'll lose control of the messaging. Better to leave with your dignity intact. Enjoy married bliss for a while. In a year or two, you can reinvent yourself. I see you with a podcast and a book deal."

He heads inside, and I follow, but our host intercepts us.

Red-faced with self-importance—he's just bought a Picasso, hence the little party—Marty wrings Jason's hand.

"Have you met Kaz? He's the one I was telling you about. The next Allbirds, I'm telling you." He kicks out a foot clad in a white high-top. "I'll introduce you."

Jason nods to me, politely, as he goes, like I'm some idiot trying to pitch him, like he can just walk away from our conversation. Like he's in charge, or will be sooner or later.

I'm shaking. As if I would ever leave Radical quietly! As if Maggie could replace me! She's conservative. A literalist, to her bones. She's not a storyteller. She doesn't believe in magic.

On the heels of this thought is the obvious. Jason will close the Well. Radical will be the app, Radical will be data. Without the Well, the business may temporarily thrive, but the brand will wither. They'll outsource production to some third party, but bereft of the story of our ingredients, the promise of purity, the spirit of our quest, our products will feel prosaic, our Voice will ring hollow. Our community will scatter. Eventually, after they reduce all I've built to rubble, they'll sell it off to some behemoth beauty or health conglomerate, cash in.

Give Radical a fighting chance, he says. So he can ruin it. I don't think so.

Gavin is drinking a bottle of beer and leaning against an enormous fish tank built into the wall. A small, pale shark noses the glass. I want to rescue it. Feed it live things, teach it to be a shark. I take Gavin's beer and gulp.

"I told you so," he says.

Across the room, a security guard stands, yawning, beside a Picasso the size of a golf scorecard scribbled with all the panache of a bored child with a broken crayon. The guests have undergone the obligatory admiration. He might as well take it down and seal it in the airless tomb where it will spend its next decades, invisibly accruing value.

"I don't want to be here, but I can't miss it. Is there a solution for that philosophical conundrum?"

"Driving home."

I laugh. I want to look as if I'm perfectly relaxed, standing beside the darting fish. I won't hide away, as though I have reason to be guilty. I refuse to vanish. I'll appear every day, until the story fades. This is a test of endurance. I only need to hold on.

I watch Jason join Maggie Walker on the couch. He crosses his ankle on his knee, dandy in his mushroom-colored trousers and bright socks. Maggie's own feet are planted on the ground, her bottle of beer secured between her knees. Their heads tip together conspiratorially.

In the aftermath of the scandal, I thought Jason would be reluctant to rock Radical. Stupid. While I swallowed candle smoke, he was wining and dining Maggie. He'll sell her to the board as a reset. The practical minivan to my vintage convertible, the dependable ride that will motor us through.

I snap a few photos of their cozy chat, making sure their faces are clear. The head of a public company shouldn't be so brazen.

Dani

Monday

The boar bristles feel soft at first, when Dani places the dry brush against her ankles, but as she sweeps it up her leg, they scrape, roughly. Her skin flares pink. Up one leg, then the other, until the ritual switches from uncomfortable to enlivening. Each pass of the brush wakes her.

She draws the brush lightly up each hip, then up her arms. *Always toward the heart,* Rhoda says. Dani imagines her blood waking, cycling through her body, swelling through the placenta, looping back again. Delivering oxygen, energy, life.

Stepping under the hot shower spray, she feels settled in the soothing surety of wellness. As if a shield of protection has lowered around her, a shell of calm. Her posture is drawn up like a marionette on a string. Her back has briefly stopped its aching.

The feeling can't last. On the broiling bus, it withers, and when she arrives at Radical HQ, it evaporates. A crowd of protestors marches on the sidewalk, screaming with hoarse throats: "Bitten by a snake! Bitten—by a—snake!"

A lurid green snake coils up a posterboard. The words ONE BILLION AT WHAT COST? twist down its length, scrawled in glittering red pen.

The poster waves in the air like a metronome, blockading Dani's path from sidewalk to doorway.

"Bitten by a snake!"

A building security guard tries to usher the protestors down the sidewalk. "Let folks through!" It's the cheerful man who teased Dani the week after the party. The sign comes down on his temple. More security runs in, a whistle blows, the protestors shout. Dani hurries inside.

*

"Thank you all for making it in this morning." Rhoda stands before the All-Hands in a crisp white shirt, her hair parted in a clean line. "We're working with the building to make sure it's safe to come and go. For today, security recommends that people stay inside, if possible."

"We don't all have bodyguards," a woman in front of Dani mutters.

Rhoda speaks slowly, like the Meditation Monday instructor. As if she can change the energy in the room—in the entire city—by force of her will.

"If you're feeling the effects of stress, we'll have a counselor on-site all week. In the meantime, we need to practice patience."

"Or party," someone whispers. The crowd ripples as everyone turns, then pretends they didn't.

Over the weekend, someone snapped a photo of Rhoda at a party, and the image spread across the internet, proliferating until it was as well-analyzed as *The Mona Lisa*. Rhoda stands beside Gavin, elbow to elbow, his fingers brushing her hip. (*Cozy*, someone said.) She wore a slinky black dress (*brazen*). A beer bottle dangled from her fingers (*callous*). Her mouth, bright with plum-colored lipstick, was slightly open. (*Watch out, she might bite!*) Gavin, dressed as if for a different party in faded denim, leaned against a huge fish tank. The internet hive mind identified five endangered species in the cerulean water. (*How many laws can you break in a single image?*)

Leandra French juxtaposed the photo with one of Rhoda somber at the vigil. *Which is truer?*

Rhoda ends the All-Hands without acknowledging the disruption. She must know about the photo. Her appearance is deliberately opposite, clean as a blank page. It reminds Dani of her nightgown, floating around her body as she paced the kitchen. The soft glow of the pendant light over her, the dark windows behind her.

In her memory, Rhoda looks like she's on a stage. *They thought I was dead?*

Her voice rising, angry. Nothing like this morning's serenity.

Which is truer? a voice sneers in Dani's head.

*

Cecelia is haunting Dani. She hangs over her shoulder and smirks as Lis-beth announces a pause on Wedding content. "Everyone needs to come up with five noncontroversial newsletter ideas to fill the gap."

Crisis, Cecelia whispers: *How to sell snake oil without the snake charmer?*

Cecelia stalks the pod. Cracking her knuckles, she inspects the rolling bulletin board covered with photos of Rhoda in her satin wedding dress. Her lip curls.

Her suitcase is back in the hall closet. She didn't leave a note. Dani will never know what she wanted to say. Dani spent the weekend clean-ing, mopping, scrubbing baseboards, emptying drawers, folding her own clothes as neatly as she'd refolded Cecelia's. Trying not to torment her-self.

Jia opens the news on her phone, and a tinny clip of the protest shrieks: "Bitten—by a—*snake!*"

She scrambles to mute it. "God, sorry. Did you know they're still out there? The security guard needs stitches."

Dani flexes her leg. The back of her knee stings where she pressed too hard with the dry brush.

At eleven, she closes her laptop, on which she's written a dozen bad ideas for newsletter content. Her weekly check-in with Rhoda is still on her calendar, but she fully expects Rhoda to cancel, for her assistant to wave Dani away from a hectic scene.

But Rhoda's alone. Sitting intently at her desk, knuckles digging into her cheekbones, computer glow on her face. Dani hears a shrill "sna—" before Rhoda presses it shut.

Dani apologizes. "I wasn't sure if we were still meeting."

"We absolutely are!" Rhoda's voice is bright, as if to show she's un-bothered by the chant. When she crosses the room to sit on the couch, her movements are stiff, as though she's pulled a small but crucial muscle in her neck.

"I expect you've heard that I've decided to pull Wedding content. The atmosphere isn't right for a big celebration. Instead of being a chance for connection, it will only make the discord worse." Her foot kicks under her heavy skirt, her restless energy not completely bridled.

She smooths the fabric over her knees. "All weekend, I asked myself, what can I do? How can we help heal our community? That's Radical's mission. And the answer was so simple, it floored me. What we need is something to lift us up, literally."

She raises her palms, waiting for Dani to get it. "*Lift*. We were going to release in the fall, but I don't want to wait. We need to remind people what Radical is all about."

The simplicity of the idea soaks into Dani like a dose of Lift. All week, she's looked forward to the pill dissolving, calm descending. The spinning arrow of her mind tuned to north, for a little while. Lifted up. Literally.

"You see it, don't you?" Rhoda smiles. Understanding leaps between them.

"I've always taken center stage at launches," she says. "But this time, I want to feature other stories. This isn't about me. It's about our community. Our followers. Radigals. You, Dani. I want your words on the page, your experiences, your lens."

"Me?" Dani laughs, nervous. Really, she recoils from the idea. Her journal is private. She enters a near-dream state to write it, bypassing her conscious, filtering mind to access some deeper vein.

"Yes, you," Rhoda says. "I read your entry from the other day. About your mom staking her plants to keep them from bending in the wind. It's such a rich image. The balance of our responsibility to participate in the real world, even when it's harsh, with our desire to shelter our psyches, to care for ourselves."

She doesn't miss Dani's unease at her journal being read back to her, but she thinks Dani is only reluctant to share her words.

"You are the Voice, after all." Her tone is light but final.

She launches into an overview of the work Dani must do, the webpages to outline, the copy to conceptualize, the testing data to compile.

"You should have access to all the materials, but I'll connect you with someone in the Well in case you have questions."

"Mari?" Dani asks, still scribbling notes. "She gave me a tour last week."

Rhoda's foot kicks. "Mari has offboarded."

For a second, Dani blanks. Then she remembers Mari said she was leaving. Her dry, formal tone not suggesting regret or inviting questions.

"Sadly, Mari was a quasher." Rhoda tugs at the cuff of her sleeve, like it's too tight. "You may need to disregard what she told you."

Dani thinks of Mari showing her the walk-in cooler, pointing out various ingredients. Dani was awed, overwhelmed. Her first week on the job, pressure humming like white noise in her brain. She can't remember anything Mari said.

Rhoda claps her hands, startling Dani.

"Your first major project! The workload might be daunting. Don't hesitate to reach out about anything. Questions, concerns. Middle of the night ruminations."

Does she know Dani's had trouble sleeping? Dani's bracelet warned her this morning, as she tipped back the last drops of a Reboot, hoping to jolt herself awake.

After lunch, the People Team rolls a whiteboard outside the cafeteria. TAKE A BREAK! SWEETEN UP YOUR DAY! A barbershop quartet croons over the speakers.

They've set up an ice cream sundae station. Cara herself, wearing a white cap and apron, is scooping vanilla on demand. Radigals mill about with mounded bowls, dripping sprinkles on the floor.

Olga, Dani's old CW teammate, is ahead of her in line. "Might as well enjoy the perks." Her phone is gripped in her palm, the blue banner of Twitter on the screen.

Dani resists the urge to lean over her shoulder and read whatever Leandra French is saying. The whirlpool tug of negative energy.

Dani asks for a small scoop of coconut milk vanilla. Cara plunks a maraschino cherry on top, the lurid red food coloring spreading a pink stain. She's slightly breathless from the effort of digging into the huge tubs.

"Look who's here!" She waves her scoop.

Rhoda and Lisbeth stroll in. Rhoda wears her public smile as she orders chocolate.

Cecelia would mock this ruthlessly. Distracting adults with ice cream. But it's working. The standoff atmosphere of the All-Hands has relaxed. Rhoda moves from group to group, giving every appearance of random, unhurried ease.

Lisbeth doesn't deign to get ice cream. She joins Dani at the windows. "I heard Rhoda wants to launch Lift in three weeks. Quite a pivot!" She raises an eyebrow. "You know the expression. If you don't like what people are saying, change the conversa—"

Her gaze goes over Dani's head, across the room.

Dani turns. The detective, Lowell, is walking into the cafeteria. He passes the sundae bar, his nostrils flaring at the sweet smell of melting ice cream.

Radigals have backed away, leaving Rhoda alone with her bowl and spoon. She's activated her aura of calm. She stands perfectly still, waiting for Lowell.

His voice is too low for the rest of them to hear, but it makes Rhoda turn to the door. Dani sees her stiffness, again. This time, there's anger in it, drawn tight.

"They're searching the office," Lisbeth whispers. Police are filing past the open double doors, dispersing between the pods.

Rhoda drops her bowl on a table and follows Lowell out.

Cara claps her hands. "Change of plan! The police need to do a quick search of the floor. We'll stay here while they work. Hang tight."

As if she's demanded silence, everyone stops talking. They draw out chairs and sit, hands folded. The Core Team clusters at the exit, like protective chaperones. They stare into the office, watching whatever's unfolding.

Ten minutes pass. You can hear the ice cream melt. Dani's back protests at the hard fiberglass shell of the chair, its curvature arguing with her spine. Fifteen minutes. Lisbeth is bent over her phone, thumbs typing furiously.

Finally, Cara calls the all clear. She assures them that their personal things weren't touched.

"A general sweep," she says, trying for brightness, like decluttering experts have been through, not police.

The energy in the office is disturbed. Chairs are pulled out from the pods, spun in random directions. Team Leads hand out bleach wipes. The floral chemical smell fills the air. Even Jia is silent, wiping down her keyboard.

The papers on Dani's desk seem less tidy than when she left. Did they dig through them, searching for Cecelia's note?

Paranoid. They don't know about the letter.

She shakes out her track jacket, hangs it back on her chair.

When she saw the detective coming up the beach, she hid the note deep in Rhoda's pocket. Instinctively. Like she knew it was trouble.

She wishes she'd never picked it up. Never heard of Carlene Voose.

On the flat-screens above the pod, sales slide downward. Tickets tick up.

Police search Radical, Cecelia whispers. *They confiscate all the good vibes.*

Cecelia was always digging for dirt. She snuck into the elevator to the Well, dug in the archives of Slack. Where did she find Carlene?

Dani's avatar is still ranked in the top five CW workers. The queue is in the purple.

Dani ignores the outstanding tickets. She searches for Carlene Voose.

Six tickets appear. They're all highlighted faint gray: resolved. They're dated from three years ago, the first ticket in May, the last in August.

Dani clicks into the earliest. An error pops up: Message unavailable. Please contact Webmaster.

The other tickets throw the same warning. She's never seen it before.

Maybe her permissions have changed. Or the tickets are so old they've been archived. She adjusts the filter to pull everything from that year, and clicks at random. Every ticket opens. She even finds one she answered herself, as a brand-new Radigal.

She returns to Carlene's results. Stares at the unyielding gray until her eyes sting.

It's late. She's exhausted. She waited for the pod to empty before digging, and now she's the only one left on the floor. The pillars loom, big as trees. Dani skirts them as she walks to the elevator, her bag dragging her shoulder. Her hips throb. The tendons between her pelvis and spine are loosening, making room for the baby. It's astonishingly painful, to come unwound.

Rhoda's waiting for the elevator. She's buttoned a dark coat over her white shirt. Is it the same coat from the beach? The thick, spongy wool. The deep pockets.

What if Dani asked Rhoda about Carlene Voose? There might be a simple answer. Like a light coming on, revealing the frightening shapes as nothing but shadows.

Over the elevator, the floor numbers tick upward. At the last moment, just as they open with a ping, Rhoda glances back to the far corner of the lobby, where the police tape seals off the emergency exit. Stepping into the elevator, she lifts a fist and raps the wall, as though she's knocking on wood.

Rhoda

Monday

I can feel the energy shifting. Loosening. The ice cream social is such an obvious ploy, so relentlessly sweet it comes full circle, feels slyly ironic. "Lollipop, Lollipop" plays loudly, a tune potent enough to replace the snake bite chant stuck in my head.

Yes, I think, dipping my spoon into a dish and ambling over to a new group of Radigals, the energy is easing. The protestors are too aggressive to win much sympathy. Jason will use them against me when the board convenes tomorrow, but it's weak ammunition.

Unfortunately for him, Maggie's board received an anonymous email with the cozy photos of her and Jason, and a hint that the press could easily find out.

The head of a public company can't idly cast out their line: shareholders will panic. Maggie has only been with the company for two years, and her hiring was accompanied by lofty promises. Her departure might suggest she thinks the business is unsalvageable. Her board will summon her, urgently. As I twist my spoon upside down to swallow a dollop of chocolate, Maggie may be standing before a very long table of very disapproving faces.

There's a chance that, confronted with her treachery, Maggie might acknowledge it, and formalize her departure. But I think not. Jason can't extend her a firm offer as long as Radical still has a CEO, and Maggie's far too conservative to take it on faith.

Wrong choice, Jason. He'll have to find another option, and anyone he picks will be measured against the ideal of Maggie.

Undoubtedly the rush of sugar and fat from the ice cream contribute to my artificial sense of satisfaction. The moment the detective, Lowell, walks into the cafeteria, I know I've jinxed myself.

I follow him to my office, a search warrant crushed in my hand, a room of alarmed Radigals behind me.

"We'll be as efficient as possible," Lowell says. "Stay at the party if you like." He lifts his eyebrows, mockingly.

Cynics are like myopic people who think they're farsighted.

On the beach, Lowell kept his expression dour, refusing to be impressed with the house, with me, with Radical. When I told him I went there to unwind, he sniffed. Acted like I was wasting his time with an obvious lie, when we were surrounded by supporting evidence: screaming gulls, slate sea, clean air rushing off the water, entirely fresh since any human last breathed it.

My office door is wide open. Police are already inspecting my shelves, turning over the couch cushions.

Lowell leans a hand on my desk, smug as Columbus. His fingers are inches from my laptop. I grab it, tuck it under my arm. With my other hand, I dial Orson.

"Stay calm, say nothing. I'll be right there."

Two impossible orders, and a vague promise. I hang up and the pressure of my anger and powerlessness opens a black hole in my brain, momentarily rendering it completely blank.

I watch them rummage through my things. There's nothing to find. We're a paperless office; I don't even have desk drawers. They spend ages going through the boxes of brand freebies. They open every one, wordlessly remove jewelry and perfume and vibrators and candles. They search my coat pockets, inspect the lipstick-blotted tissue in the garbage can. Their thoroughness would be farcical if it wasn't domineering.

When they're through, they shrug. They don't apologize. Lowell looks unfazed, like a man in a poker game folding without showing his cards.

Orson arrives as they're leaving. In the lobby, he briefly confers with the detective, then strides over to me.

"You didn't speak? Good."

My office smells of cheap cologne. I light a stick of palo santo—the police shook out the box and squinted at the wood sticks as if they were voodoo. Sharp, sweet smoke fills the room.

"It cleanses the air," I say to Orson's frown.

He nods, deferential. "I apologize that I couldn't arrive sooner. My source at the police called me right after you did. They were in a hurry to act on the warrant."

He settles on the couch, in his thinking pose, ankles crossed, pen flicking in hand.

"It seems the police reviewed security camera footage and saw Cecelia entering the building carrying a purse, which wasn't recovered with the body. Hence the search. They did find it, incidentally. She left it in the fitness center, closed in a locker."

"I don't understand. Why is her purse relevant?"

"Unofficially," Orson says, "I would say the bag was simply a pretext to get a warrant. They wanted to take a look at your office, given that we know Cecelia entered at some point to take your coat."

Gripping my fists, I go to the window. The unfinished tower is beginning to look like a ruin.

"My source isn't directly involved, so the information I have is limited. But my strong impression is only that they're being careful. This is a high-profile case. The mix-up with your identity was an embarrassing mistake. They don't want any others."

A drum pounds in my chest.

"Isn't it obvious that she fell? She crashed a party she wasn't invited to, drank too much, tripped in her heels. What exactly are they trying to figure out?"

"They can't assume anything." He holds up a finger. "That's not to say they suspect anything."

He drones about procedure, due process.

I interrupt. "If they suspect nothing, why search?"

He inhales, but I go on. "Every day—every hour—they keep investigating hurts Radical. An important business in this city, a responsible, active citizen. And they're dragging their feet—deliberately, you say.

That's incomprehensible to me. Do you understand how I feel coming into an office with crime scene tape, walking through screaming protestors, complying with a search that apparently has no purpose? Do they understand the damage they're causing, to the livelihoods of the people who work here, to their reputations, to mine?"

Orson murmurs, soothingly. "You have every right to be angry."

I cut him off. "What's next? What can we do?"

"I assure you, I'm doing everything in my power. It's a delicate matter. I can encourage, but not to the point of interference. That would backfire, badly, I think."

He pauses, waiting for me to translate what he's left unsaid.

If challenged, they'll dig in. Interfere with Radical more. They could subpoena Cecelia's old computer, or crack open her phone. Might find a reference to our "observation." Except Cecelia wouldn't use that delicate word.

At this rate, my molars are going to erode.

Orson's voice flows like ink from a fountain pen. "Let me reassure you that they recognize the need for extra consideration in our direction, too. These things proceed slowly. No news is good news. There's no indication that they're building a case."

Will a lawyer ever admit things don't look good? There are always objections, appeals, retrials, stays of execution. In a court, you can get off on a technicality. You really can get away with murder.

While in the public eye, you can be convicted on the strength of a rumor.

I feel as if tight, invisible ropes are wrapping around me. My life has become a Houdini trick, a steel box wrapped in chains, double-padlocked; my hands are cuffed, I'm upside down, the box is bobbing on top of deep water, but sooner or later it's going to sink. I need to get out of it, fast.

Even if the police don't charge me, Cecelia's death needs to be resolved, or speculation will linger endlessly, poisoning Radical.

Obviously, murder isn't a possibility.

Suicide is almost as bad. They're already saying I drove her to despair.

Out the window, a low cloud drifts over Rusher. Drizzle peppers the window. I hope the rain will drive off the protestors, but at once the sun flares again, and Rusher's flag is as bright as if dipped in fresh paint. Bitter, I turn away.

The only option is an accident.

It's the obvious conclusion. A dark night, a dangerous rooftop. The fog blurring edges, smudging the distinction between roof and air.

Without evidence, even if the police land here, people won't believe it. They'll think I made the investigation disappear. A whiff of conspiracy will trail me forever, like the sillage of perfume.

I ask whether Cecelia had been drinking.

Orson's crossed foot taps at the tempo of my pacing. "As much as I sympathize with wanting to control the story, I have a gut sense that we don't want to impugn Cecelia's name. Insinuations about alcohol, about recklessness—anything with a hint of blame." He shakes his head. "As trying as it is, the passive approach is best."

He sounds so sure. I want him to appear before my board tomorrow, to tell them that our battering in the press is strategic. That, eventually, it will prevail.

I take a seat beside Orson. I mirror his cross-legged posture. "I have an unorthodox proposition for you."

Already I'm picturing tomorrow's meeting. Distracting them with my suggestion to add a new member to the board. They'll be intrigued by Orson's high profile. And I'll seem humbled, giving up some shares, ceding some voting power.

At this point, a few percentage points are insignificant. And I'll gain one voice on the board who's accustomed to difficult clients. Afraid of nothing, as Jason put it.

How can he argue? Hiring Orson was his idea, after all. And he can't deny the fiscal sense of compensating Orson via other methods than our cash flow.

Orson listens closely, nodding. No doubt he has his own angle. Everyone does.

We shake on it. "Pending approval, of course." He winks.

He slides his pen into his pocket, pats it fondly. "As I came in, I noticed that the flowers are rotting in the memorial. I'll speak to the building about clearing it. It's served its purpose, I think."

By the end of the day, my entire being sags. The office is deserted when I leave. I cross the lobby slowly, passing the yellow tape over the door. I wonder if the police took fingerprints. They must have.

On the night of the party, I left through the emergency stairs. I couldn't face the whirl of festivity, the three-legged unicorn, Jason mingling with the Ephraims. The door slammed heavily behind me, sealing me in the intense silence of the stairwell.

Not two paces from the door, I stepped on a piece of glass. The crunch might have been an explosion. My ears hit my shoulders. I was so on edge I didn't even stop to check my bare skin for shards. Bits of broken glass stuck to the sole of my shoe, grinding into powder as I ran down.

Even if he found it, Lowell couldn't possibly guess that the glass had anything to do with me. He doesn't know I went out there. If he did, he'd have said something by now.

I quickly knock on the wall beside the elevator. No more jinxes. I can't assume anything. I'm under a microscope, as Jason warned.

Dani

Tuesday

In the morning, the memorial is gone. Without it, the building looks stark. The only protestor on the cold, gray sidewalk is a woman in a black coat, mutely holding a photograph of Cecelia.

Ducking her chin into her jacket, Dani walks over stains on the pavement where the flowers withered. Cecelia's eyes follow her. She's younger in the photo. Her signature eyeliner is only a wisp. Her slanted smile is happy rather than cynical.

The police found her bag in the fitness center. She must have stashed it there at the party. People say they were looking for a suicide note. Dani is familiar with the mess they must have found: the melting lipsticks and spilled medicine bottles, bits of tissue, uncapped pens. They didn't find anything. She knows that feeling, too.

In the hush of the Well, she tries to refocus, but the journal prompt unsettles her.

What's your worst anxiety right now? As you describe it, imagine that you're handing it over, and you don't have to carry it anymore.

Dani glances up from her screen. The Well attendant stifles a yawn. The white noise in the room reminds her of the sea surging into Rhoda's beach. A black coat dropped on the sand, a dark head in the surging water. The white paper crumpled in Dani's hand, as it was crumpled in Rhoda's the night of the party. Carlene's grayed-out tickets.

Somehow, Cecelia got behind the pop-up warning. She picked the locked tickets.

Anxiety is a tide trying to pull Dani off her legs. It wants to tear her from shore.

What's your worst anxiety?

Executing on a major work project. She hits submit.

You've achieved Lift-off!

A drop of blood lands on her screen. And another. Fat enough to burst.

Her nose is bleeding. She pinches it and rushes to the attendant for a tissue.

She shoves the whole box at Dani and rolls her chair back. "Have you had this side effect before?"

"I haven't even taken it yet." Dani pinches her nose.

The tissue comes away soaked, and the next.

She swallows Lift quickly, still holding her nose. The pill rattles against her molars, dry and brittle going down, tasting of metal.

Lisbeth shows Dani decks from prior launches. Dozens of slides, complete with webpage mock-ups, financial projections, full-color logos.

"I'll handle Operations." She sighs, like she's giving Dani a kidney. "It's going to be a logistical nightmare."

Even as she keeps up her steady stream of disgruntlement, Lisbeth is the most efficient worker Dani's ever seen. She opens the Lift data package and generates half a dozen graphs in under a minute.

"The numbers certainly speak for themselves. Although a sample of fifty-five Radical employees isn't exactly representative . . ."

With a few flicks of her mouse, she populates Dani's first slides. Overall satisfaction: 93 percent. Core benefits: improved mood (91 percent), increased energy (94 percent), decreased anxiety (90 percent).

"That gives you a foundation. The details I leave to you. Good luck."

The scale of the launch is hitting Dani. Her own words have to hold up the scaffolding of Lift. *We need something to lift us up,* as Rhoda said.

Or change the conversation.

She reads through her writing test. Her excitement is pressed into the words like a flower in a book. She remembers her walk so clearly—the morning light on the pastel buildings, the brisk breeze on the cable car, the cool blue cathedral light. Her idea still feels right. The trinity: bracelet, pill, app. The ritual.

Settling into work, Dani's mind clears. The office gossip, hypercharged in the aftermath of the police search, recedes beyond the bubble of her concentration.

She scrolls through every tester's daily ratings for a dozen metrics: positivity, energy, concentration, stamina, sleep. Their app numbers feed in, too. Settings can be cross-referenced: sleep and mood, for instance, or exercise and energy. She can filter almost infinitely, search by keyword, user name, location, age, ratings. She has access to every journal entry.

The scope of the information astounds her. She feels a wave of the vertigo that overwhelmed her when Lisbeth first showed her Radical's sales numbers. Except this data isn't anonymously aggregated. It's particular. Personal.

Data is important, Rhoda said. *But the stories are our opportunity to connect.*

Dani uneasily reads about Jia's recurring anxiety dream, Olga's obsessive calorie counting, Holly's musings on her life purpose. It feels intimate, even invasive.

She skims, hunting for pull quotes. But as the morning passes, a strange shift occurs. The more she reads, the less intrusive it feels. The personal stories begin to seem universal.

She reads about a Well researcher's estranged sister, a woman in Accounts grieving infertility. She reads about ambition and frustration, romance and loneliness, hopes and plans and, more than anything else, self-criticism. *I wish I'd done this. I wish I was like this. I should. I meant to. I failed.*

They're all alike, she thinks. That's what Rhoda means. Reading the individual diary entries is like hearing an orchestra tuning up: the disparate voices, each quavering in its own off key, and Lift like the clear call of the true note, tuning them. Guiding them toward their potential. Making them beautiful.

When she looks up, it's late afternoon. She tugs off her headphones and rolls her neck. She just has time to grab a salad from the cafeteria before the Marketing meeting.

Jia and Laurel are already in the conference room, spinning in their chairs, iced coffees dripping on the table. They don't stop their conversation as Dani sits.

"She loves that cabin," Laurel says. "She features it on the blog like it's her kid."

"First of all," Jia says, "it's hardly a *cabin*."

Dani knows what they're talking about. Leandra French pulled photos of Rhoda's beach house from the blog. The airy rooms, the vast ocean view. *Rhoda's beach house is out of touch in more ways than one.*

Pretending not to listen, Dani pries the plastic lid off her salad. It pops, lettuce leaves spilling out.

"And, seriously, do you really believe it's a coincidence? She happens to go up there just after a whistleblower falls off the roof?"

Dani peels a damp leaf off the table, her appetite vanished.

Laurel sighs. "But she wouldn't be so stupid. Why would she draw attention to herself like that?"

"Rhoda has a thing for attention." Jia leans to sip from her straw without lifting her cup. She raises her eyebrows at Dani. "Sorry, but it's true."

Dani can only shrug. She picks up the packet of dressing and tears it open. She tips it over the salad, not wanting to eat a bite. The vinegar smell is sharp.

"It doesn't make any sense," Laurel says. "Cecelia was gone. The story was down. Nobody was talking about it anymore. What possible reason would Rhoda have?"

Before Jia can argue, the rest of the team comes in, and Lisbeth takes charge, and the meeting runs.

Dani doesn't hear a word. She twists her fork through the leaves.

What possible reason? A note, folded like a flower, hidden in a pocket. Rhoda, looking away from the police tape and rapping her knuckles on the wall.

The ballpark is a bowl on the lip of the Bay, circled by seagulls, swept with wind. The scoreboard and flags puncture the low-hanging fog and it sifts down in a freezing mist over the seats.

Trevor stretches his arm behind Dani's chair, jostles his foot on the back of the row ahead. It's empty—they're sitting in a private box, courtesy of Slim Riley.

"It's just a fringe theory," Trevor says. "You have to climb pretty far down the rabbit hole to even find it. People on the internet will believe anything."

He leans forward, tracking the arc of a ball as it sails through the air, but an outfielder catches it neatly. Groaning with good nature, he bounds up to refill his beer in the indoor annex behind the seats. Eric and Mekin are inside, seeing who can eat more chicken wings.

Trevor insisted on picking Dani up from work. *You need to relax. Take your mind off things.* The baseball game isn't up to the task.

Dani hunkers in her seat, chewing sticky roasted nuts from a paper bag. Her cardigan soaks up the cold like water. She watches advertisements roll across the outfield banner. *Store Your Wallet in the Cloud, Unicorns Use Our Tools, Live Life Mobile, Slow Food Delivered Fast, Our Platform Your Dreams, Does Your CEO Have Secrets?*

Dani blinks. The text transforms. *Does Your CEO Do Payroll?*

An organ belts out a manic tarantella, and a crab scuttles across the field, circling the bases in a demented dash.

"To this guy!" Mekin shouts. "Our hero!"

Dani looks up, startled. The guys are holding their beers up to Trevor. He looks proud and slightly sheepish.

"You saved us, man." Eric is beaming.

Dani makes herself smile. "What happened?"

"He stepped up. We were running out of runway, and he laid down more, just like that!" Mekin beats Trevor's back.

Trevor's smile is shy. "I meant to tell you as soon as it happened, but with everything at Radical, I didn't want you to worry. I bought more of SitFit. I went for it!"

Mekin and Eric hoot.

Dani shakes her head. She's so tired. *Dani, are you sleepwalking?*

"But how? It's your company."

They exchange glances like she's being obtuse.

"I invested more money into the business," Trevor explains. "It was double down or shut down, and I wasn't ready to quit."

"What about the guy who got us these tickets?"

"Slim loves the idea, but he had trouble coming up with the funding. His money is tied up in real estate."

"He backed out?"

Trevor looks wounded. "Well, for now."

"How much did you put in?"

Mekin and Eric retreat inside.

Trevor puts his arm around her. "It's going to be fine, babe. You believe in energy, right? Signs from the universe. The week before I had to make the decision, I met Rhoda. Her advice was stuck on a loop in my head."

"What advice?" Dani remembers Trevor's elevator pitch, his hiccupping exuberance. Her own presumptuous satisfaction that things would turn out fine.

"She said you have to be willing to do anything for your company."

That's right. Rhoda, wrapping her scarf around her neck. *It's simple,* she said. *You have to be willing to do anything to survive.*

"I still have five months of expenses saved. Experts recommend three."

Dani sits back in the hard chair. Her back throbs. Responsibility is a literal weight. It hangs from her hips, drags her spine, curls her shoulders. She and Trevor will both be parents, but she's the one altering, literally, her cells changing in tandem with the baby, her bones ceding their solidity to build a tiny skeleton, her brain mapping new pathways, her blood supply swelling to twice its usual volume. She's filling up, brimming, with care. While Trevor will be a father without a single change, his body paying no toll, the baby only an abstraction in his mind, no more real than the prospect of his startup.

At the apartment, Dani hangs her coat. Cecelia's suitcase is still in the closet, standing in a neat row beside Dani's and Trevor's. She can't just throw it out.

She misses Cecelia. She wishes she could call her, like she might have, a long time ago. Spill out her meanest thoughts. Cecelia would have backed Dani up. Too ferociously. She'd have torn Trevor apart. That's how she was. She took things too far.

You're a fraud. You should be ashamed.

So angry. And maddeningly vague.

Maybe she didn't know what was in the tickets. She might have found them locked and thought the worst. Hoped for it.

Dani switches on the kettle. Dirty dishes litter the counter. The garbage overflows. The Congratulations banner sags over the window. Dani sits where Cecelia sat, rubs her face. She's exhausted. Her worry is incubating like Naomi, growing formlessly.

Three years ago, Carlene Voose wrote to Radical. Three years ago, Radical was tiny. They couldn't have covered up a big scandal. When Dani started, there were only sixty employees. Everyone crowded into the crumbling old office, wearing thick sweaters. Cold air leaked in as though the brick wall was a colander. The single conference room was always occupied by Rhoda, Lisbeth, and Mari.

Mari! Dani can't believe she left, right before Lift's release. All those rave reviews, all the journals attesting to Lift's power.

Mari was there forever. She must know everything that happened at Radical.

A quasher, Rhoda called her, like they'd fought. So maybe Mari will talk to Dani.

She's thinking like Cecelia now. Scheming. Cecelia's voice stuck in her head.

She finds Mari on LinkedIn. She already has a new job in a small research lab. Dani clicks through their site. The language is generic, corporate, uninspiring. Who would leave the Well for this?

In her staff photo, Mari wears a new lab coat, her shoulders braced, unsmiling. Her contact info is listed under her name.

Rhoda

Tuesday

"I'm not entirely convinced it's the right time to introduce a new board member," Jason says, threading his fingers on the table, as if to keep himself from flashing his longest digit at me.

Late-afternoon light slants through the vertical blinds, striping the table. The rest of the board sits around it, arms crossed, wearing sober frowns but nodding slowly as I make my points. I've prepped them for the request in advance; on this, they're all with me, and Jason quickly realizes it. He sits forward, rapping a knuckle on the wood.

"We have more urgent matters to discuss. Since your return, Radical has weathered a series of escalating crises." He lists them, counting on his fingers. "Fair or not, your reputation has absorbed most of the damage. I believe it's an open question whether you can carry on serving the company as CEO."

Though I knew the words were coming, I feel a moment of vertigo, like the recline of my chair might drop back entirely. I hold myself straight, imagine a pillar.

Nobody leaps to defend me. Just two weeks ago, we celebrated; Faye wore sequins, Barry wore cowboy boots. Now their faces are grim, girded for tension.

If they go against me, I'm gone. Of all the mistakes I've made, this was the biggest: giving up control. Allowing the possibility of my defeat.

I clear my throat. I must remain calm. As concealed as a reflecting pool, utterly tranquil, revealing only a smooth surface.

"For the better part of a decade, I've spent every hour of every day thinking about Radical. I check our social before I go to bed. I dream about our products at night. Our community is the first place I go with good news, or to talk through hard questions. It's my life's work.

"Our situation is extraordinary. At the moment, it seems dire. But it's also in flux. We're going to come out of this, and when we do, I'm still the person to lead Radical."

Jason strokes his watch with his thumb. It's the watch I gave him, conspicuously absent on Saturday, worn today, why? To mock me?

With an effort, I keep my blinking minimal. Look alert. Controlled.

"It's important to remember that the protestors aren't customers. The tweeters aren't customers. The noise is loud, but it's coming from outside Radical."

"Are any metrics swinging our way?" Pilar asks. "Sales?"

"We saw an initial downward slope that seems to be correcting. Given normal fluctuation in sales activity, it's difficult to discern trends from so little data."

Chad sighs so hard he nearly blows a raspberry. "The plain truth is that the media is having a field day. You're a symbol for everything wrong with startups, tech, Silicon Valley." He waves a hand over his head, placing himself at the epicenter of the world he's described. "The Rhoda brand is tainted. At this point, Radical exists in spite of you."

A freezing gust blows through me. What if he's right? People fail, companies falter. Before he went to jail, my dad packed his bag and left a day early, because he wanted to kiss me goodbye on his way to a baseball game. What you don't want can happen. You can fall out of step with the rhythm of the universe.

I look down at my wrist. My old digital running watch is cinched, for luck, above my Radical bracelet. Always, in my life, the way through misery is forward motion.

Orson clears his throat. "Bearing in mind that I am new here, I still think it pertinent to interject. Internet discourse always veers toward the extreme. It would be wise to temper our response. In high winds, you hold the wheel steady."

The table nods in his direction, but I focus on Chad. I make an effort to look sympathetic. To pretend I don't know he's only sitting here because my adviser handpicked him, a malleable idiot.

"I can understand that you want to take any course of action that might help the situation. But removing me would send the message that I'm to blame for Cecelia's death. Radical would effectively accept responsibility for what happened. The fallout would be terrible. The most talented Radigals would run for the door. Customers would feel the same way. We'd hemorrhage followers.

"You'd have to rebrand, and it wouldn't be easy. You'd risk looking either callous or fake. You could try to sell, but you'd take a huge knock on the valuation."

At this, the tip of Chad's nose grows as white as his knuckles.

"Keeping me on is a risk, too, but I have more skin in the game than anyone. I'll work harder, fight harder than anyone else, especially an outsider."

Jason's lips curl, too quick for the others to notice. *Maggie's out. Who's next?*

"If I didn't believe that I was the best person to run Radical, I would resign."

"OK," Jason cuts in. "Shall we deliberate? Rhoda, would you mind stepping out?"

As I go, he checks his watch with a show of impatience. Now they can get down to real business. *She doesn't think she's the best person to run Radical; she thinks she's the only person who can. Simply not true . . .*

I pace the hall, abhorring the polished wood and hushed carpets, the art on the walls bought in bulk from galleries, piled-up squares of color whose main appeal is their inability to offend. A veneer of good taste is spread thick over every inch of this place, the polish of profits, utterly dull, with no point of view. The first VC office I visited made me feel small and scattered; now they only make me impatient. Their judgment, like their taste, hovers on the surface. They count feathers, not wings.

A secretary comes to fetch me. I'm so absorbed in my thoughts that for a second, she might be the woman who helped me all those years ago, handing me the simple code to the secret language they were all so proud of speaking.

It's not her, of course. It's a young woman who should love Radical, but instead eyes me like I'm leaving a trail of slime.

Their verdict is in. I get a stay of execution. One week.

I thank them. I ask them to reach out, any time, with any worry . . .

Listening to my little speech, Jason's face is perfectly calm.

One week is nothing, he's thinking. More time for him to select his gladiator, to sharpen his arsenal of weapons, to starve the lion so it pounces, ravenous, onto the field.

He's not sleeping on his yacht anymore. He's staying at the Bastion Club. It's an expensive front. He'll hardly see the inside of his room. He must be spending every minute schmoozing. Staging chance conversations, loitering in the themed bars, sweating in the sauna. *Just between us, we're looking for someone interesting* . . .

Under the table, my nails dig into my palms. To the room, I say, "Radical is barraged by outside noise. It will quiet, and Radical's recovery will begin."

The next morning, showered and pressed as if fresh from a solid night of sleep, I prepare to deliver the All-Hands. To face the sea of faces. To pitch my speech so it carries across the room without raising my voice. To control my expression so I'm neither smiling nor frowning; to hold my body so I'm not fidgeting but also not stiff. To run the clock and pretend I'm not just running the clock.

From my office, I hear them mobilizing. I roll my shoulders.

But when I arrive in the lobby, it's almost empty. The Core Team huddles beside the Radical Woman. The few Radigals in attendance hang back, skittish.

My assistant dashes to catch up to me and delivers the belated news into my ear: "The staff has walked out."

I feel my face morph into a weird smile. I make a remark about our getting used to the unexpected, which is mostly nonsensical but might pass as levity. I send them off.

My team trails behind me as we walk to the Core meeting. The pods are deserted. Coffee cups and pastries clutter the desks. (Free coffee, with local beans, courtesy of me; organic pastry, with whole grain flour, ditto.) In the midst of my petty rage, I pass the Marketing pod and see that Dani's desk is empty, too.

Dani walked out? Dani, who sat forward on the couch as we discussed Lift's launch, understanding my aim. Dani, who drove through the night to find me.

The toe of my left loafer catches on the carpet. I bring my fingers to my earring, feigning an adjustment.

In the conference room, I can't conjure my veneer of serenity. "Who failed to bring this to my attention?"

The silence starts to feel pressurized.

"Leandra French organized it," Lisbeth says. "I overheard."

Cam makes a show of scrolling their touch pad. "Not seeing anything in Slack. They must have planned everything offline."

"I see."

I do see. The photo opportunity they're handing to the press; the video clips that will cycle ad nauseam online. Jason capitalizing on the clamor. *She says the uproar is coming from outside Radical, but it's inside.*

"Moving on. Who wants to kick us off?" I check my watch. The All-Hands should just be ending. *Ignore the haters.* We chant it daily. It hasn't sunk in.

My top brass drops problems at my feet. The usual issues: vendors running late, an entire batch of Skin Polish made to incorrect specifications. Normally, they wouldn't even mention such trivial troubles except to brag about solving them.

We have new problems, too. A large online platform is threatening to pull our ads. The Customer Worship Team's morale is in tatters after dealing with nasty emails for days. The Engineering Team anticipates mass resignations if they lose confidence in the value of their stock options. The magazine naming me Entrepreneur of the Year—that long-ago dinner with Jeremy Krill—has floated concerns.

"They might pull the story," Lisbeth says, her tone matter-of-fact rather than embarrassed. PR is her job, after all.

"Don't let them," I say. "What else?"

They exchange glances, a collective shrug. Nothing that's on us, I imagine them thinking. The protests, the police, the walkout—all are my responsibility, as long as I sit at the head of the table.

None of them is bold enough to openly rebel, but they're all silently tallying up the ways they could do my job better than me. But without me, there never was a Radical. Never could be.

The walkout is over by eleven, just in time for the mob to dig into the free lunch of vegan shrimp. I imagine turning the lights off, throwing everyone out.

I seal myself in my office. All I can do is work.

Work is a bog with flies and stinking mud and hidden sinkholes. The Marketing Team forgot to cancel a Wedding email, and the subject line reads like a missive from an alternate universe. Our unsubscribe rate spikes. Legal calls with the news that Rusher Tower is considering suing for the work delay. A member of the Fulfillment Team emails her resignation letter to the entire Radical LISTSERV: a manifesto against business, lies, and the silencing of "voices." She must cc Leandra French, because the letter is online in five minutes.

I don't look up until my overhead light flickers on. I stand, rolling my neck. I struggled with pain for years after I founded Radical. So many grueling days bent over a computer. Only a stringent yoga practice healed it, but these things never completely heal. The body remembers. The body communicates very plainly.

I go to the window. The evening is clear. Headlights string across the Bay Bridge. I should be joining them. A dear friend is opening a pop-up in Oakland tonight, and before my calendar was wiped, I hoped to pick out something blue. Document it on Instagram, maybe have people vote.

The way it's going, none of the Wedding plans will land. Not the sneak peek into my dressing room for my beauty prep, not the photo journal of the ceremony and reception. I won't share our personal vows to the blog, won't host an ask-us-anything on the honeymoon flight. The merchandise collection will be a net loss.

The cold wind blows through me again.

Gavin made a big pot of his signature lemon egg drop soup. I chase a floating, filmy lemon seed with my spoon.

"What would you think about pushing off the wedding for a while?"

His spoon stalls midway to his mouth. "Pushing it?"

"It's not a great time. I don't feel celebratory. I can't center on any-thing."

"That's reason to do it." He looks at me, fully, and I know he's not fooled by my charade of eating. "It's a ceremony of commitment, cen-tered on us. It's going to be beautiful."

"That's the problem. It will look extravagant. They'll eat me alive."

"Who will? The guests?" Gavin picks up his spoon again.

"You know. Jason, the board, the Instagram minions."

"They have nothing to do with our wedding. Uninvite them all. In-cluding and especially the minions." An edge enters his voice.

"You know what we planned. We were sharing our grand love story. It was going to be beautiful. Uplifting. And now . . ."

"And now?" He's alarmed. He sets down the wine he was pouring.

I draw a hand through my hair, my nails caught in tangles. "We're on different wavelengths, aren't we? I spent the day in a lion's den."

He reaches across the table to take my hands. "Want to trade tomor-row? I went up to work in the garden. Check out these calluses. I'm ready to wrestle the lions." His palms are rough and warm.

"I wish," I say. "But with these lions, you have to be nice."

"Aha." He massages my palms, moving his fingers up my wrists.

"How about City Hall? We get married, no minions, no mess. You don't even need to wear a suit."

His hands still. "Absolutely not. That's not how Rhoda West gets married. You don't sneak off to a municipal office. You get married in the house you made. You face the sea. You think about eternity. You let the energy of the sun bless your vows."

For a minute, I feel like the sun is shining on me. An instant easing in my body.

Gavin does his best to distract me, moving his hands over me, his mouth. But I lie awake long after he's asleep.

I've carefully built my future. Next week and next year, and the year after that. The foundations are already laid. Construction is underway. It can't just disappear.

I have five days.

Dani

Wednesday

The bus smells like the color chartreuse. It surges along Geary Boulevard, heaves to a stop, surges and stops. Dani's nausea swells and abates with it. She leans her head against the filthy window.

She stayed up too late, writing and rewriting an email to Mari. At midnight, she hit send abruptly, and slept badly anyway. When she woke, she had to run for the bathroom. Morning sickness is supposed to be over.

She clenches her jaw. Don't think of being sick.

Cecelia's voice doesn't jibe her for riding the bus today. Trevor's savings—all that money—gone.

Her shoes peel off the floor as she disembarks. She gulps the clean, cold air. Fog hangs low, thick as ice on a pond, swallowing the tops of skyscrapers. The city is colorless, black and white and gray. This early, only pigeons occupy Radical's steps. The Well isn't even open yet. Instead of Lift, Dani settles for a cup of tea, staring at the thick fleece out the window, like it's a mirror into her brain.

The steam rising from her mug condenses on her lip and nose, and she brings her knuckles up, checks them for blood. Nothing.

She settles at her desk. Her to-do list, begun in a tidy spreadsheet, has deteriorated into a mess of Post-its. She presents the launch plan to Rhoda on Monday. Only three work days away, and she'll miss some of this morning for an appointment with her new doctor.

Work. Focus.

The office slowly fills around her. The smell of coffee drifts from the espresso bar. Dani craves coffee. Dark, almost scorched, the kind that jolts you awake just by bringing it close to your lips. She swallows the dregs of her tea and puts on her jacket. She's timed her exit poorly. Everyone is walking to the lobby, linking arms and chatting.

Laurel joins her, pulling a beret over her bangs. "You're coming, Dani?"

They're all wearing coats, Dani realizes. They're gripping yellow printouts.

"Coming where?" she asks.

"The walkout," Laurel says. "You know, to support Justice for Cecelia. Leandra French organized it."

The lobby is swarming. An elevator opens and packs full.

"Sorry Jia was so intense yesterday. I personally don't blame Rhoda." Laurel shrugs. "I'm just going for the material. I'm working on a book proposal."

"We all have NDAs." Dani stands on her toes. She's going to be late.

"When Radical goes down in flames, those won't mean anything. Even if we somehow survive, the story's too good. They can't sue everyone."

Dani startles. *Down in flames?* When the next elevator opens, she squeezes onto it. Downstairs, the crowd sweeps her along like a current. The sidewalk is jammed, everyone jostling for position.

A megaphone squeals. "Solidarity, Radigals!"

Cheers. Phones are held high, documenting the event. Flyers wave. *JUSTICE FOR CECELIA!* An elbow jabs Dani's stomach. Tears blur her eyes, and she shoves through the crowd. She emerges right in front of the speaker. Leandra French, wearing a hot pink blazer and massive tortoiseshell glasses, punches a fist in the air.

Dani recognizes her. It takes her a moment to place it: Leandra came to Dani's party. Danced in her socks to Trevor's band.

That must be where she met Cecelia—Dani practically introduced them.

"We demand a better Radical for Radigals! Radical change at Radical!"

Does Leandra know about Carlene Voose? If she did, she would lob it at Radical, screech it through the amplifier.

If only Mari would reply. *It's not unusual for tickets to be locked. Carlene was just a customer. I can't imagine why Cecelia would mention her.*

Dani's Uber draws up to the curb, and she runs.

Dr. Melinda angles a plastic probe across Dani's stomach, chasing the rapid propeller of the baby's heartbeat. For those seconds, Dani thinks only of the sound. She listens to it as attentively as a voice.

The pressure lifts, and the amplification stops.

"Good," the doctor declares, holstering the wand. "You, on the other hand, are fast. Are you drinking caffeine?" She passes Dani a towel.

"No," Dani says, wiping the rough terrycloth across her sticky skin, wondering uneasily if Radical juices have caffeine.

Dr. Melinda flips through Dani's chart. She's more no-nonsense than Dani expected from a natural birth guru, with the wiry physique of a marathon runner, hair frizzing free of her ponytail.

"Your blood pressure is low. Are you eating enough? Staying hydrated?"

She touches Dani's neck, feeling her glands. When Dani admits to morning sickness, she frowns. "That's unusual. It may be a sign of stress. Are you sleeping well?"

Dani toys with her bracelet. She knows exactly how badly she's sleeping. Her daily health score sliding from bright green to hazard-cone orange.

She says something about work.

"This is your work, too." The doctor sets her palm on Dani's stomach, palpating. "You're building a body from scratch. The best way to care for the baby is to care for yourself. Every meal, every night's sleep is a gift you're giving the baby. Like a savings plan, an investment that will grow her entire future."

Guilt clenches Dani's chest. She's neglected Naomi. She's been careless. Just now—walking through the crowded sidewalk! Her ribs still ache from the sharp elbow.

The doctor recommends high-protein meals, micronutrients to nourish cell development. Dani is to crawl on her knees, forward and backward, for ten minutes a day to encourage the baby into the proper position. Nodding along, Dani resolves to concentrate on what matters. She's making herself miserable. Folding and unfolding Cecelia's note in her mind, worrying, when she knows how Cecelia exaggerates.

Exaggerated.

"Any questions?"

Dani blinks. Her thoughts wandered, even as she determined to focus.

The doctor's earrings are geometric, tiered turquoise shapes that remind Dani of the expensive baby mobiles she's liked on Instagram.

Dani sets her hands on her stomach. "I'm good."

The earrings swing soothingly. "The natural birth experience begins today. I want you to visualize your ideal birth story. Imagine meeting your baby. Many moms find that very motivating."

Dani will return in a month. She's to gain five pounds. She imagines her stomach inflating, her body ripening like fruit. The next ultrasound will reveal the sex. Dani read that a female fetus develops her lifelong supply of eggs in the womb, which means a person's cellular life begins in her grandmother. A chain, linking Naomi to Nadine.

Dani will crawl on the floor. She will eat organ meat (how to cook it?) and take baths (lukewarm) and imagine meeting Naomi. Incredibly, in her immersion in Naomi's growth from blueberry to lime to cucumber, Dani's never skipped ahead, never fast-forwarded to the largest produce (pumpkin?), to the moment she'll meet Naomi.

She's Dani's responsibility now. Naomi, who can yawn, can hiccup, can dream. How can a fetus dream, without memories? Dark aquatic dreams, salty and buoyant.

Outside the office, the walkout is over. Discarded flyers litter the sidewalk. As Dani steps over them, a figure appears on the stairs. It's the silent woman, holding the photo of young Cecelia. Yesterday, Dani only saw Cee. Now she meets the woman's eyes. She recognizes her defiant chin, her spare, steep eyebrows.

Dani looks down. She passes through the revolving doors, her back prickling, like Cecelia's mother is watching her go. Her silence is stark, more painful than a howl.

Dani rides the elevator up, ashamed. She should have spoken, but what could she say? *I was her friend, then I wasn't.*

The cafeteria is crowded. Apparently, the walkout made everyone hungry for bottomless vegan shrimp. Their talk is boisterous, even cheerful, and suddenly Dani despises them. Their outrage is superficial. They didn't know Cecelia.

The curled pink shrimp sweat under the heat lamps. Dani can imagine their sweet, salty flavor, the squeak between her teeth. She fights the clammy rise of nausea.

Don't let the worry gestate. Focus on Naomi. That's all.

She sticks to her resolution, filling a plate with salad, adding nuts, seeds, slices of steak, until her tray is heavy as a dictionary. She carries it to her desk.

Mari's reply is waiting at the top of her inbox.

Dear Dani,

Of course I remember you. I hope you're holding up under what must be stressful conditions.

Due to binding legal agreements with Radical, I am unable to share any details about Radical customers, or about my experiences in the Well or with prior Lift launches.

I'm sorry I can't be more helpful.

Best,
Mari

Dani feels like she's been bopped on the nose with a roll of newspaper. The mild rebuke is humiliating. She can hear Mari's cool, clipped voice, shutting her down.

Maybe Dani was too direct, mentioning Cecelia. She must have sounded like she wanted dirt, like she was as superficial as all the others.

She reads the terse email again, the voice so formal, so rigid. Not even revealing whether she recognized Carlene's name.

Unable to share any details about Radical customers, or about my experiences in the Well or with prior Lift launches.

Dani bites her pen. She forgot Lift launched before. She didn't mention Lift, in her own note to Mari.

She digs up her notes from their tour of the Well.

Rhoda's white whale, Dani scribbled. *Earlier iteration, bad interactions with prescriptions—pulled.*

Dani can't remember an earlier version of Lift, so it must have released years ago, before she was at Radical.

She opens the Customer Worship portal again. The queue is thousands of tickets deep. CW must have fallen farther behind during the walkout.

She filters tickets from the same time Carlene's tickets came in, three summers ago, and searches for Lift.

Fifty-three results come in. A few are queries about whether Lift would return, but most are complaints. Racing pulses. Night sweats. Vomiting. One woman had vertigo. She tripped off a curb, spraining her wrist.

She was furious. Both Rhoda and the Head of Legal were cc'd on her ticket.

But it isn't sealed, like Carlene's tickets. It's right there.

"Hey, you!" Holly's ping springs onto Dani's screen, making her jump. "I see you lurking! I'd love if you could hop in and help, but would you mind exiting? The system is counting you as a head, and it's throwing off our projections."

"Sorry! Yes! Just checking something for a project. Sorry!"

Dani exits quickly.

She opens the Lift Trial data. She's pored over hundreds of journal entries and reviews, but she's always looked at the top ratings. Now she searches for the opposite.

Five reviewers complained of negative side effects. Nausea and dizziness. One complained of overwhelming fatigue. *This is relaxing the way the flu is relaxing.*

Her journals curtailed three weeks into the Trial. For her final entry, Mari wrote *WITHDRAWN.*

The other negatives dropped out, too.

Only a few people, out of a large group. That doesn't mean Lift is dangerous. And Rhoda wouldn't relaunch Lift without reconfiguring it.

Dani's spiraling. She can't be sure that Carlene took Lift. It's hypothetical.

Except that Mari replied to a question about Carlene with a mention of Lift. Mari is reserved, severe, precise. She would have measured every word of her reply against the boundaries of her NDA.

Dani goes back into the CW queue. She moves quickly, hoping Holly won't notice. She searches for Carlene.

Her last ticket is dated two weeks after her death. Someone wrote to Radical on her behalf. To tell them that she died? To tell them she died taking Lift?

One woman's snake oil is another woman's poison. It was the last thing Cecelia tweeted before she fell.

A drop of blood lands on Dani's desk. She pinches her nose and runs to the bathroom. She presses paper towels to her face.

Blood soaks through the towel. It films her fingertips. Dizzy, she leans over the sink, runs the water. Pink swishes down. She thinks of maraschino cherries. The detective coming into the cafeteria. Rhoda's face, still as a pond.

What if Cecelia threatened Rhoda, on the night of the investment round, on the cusp of the rerelease?

Absurd. Rhoda shoved the letter in her pocket, careless, like it was no more than a gum wrapper. She didn't go up on the roof in the rain. It's ridiculous to even think it.

Dani pinches the bridge of her nose. She stays like this, even after the bleeding stops, her fingertips sticky, her ear pressed to the cold tile wall, the bathroom echoing like the stairwell.

Dani returns to her desk. Her hands on her keyboard look queasily unfamiliar. The knuckles bright pink from scrubbing, her fingers puffy, like her skin is inflating.

She has a dozen new emails about the launch. People are pinging her for feedback. All this frenzy in the time it took her to use the bathroom. How long was she gone, ten minutes? She checks the clock. Almost an hour.

She sits up straight. Focus. She opens a link to the mocked-up product page. It looks like a magazine feature: glossy images, splashy headlines, journal passages bracketed in stylized quotation marks.

For some reason, Dani can't read the words. The text looks strange, like it's in a foreign language. Blinking, she brings her face close to the screen. Her brain can't decipher the words. The letters blur. She rubs her eyes. They're hot.

Lisbeth raps her fingernails on Dani's desk. Dani jumps.

"You've got a mock-up already?" Lisbeth leans down to read her screen. "Not bad. That photo's too big, though, see how it challenges the hero? And do you need so much text? The Voice is about substance, not volume. It's cluttered."

"I can't read it," Dani blurts. "For some reason." She laughs, panicked.

Lisbeth raises an eyebrow.

"It's lorem ipsum," she says, like she's stating the obvious. "Placeholder text? Nobody can read it. That's the point."

She looks at Dani like her ignorance is more tragic than blindness would be.

Dani can't handle this stress. It's not good for her, not good for Naomi.

She's making a pitch for a product everyone loves. She has all their data.

I've never felt this good. I used to be so scattered, and now I can concentrate. I can even meditate, my mind is so quiet. I used to worry, all the time, especially at night, but now I sleep like a baby.

Dani's own words are here. *I feel so clear, when before I felt foggy. I feel stronger. It's like I have access to a better self.*

She was sad. She was lonely, sick at the thought of never seeing her mom again. Never having her phone ring, her mom's name flashing on the screen. Dani can't tell her the baby is the size of a grape, a lemon, an onion. The baby can hear, the baby can dream. Dani's mom is missing it. Naomi won't know her, and the sadness is like cold water rising and rising, and Lift is a lifeboat, Lift makes it bearable.

Dani can't stand the idea of Cecelia's skepticism winning. She was a quasher. Mari's a quasher. They might spoil everything for Dani, and for what?

She works until the only light in the office is over her own desk.

Rhoda

Thursday

The vilest parts of the internet climb out of my phone and invade my life.

The beach house caretaker calls. Someone spray-painted graffiti on the front door. The garden is trashed, the tender new plants torn up, tree trunks slashed. There are feces in my copper soaking tub.

She keeps apologizing. I tell her I'm only relieved that the vandals were gone when she arrived. I promise to come up and help deal with it. I hang up quickly, before my voice breaks.

I slide to the kitchen floor. I've been holding myself like I'm in a full-body cast all week. I want to thrash and kick, to pummel my fists against the dumb blank faces of the kitchen cabinets. Then suddenly, without doing any of it, I'm exhausted. I stare at my legs stretched on the floor, pale and listless.

Gavin finds me there. I tell him what's happened. Vandals spoiled his garden. Our garden, where we're meant to marry. Under the sky, at the edge of the sea.

"I need to go up there and deal with it. I don't have time."

"I'll go." A vein stands out in his neck. "I'll take care of it. Maybe it's not as bad as it looks. Gardens can rejuvenate, right?" He hugs me and grabs his keys.

I want to go with him. To drive with the top down, wind buffeting my skin. But I don't want to see it. To have the aura of my beautiful house tainted.

Anyway, I have to go to the office. To sheath myself tightly in tranquility, even though every minute—every second, really—I'm waiting to hear from Orson. Waiting for the investigation to close.

Everyone is back in attendance at the morning All-Hands. No music plays before my arrival. The silence is threaded with faint muttering, almost as quiet as the subliminal messages that supposedly play beneath TV commercials.

Why is she still here? When will she leave?

I am the picture of calm. I'm wearing low shoes, a shirt that ties at the neck with a floppy bow, a shade of lipstick that sounds like a retirement home: *Shell Echo.*

I wish them good morning. I thank them for being here. I announce that Meditation Monday is expanding to a daily practice. I encourage them to take the time, that the benefits are manifold.

"I'm grateful to have Radigals who are passionate about their values," I say, the closest I'll come to acknowledging the walkout. "I share your eagerness for resolution."

Nobody is fooled. There's even a general eye roll at Meditation Monday, though many of them will go. They'll lie on the carpet in little groups, then return to their pods by way of the espresso bar. They won't register the privilege. They'll keep whispering. *When is she leaving? Who does she think she is?*

I need to reconnect with my followers. I've spent all my energy attending to my detractors, which I've always cautioned against. Never pay attention to quashers. You can't change their minds. They'll only drain you.

I need to find a way to tap into the core of Radical, the hot molten place where we forge bonds over shared emotions, reveal our deepest hungers.

I dig through my photos. Will people respond to old pictures, or is nostalgia too obvious a ploy? Do they want vulnerability? Barefoot Rhoda doing a yoga pose, Rhoda in jeans and a baggy sweater sipping tea? A nonthreatening smile, or a pensive gaze? I scroll back months, then years. I can't hear my own voice over all the others: Jason sneering at my obviousness, Leandra French hammering my privilege, followers wondering why I'm not being open, quashers demanding my head.

My bracelet drones like a trapped housefly. Why did I insist on that feature? It only makes me more tense.

I find the Advil bottle buried in the bottom of my purse, chase it with a mix of Radical supplements. I find myself checking Jason's Instagram, squinting at his morning post: a selfie beside the Bastion's Olympic-size saltwater pool.

thatjason Champions don't have breakfast: they work.

Even in goggles, he manages to look smug. His followers are all sycophants who want his money, but the four-digit likes rankle me anyway.

Even if he doesn't find a strong replacement for me, he could win. I'm entirely passive, waiting for the situation to change, for the investigation to conclude. I'm powerless.

He's already got Chad in his corner. He might tip Pilar. He's known her longer; she joined the board on his suggestion. Faye and Barry are peacekeepers; they'll vote with the group. Orson may carry on arguing in my favor, but if the dam breaks, he'll flow with the tide.

A ping from the Well project manager interrupts my circling gloom. She's emailed to ask if she should formally wrap the Lift Trial, since we have no active participants.

No participants?

Dani is the only remaining member of the Trial, so it's easy to find her data. She hasn't taken Lift in days.

Her well-being scores have plummeted. Can't she connect cause and effect? She's still entering manual inputs, so she's aware of her numbers. Yet she hasn't restarted Lift.

I tap my nails on my desk. I've even considered my manicure: cut my nails short, painted them pale cream. I've thought of every detail, bracing for scrutiny, but the joke is on me: I was so careful people are accusing me of being fake.

In the space of a few days, the persona I refined for years has turned inside out.

My no-boundaries openness about every element of my life is no longer vulnerable and radically honest. It's not a bridge between my followers and me, a chance to bond over universal emotion and experience. It's narcissistic.

My milestones, celebrated on social, aren't wins for all womankind, not #girlboss energy. I'm a heartless striver, a hustler. Greedy, materialistic, status-obsessed.

The authenticity I painstakingly proved, year after year, offers the definitive proof of my fraudulence. There's nothing I can say now that won't be drawn into this vortex.

When I faced the board, I was so certain. My connection with my followers was steadfast. It could survive this. But it's not only the quashers dragging at me. Not just outside interference. It's Radigals. It's our own Voice.

I leave the office late, my eyes so dry the lids scratch against them when I blink. I've worked to exhaustion but accomplished nothing. I may as well have stayed on the kitchen floor all day.

I tell Gavin I'll die if I stay under house arrest another night.

We venture down to my car. I walk quickly, with my head up, in spite of Gavin's presence. I keep waiting for someone to jump out, brandishing a placard.

Gavin reaches the car first and swears. Someone has left a pitted scratch down the side. I'm gutted. My beautiful car!

Then I think: Fuck them. It's a battle scar.

I drive north, surging uphill between blocks, sailing across the flat intersections. I turn west on Pine. I hit all the green lights. Lyfts and Ubers stream along with us. What did people do before Uber? Drive drunk? Take the bus? I can't remember. That's another company that takes constant flak. How exactly do people think things get done? Imagine if the industry titans of the past were subjected to the scrutiny and whining of Twitter. Rockefeller, Ford, Carnegie, Vanderbilt. Giants. It's no secret that giants are nasty. They grind bones to make their bread.

Gavin keeps turning to check on me. The wind is so loud it's impossible to talk.

I drive to Ocean Beach. The ocean like oil under the thin moon.

I rest my forehead on the steering wheel. The horn beeps, and I jump.

"I'm going to lose."

Gavin takes my hands. I'm embarrassed by my sharp knuckles. My ring spins. I'm whittled down.

"This is too much. Living in this negativity, under constant attack. You should have seen the garden. It was destroyed. We can start over, plant it again. But what about you? What kind of damage are you absorbing right now?

"I thought you were dead," he says, gripping my hands painfully. "I was as far away as physically possible, and I had to travel half the world, believing that."

"But I wasn't."

"Don't you see? Nothing else matters! We can do anything. Live our lives." His voice breaks. "Why keep up the struggle?"

I want to comfort him, but I'm too shocked at the turn he's taking.

I'm not through struggling. I'll keep going, as long as I'm in the fight. It's not a question. It hardly feels like a choice.

He goes on. "I was terrified to sell my company. It was the most significant achievement of my life. It was mine. In my gut, I knew it would start to degrade as soon as I stepped away. Eventually, it would become something so different it might as well not exist. I had dreams about being dragged by a riptide. Violent, primal fears. The brain is a cautious machine. Especially the brain trained on capitalism. You think you need to cling to what's yours. But change will come, no matter what. There's no holding on.

"At this point, Radical has been a fun ride. Even if you stay, from now on, everything you gain is going to come at a price. You'll have to make compromises to your vision. It's not worth it. Let it go."

The cold wind blows through me again.

Even before the Twitter feed, everything was getting harder. The easy, giddy leaps of the early days were long over. To win every victory, I need to hustle harder, to be wilier, to give more of myself. And with each victory, I'm less satisfied.

I scramble out of the car and run down the beach. The sand is freezing.

I scream. It's not a musical Hollywood scream; it's primal, ragged and raw and hoarse. I run, my ankles rolling, and scream again.

When I stop, my throat feels shredded. The night is indifferent. Water whispers up the sand and sighs back out.

Gavin's jacket falls over my shoulders like a throwing net. He holds me. He radiates warmth.

"It's really fucking liberating," he says. "Not to be defined by something external."

I feel the rise and fall of his breaths. If he wore a bracelet, his numbers would be steady as a metronome.

In a sense, he's right. I have no material reason to stay. We could buy his vineyard. I could retire. Throw my phone into the sea. I wouldn't be beholden to anyone. No more patiently listening as a VC explains my business to me. No more pulling off the high-wire trick of pleasing everyone, of fulfilling the contradictory demands of my investors, who want Radical to grow and grow, faster and faster, infinitely; and my employees, who want an engaging office culture that means something but doesn't ask too much in return; and my customers, who want everything: the magic of the Well churned out in frequent new releases, inspiring content that also keeps it real, vulnerability and perfection. I could let the balls drop, one by one.

Gavin and I could wander the world. (Immediately, my mind flies to Radical, places I want to write about on the blog, ingredients to scout, rituals to practice . . .)

Life without Radical would be like a meal without flavor. A road without a destination. Sports without a score.

Work solidifies the passing of my hours, makes my life tangible, solid. Work builds upon itself, accrues, laying a foundation for the next work I do, bigger, and still bigger, my days amassing something greater than myself. Work is a scaffolding for my future. Work is the promise of an ever-expanding tomorrow.

No Rhoda, no Radical, I've always believed that. But I've had it backward. No Radical, no Rhoda.

Dani

Friday

Feeling illicit, Dani enters the Well early. As usual, the hall is empty and hummingly quiet, but this morning, a sharp chemical smell pervades the cool air. Cleaners must have just come through. The black tiles are beaded with liquid.

She passes the Testing Center, where her third unswallowed dose of Lift waits for dispersal. Part of her is tempted to push through the door, gulp the pill, sink into the trance of the journal. To feel ease fizz through her body, like her blood is effervescent. To continue to believe in the alchemy of Lift, the power of incantation. To trust that the Well is pure.

Her eyes sting from the ammonia cleaner in the air. *There's poison in the Well*, she imagines Cecelia tweeting. She goes on down the hall to the Source Room.

The walk-in cooler is just as Mari left it. A meticulously tidy jungle. Dani scans the shelves until she finds a sealed brown bag holding the chaga. A foul odor seeps out.

Some testers reported issues, Mari said. Dani combed through her notes and found only the briefest mention. *Chaga—mushroom? Fungus? Strong smell.*

She must have suppressed the memory. As soon as she read the words, the details rushed back to her. The rotten odor. Mari's pointed not-quite-a-question. *You didn't report issues, if I remember correctly.*

But Dani was ill for months. She blamed it on being pregnant, even though her morning sickness went on longer than the pregnancy app said was normal, longer than her doctor thought was healthy.

Dani tucks the bag under her elbow and takes it. Nobody stops her.

Upstairs, the kitchen is quiet. The barista is cleaning out the milk frother, making a sustained hiss. She looks up when Dani tips the chaga on a table with a clunk.

The fungus is the size of a kneecap, lumpen and gnarled. Dani hacks away a slice with a compostable knife and lifts it to her lips. The noxious smell snakes into her nostrils. It's hard and dry, like biting into a wine cork.

She fills a cup with hot water and drops the mushroom sliver in. After a moment the water turns khaki. It tastes like dirt, like the breath from a cellar door, like stale traffic exhaust. She nearly gags, but closes her lips, forces her throat to swallow.

She goes to the bathroom and waits to throw up. *You Look Fabulous*, the mirror says. She looks like a ghost. Sweat prickles her forehead. The smell of chaga lingers on her hands. She washes them, holds the wet paper towel to her face.

Yesterday she checked the CW tickets again, compulsive. She tracked the customers who complained about Lift years ago, scoured their Facebook profiles, skimmed their LinkedIns. She learned that the woman who fell off the curb runs a popular Instagram account featuring her Great Dane and dachshund.

She's fine. They're all fine. One even posted a recent bathroom shelfie, her vanity crowded with Radical's bottles.

Dani doesn't vomit. In fact, in a few moments, she feels more awake, more alert. As if a breeze has swept some of her fog away. Almost as good as a dose of Lift.

Exhaling, she leans against the rim of the sink. Lift works for her. It doesn't make her sick. She wasn't wrong. She wasn't hurting Naomi.

Relief opens an easy path. Dani could pack away her miserable doubt. Move on.

Rhoda's spent years perfecting Lift. She called it her symphony. Of course she's refined it, fixed whatever was wrong before.

But Cecelia's ghost is leaning against the bathroom wall, watching her in the mirror, arms crossed. She's forgetting Carlene Voose. Her grayed-out tickets unyielding, offering no reassurance, no easy explanation. Forgetting the coincidence of Rhoda running to the beach house the night of the party. Thanking Dani for her discretion.

Doubt is exhausting. Malaise hangs over the office. At the Marketing pod, Dani alone is working. Laurel prints chapters from her novel and makes edits with Radical's lilac gel pens. Jia shamelessly scrolls a jobs site. Lisbeth is absent, but Dani spots her in a conference room on her way back from lunch (salmon, diligently chewed for the omega-3s that will develop Naomi's brain). She's alone, sitting erect in front of her laptop, nodding into the camera the way people do when they're trying to convey enthusiastic competence. So Lisbeth might be leaving, too.

Late in the day, rubbing her eyes, Dani joins the line at the espresso bar. She'll get decaf. The taste alone might trick her body into feeling more awake. The line stretches across the cafeteria. Dani stares at the gauzy fog. Her heel crunches on something hard. A bright pink sprinkle, a remnant of the doomed ice cream social. Dani's hardly seen Rhoda since. Every morning, she makes her brief All-Hands appearance, as much for proof of life as for any updates.

She's going to be fired, people say. The board is running out of patience.

When it's finally Dani's turn, she orders a half-caf latte. The barista scribbles in marker on the cup. It's the woman Dani startled with her chaga this morning. She doesn't recognize her. She's already looking to the next person, oblivious to Dani's sudden hesitation. She should switch to decaf; she wasn't thinking. The line marches forward, and she shuffles along.

Just then, Rhoda comes into the cafeteria.

The line goes silent. Everyone stares as she walks to the refrigerator and browses the packaged foods. She exudes a deliberate tranquility, like she doesn't notice the quiet. Her face is placid as she selects a cup of fruit salad.

As she leaves, she turns her benign almost-smile onto the line.

"Dani!" the barista shouts. "Latte!"

Rhoda's eyes leap to Dani's. Her smile widens, and Dani must take a fractional step back, because Rhoda's chin tips down, and she keeps walking.

In her wake, everyone exhales.

"What is she *on?*" someone whispers.

Something stronger than Lift, Dani thinks, then immediately knows that's not true. Rhoda is disciplined enough to hold herself this way. To batten down her intensity, that vigorous, pacing energy, so she shows nothing but a calm, inoffensive façade. The effort must be exhausting, but Rhoda is capable of it.

Already, Dani feels guilty for snubbing her. She imagines Rhoda returning to her office, eating her fruit in front of her computer, reading the news, barraged by the nastiness on social.

Could she really leave Radical? It's impossible.

Dani's suspicion is impossible. She's let Cecelia's voice sway her, from guilt more than logic. Rhoda went to her beach house to recharge. When Dani rang her doorbell, she was shocked. She had no idea.

A sip of coffee makes Dani's heart gallop.

At the end of the day, she gets an email from the Well attendant:

Dear Dani,

According to my records, you've missed three doses of Lift in a row. I want to remind you that the effects of Lift are cumulative, and the supplement works best when taken regularly. Let me know if we can find a new time for you to come in, or if you'd like to begin taking Lift on your own: Rhoda has given me the all clear for this.

Dani closes the message without replying, but a few moments later, another comes in. Rhoda's replied to the thread:

Dani, What do you think of building a nudge into the app, a friendly reminder for users if they miss a dose? Something like: *Of course, life gets busy, but I encourage you to recommit to the ritual. I promise: you deserve to bebetter, every day.*

We don't want to sound stern, but do want to drive success. Go
ahead and play with the wording and include with launch materials.
Looking forward to it!—Rhoda

Dani sits straight in her seat, as if Rhoda's watching her.

Did she check up on Dani, after the awkward moment in the cafeteria?
Is this a warning? *You are the Voice, after all.*

Dani's pulse seethes against the bracelet. She's caffeinated, jittery.

It's not strange at all that Rhoda emailed her. The launch is Monday,
of course she's thinking of it. She's waited years for this. Her tone is
friendly. She used an exclamation point! She wants to lift people up, literally.

Lift works. Dani's building the presentation that proves it.

All Dani needs is sleep. She leaves work on time, drowses in her Uber.
(Yes, Cecelia, an Uber, an indulgence, especially without Trevor's
money in the bank.)

She takes a bath, pouring in a generous spill of salts. She performs her
full skincare regimen, every step, dipping her fingers in the golden oil,
breathing in the reassuring smell of jasmine. She swallows a magnesium
pill. She even changes her pillowcase, so it's crisp and cool under her
cheek. She draws up the blanket.

On the ceiling, the fan spins, lightly ticking. The pull-down chains
tremble. A wedge of light sweeps across the wall as a car navigates the
parking garage across the street. Tires squeak on cement. She gets up to
shut the window. Now she can't find the comfortable angle she was just
in. The pillow is hot and crushed, the sheet too flimsy and the blanket too
hot. Don't panic. Don't think about sleep. Don't think at all.

Trevor comes to bed after midnight, shucking his clothes and slipping
into the sheets in his boxers, elaborately quiet, assuming Dani is asleep,
as he is within seconds.

Dani closes her eyes and lies still, because simply resting the body is
almost as good as sleep. Any minute she'll drop off. But soon she's staring at the fan again, the spinning white blades, focusing her eyes to try to
follow one blade in the blurred rush.

Rhoda

Sunday

Digging a hole should be simple. A productive way to release energy. But when I plunge the spade into the ground, it doesn't come up piled with a neat scoop of dirt, as I imagined. It smacks into a rock, jolting my arm. I have to shimmy the blade back and forth to pry it loose. The earth is crowded with stringy roots and pebbles. It's hostile to my efforts.

I wipe my forehead.

Across the yard, Gavin waves at me. *Disconnect. Unplug. Focus your energy on building something beautiful.*

I drive the blade with my foot and hit another rock.

In half an hour, I'm on the freeway, my phone on the dash.

If I only have three days left at Radical, I'm spending them on the grid. Even if no news comes, even if I might as well untether. I'm still Rhoda, for a little while.

Dani

Monday

The conference room windows show a world of fog.

Rhoda is waiting, alone. She seems small, at the foot of the immense table. She's scrolling on her phone, a fuzzy cocoon-shaped sweater over her shoulders.

When she sees Dani, she sets her phone down. Her "good morning" is raspier than usual, her smile tempered with a wince.

"Stress is making me sick."

Angling for sympathy, Cecelia says. *Oldest trick in the book.* She's prowling along the windows, Rusher Tower faint as a shadow behind the pale fog.

"I took two Lifts this morning," Rhoda says. "I've never done that before."

"I didn't know you take Lift." Dani can't conceal her tone of relief.

"Of course!" Rhoda sits up. "I honestly don't think I'd have survived this past week without it. I haven't been sleeping as it is. It's awful, insomnia, isn't it? It makes that nasty voice in your head louder. Whispering all your worries, all your doubts."

Her hand opens on the table, inviting Dani's reply.

Dani's lost track of who Rhoda is talking about, herself or Dani? She imagines Rhoda scrolling bracelet data, finding Dani's shrinking sleep numbers.

Rhoda's shoulders wilt. "Am I oversharing? I'm used to being an open book. It's hard to pull back." Her smile flickers. "I've been getting death threats. The beach house was trashed. The garden, just, torn up." She shakes her head, a line as fine as cracked china between her eyebrows.

"I hope you're doing OK, Dani. The energy is toxic right now. For sensitive people like us, that takes a toll." Her concern feels genuine.

Don't be naïve, Cecelia says.

Dani positions her laptop on the table. "Are we waiting for anyone else?"

She expected an intimidating group. Lisbeth and the Core Team, someone from the Well, maybe Rhoda's adviser.

Rhoda coughs. "I haven't involved anyone else with the launch. Lift is too sensitive to expose to scrutiny just yet."

The lights go down. Dani's slides come up, bright and polished, as though she has no doubts. *Sensitive people like us.* Sensitive can mean secret. It can refer to information that's potentially damaging.

"Lift isn't a product. It's a practice." Dani's voice wavers, but Rhoda will interpret it as nerves. "A ritual that centers emotional, spiritual, and physical wellness."

Inhale. Anxiety has no benefits. Remember Rhoda took two Lifts this morning. And Dani felt better as soon as her own dissolved. She surprised herself, going into the Well elevator. She scooped the pill from the little cup and held it in her fingers, felt the beetle thinness of the green shell. So light it might have been hollow.

She clicks to the mocked-up landing page. The colors are saturated, jewel-toned, connoting the verdure of the Source Room as well as stained glass. The graphic designer drew a medieval-looking cursive *L*, the top loop curled above the stem of the *L* like a snake coiled in a tree branch. The text is in readable English now.

"Each element of Lift is one part of a trinity.

"The app facilitates a mind-body connection. It encourages intentional reflection, and trains the brain to think positively and use visualization to harness the future.

"The supplement fuels a feeling of powerful, all-around well-being. Testers reported improvement in everything from energy to sleep to emotional resilience.

"Last, the bracelet seamlessly tracks your physical health markers. When you sleep, eat, work, the bracelet is always there."

A tap-tap-tap interrupts her script. Rhoda's drumming the table with her nails.

"Sorry! I just got so excited. You're a genius, Dani. This is genius." She props her elbows on the table. "Keep going."

As Dani opens the overall ratings, Rhoda leaps from her chair.

"Let me show you a trick."

She bends over Dani's computer and opens the raw data. She's no longer snuggled in her sweater; it's falling down her back, even softer brushing Dani's arm than her nightgown sleeve was.

"Aha, I thought so. These low scores are limited to a handful of testers. See? They're dragging down the overall results."

She deletes them, and the chart springs from 92 percent satisfaction to 98 percent.

"Is that—" Dani licks her lips. "Are we allowed to do that?"

"They're outliers. They're skewing the results." Rhoda returns to her seat. Her swift change of mood has altered the energy in the room as quickly as a coin flipped.

"Our job is to communicate the potential of Lift to our followers. Remember when I explained the role of Voice? The magic? We're curating an emotional response. It's a delicate task. You'll get the hang of it."

Dani only nods. Her next slides are real words from tester journals. They all believe in Lift, too. But maybe not as completely as their quotes make it seem. Dani handpicked them, culled the best, the clearest. She *curated* them.

"You'll share your story, too, Dani," Rhoda is saying. "A photo shoot with your bump, looking all glowy."

Rhoda herself glows. That's the only word. Dani doesn't understand the dramatic shift.

"This is a game-changer," Rhoda says. "We'll hit the ground running with the launch. We can get back to what matters . . ."

A game-changer. Mari said that about Lift, too, didn't she?

Finally, the weight of questions simply grows too heavy.

"Are you worried that the last Lift release is going to taint this one?"

Rhoda stops folding her laptop, hands flat on the lid. "What?" Her voice is calm but her fingernails whiten as she presses into the metal case.

"I heard something about Lift launching a few years ago . . ." Words squirm from Dani's grasp. "I heard Lift had issues, last time."

"Oh, wow." Rhoda laughs. She sweeps an imaginary hair from her forehead. "You're talking ancient history. There was an earlier iteration of Lift, ages ago, before we had the resources to scale. I had to table the plans. We certainly wouldn't launch anything with issues."

She holds her laptop to her chest and stands. "Thank you, Dani. You've given us a real start here."

On her way out, she squeezes Dani's elbow. Her energy is manic. Dani almost expects her hair to be wet from a swim, her skin freezing from dawn air.

"What about Carlene?" Dani asks.

Rhoda's fingers briefly tighten, stamping Dani's skin pink, before she lets go.

"Carlene?" The question lilts. As though *Carlene* is an entirely unfamiliar word.

"Carlene Voose. The woman Cecelia wrote about."

Rhoda's intake of breath is long, surely exaggerated. "Ah," she says. "You found Cecelia's note." Her eyes close, longer than a blink, as she gathers herself.

She moves slowly, gently setting her laptop on the table and taking the seat beside Dani. Her perfume has a smoky edge. Or she's been smoking. Portioning out her dose of the toxic. She smooths the fabric of her trousers.

"So," she says. Her voice is as controlled as her gestures, and Dani interrupts.

"Carlene died. That's why we pulled Lift."

Rhoda's chin draws back. "Carlene had nothing to do with Lift. What made you think that?" She seems truly surprised, but she also echoed Carlene's name like she'd never heard it before.

Dani explains the tickets, and Rhoda sighs. She presses her fingers to her temples. "No, that's not it at all."

Her expression is strange. Almost sympathetic.

Dani's ears are ringing, like she's overhearing a droning, half-tuned radio station. A warning crackle, just on the edge of picking something up.

"Carlene was an early Radical customer," Rhoda says, her eyes holding Dani's. "A true quester. She wrote to Radical to thank me for sharing my story, and told me her own. She'd been diagnosed with cancer, but it was still early. She was treating herself naturally. With Radical products, among other things. Acupuncture, and spiritual healing. She never felt better in her life.

"CW forwarded her letter to me, and I wrote back. I didn't endorse what she was doing." Rhoda emphasizes these words, as if she's said them before. "But I was encouraging. Weeks later, she wrote again. She'd started riding horses. Her lifelong dream. I asked if she was interested in sharing her story on the blog. We often feature inspiring Radigals, as you know. She was thrilled."

Dani's holding on to the arms of her chair, as if in danger of being thrown.

"Then Carlene's daughter wrote us, on Carlene's account. She asked me to urge Carlene to follow her doctor's advice. She accused me of pressuring her mother. Using her for marketing."

Rhoda speaks faster, defensive. "I never told Carlene what she should do. I didn't know the specifics of her condition. I was only supporting the very real passion in her letters.

"Nevertheless," she says, the formal word oddly detached. "Legal got involved. We canceled the blog post. Legal handled all communication. They thought any involvement from me would open us up to liability."

Her shoulders shrug, a fatalistic downbeat. "After Carlene died, her daughter wrote again. She blamed me. Legal arranged a settlement. Carlene's tickets were sealed."

She sighs. "I like to think I wouldn't have handled it that way, but there was a sense of risk. Especially for Jason—my adviser," she adds, though Dani can hardly follow the sudden swerve. "Radical was expanding. I'd just started sharing my story. People were connecting with it. Jason, Legal, everyone was afraid to jeopardize the message."

Rhoda's words are like waves, surging over Dani. She's talking about her story like it's an asset. The story that drew Dani to Radical, that drew all the women at the Retreat. Dani remembers the collective held breath in the auditorium, everyone under the spell of Rhoda's words. When Rhoda knew the story hurt Carlene. She carried on. Ignoring the risks. The collateral damage. *Only fifty-nine, so unfair.*

"Carlene's daughter fixated on me. She was grieving. I sympathize, but her anger was misdirected."

Dani feels queasy, seasick. An air vent in the ceiling rattles like a lid boiling off a pot, and a cold stream of air slides down her neck.

"I want to read the tickets."

Rhoda's face undergoes a clockwork of adjustments. Surprise, a second of registered hurt, and finally, disconcertingly, that odd sympathy again.

"You've already read them."

Dani is perfectly blank.

"You were the CW associate on Carlene's tickets. Holly took over, so you didn't see the end of the story."

Dani shakes her head. "I'd remember."

"You sent a very encouraging reply. You told her some of your own story. Today, seeing a CW agent write like that, I'd have moved you to Marketing sooner. But back then, everyone was passionate."

Rhoda sounds almost wistful. Dani feels sick. A bitter, metallic burn in her throat.

"I want to see them," she repeats, without conviction. She remembers Carlene's name sounding familiar.

"I'll see what I can do," Rhoda says. "If it's important to you." She seems about to say more, then bites her lip. Sitting back, she fiddles with her bracelet. "This meeting took an unexpected turn."

Dani forgot all about the meeting. Her laptop screen has gone black.

"We help people, Dani," Rhoda says. Her eyes are wide. "My story helps people. Radical helps people. We get hundreds, thousands, of letters, every week, from women we help. Women with stories like mine, illness healed with wellness. We empower women to care for themselves. We have millions of customers. I want us to reach billions. That's our potential. Lift can get us there.

"Our scale is hugely positive. You've experienced it yourself. You told me, at your Voice interview. Radical saved you, guided you. That's what we do. Carlene was an outlier. Her story is tragic, but it doesn't cancel out the good we do. I hope you can see that."

Dani's lilac track jacket hangs from the back of her chair. She still remembers stepping to the front of the All-Hands on her one-year anniversary. Taking the folded jacket from Cara and pulling it on. The whisper of the fabric as she rolled the sleeves. Tracing the red embroidery with her fingertip. *Dani Lang*. How many tickets did she answer, in that year alone? Fifty a day, then a hundred, then more. Tens of thousands of tickets. How many Carlenes among them? She didn't even notice. Her fingers so quick on the keys, brushing away complaints and questions, applauding devotion.

> Dear Carlene,
>
> Thank you for sharing your story. It is amazing, the power Radical unlocks in the body! I also discovered wellness at a low point in my health, and I was transformed. First physically, as my symptoms disappeared, and then mentally. The image I reach for is that the body is like a house, and wellness can clean up the mess, it shines every surface, brightens everything, and if you keep with it, it opens a window onto a garden that you never noticed. I hope that Radical keeps supporting your healing journey!
>
> Wishing you well,
> Dani Lang, junior Customer Worship associate

Dani wants to go to bed. To close her eyes against the miserable, soaking fog.

Instead, she's sitting in a dim booth at the Elite Cafe, sipping a mocktail that tastes of sugared vinegar and fizz.

"I'm sure you killed," Trevor says. "You worked your ass off! Rhoda loves your writing."

He surprised her with the dinner reservation. *We have to celebrate!*

Under his enthusiasm, she senses concern. He thinks he's the source of
her misery. She forces herself to meet his glass in a toast, to feign enthusiasm over the food. It's a Bay Area riff on classic Southern cuisine: fried
free-range chicken and small-batch grits. It's salty and rich. Dani gulps
water.

Their booth is high-walled, sequestered as a confessional. The seat
is wood, worn smooth but rigid against her back. Pain runs like a wire
down her spine.

"I have good news, too," Trevor says. "A friend of my parents is giving up an incredible apartment in Noe Valley. According to my research,
it's the best neighborhood for kids. They'll put in a word for us."

Dani stops slicing the skin from her chicken. Trevor's face creases into
a wide grin. He's done research, he's proud. How does he not realize
they can't afford it?

Behind the bar, a glass shatters. She flinches, splashing water in her lap.

The broken glass and the catcalls. Heat and noise, darkness, the glitter
of a disco ball, balloons and a pulsing beat. The party and the Retreat are
blurring together. Belief and excitement generating energy, making the
air electric, making it spark. Carlene and Cecelia dead. Radical growing
and growing.

She excuses herself, standing dizzily. The high booths loom around
her, blocking her path, like a maze. She's nearly to the bathroom when
she sees Lisbeth.

In spite of the cloistered seating, Lisbeth is conspicuous, speaking ani-
matedly, gesturing with her martini glass, her pale hair over her shoulder
like a mink stole. Before Dani can hurry along, Lisbeth's glance falls on
her, and their eyes meet, unavoidably.

Lisbeth's face drops, then she overcorrects with a toothy grin.
"Dani! Hi!"

Her dining companion is concealed by the deep booth, except for a
hand resting on the table. His large watch reflects the light. His fingers
are curled, tense, at odds with Lisbeth's brightness.

"You must be out celebrating your first pitch!"

Is Dani smiling? She's numb.

"Rhoda was over the moon all afternoon. I haven't seen her as pleased since the party." Lisbeth scoops the olive from her drink, smiling. "Not to bring up a sore subject."

She chews, shielding her mouth with two manicured fingers. "Did she say when she's hoping to launch?"

"Soon, I think."

"It's quite a risk. The wedding bled us dry."

Dani wraps her cardigan around herself. It no longer buttons. How big is Naomi now? An orange, a grapefruit? She thinks of the chaga root, bumpy and round.

"She seems confident," she says.

"Are you? You get an opinion, Dani." Lisbeth's interest seems sly.

The watch dial beams into Dani's eyes; it must have caught the light at just the right angle. The hand retracts. Lisbeth glances at its owner.

"Congratulations, regardless. I guess you were the right pick for Voice for more than one reason." She smiles. "Don't skip dessert. Tell your waiter it's on me."

Back at her seat, Dani plucks her napkin from the table.

So she wasn't supposed to be Voice. That's what Lisbeth means. Rhoda gave it to her because of the Megaphone article. To make it seem as though the accusation was untrue. She promoted Dani rather than fire her. She saved face.

Rhoda lies. She lies easily, and always for her own benefit.

But Dani lies, too. When she took the job, she signed a document for a lawyer that she knew wasn't quite right. She hid Cecelia's note from the police. She deleted the outliers. She made excuses for Rhoda, again and again. She entered the lion's den willingly.

Rhoda

Monday

You can tell a surprising amount about a person from simple inputs. From heart rate and step count, bedtime and calories consumed, rest and activity. From patterns and aberrations. Studied together, an outline forms. Clockwork person or spontaneous type? Night owl or lark? Outdoor, indoor? Dieter or gourmand?

The bracelet is always there, Dani said, and the idea jolted through me.

Without cameras, the rooftop was an unlit stage. The action played out in darkness. Cecelia's bracelet is a narrator.

I go directly from the conference room to my office. I don't reduce my pace, don't worry how I look. I don't even think of Dani, who stays behind, head bowed. I don't berate myself for not realizing that she read Cecelia's note. I'll deal with that later. Purpose and action surge through me, like joy. Better than joy.

Downloading the data package, my heartbeat ticks in my neck. Careful, I remind myself. No mistakes. I need to tell a story with only one possible interpretation.

Cecelia wore her bracelet sporadically, but details accumulate. I still have thousands of data points over one year. I check every input. Clear patterns emerge. Themes. As an incomplete fossil suggests its full shape, I can assemble the pieces, arrange the gaps, to construct a plausible complete picture.

Cecelia was a night owl. She climbed into bed early (her step count drops to nil after 9 p.m.), but she stayed awake late. Streaming shows, I imagine, scrolling the internet. Soaked in blue light. But these details aren't relevant.

Cecelia had terrible periods. She recorded them on her app, perhaps because they were annoying enough to override her distaste for everything Radical. They were irregular but frequent, lasting so long her blood pressure would drop.

In her emails, I find requests for time off and work from home. Cramps, weakness, exhaustion. In one message, two months before the party, she told Holly she had vertigo. *I'm too dizzy to walk to the bus.*

Breadcrumbs. I pick some of them up. I leave others. I don't want questions of chronic illness and Radical policy. No need to introduce Holly's separate documentation to the People Team, which casts doubt on Cecelia's excuses.

When I've reviewed the night of the party, I sit back in my chair. I feel as if a gargoyle has dismounted from my shoulders and scampered off.

I call Orson, walking slowly along the window, one foot in front of the other as if on a balance beam. I explain what I've found.

"Of course, the police may have concerns about anything I provide . . ."

He understands at once. "I'll review the materials. If they're relevant to the investigation, I'll take it from there."

It's only midafternoon. I count, anxiously ticking my fingers. Only one day until I face the board. I pace the carpet, the sun slanting lower, dinnertime passing, the sky cooling to twilight. My phone starts to ring.

At dawn, Cara sends an email to the company.

I'm already in the office, walking the teal path, admiring the soft colors of the pillars, pink as Himalayan salt. For the first time in ages, my body is vibrating at the same frequency as this space.

Dear Radigals,

Last night, our Legal Team learned that the investigation of Cecelia Cole's death has been closed, with a determination of accidental death.

We want to extend special thanks to the Data Team, whose analysis of Cecelia's bracelet proved invaluable in deciphering the moments before the tragic accident.

We also want to thank each of you for your faith and perseverance
as Radical weathered uncertainty and loss. As ever, you make Radical
better.

Radigals arrive early for the All-Hands. They touch their own bracelets self-consciously. It was a risk to draw attention to what they can
do, but most people will forget soon enough. Convenience outweighs
caution.

"Good morning." I'm wearing a crisp suit. My heels tower. From
where I stand, the faces look like an ocean, their shifting motion rippling
like waves.

"I trust you've read Cara's email. I hope you feel as relieved as I do to
get closure.

"I'm going to speak honestly. These past two weeks have been im-
mensely challenging. Before them, I would have said that Radical was
the core of my identity. I would have happily admitted I was a founder
and CEO in every atom of my being.

"The past days shook that belief. My entire sense of self was up in the
air. It was painful, and humbling, to realize Radical is so much bigger
than me."

The lull is pregnant. They're holding their breath.

"Radical is more than a place to work. It's a movement. It's greater
than any one of us. To work at Radical is a privilege. We change the conversation. We push boundaries. We dream the future into being.

"It's not going to be easy to move forward from here. The urgent task
of rebuilding our followers' trust begins immediately. I can promise you
I'm going to do everything in my power to restore the Radical community. I hope that every single person in this room is all in to join me."

I begin to clap. A few seconds pass before they join. They have to
recalibrate. *She's not leaving.* Let it sink in.

I hold my palms together in a gesture of prayer. "A special Well product helped me through these last weeks, emotionally and spiritually:
Radical Lift.

"Lift is the most incredible supplement we've ever made. We planned
to release in the fall, but I can't wait. I want to literally press Lift into

people's hands. For the first time ever, every launch day order will be free!"

The ocean of faces ripples. Some of them stand rigid against the current.

"Because Lift is completely tailored to the individual user's story, this will be a community launch. Our campaign will feature the voices of Radigals and followers. It's not one lantern released into the air: it's millions.

"I hope you join me in looking to the future with optimism."

At Radical, we share the Well, we quest harder, ignore the haters, always bebetter, can't be stopped, Radical, Radical, out on top!

The All-Hands generates energy again. Finally, after weeks of low wattage, we can shine. Several Radigals approach me to shyly confide that they were in the Lift Trial. Others slink off to drink cold-pressed juice and count up their complaints like the currency of a collapsed regime.

I'm willing to forgive and forget the walkout, the grumbles on Slack. But not after today. If naysayers persist, I'll weed them out. Thinning the ranks will appease the board, anyway, soften the cost of offering Lift for free. I don't want to declare victory too soon, but I'm almost impatient to meet them, to pack away the idea of a *leadership transition* for good.

Now only my customers are left to appease. I agonized about how to win them back. A rebrand? Another Retreat? Then it struck me: no need to be subtle.

A free launch. It's going to be a stampede. The only catch is that you must order Lift through the app: download it, set up a profile, all those tedious tasks that, once completed, vastly increase usage.

The Core Team meeting is like old times! The review of weekly team performance is laced with an implicit warning. *Back to work, catch up!*

Only Lisbeth ventures a challenge.

"Are we ready to launch Lift without Mari?" Her arms are crossed. She's wearing a Chanel jacket I've never seen before.

"Lift was perfected before Mari left. The logistics are our job. Anyone who thinks they can't handle it, speak now or forever hold your peace."

They laugh. They cut eyes at each other. I don't think any of them will go. Their latest batch of options doesn't vest for two years.

After the meeting, Lisbeth tails me. "Do I get to see the Marketing plan, or are we trusting the junior person on my team to handle it?"

"I'll share it with you, but I'm confident in Dani."

Lisbeth winces, as if it pains her to go on. "I ran into Dani this weekend. She seemed surprisingly unenthused for someone who just designed their first launch at the hip of the CEO."

"She's not one to brag."

"I can tell the difference between modesty and lack of enthusiasm. I told her I was surprised, after you went out on a limb giving her the Voice role."

Lisbeth strolls away, stroking her hair like she's comforting a small child.

Her motive is easy to uncover. Over the weekend, she posted a photo of her hand holding a champagne flute, the cuff of her new jacket flipped just so. From the peripheral details, the oxblood walls and jam jar water glasses, I recognize the Elite Cafe. One of Jason's favorite haunts.

How disappointing, for both of them.

Rusher Tower crawls busily. It's good to hear construction again. Like an exorcism, purging the ghost. Orson is parsing my penthouse lease for loopholes. Maybe I'll venture to a different neighborhood. Up to Pacific Heights, elbow in among the pearls and politicians.

Standing at the window, I roll my neck. My body's recovery will be slow. No way to hasten that along. Only time, and gentle effort.

I'm surprised that Lisbeth was astute enough to mention Dani. When I floated her for the Voice role, I must have gushed about her intuition, forgetting Lisbeth's sensitive ego.

I didn't spot Dani in the ocean of Radigals this morning. She took Carlene's story hard. She thinks it's at least partly Radical's fault.

Legal must have agreed—they certainly rolled the rug up tight.

They didn't see it like I did. Maybe few people would.

Carlene wasn't stupid, or naïve, or afraid. She narrated her own story. There's power in that, no matter the ending.

The question is, can Dani see it that way? She's sensitive. Insightful, even shrewd, about the power of Radical. Surely she can accept that no good thing is perfect. Some degree of gray is inevitable in any enterprise.

Dani found Cecelia's note and said nothing to the police. She didn't pass it to Leandra. Even as she nursed doubt, she planned the Lift launch. She still believes, I'm sure of it. She's too smart to join the quashers, to leave now, on the brink of all we're building.

I'm almost sure.

I sit at my desk, open a browser. What Dani needs is a gesture of faith. Luckily, I have an excellent memory for names.

Dani

Wednesday

Lift isn't a product. It's a practice.

Dani's words stretch across the wall, each letter as tall as a truck. Rhoda stands in front of them, passionately describing how she relies on Lift. Part supplement, part meditation, part DIY therapy. She pauses for a laugh.

The conference room is filled to capacity. Every Core Team member, every Team Lead, Senior Designers, Sales, Product. Lisbeth leans against the whiteboard, her sleeves rolled to her elbows. The room is humid as a locker room.

"Before some releases, I feel a bone-deep intuition that they're going to be big. Lift gives me that sense, times a thousand. It's going to change the way people think about mental health and self-care. It will generate a current that alters the direction of the future." Rhoda gestures at the words behind her. "Lift isn't a product . . ."

She moves swiftly on to the business plan. Units in production, expected sell-through, margins. People fire off questions.

Dani shifts in her seat, minutely adjusting her posture. It's strange, hearing her own words juxtaposed with sales and profits, her careful mantra turned into a catchphrase.

She feels absurdly naïve. The machine of Radical is in motion. Lift will launch, outliers firmly removed. Millions of people will use it.

Radical is about making money. Beating last month's numbers, which beat the prior month's, a ladder lifting them higher and higher, until their customers are like people glimpsed from an airplane: tiny specks, quickly left behind.

"Moment of truth," Rhoda says. "I've written the announcement myself." She waves her phone in the air. "Let's send it out, shall we?"

After a dramatic pause, she presses her thumb to the screen.

An empty x-y axis appears on the wall. Seconds pass. Rhoda's hands lace together at her heart.

Data starts to appear. A line, moving up to the right. It must be email opens. People reading the letter in real time. The line accelerates. Climbs toward the ceiling.

Applause fills the room. Rhoda turns on her heel, her smile huge.

"Let the next chapter begin!"

The cheers are giddy. Rhoda moves through the room, clasping shoulders.

Dani slips out. She feels feverish. Her bracelet must register the spike in her temperature.

Sun floods the office. Dani is dazzled by the pixelated grid of computer screens, the flush of people's faces. Everyone is hurrying. Rushing between pods, hustling in and out of conference rooms. They clench their phones, constantly twisting to check the time, to read an email or take in a chain of Slack notifications.

Back to work! I hope every single one of you is all in. Rhoda's rallying cry—or threat. Either way, it's worked. They're back to business, as if the past weeks are already a distant memory, the present metabolizing the past at an alarming rate.

As if the question of how Cecelia died was all that mattered, not the fact that she did.

Dani bypasses the pod and shuts herself in the meditation room.

The dim silence envelops her. The waterfall trickles down the wall, bubbles into a dark pool. Dani hasn't been in here since Cecelia caught her sleeping. Before the Voice interview, before Leandra French, before Cee knew Dani was pregnant. She might have guessed, watching Dani peel her cheek off the rubber yoga mat. She only stared at her phone. She'd built a firm, transparent wall around herself. Negativity, Dani thought. Cecelia was a complainer. That's just how she was.

Really, Cecelia was sick. She withdrew from Dani, from everyone.

A coping mechanism, self-defeating but understandable. Unhappiness curls around itself. Dani should have recognized it: she'd been there, too.

She stares up at the shaggy bonsai trees shading the false stream. Her bracelet digs into her wrist bone. She tugs it off. Her bare skin registers the tiny change in weight, the easing of pressure. A thin pink line crosses the blue of her veins where the bracelet was tight enough to take its readings.

Cecelia used to spin her bracelet on her desk like a top. She mocked it, but it was collecting her data points, proving that she really was sick. Her pain was real.

Cecelia told her, but Dani ignored her. She thought Cecelia was exaggerating. Maybe even faking it. *She's just negative. That's how she is.*

The rest of the day, Dani's hyperaware of her naked wrist.

Though she is theoretically at the center of the launch, her inbox full, her chats chiming, she feels static. She's referenced, consulted, eyed as if for luck, like the Radical Woman.

She develops a tic. Swiping into her phone, opening the Radical app, and blinking at the question mark that's replaced her daily health score. Her data inputs are grayed-out.

Each time, she exits the app, puts her phone face-down on the desk, reminding herself there's nothing to check, only to find herself back again a few minutes later.

She never realized how often she opens the app. Without it, she's unmoored, slipped off of the grid. It almost feels illicit.

Cecelia laughs at her. *You don't need it,* she says. *You can spit out the Kool-Aid.*

But her amusement is also angry. The caution tape has come down from the lobby. Rusher Tower hammers and grinds. The flat-screens over the pods are already back in the yellow. Leandra French has taken down her website. The landing page shows a stylized megaphone logo. *Back soon . . .*

Dani moves between meetings in a daze. The Marketing Team needs to get sales back up, stat. Product needs to deliver thousands of extra bracelets in preparation for launch. Dani needs to choose Radigals to share their Lift journeys on the blog. Rhoda's already put Dani's name on the production schedule. Her photo shoot is next week.

Radical is accelerating. Faster, higher. Leaving Cecelia behind. Soon she'll be a distant memory, like Carlene. Discarded like an outlier, so the rest of them can go faster.

The bus's chartreuse smell is in Dani's hair. She climbs the stairs slowly. (Four flights! How will they do it when the baby arrives?) She kicks off her shoes. She can tell Trevor's not home: the apartment is gloomily dark. Outside the fog is so thick it threatens to burst at any second, fill the air with rain. Exhausted, aware of the germs on her jeans, embedded in the wool of her coat, she crawls into bed and pulls the covers up.

Dani sleeps.

The gray windows darken to black. Makeup smears her pillowcase. Her coat sash tangles around her ankles. Inside her, the baby gives an experimental spin, settling a foot into the canoe of her ribs, lifting and lowering with her breaths as though on steady waves. Naomi might be dreaming, but Dani is not.

Outside, a car door slams. There's a frenzied jangle of keys dropped, retrieved, and crammed into the lock. The curving staircase shakes under stomping feet.

"Babe!" Trevor runs into the bedroom, carrying the smell of beer and expensive New American cuisine—fat and salt and lemon—on his clothes.

Dani's eyes open. She rolls to peer at him. "What's wrong?"

The hallway light spills into the room, and she rolls away again. The door to the thick velvety world of sleep is still open. She only needs to shut her eyes . . .

The lamp clicks on.

Her fingers cage her eyes, but it's too late. The world crowds in. Her purse dropped on the floor, her phone humming with emails, the bracelet on the nightstand. The alarm clock snaps away the bottom left segment of an eight, turning into a nine.

"You're not going to believe what happened." Trevor bounces his knees against the bed. "It's real this time. The ink is on the contract. Proverbially. Is that an adverb?"

He tugs down the zipper of his SitFit sweatshirt, worn with matching SitFit T-shirt. The tails fly as he spins across the room.

"We got a call this morning, from some lawyer. Super abrupt: my client wants to see you, ASAP. Are we free after lunch? Normally, we vet everyone. We're not amateurs. But today, we said, fuck it, let's go. We all Ubered over, pregaming on Monster. The tension was intense. Nobody said it, but it was like: last chance, nail it or die.

"So we go inside, and guess who's sitting at the table? Dani? Can you guess?"

Dani opens her eyes. "What?"

"You mean who! Rhoda! Rhoda fucking West! We snap into action. And we are on. Boom, boom, boom, transitioning, hitting every point, dunking it. And Rhoda's poker-faced, firing off questions. But she signed. She's in, Dani. It's happening!"

He hoots.

Forgetting that she's supposed to roll onto her side and push herself up with her arms, Dani sits up, struggling, her stomach like a heavy bowl on her pelvis.

"You mean, she bought your company? Just like that?"

"Yep! I pitched her in the elevator, remember? I work for Radical now. Wait until you see the check, you're going to freak out."

Punching the air, Trevor struts off to the bathroom.

Dani slouches against her pillow. She came up too quickly from sleep. Her brain feels pressurized, like a diver with the bends. Her fingers reach to toy with a bracelet that's not there. Did Rhoda notice that she removed it?

Only this morning, Rhoda was celebrating in a crowded room, announcing Lift to the world: the busiest person in the busy office. Yet she found the time to meet Trevor. To organize the complex paperwork needed to acquire even a tiny company, though her check can't have been tiny, based on the fight song Trevor is belting in the shower.

A tipsy elevator ride can't possibly have persuaded Rhoda to acquire SitFit.

Dani circles her wrist. She imagines her pulse quickening. Her deep sleep line broken off. It won't resume tonight.

Rhoda

Thursday

In the morning, I drive down to face the board. Traffic is murder, but I'm cheerful. Gavin texts a picture of the garden, where he's working alongside landscapers to rebuild the destroyed meadow by tomorrow. Already, it looks lush.

For once, I beat Jason to the meeting, and it's at his own conference table.

The murmurs of good morning are cordial. As chairman, Jason is in charge of running the meeting. Nobody wants to set the tone too soon. The vote for my removal remains on the agenda, though it's not even a question at this point. They're following my Lift launch updates with rabid interest.

I didn't quibble. There will indeed be a removal, though not mine.

Jason arrives a moment later. He's applied his cologne with more of a splash than a mist.

It's probably difficult to get dressed on the yacht. He's checked out of the Bastion Club. I imagine him on deck, drinking and staring at the sky until the stars turn to milk.

"Everyone ready?" He pushes his glasses up the bridge of his nose, his watch flashing. "Thank you all for coming today.

"I want to lead off, although I have no doubt that Rhoda has prepared a persuasive, heartfelt statement." His smile is as small as the last shrimp on a platter.

Our eyes meet. Old habit. We could communicate a memo in the span of a blink. Strategy shifts, questions, apologies, amusement. Now all I think of is meeting his eyes in the mirror the night of the party, finding disdain.

I'm curious to see what hand he'll play. My sullied reputation? Wipe the slate?

He sets his hands flat on the table.

"It's no secret that I doubted whether Rhoda could continue to serve as CEO. In my consideration of replacements, I found better business minds, more competent operations managers, and steadier tempers. I did not, however, find anyone with Rhoda's knack for pulling just the right card from the deck at just the right moment.

"As such, I personally move to keep Rhoda West on as CEO. This past week, she's soundly rebutted my strongest concerns. However we may diverge in opinion, we share the desire for Radical to thrive. I'm convinced that Rhoda, together with the varied minds and viewpoints at this table, will competently lead Radical into the next phase."

He turns to me, offering a little bow. "I hope I didn't embarrass you by delivering the speech here and now, without the customary ritual of sending you out of the room. I wanted you to hear my endorsement, on the record, so we can continue our strong working relationship."

An electric current is zinging through me.

Pilar is already seconding the motion, and Faye is offering her support, and Orson lifts both thumbs, and Barry gives a nod, and finally Chad, having no choice but to fall in, taps his pen to his temple in a sailorly salute.

"It's unanimous." Jason smiles, sly as the joker card. "May she climb to towering heights."

The meeting dissolves, rushes away from structure, like champagne spilled from a bottle. Against his endorsement, I can't formulate an argument, can't articulate his betrayals, can't point out that, while the CEO has proven her worth, the chair has not.

He's called off the game at check, before I could call checkmate. He tapped out before the knockout blow. He's a coward, and he smiles, delighted, rapping his knuckles on the table to call for order.

"I'm sure I speak for everyone when I congratulate Rhoda on her nuptials. I'm keen to enjoy the ceremony without a cloud hanging over us."

Dani

Friday

The morning of Trevor's first day of work, he brings Dani a glass of fresh-squeezed orange juice, made in a fancy new machine taking up half their countertop.

"I know what's going on," he says. "People crash after huge projects. I've seen it. It's like a return to earth after riding a rocket. Your system is shocked. It'll pass."

Dani took a sick day yesterday. She really did feel ill. She nearly put on her bracelet to see if she had a fever. Her bones ached. (She sounds like Cecelia! The pain in her pelvis sharp as a knife, hot as oil.)

"You better get up," Trevor says. "The car is coming soon."

He's already dressed, his hair wetting his collar.

She drinks the juice. It's sweet, delicious. Paid for by Rhoda.

She won't let Trevor tell her how much he got. Clamps her hands over her ears, making him laugh because he thinks she's afraid of jinxing it. *We don't have to worry anymore*, he says.

Dani takes a long, weak shower, washing with a cheap bar of soap that stings her eyes and films her mouth with a chemical taste. She longs for Radical oils, the rich gloss on her fingers, the practiced gesture of dry brushing, visualizing her energy flowing, surging. She misses her affirmations. And Lift. Most of all, she misses Lift.

Cecelia would mock her. Longing for comforting routines, her self-centered rituals. With everything she knows, how can Dani possibly miss Radical? She should hate it, as purely as Cecelia did.

The truth is, the structure of Dani's days was trellised to Radical. Without it, her routine has collapsed. She forgot to look at the pregnancy app to learn how Naomi is developing. She didn't add collagen to her tea, skipped her vitamins.

Her brain is still loaded with fragments of Radical's wisdom. Drink a full glass of water as soon as you wake up and finish your shower on a cold rinse to close the pores and pat your face don't rub it and dry your hair with an old T-shirt instead of a towel to prevent split ends and skin-care is more important than makeup and chew your smoothies because the digestion process begins in the mouth and inhale into the diaphragm not the lungs or the stomach and exhale for longer than you breathe in and meditate every day and choose an affirmation, which isn't exactly the same as a mantra, though the difference is subtle, the kind of thing only really understood by those who get it, all of it: the merino wool underwear and the rose quartz rolling up your cheeks and across your forehead like your mom's fingertips used to trace before bedtime, and the oils applied to pressure points, and the cotton string bags instead of silky plastic grocery bags and glass water bottles filtered with a stick of charcoal, and all the habits that stack up, brick by brick, to build a secure foundation for life.

Where can she put that knowledge now? She can't simply delete it from her consciousness, when it's woven through so completely.

At precisely eight thirty, a black car draws outside Dani and Trevor's apartment, just like the one Rhoda takes to work. The atmosphere inside is frigid and pure, like the air over a glacier. Dani slips on the leather upholstery, her back shrieking. She holds the handle over the door, bracing herself. They drive on the street she walked, brainstorming for Lift. The pigeons pecking at the sidewalks are the same she scattered with her feet. Concierges hose the sidewalks outside tall stone buildings. Here's the hotel Dani stayed in when she moved to the city. Its grimy awning is coated with an extra three years of dust. She was so thrilled she didn't even notice the dirt.

"What if I decided to quit?"

Her voice is jarring in the silent car. The driver's head twitches, though he's too professional to turn around.

Trevor turns toward her, bewildered. "But you love Radical."

She shrugs, avoiding his wide eyes.

Trevor completely believes in Rhoda's enthusiasm. *We're at the vanguard of wellness—she said that!* She can't tell him Rhoda bought his company to appease Dani. To persuade her to ignore the outliers, twist the magic of the Voice into an excuse for lying.

They ease to a stop at a yellow light. A cable car jangles through the intersection, ringing its bell. Dani wishes she were on board, hanging on to the strap, wind in her hair.

"You must be exhausted. You've just come off a huge project. And, of course, losing Cecelia, that was horrific. A complete shock. You've been dealing with a lot."

He picks up her hand, but rather than squeezing it, he turns it in his, touching her fingers, her rings, like an engineer inspecting a malfunctioning gadget.

"You shouldn't make such a big decision right now. Give it some time. Let's see how this next phase feels." His voice grows more certain. "Whatever you decide, we'll be OK." He strokes her bracelet.

He didn't notice the drama of her taking it off, or the tentative way she cinched it back on this morning, just before walking out the door. She imagined the sudden leap of data into silence. Like the start of a musical score, a jump on a seismograph.

The peppy soundtrack is back. *I'm happy—happy!* The Radical Woman shines. Trevor grips his backpack straps, rising on his toes. He looks like Dani must have looked on her first day. Awed. All in. He spots Eric and Mekin and makes his way to the front.

Dani hangs back, answering his confused pivot with an apologetic wave. The music cuts off, and his attention turns.

Rhoda strides into the room.

"Good morning, beautiful humans!" Her voice is as enticing as ever. Hoarse and deep, compelling you to lean forward. "It's a beautiful day for good news."

Dani watches the faces track Rhoda, like sunflowers turned to the sun.

"I have an exciting announcement. Radical has acquired an experimental health company, which is right in our sweet spot of technology and wellness."

Rhoda calls Trevor up, and he shakes her hand, winningly confident.

She scans the crowd, looking for Dani, as if she expects Dani to be up there, clapping. As if her money promises a future so bright it can obliterate the past.

But she doesn't see Dani. Her jaw seems to tighten, though Dani may be imagining it. In the next breath, she begins the cheer. *Ignore the haters, always bebetter, can't be stopped!*

Dani's already weaving between the pods, gone before the final shout.

To whom it may concern, Dani writes. Meaning Rhoda. Lisbeth won't be concerned. *I tender my resignation, effective immediately.*

The language is unnatural, stiff and constricting. It takes forever to write a few sentences.

Her bracelet buzzes. It seems ultra-attentive this morning. She wonders if some tiny change, a break in the pattern, gave her away. *A quasher,* the system will flag.

Radical is like a web woven around Radigals, capturing the motions of each day and the shape of their striving in its weave. What story could Rhoda spin from Dani's data? She already guessed at Dani's insomnia. She could blame Dani's unhappiness on lack of sleep, poor nutrition, pregnancy hormones, her cold-turkey withdrawal from Lift. She could choose the facts she liked, tell a story that suits her needs, like she did with Carlene. And Cecelia.

Dani logs into the data aggregator. She's only ever looked at the Lift Trial, but the bracelet data is easy to find. With a click, she opens Cecelia's archives.

The office seems to retract, as if Dani has slipped behind a curtain, or through a secret door, behind which a vast machine covertly churns.

Cecelia's tracking began at six, the night of the party. She must have slipped on the bracelet, hoping it would help her get past security. A flash of the ubiquitous silver band to prove she belonged. Her heart rate ran quick. Nerves, or excitement.

Dani scrolls along the tracking line, as it wanders up and down—was Cecelia ducking through the lobby, here? Joining the group photograph? Did she get a drink at the bar? When did she leave the note on Rhoda's desk?

At 9:46 p.m., her heart rate elevated. At 9:51, it soared. It rose through the levels of alarm color-coded on the chart: yellow, orange, red-orange, red, maroon.

Then it stopped.

Dani holds her breath. She doesn't want to see this. Cecelia's last minutes recorded, like a film without image or sound. Although Dani can't help imagining both.

At 9:46, Cecelia must have been climbing the stairs, breathless, giddy from delivering her note. Her bracelet registered an ambient temperature drop at 9:47 as she stepped outside. Her pulse steadied. Was she gazing at the city lights, gulping breaths of air, triumphant at scoring a point over Rhoda? Or maybe she was hiding from the party. The chanting, the speeches, the Radical fervor. It must have depressed her, seeing Rhoda unscathed.

But her heart rate was normalizing. She was calm. She wasn't gearing up to jump.

She only stood for a few moments. Suddenly, without preamble, at 9:51, her heart rate flew. Her panic lasted several seconds, awful to imagine. Horror expanding like a parachute in her heart and lungs, flailing and futile.

Then a sudden, full stop.

Dani closes her eyes. Don't picture it.

"Dani?" Fingers rap her desktop, inches from her laptop screen.

She's jolted back to the office. It's a surprise not to see everyone dressed for the party, the lights dimmed and balloons drifting across the carpet.

Laurel is standing by her chair. She doesn't glance at the strange netherworld on Dani's computer but gestures for her to get up. "Come say goodbye."

The team is huddled around Lisbeth. She's packing a box with rigid movements. Her mouth is fixed in a smirk, as though the side of her lip is tacked to her cheek.

Jia touches her elbow, and she jerks away. "It's fine. It's not like I'm surprised."

Her voice is clipped, as if she wants to be curt, but she can't resist going on.

"I committed treason, after all. Disagreeing with Rhoda. It's funny, the bigger she's gotten, the more closed off she is. I remember when she listened to other people. When you could have a different opinion and debate. Now it's Rhoda's word or nothing."

Her cold blue eyes land on Dani, and her vitriol seems to, as well.

"Learn from me. Take credit for everything you do, or she will. If you stay, that is." She snorts. "If any of us stay. More heads are going to roll." She hoists her box onto her hip. "Don't be strangers."

The team lingers around her empty desk, dumbfounded.

"Shit," Laurel says. "What do you think she did?"

"Do you really think the rest of us will be fired, too? I've heard of whole marketing teams just—pfft!" Jia mimes slicing her throat.

Dani returns to her computer. Cecelia's data is still up. Dani adjusts the filter to show every bracelet, and thousands of rows run down the page. All this data. It can answer the question Dani hardly wants to think of.

Was Cecelia alone on the roof?

Holding her breath, moving as fast as Lisbeth built her charts, Dani filters by location, and adjusts the ambient temperature field to pull drops between 9:45 and 10 p.m.

The results page empties—almost. Two bracelets remain. Cecelia's. And another. A bracelet labeled with a number rather than a name.

At 9:48, bracelet #713 left Radical HQ. Five minutes later, they came back in.

It might be a coincidence. Someone stepped outside to vape, or meet a car.

Dani checks the heart rate data.

The line syncs with Cecelia's, almost exactly. Ten seconds before Cecelia's heart leapt, this line leapt. When hers stopped, it stayed high, holding a long, frantic solo note, even after the bracelet came inside again.

Someone was on the roof with Cecelia. Someone whose emotion surged before Cecelia fell.

It can't be a coincidence. It can't mean anything else.

Dani's bracelet buzzes and buzzes.

Does Rhoda have an anonymous bracelet? Palms slick, Dani searches.

No. Rhoda's data is entirely accessible. Her every action is tracked all day, every day. Radical transparency, like she says.

Dani sits back. She feels alert, awake, for the first time in days. Like she's taken a dose of Lift—several doses.

She looks at the profile for #713. The data begins on the night of the party and cuts off at 11:49, never to recommence. As if they threw their bracelet into the sea.

Dani stands, her chair spinning behind her. "Has anyone seen Rhoda?"

Her teammates startle.

"You mean, since she fired Lisbeth?" Jia asks.

Dani doesn't bother explaining. She tugs her laptop from its cord.

She hurries along the teal path, peering through conference room windows, scanning pods. No Rhoda. She spots Trevor in a conference room, scribbling on a whiteboard, and speeds up, hoping her alarm is invisible.

Rhoda's office is dark. A note pinned to the door reads *Gettin' hitched!*

Dani parked Trevor's car under a red-flowering tree three blocks uphill, and hasn't touched it since the morning of Rhoda's return. Now, rotted rusty blooms dot the windshield, pooled in sticky sap. She stops at a gas station to scrub them away, ripping the sleeve of her blue dress in her haste.

Trevor texts that he's going out with new coworkers tonight, want to meet up?

Have fun, she writes, one-handed, pulling into traffic. She can't slow down.

Out of the city, across the Golden Gate, through the suburbs, into the country, the same journey she made that strange night, when instinct told her to find Rhoda, before her quiet certainty was replaced with corkscrewing doubt. The low sun smears the scenery with light, but it's still sinister. The windmills spinning out of sync, the thorny wire fences, the blackbirds dense on the power lines.

Dani drives as if someone is following her, slowly gaining.

She speeds through Rhoda's town, up the narrow, private road. This afternoon, it isn't quiet. Ahead of Dani, two gleaming black SUVs turn into Rhoda's driveway.

Dani idles in the road. Through gaps in the trees, she watches the cars wind up the drive. They stop. Doors slam, and Dani sees flashes of bright clothing, hears the muffled sound of voices and laughter. Music is playing, a rattling cymbal.

Rhoda's having a party. She's getting married tomorrow. Dani forgot.

A yellow Corvette pulls up behind her, beeping its horn, and Dani drives up the road. High fences surround unseen estates. She parks on the shoulder, lowering her window. The trees shake in the ocean breeze. She can just hear the festivities. It's cocktail hour. Dani imagines Rhoda eating and drinking, her face bright.

Dani waits.

Rhoda

Fríday

Candles collapse into puddles, releasing the mild sweetness of beeswax. The white tablecloth pools in my lap, and Gavin's hand tunnels through the fabric to find my thigh. My feet are bare in the grass. Paper lanterns glow overhead. The wine-warmed laughter of my guests drifts into the night.

Peace, finally. I sit back in my chair. Inhale the tang of topsoil. The garden rustles in the breeze.

A fork sings against a glass. I pretend to protest. "That's for tomorrow!"

More glasses chime, and Gavin kisses me. He stays close a moment, cupping his hands around my face, shielding us.

"Are you all right?"

I nod. Kiss him again. The scratch of his beard. His taste, like bread. All is well.

A wolf whistle zips up my spine. It's Jason, from the far end of the table. His glasses flash in the lantern light.

My fingers tighten on the tablecloth. His presence is like a beetle, small but utterly spoiling. He should be drinking alone on his yacht, ousted, out of my life.

I smile. I'll pretend his insurrection is water under the bridge. I'll wait. He thinks he's more patient than me. Eventually, he'll relax, and an opportunity will open.

I stand, arranging the taffeta ruffles of my skirt. I'm wearing bright red, like the flamenco dancer emoji. I'm celebrating. The battle is won. Radical lives another day.

"Thank you all for being here, wonderful humans. I can't tell you how good it feels to feel good!"

I take Gavin's hand. His nails are marked with dirt from his patient work. He's looking up at me, his shirt open at the throat, a gold chain dipping down to his heart.

"Tomorrow, I marry this man. How lucky am I? Gavin has kept me alive these last few weeks. I mean that very literally, as in he's made sure I've eaten and slept."

I pause for the smatter of soft laughter. I can't joke too openly, absolutely can't complain. Let it go, Gavin says. Keep moving.

When I didn't quit, I thought he might be disappointed. That after imagining a future without Radical, he wouldn't want to go back to the frenzy of it. Most men would turn bitter, ferment like booze. Not Gavin.

We put in an offer on the vineyard this morning. We'll grow grapes, and an herb garden for Radical. My instinct is that we should veer toward the elemental.

Gavin stands, rocking on his heels. "The last time I spoke to such an important crowd, I'm pretty sure I had printed MapQuest directions sticking out of my pocket."

He grins through their laughter, at ease with himself. "I'm glad my pitch worked on Rhoda."

Tomorrow night, we'll set off fireworks on the beach, a grand finale to the wedding. Tonight, the candles quietly sputter out. Two by two, and then en masse, the guests depart.

Gavin and I kiss good night. His parents no longer drive in the dark, and he ushers them to his car. He'll stay at their hotel. I want to sleep alone tonight, not see him until I walk up the aisle. Old superstitions have power.

Inside, the caterers are wiping the last wineglasses. My planner, a miracle of efficiency with a steel braid, promises to return first thing in the morning.

The sound of the last retreating car engine is so sweet I could weep. I haven't had a break in weeks, a clear breath.

The moon is as round and yellow as my paper lanterns. It lights the water like a spotlight over a stage. It's bright enough to take a walk on the beach.

"Stunning," a voice says, making my heart kick.

It's Jason, prowling across the grass. His hands are clasped behind his back, as if it's perfectly ordinary for him to be lingering in my yard. Malingering. Is he drunk? Or only delusional? A Napoleon, refusing to go off to Elba.

He draws alongside me. The steps are before us, railings bright in the moonlight.

"This must be spectacular in the daytime. You never invited me." His voice is wounded, teasingly, or maybe not quite.

The sand glows along the dark curl of water. My idea of a walk is spoiled. I lean against the stair rail.

"The party is over," I point out.

His smile is opaque. "We didn't get a chance to talk. I wanted to make sure to congratulate you."

"You don't congratulate a bride. You offer best wishes."

"For you, I'll wish the best of luck." He chuckles, an oily, satisfied sound. "But I wasn't referring to the wedding." He crosses his arms. The dial of his watch flashes in the moonlight.

My vision clicks into sharpness, as though a correcting lens was held up to my eyes, revealing the painful brightness of reality and the extent of my myopia.

His watch dial is unbroken, shining. No scratch. No patina.

I reach back to grab the rail.

Running down the stairs, the night of the party, I stepped on a small piece of glass. It crunched under the sole of my shoe, and fragments of it ground into the steps as I ran down. I didn't stop to wonder what it was. I only worried that Lowell would know I was there.

"I hope you'll forgive me," Jason says. "I was only acting in Radical's best interests." He's toying with me. He doesn't think I know.

I picked out the watch myself. I asked the dealer which was the most valuable, and he lifted it from his velvet-lined briefcase carefully, as if handling an egg. I remember the weight of it in my palm, the cold disc of the dial. I wasn't impressed with the banged-up face. I ran my nail along it, scraping the nicked glass. *Patina.*

On Marty's balcony, the week after the party, it wasn't on his wrist. It must have been at the jeweler's. He was wearing it again a few days later, at the board meeting. Sweeping his thumb along the new dial.

He's telling me that he hopes we can move on, put the unpleasantness behind us.

"What time is it?" I ask.

He's surprised, slightly irritated, at the derailing of his little honeyed speech. He hasn't yet unwrapped whatever poisonous morsel is at the middle. He twists his wrist.

"Nearly ten. Has Gavin instated a curfew?"

"You've fixed your watch."

"Ah. I wondered if you would notice." He shakes his wrist. Nerves. They don't enter his voice. "A silly mistake. It came unclasped, and I stepped on it in the dark. Clumsy." He coughs. "I considered scratching it deliberately, but that felt like cheating."

"I stepped on it, actually," I say. "In the stairwell at Radical."

He stiffens. His glasses flash white.

"Maybe if I hadn't crushed it, the police would have found it. Asked different questions." Anger enters my voice, a tightness like something coiled around my throat.

I realize I've lifted my hands, that my fingers are gripped into fists.

He clears his throat. "Don't be ridiculous. Are you suggesting I killed Cecelia Cole? That's a wild swing."

He's perfectly still, watching me. I recognize this stance. He's proud of his poker face, his flat blandness in the face of argument. He sees my raised hands as excessive emotion, a weakness. I lower them, but can't unclench my fingers.

I can read him exactly, yet I missed all the signs. I underestimated him.

We fought in the glare of the bathroom. I left him, his face red, his shoulders stiff. I went to my office. He came after me. But instead of turning into my hallway, he must have seen Cecelia, crossing the lobby in my coat. She went out the emergency stairwell. He followed. Up the stairs, her heels clicking. Out the door, into the dark.

"You killed me," I said. "Or meant to."

I feel the heat of the day through the soles of my feet, and it might be my anger.

He didn't look for me. An unidentified body outside Radical, and Jason didn't check the beach house. He let the police presume it was me, because he thought it was.

When I walked into the boardroom, he stumbled back. His blood drained. I was a ghost, haunting him. Only I wasn't dead. That must have been much worse.

"Don't be ridiculous," he says. His lips are curled. He's smug. He's going to deny it but not bother to be convincing. "I could never do anything like that. I'm not capable of real action. You said so yourself. I'm as flimsy as a checkbook."

His face is as tight as it was when we confronted each other in the bathroom mirror. He has the audacity to be angry with me!

"A bit of glass means nothing," he says. "You'd better be careful. You've only just convinced the police it was an accident. I'd hate to see them doubt your word."

I step toward him. "You—" My hands are still in fists at my side, but my anger is a force, like electricity.

Jason flings out his hands, warding me off, his snarl cracking the smooth arrogance in his face. I hear a whimper, high-pitched enough to pinch at my ears, but it doesn't come from Jason. It might be a strange birdcall or a mouse being devoured by something in the grass. Jason turns his head, with a city person's alarm at wild sounds.

Then, in an instant, the snap of a finger, his face goes slack with shock, like he's seeing a ghost, again.

Then he's gone. He drops off the stairs, vanishes without a sound.

Dani

Friday

The force of the push sends Dani stumbling backward. She lands clumsily, the impact singing in her wrist. Maybe it's broken. It's buzzing, buzzing, her bones reverberating with it.

It's her Radical bracelet, humming out an alarm.

She grips her wrist, feeling the panicked quick of the bracelet, like a rapid heartbeat, dut-dut-dut, and worry for Naomi crimps her throat, makes it hard to breathe. She looks up at Rhoda.

Rhoda's hands are held high, a gesture that makes Dani think of surrender, entirely unlike her.

A wave of dizziness makes Dani lie flat on the grass. All the stars look like comets, racing. She shuts her eyes.

Dani had been crossing the lawn, hurrying. She'd waited what felt like hours for the party to wind down, for the guests to depart. She was half-running, eager to find Rhoda, her news coiled in her throat. Rhoda didn't answer her doorbell. She wasn't at the trestle table in the garden, under its constellation of paper lanterns.

She was standing at the edge of the yard. A man was with her, standing very close. Not Gavin, but her adviser. The moon shone on his skull.

Their conversation was intense. Their voices rose, carried across the lawn.

Dani slowed, uncertain. Then Rhoda lifted her hands into fists. For a second, she looked like Cecelia, pugilistic, defiant.

Dani's knees hollowed, as if she was on the swaying roof.

Rhoda's hair was piled in a bun on top of her head, as Cecelia often wore hers. They didn't really look alike; polar opposites in manner, voice, movement. But in the dark, if they stood still. You'd see a woman's silhouette, the hem of a dress blowing in the wind, high heels. Rhoda's coat.

Someone might have seen Rhoda that night. Someone who knew she went up to the roof. Someone whose bracelet sang in unison with Cecelia's, and then disappeared.

An outsider could throw away their bracelet with no one noticing, while a Radigal never could.

#713.

Dani began to walk faster. Rhoda cried out, her voice distressed. "You!"

She didn't need Dani to tell her, but Dani was running anyway.

Rhoda was backed against the railing at the top of the staircase. All those steps, plunging down. Jason reached out, grabbing at her.

Dani didn't think. Her instinct was fierce, protective, total.

She ran, a shrill protest in her throat, frantic as her buzzing Radical bracelet. Her arms were stretched out as she collided with Jason, the jolt knocking her back.

She sits up, awkwardly, wincing as she pushes off her sore wrist. Rhoda is still standing, eyes wide, chest rising like she's the one who ran.

Jason isn't lying on the ground, Dani realizes. He's not groaning and staggering to his feet. He's not gripping the stair rail, stunned. There's no outraged shout. Only the ocean, and the accelerated beat of Dani's bracelet.

Jason's gone. He's gone. Dani's pushed him.

Rhoda

Friday

I'm not dead. The joy of it shoots through my body, from my toes to my fingers, the pure physical delight of being alive. *You don't have a body—you are a body*. It sounds like a warning, but really, it's an exultation. You are a body! Your senses skim meaning from the soup of the world, your muscles spring, your heart beats, your mind fires off electric sparks. You're a body, a body!

There was a moment, facing Jason at the top of the stairs, that I could imagine the drop of gravity, the terror of a fall.

I can see him, a dark smudge on the white stairs far below. He tumbled nearly to the beach. It's a steep staircase. Built sixty years ago, with the house, before modern safety regulations.

The triviality of this thought makes my throat tighten, suppressing a laugh, or vomit. Jason has fallen down my stairs. The stairs where, tomorrow, Gavin and I will pose for photographs, where our guests will venture during cocktail hour, daring each other to take off their shoes and dip their toes in the surf.

Jason, who intended to push me. Jason, who almost ruined me. The sheer force of my fury might have shoved him off the edge.

But it wasn't me. It was Dani, letting out that high call, that soft, stricken battle cry, rushing out of the dark and colliding with Jason. Where did she come from?

She's fallen back onto the grass. Her eyes meet mine, dazed.

I turn away. I need time.

I descend the stairs carefully, holding my dress up to my knees. I stop just above Jason. Blood angles across his brow like a beret. His arm is caught on a stair post, bent at the elbow, as if giving me a final salute. *Good luck, my dear.* I bring my knuckles to my teeth, tapping them hard. I can't panic. There's no time for grief or fury. I pass through the narrow aperture of shock into the heightened, wide lens that opens when I'm under pressure. My mind leaps ahead. To police, thronging my yard. Orson making his way up the shore, a mint rolling against his gums. And, soon, the press. Wolves circling Radical, incisors dripping.

I shake my head, blink this image away. My mind runs through scenarios. I might go inside, pretend ignorance. An accident. He was drinking.

It will never work. Another fall, another body. The police, the press, disaster.

The night is cold and shining. A line of white moonlight stretches along the water to the horizon. It looks like a road.

Jason swims every morning, without fail. Tomorrow morning, he would do the same. There's a public beach a few miles away. He would drive over early, swim out. After tonight's party, he would be hungover, dehydrated. He's not used to the ocean. He might find himself deeper than he expected. The waves are larger than they look from the beach. Riptides stalk the shore. It wouldn't be unusual if his body were never found. In the unlikely event that it is—well, the story's told itself. No reason to look too closely.

Six steps down to the beach. Then a tug into a boat. The tide is obligingly high.

I take another step down, then stop. I've forgotten Dani.

I grip the railing. The image of the empty stairs in tomorrow's bright sunshine flickers, threatens to blink out.

I left her dazed on the grass. Dani, who appeared from nowhere, as though I manifested her. She seemed expectant, as if waiting for me to explain what she'd done.

Dani's curled herself tightly, her knees drawn to her chest and her chin tucked.

I kneel next to her. "Are you all right?" I keep my voice neutral. An excess of emotion, even sympathy, might undo her completely.

"Is he?" Her eyes are wide, pleading.

I pause, give her a few seconds to understand. "That was quite a fall."

She clumsily stands up off the ground. "We need to call an ambulance."

I grab her hand. "Slow down, Dani. Take a breath. There's no rush."

The implication jerks through her. She leans toward the steps, craning to see, still tethered by my hand. It's best if she doesn't see him.

"You came out of nowhere." I keep my amazement gentle. I can't express the shock of it—Jason flying, and then turning to see Dani, ferocious, avenging, certain. "How did you know?"

"He was on the roof with Cecelia." Her words are halting. She's still staring at the gap between the railings. "I found his bracelet data from the party."

My breath comes fast through my nose. The bracelet! I gave one to every investor for the photo op; I set them up myself. I forgot about them. What an oversight! No wonder Jason sneered at me. He thought he was invincible.

"I came here to tell you, but then I saw you fighting. I didn't think. I just ran. I didn't mean—" She's on the verge of overwhelm. If she panics, we'll be lost. I can't hurry her along. Slowly, slowly . . .

"He just told me. He said he thought I was Cecelia, in the dark."

A bitter, curdled laugh escapes against my will. The reality of the situation closes in on me like a trap. The fact of a body, lodged on my stairs, spotlit by the moon, the night before my wedding. I feel feral. I press my lips together. I cannot lose control.

But my panic calms Dani. The pull on my hand eases as she steps toward me.

"We'll call the police," she says. "We'll explain everything. It was self-defense."

"Was it?" I watch her closely, her frown of confusion.

"He was going to push you." She's sure of it. Certain that the truth is objective. Simple.

"You hit him from behind. He was no threat to you."

She protests, but I go on.

"I'm fucking grateful, believe me. You saved my life. But we can't prove he was threatening me."

"The bracelet—"

"I believe you. But what will the police think? They've just accepted bracelet data telling another story. Now I'm going to contradict that? Tell them I got it wrong, but this time it's right?" I shake my head. "They won't trust the bracelet again. They'll think we made it up. Manufactured new data to cover ourselves."

She's about to argue, but I can feel time ticking on as though Jason's watch is on my own wrist.

"You'll be dragged into it, and because of who Jason is, and who I am, you'll be infamous. You'll be in the news. They'll dig up anything they can on you, and fixate on the most damning details. They'll twist your friendship with Cecelia, your work at Radical. They'll slant everything, until you don't recognize yourself at all, but everyone will believe it."

This is brutal. I lay it out matter-of-factly. It's not a threat. It's reality.

"You don't want that, Dani. You don't want to go to a police station, get your fingers printed, pay for a lawyer, maybe go on trial."

She's covering her own mouth, as if it'll stop me talking.

"He killed Cecelia. He was going to push me, too."

I say the lie swiftly. It's what she already thinks, anyway, and it's a much better story than the truth. That I was reaching for Jason, and we were both angry. That if she hadn't come along, we might have fought, and he might have fallen, or I might have, or he might have feinted my swipe, laughed me off, made a tactical retreat, gotten drunk at my wedding reception. That, ultimately, it doesn't matter. The past is only relevant in as much as it shapes the future. Not every story gets told.

"You can't ruin your life for him. I won't let you."

"What are you saying?" she asks. "What else can we do?"

I need to be calm and sure. She needs to see it the way I can, to visualize it, to believe in our success.

"I'll take him out." I point at the ocean, wrinkled under the searching beam of the moon. Waiting. "I have a boat. I'll drop him far out."

Dani's face is entirely blank, my words so strange she doesn't register them.

"I'll leave his car at the beach, just down the road. People will think he went for a swim and drowned. That he cramped, or caught in a riptide. It happens."

"What?" She's shivering. I'm hardly aware of the cold, though the wind is battering my dress.

"Concentrate, Dani. It's a story. We're telling a story."

Her eyes are wide. Maybe not as wide as I'd expect, though; she's considering it.

"I'll drop him far out," I repeat. "Nobody will find him. No one will miss him."

For the smallest iota of an instant, I pity the ruined figure down there. Once, he would have been the one I huddled with, shaping a plan, doing whatever it takes, even this. Living to fight another day.

But Dani shakes her head. "You'll never get him out far enough, or you'll capsize. Someone will see you driving his car. There are cameras everywhere. And his body might wash up. They'll find out what really happened."

"We can mitigate those risks. I will take him far enough. There aren't many cameras here. It's a point of pride to be analog. And if they find him, it might be days from now, weeks. They won't know he was here. They'll have no reason to suspect you."

She blinks, surprised at my point-by-point rebuttal to her wild, frantic list.

Every word now is deliberate. I've learned my lesson. I'm under a microscope. Every syllable matters.

"If we call the police, we have no control. We'll be caught in the story other people tell, and it will be nasty. You're having a baby. You're going to be a mother. You don't want to be associated with this for the rest of your life. Believe me, I know from experience." I rake my hair back, startled at the thought of my father, the accusation I never speak. I trust that Dani knows the story, that she's making the connection. Her face crumples, tender as fruit.

"I owe you, Dani. You saved me. I'll take him out. Let me take a big risk, and we can go on with our lives."

I don't say that Radical can't survive another scandal, that everything I've built would be destroyed. That I would take almost any risk to prevent that.

I think of the view from the rooftop. The skyline's buildings and bridges and streets. Every single one of them has a few bodies buried in the foundation. That's the cost of progress.

"The future isn't a track laid out like a railroad. We invent it every day. When necessary, we can use dynamite."

She rubs her stomach, her hand circling, unconsciously. Her eyes have moved past me, to the horizon.

Come on, Dani. Come on.

At last, she takes a breath. Bites her lip, then speaks.

"We'll need to leave his glasses at the beach. He wouldn't swim with them on."

After

Dani drives a cream-colored convertible up and down twisting hills. The moon lights the scene in shades of blue and black and gray. The night is cold, and she's wearing a thick coat, soft on her bare legs. She stretches her toes to reach the pedals. She's following another car, but she's fallen behind. A rim of light appears over the hills. She feels an enormous pressure, watching the yellow seeping upward into the sky, creeping across the grass. As if she can't let it touch her car, or something horrible will happen.

Even as she's sliding down in the seat to press the pedal, even as she's lifting fingers to hastily, ineffectively adjust the rearview mirror, she's aware, on some level, that she's dreaming. This isn't real: the rising sun, the spit of gravel pinging under the car. It's a dream.

She wakes before it ends, as she always does. Her bracelet singing on her wrist. The full moon shines through a gap in the curtains. She rubs her eyes. She feels queasy. Dread in her stomach, like something's going to happen.

She kicks away the long, tubular pillow that circles under her hips, twists around her stomach, reaches up her back. It seems to be strangling her.

The hallway rug Trevor bought has a tunnel in it already, worn from her bare feet in the middle of the night. He bought a new couch, new TV, new table, then ran out of energy. Dani lies on the couch, tugs up her T-shirt so the material won't touch her stomach. Her skin is stretched to impossible thinness, her belly button like the knot in a balloon. It itches.

One of Naomi's limbs bulges out below Dani's ribs. Dani rubs the swell, feels for the bend of the bony elbow or knee.

"Hi, Naomi," she whispers. She must be as uncomfortable as Dani.

On the marble mantel, there's a framed photo of Trevor and his cofounders from the early days of SitFit, and the taped-up acrostic Cecelia made, and a photo of Dani and Trevor on the courthouse steps with a bouquet of daffodils, and Naomi's thirty-week ultrasound.

Hanging on the wall above everything is an oil portrait of Dani. She sits in a garden, wearing a canary yellow dress, the voluminous fabric draped over her belly. She holds an inkwell and a pen. Around her neck, an open locket shows a tiny likeness of Dani's mother.

The garden is lush with healing plants, needled leaves and scalloped mushrooms. At her feet, a white-flowering herb waits to be planted in a patch of churned-up ground. Its root ball is wrapped in burlap, soil spilling on the grass. Bits of soil dapple her skirt. In the dark paint of the disturbed ground, there's an aberration: a narrow silver curve, glinting like a piece of glass catching the light, nearly buried in the dirt.

The painting was a gift from Rhoda. She delivered it herself, just after Dani and Trevor moved in.

"I didn't realize people still had their portraits done," Dani had said.

She'd studied it, hand on her stomach. It was uncanny, seeing herself rendered in paint. Was she really so plain? Her face like a soup plate.

"I have one myself," Rhoda said. "It's a reminder of what I've done, and a kind of challenge, for what I need to live up to." She smiled, watching Dani assess her gift.

"It's beautiful," Dani said.

"It's fierce," Rhoda corrected. "It's your legacy."

They never spoke of it. Dani went home. Rhoda got married. She left on her honeymoon, and Dani was alone in the city for a week, waiting every day for Lowell to appear from behind a pillar, to level her with his cool stare.

Rhoda returned, tanned and energetic, greeting Dani at their weekly check-in meeting with a proclamation of how many ideas she'd had since she went away, and how thrilled she was to get back to work. She led Dani to the couch and squeezed Dani's hands between hers, two quick pulses. *Thank you*, maybe. Or *trust me*.

Or, maybe, *forget*.

And Dani did. To her astonishment, it wasn't difficult. She pretended the night never happened. She didn't think of it. She moved to her new apartment. She got ready for Naomi. She crawled on the floor, she ate ninety grams of protein a day, she went to bed at nine, dabbing Sleep Potion on her wrists. She immersed herself in Radical. She centered her body, her rituals like a shield warding out the negative. She thinks Carlene must have felt this way, too. Protected, buoyed up, by Radical, by the sheer force of her own belief. She might have known the risks and found them worth it.

A cramp tightens Dani's stomach, taking her breath away. Her queasiness isn't fading with wakefulness, but intensifying.

Naomi's coming. The realization is a surprise, even though this is exactly what the pregnancy app says to expect. She's supposed to get a timer, call her doctor. She's supposed to walk, or drink water.

She smiles into the dark. As her contractions rise and fall, she watches her own face, still and calm, wide as the moon, her feet set firmly on the ground. Her Radical bracelet shining at her wrist.

Baby Naomi is on her way!

I'm walking to work when I get Dani's text. The morning is fittingly sunny and warm. Summer has arrived at last. I send a bouquet of emojis, rainbows and suns and crowns. Then I text a quick heads-up to the photographer.

As I pocket my phone, I falter. A police car cruises past Radical and parks across the alley.

I cross from the sun into the shade, walking slowly.

A cheer bursts into the quiet. I forgot: it's Rusher Tower's delayed grand opening. There's a small crowd outside. Some local politician has just cut a ribbon. Bunches of balloons are tied to the fence, tugging at their tethers in the breeze.

We can see the penthouse from the boardroom. The chair at the foot of the table stays empty, by unspoken agreement. It tilts back, as if an invisible occupant is reclining, silently observant.

The murmurs of good morning are subdued, but only in deference to the empty chair. Everyone is happy. The Ephraims and Pilar became unlikely friends, having invested in the same media-darling pet rental startup. Chad's Instagram features a rotating cast of designer dogs: visiting his yacht, cavorting with his daughters, sitting at attention in a bow tie between the brothers. Faye made a fortune when a female-centered dating service, for which she was an angel investor, went public. Barry is contemplating running for office on an independent ticket. Orson welcomed his tenth grandchild.

"It's wonderful to see you all," I say. "Before I go over the last quarter, which is full of good news and big wins, I want to say how strange it feels that Jason isn't with us. This is my first review without him. He was always leaning back in his chair, listening carefully, jumping in every time I was vague, catching everything I was trying to downplay. He always pushed me to be better. The hashtag might not exist without Jason. Radical might not exist if I hadn't met him."

The board looks sympathetic. Maybe a tad embarrassed. They're not sure I realize how badly Jason wanted me out. They think I'm naïve, but it's better that way.

The response to Jason's disappearance was rather muted. It wasn't until his car was flagged as abandoned that concern was roused. Jennifer, poised to inherit everything, didn't raise a fuss. She was kind enough to sell me his shares.

I never imagined how much work it would be. Taking the boat out so far, and then lifting and hauling and dropping. By the time I made it back to the beach, the sky was nearly gray, the cliffs visible against the misty dawn, like an old, faded photograph.

I drove his car. Ducked under the silly wing doors, not adjusting anything, not even turning down Bruce Springsteen's holler. Jason's driving gloves on my hands. Dani followed in my car. In my headscarf, she could have been my clone. Faster, faster. The dawn was gaining on us. From purple to red to gold. Shapes appearing like hastily drawn sets, shrubs and signs and fences, and by the time we got to the beach, the details of things were etched in. Leaves and lane stripes and colors, the wet red of a stop sign, the silver of a crushed can.

We drove back together. Neither of us breathed until we were back in my driveway. The sunrise shone off the windowpanes. A fine morning for a swim.

The wedding went on. Gavin and I boarded a plane that night. The jet barreled down the runway, leapt into the air, and banked over the ocean. The floor vibrated under my shoes.

My assistant clicks a button, and the shades lower over the windows. I blink. I'm back in the conference room. The smell of apple turnovers and vegan banana cake and roasted coffee. The gleam of the wooden table, the click of pens and riffle of paper packets opened to the numbers page.

"We have lots to cover, so I'll jump right in."

The launch of Lift was phenomenal. The site crashed twice on the morning of release. We sold out by noon, then restocked the following week, $149 for a month's supply, less than a daily latte. Almost two-thirds of subscribers complete their Lift questionnaire every single day.

I click to a fresh slide.

"What's coming next is going to be bigger still. It's not a single product but an entire channel devoted to one of the most valuable and underserved demographics in the country: mothers."

I unveil our line of supplements, the pregnancy app, all designed by Dani in a burst of creative energy that kept up until the last hour.

They pepper me with questions. Chad asks if I'm worried about a repeat of Wedding, and everyone laughs nervously, not wanting to offend me. I have a slide ready: the vast, untapped market opportunity, the few weak rivals in the space, all of them corny or condescending or decades old.

"I don't think I need to tell you how interested advertisers are in mothers. With Lift, and the bracelet, we're able to capture the earliest signifiers of pregnancy, which is like the Marketing equivalent of cracking nuclear fusion. I've always said Radical's most valuable asset is our community."

The board files out, congratulating me. The glow of a positive quarter is on us all.

I walk back to my office. I exhale. I stretch.

A movement out the window startles me. A balloon is bobbing against the glass, pinned by the wind. It drags against the window, like someone panicked.

I don't have time to parse the way the balloon unsettles me. My assistant knocks, bringing my daily itinerary and green juice. Before she goes, she hangs the framed cover of *Entrepreneur*. "Rhoda West Has Weathered Storms. She's Not Afraid to Think Radically." My arms are crossed, my skin airbrushed to silicone smoothness.

It fits in among my other clippings. Another hurdle bounded. A triumph, not a struggle. Just one chapter in the story I'm telling.

Dani leans forward and the tub's murky water ripples beneath her breasts.

The pregnancy app said contractions are like waves, starting small, rising and rising, then, more importantly, falling. Not so. Her contractions have no pattern, except relentlessness. Again, again, tighter and tighter. The pain lets up, and she collapses, releases her guard, and at once the pain is back, tighter, as if it only paused to get a better grip.

She climbed into the tub in another life, eager and nervous, innocent. Ages have passed. The window is pinkish gray. Sunrise or sunset? She doesn't know.

Her doula sits on the toilet, sleeves rolled, hair falling from her ponytail, counting and breathing as seriously as if she's doing it on Dani's behalf.

Behind her, a photographer kneels in the sink to get a shot. Dani agreed to share her story on Radical Motherhood, but that was back in her innocence, when she expected to bounce on a birthing ball, to visualize walking through a garden as the pain crested and fell. Instead, she feels like an insect, pinned down by her own weight, curling closed at the pain instead of opening up. She's reached the end of tiredness. Even in an imaginary garden, she couldn't take a single step.

She closes her eyes and falls down a spiral of pain.

The doula sweeps the tub with a small net, chasing away bits Dani chooses not to see. Then she tops the tub with a bucket of hot water, like Dani's mom used to do. Dani curls her toes in the mix of hot and tepid water, as she did as a child. What wouldn't she give to look up and see her mother? A towel over her shoulder, her sleeves rolled. Wearing her blue blouse, with the red buttons shaped like flowers.

A towel dabs her forehead. A straw prods her lips, and Reboot cools her throat.

"You're doing beautifully, Dani," Dr. Melinda says. "You were made to do this. Your body is ready."

On her knees, Dani grips the side of the tub and pushes until the white tiled walls go dark. Someone is burning a candle, and it smells like Radical. Maybe she's in the Well. She's in the cathedral. Someone is singing a long high note.

"Again," a distant voice says.

She crawls deep into herself. Her ears buzz with the noise of bees in a garden. She smells a familiar lipstick, hears her name in a familiar voice. Fingers lace between Dani's. Her mom is here, reaching to pull Dani across the gap into motherhood. She did this, too, made a link in the chain that pulls Dani along.

With a massive effort, a strain that draws every bone and tendon and vein taut, bursting into a searing schism, and then a slippery drop that releases the pressure, a feeling so welcome Dani opens her eyes in euphoria, and Naomi is there, at once smaller and more intensely real than Dani expected, her mouth wide and furious, her body opening in rage and then curling into Dani's chest. Naomi. Trevor's kissing her, his shirt shockingly filthy, smiling at Dani, touching Naomi's tiny fingertips.

She's just as Dani imagined. Her eyes curved and closed like clamshells, her frog cheeks, lips jutting and twitching. Her skin is tacky, gooey with white gunk and blood, her soft, shriveled skin hot as bread.

The photographer looms, his lens zooming. Dani's weeping. Joy has split her from her temple to her toes, and light pours from the cracks.

Already, she's forgetting the fullness of the experience, reality as transcript of passing time. Already, in her mind, she's revising the story. Grasping for the feel, not the facts. Transcendence is all that matters.

Acknowledgments

I was incredibly lucky to have so many smart, patient, enthusiastic, generous people help with this book. Many thanks to Kate Nintzel, Molly Gendell, Jessica Vestuto, Ana Deboo, Laura Brady, and the team at Mariner; Vicki Mellor, Gillian Green, and everyone at Pan Macmillan; Dan Conaway and the team at Writers House, especially Peggy Boulos Smith, Maja Nikolic, Tom Ishizuka, and Chaim Lipskar; Sylvie Rabineau and the team at WME; Liz Van Hoose, who provided invaluable help with early drafts; Jacqueline Wein for her galvanizing enthusiasm and helpful notes; Nick Petrie for writerly insight; the brilliant booksellers and readers I've met over the years; to my family for love and support, with endless appreciation to my mom and dad; and to Greg and Nolan for being the best.